THE SORCERERS' PROPHECY: SECRETS OF EILEEN

BOOK 2

by

TAYLOR EVANS

TELEMACHUS PRESS

The Sorcerers' Prophecy: Secrets of Eileen

Cover designed by Telemachus Press, LLC

Cover art:
Copyright © 99 designs/Rebecca Harrison, artist

Author photo copyright: David Evans

Map image: Robert Altbauer

Published by Telemachus Press, LLC
http://www.telemachuspress.com

Visit the author website:
http://www.facebook.com/thesorcerersprophecy

ISBN: 978-1-942899-96-9 (eBook)
ISBN: 978-1-945330-16-2 (Paperback)
ISBN: 978-1-945330-17-9 (Hardback)

Version: 2016.11.03

10 9 8 7 6 5 4 3 2 1

Dedication

To my wonderful sisters, brother, parents, family and friends who were my first editors and embarked on this journey with me. Your unconditional support made this dream possible.

IA

Shadowlands

EILEEN

Hunters

Emberrun

200

CANABAR

THE SORCERERS' PROPHECY: SECRETS OF EILEEN

BOOK 2

Prologue

AIDEN REMEMBERED SITTING in the same spot every year for the last twenty years, asking the same questions. Some of those years stood out in his memory, but most of them blurred together, indistinguishable from each other. Time is a funny thing, though. When one doesn't age, the weeks, months, and years lose their meaning. How couldn't they, when all that changes is one's hair length? Years had passed, but Aiden had gone through time untouched by its hands. He gazed up to look at his old friend. His face, his hair, his skin, his stature, everything ached with what those years had taken. But Aiden was never after those physical attributes when he hired him. He only wanted the vast knowledge concealed in his mind.

"How are you, Aiden?" Professor Hugo Blakemore asked, as he slowly settled into a plush sofa.

He wore a beige tunic and loose-fitting pants of the same color. He had several colorful rings on his fingers, and his once-black hair was now a dark grey. Wrinkles streaked across his forehead, formed at the corner of his eyes and around his mouth. Regardless of his aged body, Blakemore had maintained his wide smile and alert eyes. He swatted at a bee that had landed on the edge of his cup of herbal tea.

"I'm doing well. It was nice to get away from the city for a few days. Jobs have been quiet for a while now," Aiden said, as he signaled to a house servant that he had enough sugar in his tea. "How is everything going here?"

"Very well. I expect that he'll be prepared far before his twenty-fifth birthday, as we originally planned." Blakemore set his tea down and leaned towards Aiden. "He will be a great leader, Aiden, and it's because of you."

"Alagia could use a king like him, especially since we seem to be on the verge of war."

Blakemore nodded slowly as he listened. "You are still planning on carrying out your original plan of action?"

Aiden thought back to when he first brought Blakemore and his pupil here. That was a year that stood out in his mind. Another was when Blakemore's student was eight years old and had just fallen in love with riding. Aiden also remembered when the boy could name all of the most influential rulers of Alagia, and he would sit on the balcony while Blakemore's student told Aiden their brief biographies.

Even so, the visit Aiden remembered most happened over ten years ago. They had been sitting on the edge of a fountain as they fed the koi fish that circled below. The student had asked what happened to his family. For years, Aiden had known this question was coming. Aiden knew he owed him the truth. After all, he was the one responsible for their deaths—though murder was more accurate.

Blakemore's student was the central piece to a vision that was now twenty years in the making. This plan had evolved into something greater than its initial vengeful purpose. It had become a new hope for the people, for Eileen, and for Alagia. It was meant to achieve some good out of all the bad that had resulted from Aiden's last mission in Eileen. Its very essence embodied his since-deceased brother, and that was why Aiden couldn't let it fail.

"Yes. It's the only way all of this will have been worth it," Aiden replied.

Blakemore's eye caught something in the distance. He smiled warmly, leaned back, and stretched out a welcoming hand. Aiden turned to find his twenty-year investment and Blakemore's royal pupil: Lysander Tennenbay, future king of Eileen.

Aiden was prepared to die to put him on the throne, because it was the only way to reconcile the murder of his friends and younger brother. But first, he wanted the blood of the woman responsible.

Chapter 1: Casey

I LEANED FAR into the car, my finger just brushing my suit-case as I tried to balance two other bags on my back, juggling them just right so they wouldn't slide down and smack my side. I finally hooked a finger under the strap and yanked it towards me. As I straightened, muffled whimpers could be heard from one of the duffels pressing into my hip. I hushed the bag, trying not to jostle it too hard. I thanked the cabbie, threw the final bag over my shoulder, and started pulling my suitcase in tow.

My grandmother was just handing the driver some bills when I heard brakes halting to a stop. I cringed at the sound, but didn't turn. It wasn't until I heard my name that I stopped. The voice was deflated and breathless. In fact, it sounded more like a whisper than anything else.

"Casey," the voice said again.

I knew who spoke right away, but I hadn't expected to en-counter anyone I had left behind three months ago for at least a few more weeks. I spun, my face wavering between a grim smile and a frown.

When my eyes fell on Connor, the tone of his voice suddenly made more sense. He used to stand tall, with his shoulders back and chin slightly tilted to the sky. While I wouldn't say his eyes sparkled, they were always flitting around the room, constantly looking for something amusing. But now his gaze settled on one thing, moving languidly, if at all. He looked hunched, and his lips tugged downwards at the corners.

I stole a glance at my grandmother, who watched us cautiously. The whole moment felt breathless. She finally sent the cab on its way and approached me carefully. I let the bags I held slip from my shoulders. After hushing Adalia, who whined from her pet carrier, I handed the crate to my grandmother.

"Can you take her in, please?" My grandmother cradled the carrier in her arms and left Connor and me alone on the street. The only thing that separated us was the narrow sidewalk.

I abandoned my luggage and walked towards him as he rounded his car. When his familiar scent invaded my nose, I fell into his arms. It wasn't a warm embrace, or even a friendly one. It felt desperate. I thought about the last time we hugged. My silent tears had soaked through his shirt, and his ragged sobs rung in my ears. A couple weeks later I had sent him a message.

I'm leaving.

Are you coming back?

I don't know.

We pulled away from each other. I wondered if he saw all the changes in me that I clearly saw in him. "It's been three months."

"I know," I muttered. I gazed at the trees behind him. They had shed their green foliage and donned bright yellows and oranges.

"I didn't think you'd come back," Connor said. His words were as hollow as his eyes.

I was expecting him to be angry with me for leaving him without an answer or any means of getting in touch with me. I just stared. I didn't have an answer for him then, and, three months later, I still didn't have one.

I uttered the only words I thought could mend the rift between us. "I was a shitty friend for doing that to you. I'm sorry."

He shifted his weight and shoved his hands into his jeans pockets. "His mom called me, you know..." he began. My eyes slid back to his face, but I wasn't used to holding his gaze for so long. "She started to invite me up to the lake house—but then she hung up. She called back, saying she was sorry, and that they couldn't go this year and to forget she had called." He shoved his hands deeper into his pockets.

Jackson and his family practically lived in the lake house over the summer, and Connor always went with them. He was the second son they never had. Ever since I'd known Connor from back in grade school, he always talked about his summers at the lake house, roasting marshmallows at night, and falling asleep to a cricket orchestra that played in time with the fireflies that twinkled in the grass. He didn't have summer plans outside those, so with Jackson gone, I never thought about what he would do instead.

"I know how it feels...expecting him to be next to you and he's not," I said softly.

He breathed deeply and stepped back to lean against his car, which was still running. His eyes were downcast, and he had a contemplative expression on his face.

"I thought a lot about what I was going to say to you, if I ever saw you again—but none of that came out the way I wanted," he said again, sounding down.

My gut clenched with anger more than sadness. There was only one person to blame for Jackson's death, and now Connor's decline.

"None of this happened the way we planned," I replied, as anger crept into the edges of my voice. Connor's expression looked pained. "How are the other two?" I added, referring to our small circle of friends.

"They're on and off. They just don't know what to do with themselves." I nodded slowly. "I guess none of us do." His eyes rose to meet mine again.

Just like at "Kate's funeral," I would feel the deep sorrow weighing on Connor's every move, every breath. Everything he did now seemed to float in slow motion, without destination or purpose.

As though something grabbed his attention again, he pushed away from his car and straightened. "I was actually headed to meet them. Would you—"

He paused, making a curt gesture towards his car. My lips parted at his offer. I didn't expect to see him today, never mind the rest of our now-shattered group. But something in his eyes wouldn't allow me to avoid my friends anymore.

I'd returned. Saying I was home was still a bit strong, but I *was* back, so that meant I had to start acting like it. I'd gotten what I wanted: to run. I'd been running for three months. It was time to face the wreckage I'd left behind.

Our drive was as normal as it would have been a year ago. Windows were rolled down, and the autumn breeze washed over us. Our seats were reclined just enough to be sitting up and lounging at the same time. The back seat was littered with clothing, water bottles, and CDs. Everything was the same, except for us.

Connor should have had one arm draped lazily out the window, his hand riding on the wind, while the other confidently steered. I should have had both feet propped up on the dash as I looked ahead. Instead, Connor had both hands firmly on the steering wheel, his hands at ten and two o'clock. I had my legs folded over one another, and my arms crossed in my lap. At least Connor's music remained the same, as it still blared as we drove along. It seemed to be the only thing that could bridge what had been and what now was.

We were meeting Brenna and Nick at a coffee bar. It wasn't the typical metropolitan area with overcrowded streets and screeching cars that I had witnessed in London. Instead, the neighborhood was an older and quaint part of town with brick buildings and gaslight lamps. Small businesses and restaurant patios staked claim to parts of the sidewalk and various trails made for relaxing bike rides and beautiful photos. Every year my grandmother would bring Kate and me out here to take pictures for our Christmas card. Afterwards, we would escape from the cold and curl up by the fireplace with hot chocolate. I could just see the setting of last year's picture when sadness hit me like a punch. Yet another memory of my old life had been destroyed by the present.

I ducked my head as we passed the store window of the little boutique where Kate and I used to work, as Connor pulled into a small lot behind a white brick building. A couple of other cars were parked in the lot as well, and I immediately recognized Nick's blue Toyota Camry and Brenna's red Beetle a few spaces away. I could just make out the black bear sticker on Nick's back windshield, Bellemont High School's mascot. I shuddered at the thought of school, and exited the car. Connor waited for me as I shut my door and followed him around the building.

Black patio tables scattered the sidewalk, inviting people to dine outside. A few had large umbrellas, further enticing outside dining. Kids rushed past Connor and me on their way to an ice cream parlor down the street. A young couple, with a toddler seat connected to the back of the mother's bike, rang their bells as they pedaled past. The strip was exactly how I remembered it. It was strange coming back after so long and realizing that virtually nothing had changed. For some reason, I had expected it to be much different. I had experienced many transformations—in this world and Alagia—but my hometown had not changed.

As I walked behind Connor, I noticed his whole posture seemed to have diminished. It only made me more nervous about seeing the other two. As we approached the coffee bar, aromas of espresso wafted past my nose. I was deeply inhaling the smell for the second time when a sharp gasp stopped me short.

My eyes fell on two figures sitting at a high table. They looked the same, and completely different, all at once. Brenna's once long, dark hair was cropped to her shoulders and was now an auburn color. Her small lips, that were normally pursed together, had fallen into an "O" shape. Even her eyes, usually narrow and calculating, were opened wide. Nick's black hair was shaved close to his head with a small tuft spiking wildly in the front. His olive-toned skin was darker than I remembered, and I could see flecks of freckles on his cheeks. His eyes weren't wide like Brenna's. They just stared blankly, as though deciding whether to believe what they saw.

Brenna jumped down from her stool and rushed towards me. Connor smoothly moved out of the way as Brenna came crashing into me. "Oh my God, you're home. You're finally home," she gasped, squeezing me. She pulled away. "We thought—Connor told us—we didn't know where you—or when you'd—it's been an awful summer," she finished breathlessly.

She reluctantly stepped aside as Nick approached us. "Hi, Nick," I greeted him, weakly, as he yanked me to him. When we stepped back, his expression was difficult to read, as I imagine mine was, too. He struggled between looking happy to see me and guarding how he felt. He fought for the right words to say— the words that would close the gap that had grown between us.

He tentatively spoke. "Want to sit?"

Connor and I followed Brenna and Nick back to their table. I thought about how, if our whole group had been there, it would have been less roomy.

Brenna's newly painted nails tapped impatiently, or nervously, on the table. Nick still couldn't figure out exactly what he wanted to say. Connor slipped away to get us drinks. "So...how has your summer been?" I broke the silence.

Brenna's lip twitched, and Nick stole a glance at her, as though searching for a cue. "There were a lot of concerts and parties. We went out on a boathouse for the Fourth with some people from school. It wasn't nearly as fun as just the six of us going up to Jackson's though," Brenna admitted.

"This summer sucked," Nick added.

I noticed that even though they sat next to each other, they both made the very conscious effort not to engage with each other. When Brenna shifted in her seat, Nick glanced the other way. If Nick reached out to grab his drink, Brenna propped her elbow on the table as though to create a barrier between them. It couldn't have been that long ago when Brenna stretched carelessly across Nick's lap as he peppered her with kisses. I guessed this was just more fallout from the unexpected deaths in our circle.

I thought about how unfair this all was. My friends were left to believe that two people from our circle were dead, buried, and left to be forgotten. Jackson was gone, yes, but his killer was not. That knowledge kept me from grieving publicly, and I wondered how callous my friends thought I was about my sister's "death."

"How are you doing?" Brenna asked. Her voice was low, and I recognized that she wanted a serious answer.

"I'm better," I said truthfully. Brenna nodded earnestly. Connor returned and placed my usual, a cappuccino, in front of me, then slid into the chair beside me. I thanked him and saw that Brenna was still staring at me. My answer wasn't sufficient. "Honestly, I am. I've had a lot of time to think, and it's helped a lot."

And it was true. When I finally told them I had been in Europe, I could see their expressions mirroring my own initial excitement when my grandmother had told me we were going. However, once I was there, the streets of Rome; the Seine; even the West End, though bustling with people, felt empty. The loneliness I'd experienced was a stranger I'd never known. My whole life I had wanted to walk those streets with Kate at my side, laughing at street performers and strolling through galleries. Instead, I was left to glance over my shoulder, wanting to share a joke, only to find no one next to me. I became so miserable and distraught that my grandmother finally had to take me to her friend Charlotte's cottage in the English countryside. It was there I had my mental breakdowns, where I cried in the overgrown groves, and where fitful tantrums scared me out of sleep. I was only able to quell the depression by practicing spells.

So, what should have been three wonderful months spent exploring Europe with my grandmother had turned into three gloomy months spent cooped up in a cottage, miles from civilization.

"We're so glad you're home," Brenna breathed. There was that word again.

I lifted my cup and sipped gingerly at the foam. My friends watched me, studied me. They all searched for suggestions of what to say, how to behave. They were tiptoeing around a land mine that had already detonated.

"Guys," I said, putting my mug down. "It's all right—I'm all right." When no one said anything, I added, "So, who performed this summer? Anyone good?"

Nick made the first sound, and it was the first time that he and Brenna exchanged glances. As he started talking about the concerts, Brenna would glance at him and then add bits of commentary here and there. It wasn't their usual seamless way of telling a story together. It was choppy and uneven, but they tried for me. Connor drank his coffee noiselessly, his eyes trained either on his cup or the napkin holder in the center of the table.

My insides twisted sharply as I saw that my friends had been reduced to this. We were no longer the "Sensational Six," as Brenna liked to call us. We were the "Fractured Four," and even now I could see us splintering more.

I hugged Brenna and Nick goodbye when our coffees had grown cold and accounts of the "awful summer" ran dry. We parted in the parking lot, and I watched as Brenna and Nick, once an inseparable couple, settled awkwardly into their cars.

Connor drove me home, and we sat the same as we had before. When he pulled up to my house and parked, I wasn't sure how to leave. Before, we would have shared some playful banter. But now we just sat in silence as his car hummed beneath us.

"Thanks for the ride." He smiled bleakly. I slipped out of the car and shut the door. As I was turning to leave, he called out.

"See you later." It sounded like a question, rather than a promise. I nodded and lifted a hand to wave. He pulled away from the curb and drove down the street.

I faced my house and, again, nothing had changed. No, I shouldn't say that. The bushes were overgrown and unruly, dried up flowers wilted in the sun, and half the lawn looked dead. But the walkway was still cement, the blue shutters were still blue, and the panels on the house were still wood. The porch was still a porch, but without the two armchairs my grandmother normally had on it, it looked empty and cold. Even the door looked barren and sad without the fall wreath we always hung this time of year.

I walked up the pathway, entered the front door, and came to a stop.

Something crawled under my skin, and my hair stood on edge. I wasn't sure how I had missed it earlier, when I carried my luggage inside and dropped it at the foot of the stairs. I couldn't even try to ignore it now.

My grandmother glimpsed me, frozen by the door, and came over. "What is it?"

Adalia growled furiously. She sensed my apprehension. Her snarl was low and guttural, and warned of danger. "Casey…?"

"Kate's been here."

Chapter 2: Kate

THIS NIGHT, AND every night, I killed my sister. Whether it was with my powers, a sword, or a dagger, every night I ended up standing in a pool of Casey's blood as she gasped her final breaths. I used to wake up from these dreams shaken. My heart would race, and my skin would be cool with sweat. But after having the same dream every night for months, I had become immune to the emotions I used to feel.

This was the outcome I wanted. It was why I faced Casey in Azlaya's castle. I was ready to kill her, and yet her hesitation was so evident that a small part of me deep down inside made me question my own commitment to my so-called destiny. Regardless, Casey stood in the way of my reunion with our mother. She was blinded with lies told to her by the Hunters—our mother's murderers. Thinking about our mother's betrayal among the very people Casey was fighting for made me sick to my stomach. They took her away from us— from me—and now I wanted nothing more than to avenge her. I wanted nothing more than to see her again, and for her to see what I had become—the only sorceress to ever match her power. These thoughts always managed to reignite the drive for my purpose.

I suppressed them into the deep crevices of my mind, knowing that it would help me focus better when training began. I pushed the deep purple covers from my body and sat up in bed. The rectangular window across the room had no panes, just some grating. To me, it had looked like a prison cell the first time I entered the room, and in all actuality, it was, even though no one else would admit it. The door was locked at night from the outside, and the entire room was coated in a powerful curse, making it impossible for me to break out.

I was being "held for my own protection." At least that's what Azlaya told me. After her brief meeting with the queen of Eileen, Azlaya brought me to train further with the Sagen. However, my impatience grew, and one night I used my necklace as a doorway back to my world and stepped through the front door of my house. I was shocked to find it empty. I searched every room thoroughly, making sure I hadn't missed anything, but Casey and my grandmother were gone.

Frustrated, I returned to Alagia to face a furious Azlaya. She confiscated my necklace, brought me to my new room, put a spell on it, and handed the keys over to the Sagen. She thought I was too taken by my emotions to safely battle Casey, and that I needed more training. She wasn't going to jeopardize her chance at winning the war, and she definitely wasn't going to have me running after Casey and getting myself killed. Hence, the curse on my room which prevented my escape.

At first I was indignant about where our partnership had left me, but after several weeks of channeling my anger into my training, even the Sagen couldn't deny my powers' new strength.

I was eager to continue to learn more sorcery, especially Dark Magic. I knew a little about a lot, so now I had the opportunity to know a lot about a lot. I finally came around to understanding her point of view, but the sealed window, the locked door, and the curse remained.

I walked over to the window and wrapped my fingers around the bars. The sky was bleak, gray, and depressing. An expanse of thick, dark clouds constantly hung overhead. Dark purples and blues painted the sky the color of storm clouds that roll in on a humid summer day. I'd gotten used to the absence of the sun, but that didn't mean I didn't miss seeing it. The landscape fit perfectly with the sky. Everywhere I looked, all I saw was black. Black ground, black grass, black sand, black mountains. Black. It looked like a volcano had spewed ash everywhere and it never went away. I was in the Shadowlands, and the Sagen had become my gatekeepers.

I stepped away from the window and crossed the room to the chest that sat at the foot of my bed. Inside were layers of training clothes: padded shirts and pants, thick boots, and various cloaks. I pulled on some dark pants, a black long-sleeved shirt, and boots that covered my knees. A pitcher of water and a bowl served as my sink. They sat on a side table that rested against the wall. I splashed some water on my face and rubbed the sleep from my eyes. I really missed my large mirror at home. Oftentimes, my fingers would wander down to try to pick up a bottle of perfume that wasn't there, or they'd try to open a drawer that didn't exist. I swiftly pulled my hair into a high ponytail and walked over to the door.

I bemoaned the fact that no one acknowledged that I was a prisoner. Just one look at the door and anyone would agree that a door of that size and width wasn't exactly meant to be a bedroom door. I knocked three times on the door to let the Sagen outside know that I was ready to exit. I heard a couple clicks and the door swung open. I was escorted from my room and down a dark corridor to yet another jail-like door.

I followed the Sagen out of my humble abode, which looked like a jagged, one-person castle jutting out from the haphazardly placed rocks. There were two distinct floors, separated by rows of windows. I resided on the second floor: my servants, cooks, and maids stayed on the first. At least I was well cared for while being locked up.

I entered a shallow valley. Ash covered my boots and kicked up dust when I walked. Across the way, I saw the Sagen that was my instructor. It looked just like the rest of them, except for the silver pendant that hung from its invisible neck and rested on its chest. I approached it and bowed my head in greeting.

"Describe your dream to me in full detail," it told me in its raspy voice. That was how every training session began. I went into detail about yet another dream of me killing Casey. Last night I had killed her with a spear. I hadn't dreamt that version in a while. I had to describe everything: where I was, what I looked like, what Casey looked like, what the weapon looked like and how it felt, and finally how I ended Casey's life.

When I finished, it nodded with approval. "We will not engage in much physical training today," it said. I felt my body sigh a little with disappointment. I was already dreading what was to come. "Instead, we will work on your mental defenses."

In other words, the Sagen was going to attack my mind for hours on end while I tried to keep it out by rebuilding barriers that kept getting knocked down. It was arduous work, and the Sagen didn't believe in taking breaks. By the end of it, my defenses were more fortified, but the pounding headaches that followed always made me wary of the sessions.

"You are unhappy with our plans?" the Sagen questioned.

"We've already done it four times this week," I explained. Even though it had no real face, I imagined that its eyes narrowed at me.

"When I can no longer penetrate your mind, then we may discontinue these lessons. Until then—" The Sagen gestured to a boulder, telling me to sit.

"I just don't think my sister is as strong as you, so I believe I've trained my mind enough to face her." The Sagen ducked his head a little to gaze down on me. I sat still, knowing that shying away from this dispute would only earn me harsher memories to combat when the lesson began.

"Do you wish to be unstoppable by your sister's standards, or do you wish to be unstoppable?" The menace in its voice matched the feelings that consumed me when I thought too much about Casey and the Hunters.

"I get it," I replied. I folded my hands in my lap, and shut my eyes.

The memories came in a deluge. There were so many at one time that I couldn't even make out faces, let alone place them in chronological order in my head. Finally, they began to slow, and I found myself in my room. It looked just as I remembered. The full bed was tucked in the corner, next to a white nightstand that held my alarm clock and random books I had yet to finish. My closet door was ajar, and my vanity table had bottles of perfume strewn about it. I was about to turn when a familiar smell hit my nose, and someone's arms snaked around my body, pulling me in.

The arms twisted me around, and I was gazing into Jackson's eyes. They were warm and adoring, the way he sometimes looked at me. A mischievous grin grew on his face. "Kate, where have you been? I've missed you."

I knew this trick all too well. The Sagen used an old memory to get me to let my guard down as I got caught up in the emotion of the moment. Meanwhile, it was calculating a wicked blow from another angle. My face went blank. I didn't return the look that I received from Jackson.

"You aren't real," I told him coldly. He ignored me and pressed his lips to mine. At first it was gentle, but very quickly it became more passionate, almost desperate. The warmth I used to feel when we kissed began to tingle inside me, but I hastened to suppress it.

He pulled away. "I love you, Kate. I love you, Kate. I love you, Kate."

He kept repeating those words over and over again. I stepped away from him, but he stood still with the same stupid look on his face, sounding like a broken record. I turned from him to where the door to my room should have been, but of course it wasn't there. I had to take control of this memory. That was the only way to win the twisted game the Sagen and I played.

I noticed that Jackson's words had slowed and no longer came out in quick bursts. He began saying something different. I returned my attention to him. "I loved you, Kate. I loved you, Kate. I loved you, Kate." I cursed under my breath. The memory had shifted, however slightly, and I wasn't the one who had done it.

When I tried to take control, I lurched forward. I found myself in the woods behind my house. I felt goose bumps rising on my arms. The wind bit at my clothes. I felt warm blood dripping down one of my hands, and I looked down to see that I was clutching a bouquet of roses. The thorns were lodged deep into my skin. I tried with all my might to cut the memory off, but the Sagen's resistance to me was stronger. My teeth gritted together. I was riding this one out.

Jackson suddenly materialized a few feet in front of me. He was tall, had cropped hair, and wore jeans and a letterman jacket. His lips were pressed into a thin line, and his eyes screamed with pain. It made me want to return to the previous scene when Jackson was enamored with me.

I glanced at the roses again and noticed that blood was dripping from the petals too. I turned back to Jackson and saw that blood was slowly running from his eyes, mouth, ears, and nose.

"How could you let this happen to me?" he asked. "Why would you do this to me?"

His voice was heavy with pain. *Don't show remorse, Kate. Don't show remorse, it only makes it worse.* I felt a pang in my head. My body tensed, already knowing what was coming next. A shattering, strangled scream sprung from his mouth as he crumpled to the ground. He curled up in agony and continued to split my ears with his cries. My heart raced, and I closed my eyes. My hands squeezed the rose thorns tighter. *Take control, Kate.*

I opened my eyes and hardened myself against what I was witnessing. He was begging me to make it stop, but I didn't move.

"You deserved it," I shouted at him. "Did you hear me? You deserved it!"

I watched him writhe in pain for a few more seconds. I had completely blocked him out now, and the initial pangs of guilt I felt began to vanish. Relief set in.

"I have no pity for you."

The scene changed immediately. My senses returned to me, and I was standing in a spacious tent. There was a bed big enough for two people, an animal skin rug on the floor, and across the tent, what appeared to be a bassinette. I oriented myself in the room, trying to anticipate how I could take control of the scene from the Sagen. I walked over to the bassinette and saw two babies sleeping calmly inside. Then, one began to scream shrilly, and a man entered the tent. I recognized right away that it was my father. He bent over and lifted the crying infant into his arms, but he didn't try to calm it. He gazed at the thing with contempt as its face turned red as it cried.

"You've always been a menace," he spat. "Look at what you've done," he said pointing at something behind me.

I turned and saw piles of skeletons that seemed to stretch on for miles in every direction. The tent had suddenly disappeared, but my father still faced me. Under my feet were more skeletons, their empty expressions staring up at me. I stayed calm, forcing myself to focus, before yet another scene got out of control.

"You're a cold-blooded killer, a vile human. You're a monster."

Something began to crawl over my skin. I had never had this happen before. Suddenly black scales began to sprout all over my body. My fingernails grew into razor-sharp claws, and spikes started forming on my forearms. As if to confirm what my father had said, I felt myself turning into what appeared to be a human-dragon hybrid. I grinned wickedly.

"Yes, I am." I stepped forward and my arm shot out so I could wrap my talons around his neck. His face was consumed with fear. "Don't ever forget it," I hissed as I pinched my fingers together. The talons sunk deep into his neck. The scene ended.

I breathed deeply, waiting for the next scene to materialize. One minute I was in complete darkness, the next I was standing in the woods with Sagen and Hunters battling all around me. That is how the duration of my morning went. As soon as I broke free from one scene, I was unceremoniously thrust into the next.

Several hours later, my eyes fluttered open. My head was a little foggy, but I regained my composure quickly. It was nothing like my first lesson when I tried to come back to my senses too quickly, doubled over, vomited, and then passed out. I blinked away any haziness in my mind and located the Sagen who still stood over me.

"You did well," it told me. My chest bubbled with excitement. Maybe I'd done well enough to discontinue these lessons. "You've not done *that* well." It silenced any hope I'd just had. I restrained myself from making a sour face. The Sagen motioned for me to stand.

I rose to my feet and ignored the creeping headache, as the Sagen studied me. I raised my chin a little to prove, yet again, that the shadow creature it was didn't intimidate me. When it had finished making sure my mental health hadn't been obliterated, it spoke.

"Azlaya will be pleased with your performance today."

"Will she be back soon?" I waited for yet another excuse explaining where Azlaya had been.

"We've received word that she will return within the next few days," it replied. My ears perked up. "She and the queen of Eileen have a few more things to discuss before you will be allowed to enter the city."

"Why am I going to Eileen? I should be looking for my sister."

"That is for Azlaya to tell you. All I know is that you'll play an instrumental part in building Azlaya's army."

I shook my head in irritation. I hadn't spoken with Azlaya in weeks and I was tired of receiving news and commands through the Sagen. I pointlessly averted my eyes from the Sagen; it could surely feel my inner frustration without seeing the emotions on my face.

Suddenly, I froze and my vision went black. When it returned, I was standing in my house, watching Casey push the door open and enter the house. As though she had tripped a trigger, I watched as she walked through the spell I had placed over the door when I was home. She'd returned. I blinked again and was back in the overcast valley with the Sagen.

I slowly lifted my eyes to look at where it should have had a face. "Did you see that?" My heart began to beat faster. My initial fears that she and my grandmother had abandoned the house left me in an instant. "She's back. I could go—" I said as my fingers searched for my confiscated necklace.

The Sagen held up a warning hand. "You are not to leave the Shadowlands." Its tone usually left the slightest room for dispute, but not this time, which made me even angrier. A couple words, a few gusts of wind, and I would be back in my house with an unsuspecting Casey right in my clutches.

"Oh come on, she's right there! I can literally sense her in my house. I can smell her." I lied about the last part, but I was desperate to get more slack on the invisible chain Azlaya and the Sagen had wrapped around my neck.

"You are not to leave the Shadowlands." I wondered how hard it would be to create a portal and run through before the Sagen stopped me. "You wouldn't even summon the spell before I stopped you," it threatened. I tightened my jaw, always forgetting that it could read my mind, even though I couldn't do the same to it.

"I'm ready," I argued.

"That is for Azlaya to decide."

I rolled my eyes in the smallest circle. "We should be doing more to capture her," I told it, with an edge.

I thought back to when I roamed my house searching for her, but she wasn't there. Not even the necklace was in the house. The necklace was the key. It was her doorway into Alagia, where she would most likely land right in the Hunters' camp. Without it, though, she was trapped. Without it, she had no way to enter Alagia, and there would be no way for anyone else to reach her. In the few moments it had taken me to think all that through, the Sagen hadn't budged. I think it was preparing to stop me if I tried to bolt.

"Did you catch all that?" I asked, referring to what had just run through my head. Its hood dipped slightly, and I took that as a nod.

My instructor floated away, moving silently as it went. I wasn't surprised that it wasn't going to explain what it had in mind for stealing Casey's necklace, but I didn't think about that. Instead, I thought about Casey, whom I thought had run away for good, but there she was, right where I needed her to be.

I turned my attention to another pressing matter. I still hadn't figured out what was so important about the kingdom of Eileen. I knew the Queen and Azlaya had some sort of deal with each other, but I had no idea how it related to our cause and the war in any way. *Building her an army.* How was I supposed to do that?

I was eager to finally see Azlaya again. It had been over a month since we'd last seen each other, and I was ready to leave the Shadowlands and hunt for Casey again. While I felt my powers and abilities getting stronger, I wanted to put them to use, and not just spend hours a day training them. The war had been put on pause for too long. I was ready to put it into motion.

My escorts from earlier returned to me. I felt the energy from their powers radiating from them and it made my own skin tingle a little. Azlaya really didn't want me leaving that place. I knew I was strong and able to take on several Sagen at once, but not the twelve that constantly escorted me from place to place.

"We are here to bring you back to your room," one of them said. I didn't know which because nothing distinguished one from the other, and especially not their voices.

"Prison cell," I snapped. "Call it what it is."

Chapter 3: Casey

I THINK I made my grandmother's heart stop one too many times in the past months. I would think I saw something and freeze, or catch my breath, or stop mid-sentence, leaving her frantic with anxiety. I cried wolf too often, and yet, she still responded as though it was the first time. I made the same mistake when I mentioned Kate had been at the house. Her eyes grew larger and one hand flew to her throat like it often did, as though it were holding her head on her shoulders.

I walked cautiously around the house. Kate's energy was strong—unnervingly strong. I picked my way through each dusty room, but they were all empty. While it seemed as though her very presence tainted the house, she wasn't actually there. She had spent the most time in my room and our mother's room, and her energy lingered on just about everything.

"When was she here? And how long?" My grandmother questioned anxiously.

She kept glancing over her shoulder, expecting Kate would be there. But I couldn't tell, and quite honestly, I wasn't sure I wanted to know if she had crept through the house two months ago or two minutes ago. Regardless, I was sure she wasn't there anymore, because I would definitely be able to feel her presence. I reassured my grandmother and diverted her attention to unpacking our things. Our ghost house had been empty for far too long. So, like I said, it was another false alarm.

Two weeks later I found myself sitting in Connor's car, backpack between my feet, and phone spinning nervously in my hands. I still couldn't believe the rest of my time "easing back into things" was already over. School was starting today, which meant I was about to be thrust back into life. I'd spent last night and that morning deciding how to act: still depressed; sad but trying to move on; or completely okay and ready for senior year. It was like choosing a flavor of ice cream. I settled on the one I felt I could pull off the best.

"You ready?" Connor asked as I approached. I smiled grimly and nodded: *sad but trying to move on.*

We pulled into the school parking lot twenty minutes later. I was grateful Connor had offered to give me a ride. Had I been behind the wheel, I might not have driven myself to school. Part of me was ready to resume my normal life, and another part longed for my newly-found home. Still another part of me was anxious to see how the students had interpreted my sudden disappearance and subsequent summer flight. I swallowed these thoughts hard as the car jolted to a stop.

Connor exhaled a drawn out sigh. We acted like it was our first day at a new school, with no friends, and nowhere to belong. That was honestly how it felt. The dynamics of the school day would be different now, because both of us were missing someone we had always expected to have at our side.

"Senior year, here we come," he said, with such dread that the air became harder to breathe. His mouth was pulled thinly across his face and his eyes looked hollow again.

We slid from the car, braced ourselves, and started walking towards the school. The lot was a mad scramble of students and teachers trying to get to their parking spots without hitting each other. I used to joke all the time that if I were to die anywhere, it would be on that uneven asphalt. That thought was no longer funny. Connor and I weaved through the cars and students with relative ease. Three years of practice trained the mind to locate the most efficient path to an empty space, and we were well-versed in spotting careless drivers in our periphery.

As we walked inside, I noticed that Connor hung a little closer to me than usual. He was still coiled up, his hands thrust deep in his pockets, and his shoulder brushed lightly against mine. A few passing students in our grade greeted Connor as we passed, but all he could give in return was a curt nod or a flick of his eyes. I was given shocked looks, so both of us were uneasy.

The hallways swelled with kids. Freshmen dodged around people, frantically trying to run through their schedules. The sophomores laughed, but still shot furtive glances at room numbers and school maps. The juniors walked through the hallways with ease, only stressing about their upcoming, and supposedly most challenging, year. The seniors were the calmest of everyone. They were on their way out. They had finished the hard part and were hurtling fast towards graduation. I guess I should say *we* were hurtling fast towards gradation. However, listening to everyone talk about their test scores and college applications sounded foreign to me, especially having spent the summer in total seclusion without devoting a single thought to what I would do once I returned to high school. College hadn't even entered my mind.

Connor and I went to the common area where students gathered to socialize and finish eating breakfast before class. At a high table in the corner, I spotted Nick and Brenna and careened over to them. Nick wore beige pants and a white t-shirt. The front of his hair was spiked, and his shades were hooked in the V-neck of his shirt. Brenna's hair was flat-ironed, and she wore a pair of jean shorts and a floral shirt. They looked like they had stepped out of a magazine ad.

"Hey guys," Nick greeted us. "Brenna's already stressing about her schedule."

"You would too if the counselors had messed up and put you in AP Physics!" Brenna snapped. She turned to me. "I haven't even taken regular Physics, and I suck at science. You know that."

I made what I thought was a reassuring face. "The counselors will work it out, I'm sure."

"But they're being really strict this year. What if they don't change it? I'm going to fail that class, my already average GPA will be ruined, and then what do I tell colleges? I won't get in anywhere and have to live with my parents forever!"

"That escalated quickly," Connor said dryly. I stole a glance at his face. It didn't match the comment he made, but I still chuckled. There was still part of his old self inside him somewhere.

Nick was trying to talk Brenna down. His logic was indisputable, so I left her to take his advice. I turned away from my friends and caught the furtive glances of a group of other students staring at our table. When they saw me look over, they all shifted their eyes elsewhere, or completely turned around. I didn't need to use a spell to enhance my hearing. I knew what they were talking about from the pity in their eyes.

Five months had passed, and I was still the girl whose sister died in a tragic car accident. I was still the girl who vanished over the summer just to turn up again when school started. I was still the girl who was known by just about everyone in school. I was still Casey Coles—but at the same time, I wasn't. It was as if the "new me" still occupied my old body, but the two wouldn't merge.

Brenna had to call my name twice to get my attention again. "They called the seniors to the auditorium," she explained as she gathered her things. We all filed in behind the other seniors and headed to the auditorium. I kept catching people glancing at me or gesturing in my direction and thought about how Kate would have loved this extra attention. I, on the other hand, wanted to pull the hood of my sweater around my head and block everyone out.

The assembly had one purpose: get the seniors excited about the school year. While my fellow classmates were unusually rowdy, I didn't think it was about school. In fact, I thought it was due to the fact we were getting catered food afterwards. Either way, that cinnamon bagel was the highlight of my day. The remaining hours dragged on with the typical "first day of school" proceedings. The teacher would greet his or her class, list the course expectations, assign some light homework, and then we'd be on our way. It was dull and dry and everything I expected on my first day back. So, when I fell into Connor's car at the end of the day, I was glad it was over. I was rubbing my face as Connor sparked the car to life.

"Rough day?" he asked casually.

"I've had worse. But as far as first days go—it was rough." He breathed outward sharply. I counted it as a laugh.

Getting into the parking lot in the morning may have been chaotic, but getting out was much worse. First, all two hundred cars were trying to leave at the same time. Second, there were only three exits, so everyone rushed to get to them before they got backed up. Third, beating the buses out of the lot was crucial and determined whether you'd get home at 2:34 or 2:44 (a huge difference to impatient high school students). And last, the lot was packed with too many teenagers who thought their driving skills were superior to the kid's next to them, so it felt like hell was being unleashed promptly at 2:15 every day.

Connor had been maneuvering through this chaos for years now, and effectively cut his way through to an exit and got us on our way home just as underclassmen were beginning to board the buses. My mind wandered back to when Kate and I used to race to our car to be one of the first ones released from the lot. We rarely socialized with our friends at the end of the day, because everyone was making the mad dash to the parking lot. I was comforted by the fact that at least *that* hadn't changed while I was away. I rolled my window down and watched the fall trees whiz by. One of the roads back to my house was a winding one through a thick part of the woods. It wasn't travelled much because of the potholes and deer. It was a beautiful and convenient shortcut to my neighborhood, though.

My eyes rolled over to Connor. Just like this morning, we weren't saying much to each other. His hands clutched the wheel and his knuckles were pale. It pained me to think that he doubted his driving skills only because he believed Jackson's carelessness had caused him and Kate to go flying into a ravine to their deaths. I wondered how many times he pictured that image in his head while he drove, and immediately cursed myself for not thinking of a better, less traumatic way to have staged my sister and her boyfriend's deaths.

I pressed my lips together and started humming, audible enough so he could hear me over the rushing wind. He broke his fixation on the road and kept stealing glances at me. Getting his attention once again reassured me that there was part of his old self that could be recovered in moments like this.

"What're you singing?" he asked.

"I think you know," I replied lightly. I stuck my hand out the window and let it flutter on the wind, and kept humming.

I caught the first genuine grin when I checked his face again. "Sweet Caroline," I sang.

Then, on cue, he burst out, "Bum, bum, bum!"

"Good times never seemed so good," I chimed in, giggling at his welcome effort to sing with me. "I'd be inclined—"

"Bum, bum, bum!"

"To believe they never—" I gasped so suddenly it was almost a shriek. "LOOK OUT!"

Connor snapped his attention back to the road as he slammed on the brakes. They squealed furiously in protest, but we couldn't slow down fast enough before barreling right into the young man in the middle of the road.

He hit the hood of the car and was sent sailing through the air. The car finally came to a violent halt, slamming Connor and me into our seats, as the person's body hit the ground. I stared in shock, mouth hanging open. My hands were trembling. Connor clenched the wheel even tighter, if that was possible.

"Holy shit," he breathed shakily.

We sat frozen. I don't think either of us wanted to believe we had just hit a person, but there he was, lying in the road. Neither of us knew what to do.

"Do you think I killed him?" Connor finally voiced what we both were wondering. As I was about to answer, rather untruthfully, the body twitched.

"Oh my God, he's alive," I said with disbelief and relief. I threw the seatbelt from me and jumped from the car. The man's body had landed a good twenty feet from the car. I rushed over and knelt beside him.

He lay face down with one arm propped under his head and the other across his face, covering it from view. His legs were splayed wildly, and he looked like a crazy sleeper in the middle of the road. It wasn't until I saw the thick riding boots on his feet that I noticed that his clothes weren't normal. I didn't know any guys around here who wore tight pants and a leathery, quilted shirt. The long cape-like thing draped haphazardly over him only confused me more.

"Please tell me he isn't dead," Connor said shakily between a string of curses. He'd gotten out of the car and left it idling as he hesitantly approached.

I was about to reach out to shake the young man's shoulder when I heard an agonized groan as his head rolled to the side.

My eyes doubled in size and my mouth gaped. For a moment, I completely forgot that we'd just bulldozed into this guy as I violently grabbed his shoulder and pushed him over. I couldn't believe my eyes.

"Brennon!"

"I hate your world already." He cringed from an internal pain. Connor called to me again, and I jumped into action. I started inspecting Brennon for any major bleeding, but somehow, there was none. His hands and forearms had multiple scratches from skidding across the gravelly road. I decided to tend to those later, knowing they weren't too pressing. What, then, was the cause of the moaning?

Connor stood over me. "Holy shit; he *is* alive."

I placed a hand on Brennon's abdomen, and he stopped moaning and snapped to attention. "CASEY! At least sedate me before you start poking around!" he growled through gritted teeth.

I didn't bother to address the confusion on Connor's face. "How does he know your name? Do you know him?"

"Can you stand?" I called to Brennon, because he seemed to be fading. "Brennon! Can you stand?" He looked up at me, a hard glare on his face.

"I'll call an ambulance," Connor offered.

I kept my gaze fixed on Brennon. "No, Connor. Help me!" I yelled over my shoulder. His feet shifted, unsure of what to do. He finally dropped next to me, halted any questions for the moment, and helped pull Brennon to his feet.

"Let's put him in the back seat," I instructed.

"Shouldn't we call an ambulance? They'll know what to do."

I brushed off Connor's questions and concerns. "Just get him in the car." We ungracefully dragged Brennon over to the vehicle. The moaning had turned to pained grunts. I pulled the door open, and we clumsily managed to slide him onto the seat.

Connor stepped back from us, but I stayed a few inches from Brennon's face. His breathing was ragged. He eyes suddenly shot open. They revealed a mix of fury, disbelief, and distress. He tried his best to blink the emotions away.

"Where's the necklace?" His eyes flicked to my chest, where it should have been hanging.

"I left it at home. Why?" I responded, matching his angst. Connor made a puzzled sound, which we both ignored.

"We need to get there, now. The Sagen are coming for it."

Every bone in my body doubted what Brennon had said, but a few minutes ago, they would have doubted the possibility of ever seeing Brennon here. I quickly turned to Connor and told him we had to get home. He was still too confused to refuse my demand.

As the three of us sped towards my house, Connor kept glancing in his rear-view mirror, watching Brennon and me huddled in the back seat. Brennon's body stretched across the seat, and his head rested in my lap. I placed my hands on his chest and abdomen and used my healing abilities to mend what had been fractured, torn, and bruised underneath. I kept whispering 'sorry' every time I caught a glance of his scrunched face.

"How do you know they're coming for it?" I asked him, to distract him from the pain.

"Myra sensed they were after your necklace, built a portal to reach you, and chose me to come warn you. Then I get run over by this monstrosity!" His voiced grew louder with each word, which meant that his insides were mending. "I mean, what is this thing, anyway? A glorified wagon?" he spat.

Connor stole another glance. "Portal? Wagon? Are you sure he's okay, Casey?" His eyes shifted between looking at the road and at me.

I tried to brush off his concern as coolly as I could manage, but my heart raced uncontrollably. "Probably a small concussion. He'll be fine."

"I'd be even better if your friend hadn't nearly killed me. I can maneuver Danzinar better than this piece of shit!"

"Dandazar? Is that a car model?"

"No. *Danzinar* is my dragon," Brennon shot back before I could clamp my hand over his mouth.

"Brennon," I lowered my voice. "Stop talking."

"*Dragon?* I think he's lost it," Connor said. I made an affirmative sound.

I decided to let Connor think that Brennon was crazy and ignored the scattered 'hmms' and 'huhs.' My hands hovered over Brennon's cracked ribs. I hadn't healed anything this major before, so I blocked the guys out and focused on the splintering bones. It was like a jigsaw puzzle that needed to be reassembled. As I was pulling his last rib into the proper position, I heard Kate's name, and my attention was jerked back to their conversation.

"What does he mean that Kate's been looking for you?" Connor asked.

My eyes shot up to meet his. "What?" Brennon's last bone snapped forcefully into place. He bolted upright, almost knocking his head into my low-bent chin, and jumped to the other side of the car. I tried to tell him with my eyes that Connor believed Kate was dead. Brennon didn't catch any of it.

"Of course she's looking for her," Brennon said. I raised a threatening hand, and Brennon's mouth formed a large "O" shape. "I figured he knew."

I shook my head furiously. We were just pulling into my neighborhood. Connor parked sharply next to the curb. "Knew what?" he asked me.

"Nothing," I replied hastily. I leaned over Brennon to unlock the car door and shoved him out. I climbed out after him. As I was sliding out of the car, Connor vacated the driver's seat and dashed around the car to block me from going anywhere. I thought he was anxious before, but now he couldn't try to hide it.

I tried to duck around him, but he grabbed my shoulders and anchored me. "What the hell is going on? Who is this guy?" he glanced at Brennon. "And isn't your collarbone broken or something?" Connor snapped. The way Brennon stood would never lead anyone to believe a car had just run him down.

"My ribs were, actually," he replied lightly, "and they're still a little sore."

"He's fine," I broke in. "Connor," I said, bringing his attention back to me. "Look, I know this isn't making sense, and I promise I'll explain later. But the two of us need to go inside, now!"

I gently pushed him away. He wavered, and his eyes harbored thousands of questions. I couldn't tell if he was scared for himself, or for me. It may have been a mix of both. I steadied my breathing and softened my face to convince him to leave. Just as I thought he was going to climb back in the car and drive away, Brennon ripped his sword from its scabbard. I wondered how we hadn't seen it before then. It must have been hidden behind his cloak.

Connor jumped back. "Shit, man!"

"I think they're already inside," Brennon said to me, but he faced the house, searching the windows with his eyes.

I tried to pass Connor again, more forcefully this time, but he wrapped tense fingers around my arm, pulling me back. "He has a sword!" It sounded like a question and realization at the same time.

"Connor, let go!"

"Hey, get your hands off her!" Brennon shouted.

"Be careful with that thing! Why the hell do you have a sword?" Connor snapped at Brennon, and then said to me, "I'm not letting you go anywhere with him."

"Connor, it's fine. Let me go. No, Brennon, don't hurt him!" Brennon had latched onto Connor's other arm. I tried frantically to pry fingers away, but I had no idea who they belonged to anymore.

The situation was spinning out of control. I couldn't explain myself to one of them without giving away secrets to the other. Our confused wrestling with each other was interrupted by a shrill scream.

"Grandma," I gasped.

Both released their grips on me, and I darted forward. I raced up the walkway, whispered an Unlocking spell, and threw the heavy wooden door open. It banged against the wall as I moved past the narrow hallway into the kitchen. I turned the corner and skidded to a halt. My grandmother stood behind the island in the middle of the room. She trembled as a long, jagged knife rested at her throat. The creature that held it sent images hurtling through my mind.

I'd encountered the Sagen on multiple occasions, but that didn't make seeing them any less frightening. However, it wasn't the warriors that actually sent shivers up my spine. It was the fact that they stood, solidly, in my world. I'd always envisioned the line drawn between my world and Alagia as one that only Kate and I could cross. I never really entertained the thought that other people, and things, could cross over, too. I suppose Brennon's presence had already shattered that comfort, though.

I heard Brennon curse furiously behind me, and Connor sucked in a sharp breath. I spun and saw that three other Sagen restrained them. Brennon was fuming about being jumped from behind. I turned back to my grandmother, and two more Sagen had appeared. I wondered where Adalia was, but she was nowhere in sight.

"Where is the necklace?" one warrior hissed. The snake-like sound made me recoil.

"It's not here," I said without thinking.

An airy *sss* sound came from the Sagen. "We can sense when a portal to our world is near." It made a sweeping gesture towards my grandmother, and the Sagen holding her pressed the knife a little deeper. A small trickle of blood started to form along the edge of the blade. I made a move to stop him, but hesitated. I wouldn't be able to cross the room and stop the warrior before it slit her throat.

"All right, all right; it's here." I raised my hands as a sign for the Sagen to stand down.

"Casey," Connor whimpered. I angled my body towards him so that I could still see my grandmother from the corner of my eye. His normally large build looked tiny in comparison to the even larger Sagen. Connor's face was a mask of terror. My heart seared with pain, longing to give the comfort I couldn't provide him.

"I'm going to get you out of this, Connor." I kept my voice even to be as reassuring as possible.

"The necklace. Your sister is not very patient."

Connor's eyes shifted from my face to the Sagen behind me, and then back to me. I could feel my carefully constructed expression fading.

"She's alive?" Connor whispered.

I opened my mouth to respond, but pressed my lips back together when I realized I had no explanation.

"I'll go get it." I spoke to the Sagen, but kept my defeated eyes on Connor. His entire body seemed to have fallen slack.

I felt a cold hand on my shoulder and a chilling voice in my ear. "We're coming with you," the warrior said as it pushed me forward. I shrugged it off and headed towards the stairs. I caught Brennon's gaze just before I turned the corner. *Get them out of here,* I said to him, mentally. His eyes ignited with these words as we exchanged glances.

I left Connor, Brennon, and three Sagen behind in the kitchen and climbed the stairs with three more Sagen floating on my heel. I slowed outside my room, thinking of how I was going to grab the necklace before they could; get Connor and my grandmother to safety; and do so without alerting the entire world that mystical creatures were in my house.

A violent push from behind made me fall forward and into my room. Once I regained my footing, I was thrust against the wall as the other Sagen stepped forward. A bony limb pressed into my neck to keep me from moving. I peered towards the stairs, hoping Brennon could handle everything downstairs.

"Where is it?"

"I thought you could sense its presence," I croaked, my throat half closed. The Sagen grabbed my face with black, skeletal fingers. My cheeks and lips were smashed together under its grip. "I won't ask again."

I couldn't form comprehensible words anymore, so I flicked my eyes towards my closet door. The Sagen stepped back and wrenched the door open. "Top shelf," I croaked.

I heard a crash come from downstairs, and then something that sounded like a vase shattering into a million pieces. My mind grew restless from worrying about what was happening downstairs. *Please keep them safe, Brennon.*

The Sagen emerged from my closet, music box in hand. It opened it, and the third Sagen that had been guarding the door lifted the necklace from the cushion.

It swung like a pendulum, taunting me with each swoop. I randomly caught the smell of smoke, and my nose wrinkled.

"What do you want with it?" The Sagen ignored me and laid the necklace on my desk. Then, the other Sagen removed a menacingly sharp dagger from its belt. "Hey! What are you doing?" I shouted frantically.

"Bid your door to Alagia farewell."

I thought quickly. It had been months since I'd used my powers for combat, but trying to formulate a plan wasn't an option.

I threw my hands up and clutched the arm of the Sagen that restricted me. My handprints burned into it, as it doubled back, howling in pain. I broke from its grasp and rushed at the Sagen with the dagger, which was poised right above the necklace. I hit it in the chest and sent it skidding back across my floor, leaving scorched marks on the wood.

I eyed the smoky trail, annoyed. "Thanks," I scoffed. Suddenly, flames burst through the door. The Sagen I'd burnt had completely ignited. I jumped back in surprise, but didn't have time to think about the source of the fire.

I rushed back to my desk and snatched up the necklace before the other Sagen could grab it. It started to come around the desk. With a flick of my wrist, I threw the large wooden desk into it. The Sagen and the desk broke through my wall, through my closet floor, and went tumbling to the first floor below. My mouth parted in shock as the heat became extremely uncomfortable.

I whipped around. I still had one more opponent. It rushed me, but I ducked out of its way. My head jerked back, and I shrieked in surprise. The warrior had caught my hair and was dragging me towards it. I tried to twist away, but I couldn't go anywhere. I threw my arm out and cracked it in the jaw. The Sagen released my hair, and I spun and kicked it in the gut. It snarled and started to come at me again. With a sweep of my hand, I yanked my mini-chandelier from the ceiling and brought it crashing down on top of the Sagen. The warrior easily evaded it as it went crashing to the floor.

Then, the Sagen made a motion as if it was pushing the floor down. The wooden boards under me collapsed, and the floor fell through. Somehow, I managed to catch myself on a wooden beam and hold on as the rest of my room's contents fell in a chaotic heap around me. I still clutched the necklace in my hand as my lower body dangled. Hot flames licked at me from below. I searched for Brennon, Connor, and my grandmother, but all I saw was fire eating away at everything in its path.

The Sagen warrior kneeled next to the edge of the new hole in my room. It stretched its hand out to me. "The necklace," it demanded.

I glared at it. "You'll have to try harder than that," I spat. The beam I clung to started groaning under my weight. The fire had severely weakened the wood. I nervously listened to it creak.

"Give it to me, and I will help you," it offered.

I held out my hand that clutched the necklace. The Sagen stretched down and grasped my hand. I smirked, and before it had time to retreat, I yanked the warrior down and watched as it crashed into flames below. It disintegrated upon impact. Then, my heart sank at a snapping sound. I screamed as the broken beam and I went tumbling to the ground. I hit my back and head on the wood floor and furniture. Ashes flew up into my face, but I couldn't cough. I was still struggling to get my breath back. I lay in the rubble, the necklace still clenched tightly in my hand.

The world spun, and though my mind screamed at me to get up, I couldn't move. My head was pounding and I couldn't dismiss the sudden heat that suffocated me. That's when I remembered the fire. I closed my eyes, willing every ounce of my body to focus, or else be burned alive. I remembered Myra telling me that I could become "one with fire" for a brief period of time, during which the flames wouldn't burn me. I slowly felt the flames become less oppressive. A few moments later, I opened my eyes and noticed that I didn't feel hot anymore, even though I was surrounded by an inferno.

I turned my head and my fuzzy gaze fell on a picture on the mantle above the fireplace. It was of my mother and father, before Kate and I were born. They were sitting under a maple tree in the fall; the hues of orange and red were all around them. My mother's full laugh was forever frozen in time and my father's smile was knowing. My grandmother had revealed that picture to me soon after my return from Alagia. I reached out for it, willing it to come to me, but my head was so foggy I couldn't even think of the spell.

I heard a bang that sounded like a gunshot, and then feet pounded their way into the house. Firemen suddenly burst into the room. They began scrambling everywhere as they searched for something. I heard them breaking down doors, shoving furniture, and shouting commands. I wanted to call out to them, but I couldn't find my voice.

Suddenly, several panicked shrieks cut through the air and sent my head spinning. "Over here," one yelled to the others.

Hands began pulling the heavy wood that had fallen with me. I just lay there like a rag doll, limp and expressionless.

"What the hell happened?" I heard a voice shout. He must have been referring to the ceiling. "She's not burned!" another exclaimed. In my disoriented state, I wondered what he meant.

Two arms wedged themselves under me and lifted me up. I was carried from the smoke-filled room and rushed outside. As I lay helpless in someone's arms, I thought of all my books, my mother's journals, Kate's clothes, my grandmother's collectible quilts, second grade art projects, and years worth of math notes all being devoured by an indifferent fire.

Once outside, I breathed deeply, greedily taking in air. I was resting on a stretcher. Hands started poking at me, and I heard voices marvel at my unburned condition. Everything sounded like it was under water. Several minutes passed in this manner, until the medics were called away to help with my grandmother. The firefighter who was told to stay with me was ordered to help somewhere too, so I was finally left in peace. My head was so cloudy that I began to welcome sleep before a sharp bark jolted me back to the present. Adalia nudged her nose into my hand as Brennon rushed over.

"Casey!" Brennon shook my shoulder. I peered at him, my head instantly clearing.

He placed a hand in the small of my back and helped me sit up. "The Sagen?" Brennon asked.

"Dead. My grandmother?"

"With your yellow people," he replied. I would have laughed at what he had called the firefighters, but I was too caught up in everything.

"How did my house catch on fire?" I turned to Brennon, who watched the ruckus of the scene before him.

Brennon's mouth twisted. "The Sagen threw an Incendiary spell at us."

"Connor?" Brennon made an uneasy noise, as though he didn't know how to respond. "What happened? Where is he?"

Brennon gestured to the black woods behind my house. The dancing light from the fire wasn't able to penetrate the deep darkness of the trees. "He's back there. He was hit by a spell," he admitted.

My eyes flared with anger, until I remembered there was nothing Brennon could have done to protect Connor from the sorcery. I stole one more glance back at the commotion that was now mounting on the street in front of my house. I caught a glimpse of my grandmother being treated by a medic. She looked a little distraught, but unable to move at the same time. Either way, she looked unharmed, at least physically anyway. Firemen darted about fighting the fire. They seemed to have forgotten I was left on the gurney, so I slid down, with Brennon's help, and followed him to the wood's edge.

Brennon and I ducked behind a thick trunk and found Connor propped against it. Or rather, he had been. Now he slumped over and writhed with pain. I knelt beside him and grabbed his hand in mine.

"Connor?" I didn't try to steady the fear in my voice. "Connor, can you hear me?" He ducked his chin, which I counted as a nod. I leaned back and noticed a festering wound on his bicep. It was black and boiling, with smoke rising from it.

Seeing his deflated and hurt expression on my first day back home had broken me down inside. But now, seeing raw pain tear into his face completely snapped something inside me. I hated myself for involving him in a world for which he was utterly unprepared.

"Bite on this," Brennon told Connor, handing him a torn bundle of his cloak. I silently apologized before I placed my hand right on his wound. Connor bit the fabric and a strangled, but muffled, cry burst from him. Brennon stood back to give us space and watched helplessly. After several excruciating seconds, I pulled my hand away. The wound was smaller, but not healed. I was too weak. I gave in to Connor's eyes, which were worn thin with fear. I hushed him gently, placed a hand on his cheek, and infused a Sedative charm into his skin.

"Did you get it?" Brennon asked me. I opened my hand in response. The necklace shone in the moon's light.

"We need to go back—now. I can't be here for much longer."

"We're bringing Connor with us," I added.

There was a full pause between us. "That's not a good idea."

"I can't heal him completely. I need Myra's help." Brennon made another queasy sound. "I'm not asking for your permission. I'm telling you, I'm bringing him."

Brennon saw the resolve in my expression and sighed in surrender. "Fine. But know that, just like I can't be in your world for long, he can't be in mine for long, either." I nodded my understanding. "Okay, let's go."

I felt the charm in my hand, when suddenly I sucked in a sharp breath. "The music box!"

"What about it?"

"I left it in the house." Brennon raised an eyebrow. "It has the inscription on it that opens the doorway."

His mouth hung open with an absent answer. "Well, can't you make something up?"

I shrugged. "I never had to try. I've only done it once," I said sharply. Brennon brushed aside my comment and coaxed me to try something—anything.

"Okay..." I responded. I thought for minute, trying to remember the poetic words I had spoken last time to gain entrance into Alagia. *Take me to a world where few have gone, where destiny can finally become my own.* "Return us to the world where our destinies are not complete," I intonated awkwardly. I glanced sideways at Brennon, who smiled with only a fraction of his face.

I was about to add something when the trees began to chatter. A wind rustled the leaves, and a thick wooden door began to materialize in front of us. My hair flew about wildly with the wind. The door swung open and a shower of light spilled over us. Brennon expertly hauled Connor onto his broad back and balanced him effortlessly. The glaring light made the dizziness I had felt before come rushing back, and my whole body swayed. Brennon placed a solid hand on my shoulder and steadied me.

"Looks like you need a visit from Myra, too." He pushed me ahead of him and let me lead the way back to Alagia, with Adalia on our flanks.

As I was stepping over the threshold, I wondered about my future. At best, it was uncertain. Now I wondered if I would ever see my school again, if I would ever sit with Nick and Brenna again in the commons, or do homework at the kitchen counter. I wondered if I would ever see my house again, or my grandmother, or come home to freshly baked breads. I wondered if I'd ever see all the kids that stole glances at me in the hallway and whispered that I was the surviving twin. I wondered for how much longer I would *actually* survive, now that it seemed I was going back into the snake pit. Above all, I wondered if I was finally leaving my old life for good.

At first, the pain crept over me slowly, and then it came as an onslaught. Suddenly, all the adrenaline I'd felt before fell away, and I collapsed under crushing agony. I cried out as I felt the sensation of my body being torn apart. Adalia barked madly in fright. Someone supported my weight and called out to me, but I could only make out indistinct sounds before I passed out.

Chapter 4: Kate

I COULDN'T REMEMBER the last time my boots had been free of a thin layer of black soot. I couldn't remember the last time I went to bed without first having to wash ash from my skin. I couldn't remember the last time I saw the sun, or a blue sky. These thoughts crossed my mind as I pushed a few strands of hair behind my ear and straightened to face my targets. Four burly men waited patiently for me to make my move. Since the Sagen were not suitable sparring partners, they configured human projections to simulate fighting with people.

I targeted one and ran towards him. Once I had engaged with the first one, it was like I had clicked an "on" switch for the others. They all jumped forward. The first man crouched low and ran towards me as if he was a linebacker. I dropped to the ground and slid past him, knocking his feet from under him. I rolled over and just missed getting a solid punch to my chin. I landed a hard kick in my attacker's gut, jumped up, and landed another blow to the side of his skull. Just to make sure he was "dead," I stomped hard on his neck. A third and fourth man approached and began throwing punches. I would block one, get hit by another, land one, get hit by another. I ducked low and kicked hard at one man's kneecap. He crumpled to the ground. As I was spinning to locate the other man, I felt my jaw crack and my head jerk in the opposite direction. Even though these men weren't real, the Sagen made sure to include pain as part of the simulation.

As I regained my balance, I felt my arms being twisted behind my back and a knee was being driven into my spine. I gritted my teeth and threw all my weight forward, which catapulted the man holding me over my back and onto the floor. He rolled over, stood, and produced a knife from his belt. I fleetingly thought that it wasn't fair that I couldn't use weapons during these sessions, but my attackers always seemed to have them.

The man jumped forward and slashed the knife through the air, as I ducked to the side. I caught the arm holding the knife between my own arms before he spun away. He came at me again, slicing the knife back and forth, but I kept blocking his swings with my arms. Finally, I miscalculated his move and turned the wrong way. I envisioned the cut before I felt the knife rip into my upper arm. I cursed the Sagen's wicked game and burst forward with new energy. I lunged to one side to miss his swing, spun, grabbed his hand holding the knife, and gave it a violent twist. His whole body shuddered as I felt his shoulder dislocate. I snatched the knife and kicked his injured shoulder so that he fell onto his back. As he writhed in pain, I lifted the knife above my head. As I was about to drive it deep into his chest, he and the knife disappeared. My arm no longer stung, and the simulation was over.

I pulled myself from my crouched position and stood to face my hooded mentor. "You could have at least let me finish,"

I complained, as I brushed some sweat from my brow. "And will I ever get a weapon of my own during one of these sessions?"

The Sagen ignored me. "Azlaya has returned."

I stopped short. "She has?"

I brushed past the Sagen and back towards my abode. The trodden path to my training site was easy to follow, up a slope and onto a flat plateau. I walked briskly and kept a keen eye out for Azlaya. It had been much too long since I'd heard from her, and even longer since I'd seen her. Once up the slope, I could see my homestead erupting from jagged rocks. I rushed quickly to the door, rapped twice, and was let in by a house servant. He ducked out of my way as I went past and down a corridor. At the end of the hall, I descended a flight of stairs into a cave-like room. A long table made of the same rough stone as the exterior stretched down the middle, and chairs that looked like they could draw blood surrounded it. At the end sat Azlaya.

It had been weeks since I'd seen her, and, as expected, she hadn't changed a bit, except for her eyes. They looked worn. Her black, curly hair was pulled up into an unruly bun, and small wisps framed her pale face. Her lips were a deep, red color, and her eyes were dark. Her jawline seemed tight and her mouth was more downturned than usual. Even the creases on her forehead seemed a little more defined. I knew it wasn't a result of aging, considering that she didn't age, so I figured she was especially anxious about something. When her eyes fell on me, she beckoned me over with a sharp movement.

"Kate, come sit." It was an order, not an invitation.

I lowered myself into the chair next to hers at the head of the table. I never liked the meeting room. It was musty and dank, and nothing like the dry world above that I'd gotten used to. "How was your trip?" I asked.

A servant entered the room and placed some refreshments before us. Azlaya batted her away with a dismissive hand. "I've been receiving progress reports on your training." She plucked a slice of cheese off the plate and placed it on her tongue. I held my breath as she chewed, wondering if the Sagen had told her about my frustration with her absence, or my restlessness to find my sister. She swallowed. "I'm very pleased." I silently let out a sigh of relief.

"Does this mean I'm coming with you the next time you leave?" I asked eagerly.

"No," she replied, between sips of wine. "But you are going to help me with something. This war is going to be fought, not with iron weapons, but with spells. You're going to help me build an army that can do that." I remember my Sagen mentor telling me the same thing days ago.

"How?"

"Do you remember what I told about how the Sagen get their powers?" Azlaya looked at me keenly. This was a test. The training never stopped.

"Sure. They take the sorcery abilities from humans and it results in Dark Magic."

Azlaya nodded. "What I didn't tell you at the time is that their powers can be amplified by passing it on to other Sagen. Each time one's powers are passed along, the magic becomes even more powerful," she explained.

"If that's the case, then why doesn't one Sagen pass its powers on to the rest?"

"The sorcery can only be passed on a limited number of times. The more powerful the sorcerer, however, the farther his or her powers can be passed."

I sat in silence trying to run the numbers in my head. I never had an affinity for math, but I could envision the process of Sagen with sorcery multiplying like bacteria. "All right, but where do I come in?"

"I need you to find the sorcerers." I stared at her, but her expression remained firm. "I'm going to send you to Eileen to hunt down sorcerers that the Sagen can use."

"I finally get to leave the Shadowlands?" I asked with a little too much eagerness. Azlaya's stare cut my celebration short.

"Yes, you will be allowed to roam Eileen freely to find these sorcerers. Your sister, and anything concerning her, shall remain peripheral." Azlaya could see protest in my eyes, because she quickly added. "Your sister's powers will have grown stronger, just as yours have, but soon you'll be unbeatable. Until then, you will focus on this task. Am I clear?" I nodded my response.

"What about the other kingdoms?"

"I've had Sagen scouring them while I've been away." I wondered briefly what else had been going on under my nose while I was preoccupied with my training. "However, the most powerful and largest concentration of sorcerers will be in Eileen."

"Why's that?"

"Eileen is home to some of the best sorcery academies. It's where the most gifted sorcerers are sent to train, and where the most powerful sorcerers teach. You'll find the best specimens there, and in and around the kingdom."

I nodded in understanding. It finally occurred to me that Azlaya's plans for me did not involve her at all. "This is something I'll do on my own?" I asked her.

Azlaya made a repugnant expression. "Well, I'm not your nanny. I'm just trying to keep your ego from getting you killed. Besides, I believe you're well equipped to handle Eileen on your own."

"Where will you be?"

"I'm making provisions to make sure our rule goes unchallenged after you kill your sister. Sagen enforcing our authority throughout the kingdoms will help, but I'm looking for something that will make us—invincible," Azlaya said, with so much conviction that a chill settled on my skin.

"What is it?" I asked. Azlaya's gaze had become a bit distant, and my question made her focus back on me. She often let her thoughts wander when she spoke of her rule after the war. She *had* been waiting a long time to be recognized as a ruler by Alagia's people.

"It's a sorcerer. One that even your mother would fear. That's all you need to know now. I want you to stay focused on your mission. Doing so will allow me to focus on mine."

A part of me jumped with anticipation at the mention of my mother. Azlaya rose from her chair and rounded the table so that she loomed over me. She took my left arm in her hand and pressed two fingers to my wrist where my pulse beat rhythmically. Suddenly, I felt stinging under her fingers. I knew better than to show pain, so I bit the inside of my lip and waited for the searing to subside. When Azlaya pulled her fingers away, a Celtic-looking tattoo was burned into my skin. Slowly, the inflammation subsided and the design settled into a black coloration. "When you've found a sorcerer that the Sagen can use, put a finger here," Azlaya said as she pointed to the marking, "and the Sagen will appear to take them away."

I was too busy examining the design to notice a Sagen stood in the doorway to the stairs. "He's ready, My Lady," it said to Azlaya.

She dipped her chin in the Sagen's direction and turned back to me. "Go pack a travel bag. You'll leave for Eileen tonight." I nodded to Azlaya and stood. She produced my necklace from the inner folds of her cloak and held it out for me to take as I passed. I slipped past the Sagen and started climbing the stairs. "Bring him in," Azlaya ordered the Sagen below.

When I'd made it to the top of the stairs. I heard the sound of something being slammed on the hard table and a grunt. I knew better than to spy on Azlaya, but I couldn't get my feet to pull me away.

"I won't tell you anything," a new, human voice said.

"Would you like that inscribed on your gravestone when I'm done with you?" I heard the slamming sound again. "Where is the tomb?"

"You'll have to kill me first."

"Don't give me an offer I won't be able to refuse," I heard Azlaya say playfully. Strangled screams erupted from the meeting room before they were abruptly cut off. *Silencing spell*, I thought. I figured that was as good as any cue to leave before I was discovered eavesdropping.

I practically ran to my room and hurriedly shut the door behind me. I didn't remember seeing anyone else in the room while I spoke with Azlaya, so where did the other person come from? I realized there must have been another door down there that led to another passage. I didn't put hidden entryways past Azlaya. She seemed to like that sort of thing. But what were they talking about? Where was whose tomb? Who was this sorcerer that Azlaya sought out for help?

I caught sight of my new tattoo while these thoughts raced through my head. Azlaya was hunting something, but so was I. I would have to worry about her endeavors later, because I had a mission of my own.

I drew a black knapsack from under my bed and knelt next to my trunk of clothes. I packed several rugged outfits and my heavy-soled boots that laced up to my knees. I remembered being told about Eileen's harsh climate and dug up a long, black coat that was lined with warm bear fur. I wondered how quickly I was going to adjust from the Shadowlands dry weather to Eileen's frigidness.

As I continued to pack my things in my travel bag, my excitement at getting away from what had become my prison kept growing. I was finally being released into the world; my leash was getting cut. I was to help build an army of Sagen to conquer the four kingdoms, and then I'd be able to reunite with my mother. It all seemed so simple in principle. Essentially I was acting as the Sagen's bloodhound while they fortified their strength and power. I didn't know what Casey and the Hunters were planning, but it had to be weak in comparison to this ambitious plan. A new sense of purpose burst inside me, as I felt my invisible chain fall away.

Finally.

Chapter 5: Casey

I HURT. EVERY movement, every breath, even every thought hurt. It felt like someone was smacking the side of my head with a wooden plank. A glaring pain engulfed my back as well. My entire body ached so much that I knew I must have fractured bones somewhere. Every time I inhaled and exhaled, an excruciating pain stabbed me in the chest and made me wish I'd black out again. If breathing hurt this much, I didn't want to imagine what other actions would do. My heavy eyelids fluttered open, and the sudden light made me squint.

Myra crouched over a boiling pot of herbs and incense in the tent. Now, more than ever, she looked like a stereotypical witch. She poured the pot's contents into a cup and brought it over to me. I winced and whimpered when I pulled myself upright. My hands wouldn't stop shaking, so Myra had to help me hold the cup and bring it to my lips. She took it back, and I gratefully slumped back down. Myra called to a Hunter outside, and she entered the tent. I recognized her as one of Myra's students, so that made me the temporary guinea pig.

She came to my bedside and instructed me to roll onto my stomach. I bit my lip and squeezed my eyes shut, willing myself to just flop over. Inch by painful inch, I turned over; it seemed to take an eternity. Myra and the Hunter placed their hands under me to try to be of assistance. Between the combination of moving my head and twisting my back, I thought my body was being ripped apart. A sharp pain erupted through me. I couldn't even scream. That level of pain needed a different sound, and screaming wouldn't have done it justice.

Myra gently lifted my shirt up to my shoulder blades. The Hunter started moving her hands over my spine. The dull pain I'd felt earlier started becoming more pronounced. I dug my teeth into my pillow to try to still my body. The grinding sound, I realized, wasn't from gritting my teeth, but from the Hunter literally realigning the bones in my spine and rib cage. After several minutes, my body trembled. She finally pulled her hands away, and the sharp pains faded to dull ones again.

"I have to do that to make sure your spine doesn't lock up," she said apologetically. They helped me turn back over. "Just relax," the Hunter soothed me.

"Out…how…how long…" I couldn't form a coherent sentence. Words swam in my mind, but I couldn't piece them together in a sensible way.

"Worse than I thought." Myra mused, as she and the Hunter exchanged glances.

The Hunter hushed me and placed a warm hand over my forehead. Her healing abilities slowly started to return my vision, and I could begin to locate words in my head without delays. It was as if she had wiped the residue from my head and allowed me to think clearly again. Everything was in focus again and there weren't fuzzy spots in my vision anymore. The incessant, pulsing headache was finally disappearing.

"You couldn't have done that sooner?" I breathed a sigh of relief when the last remnants of my head injury were gone.

"We wanted to wait until you were conscious again before messing around in your head," Myra said in a tone that made it impossible to question her judgment. The Hunter pulled her hands away and took her leave to go.

"Your back and ribs will still be sore for a couple more days, but how does your head feel?"

"Tired, but almost normal again. Thank you," I replied. It was the first time I noticed how Myra's eyes dragged with exhaustion and how striking her pallor was. "How long have I been out?"

"Two days."

"Are you all right?"

"A little drained," she replied dismissively.

I organized the scattered thoughts in my head, and one, which had been skirting around the edges of my memory, jumped out at me. "Connor."

If Connor had died, I wouldn't have known it from Myra's expression. She always seemed to be able to keep her face calm and collected, regardless of the havoc that could surround her. Now, she showed off that impressive, but sometimes infuriating, talent of hers. "The boy you brought back with you?" I heard disapproval in her voice.

"Yes. Is he—" I didn't know how to finished my question. *Is he actually here? Is he angry? Is he wondering what the hell is going on? Is he alive? Is he dead?*

"He's alive."

"The spell—will it...is it still in him?"

Myra smiled, though limply, with the approval that wasn't evident in her voice. "That was a very dark and strong spell. You managed to hold it at bay until I saw him."

I thought back to kneeling next to Connor as he trembled. I had wrapped my hand around it and thought about absorbing the spell in my disoriented state. Thankfully, it had worked.

"You absorbed it?" Myra asked.

"I think so." I held out my hand as some sort of evidence. Myra took it and ran a delicate finger over my palm. Her eyebrows furrowed and her normally peaceful face wavered into a flicker of consternation. "I don't know many sorcerers who possess that kind of power." She tapped her bottom lip as she thought.

"Myra?" She returned her gaze to match mine. "Connor. Can I see him?"

"Do you think you can walk?"

I pulled myself upright and slid from the bed in response. Myra motioned for me to follow her. Connor was in a tent next to the one we had exited, and I anxiously pushed my way inside. A different Hunter sat at his bedside with a hand on Connor's chest. Myra explained that the Hunter was using her sorcery to pull energy towards Connor. Without the extra energy, he wouldn't be able to remain in Alagia for very long. The Hunter lifted the Sleeping spell before exiting the tent. Before Myra turned to leave, too, she told me I had no more than an hour before he would start feeling the effects of the foreign world on his physical and mental state. I didn't want to know what that entailed, so I nodded my understanding, and Myra stepped aside to allow us privacy.

Connor had several pillows under his head, propping him up. His hands were clasped over his stomach. I dragged a stool to his bedside and collapsed on it. My hands fiddled with each other in my lap as Connor slowly regained consciousness. Once he was fully awake, he took one glance at me before training his eyes on a spot somewhere above him.

The silence was a thick fog, both tangible and impenetrable. I wished Connor's music were there to fill the silence, as it had before.

After what felt like a lifetime of this, I shattered the quiet veil. "Just say what you're thinking," I murmured.

"I'm trying to figure out how without cussing every other word."

"Okay," I replied softly.

There was another drawn-out pause. He finally sat up, but his eyes still didn't meet mine when he spoke again. "I just want the truth."

I nodded so slowly that it was hardly visible. I swallowed hard and let out an uneven breath. "You'll have to suspend your disbelief."

Connor nodded. "Where are we?"

"This world—it's called Alagia. It's where Kate and I were born."

"Is this where you were over the summer?"

"No. I really was in Europe."

"Those things that were at your house?"

"They're called Sagen."

"And you are?" He glanced so quickly at me that I nearly missed the shift in his eyes.

"I'm a sorceress."

"Sorceress?"

I opened my mouth to answer, but then I figured showing him would be the best explanation. In the hand I held out, I produced a simple Light spell. The little ball shriveled and died after a couple seconds.

"Have you always been able to do that?"

I shook my head. "No. I only discovered my powers recently."

"And Kate?"

"She's known about them for a while."

We both stopped to take a breath. "Is Kate actually dead? Those things at your house mentioned her. That guy did too."

I wet my lips, because I already knew the question that would follow this one. "No, she's still alive," I said shakily.

"Is Jackson dead?"

At my hesitation, his gaze finally shifted from the ground and fell heavily on me. The deep sorrow that had burrowed its way into everything he did was surfacing in his eyes. I tried swallowing a lump in my throat, but it wouldn't budge. "Yes, he really is."

"What happened?" He asked airily, trying hard stay in control of what he had bottled up inside.

I avoided his gaze and balanced my head in my hands. Connor moved on the bed and finally faced me, full-on. His knees knocked against mine, and when I lifted my head, his face was inches from mine.

"What *really* happened?" He wrapped his hands around my wrists and pulled my hands away from my face.

"Kate—she lost control of her powers and killed him." Connor's eyes fell to the floor. I placed a warm, but firm, hand on his arm. "I would do anything to bring him back to you," I whispered. Connor looked up; his unsteady breathing tickled my face. "But I can't. I can't bring him back, and I can't say 'sorry' enough times for that." I was choking back sobs.

Maybe Connor had done all his crying over the summer. Or maybe he was relieved to finally know the truth about his best friend's fate, but his face suddenly seemed more relaxed. He leaned closer and pulled my head onto his shoulder.

"I had to make up something for everyone to believe," I admitted, referring to Kate and Jackson's staged deaths. "I'm sorry—I'm so sorry."

I leaned back to see his face. I needed to know how he was absorbing everything I was saying. "I wish you had told me," he said.

I laughed emotionlessly. "I couldn't have without explaining all of—" I gestured around us. "All of this."

"How can any of this be real?" Connor asked.

I scrunched my shoulders up and pressed my lips into a tight line. "Even I haven't had that question answered." He seemed to grasp what I'd said relatively well—much better than I had, at least. Maybe the shock of the seeing Sagen and having a spell come hurtling at him had desensitized him.

"What happens now?"

I thought back to what Myra had warned me of earlier. "You have to go back home. You can't stay here, and I don't want to find out what'll happen if you try."

"Just like that? You tell me all this and then you're just going to ship me back home?" He seemed more hurt than I would have expected.

"Connor, you don't belong here," I replied gently. "And I won't risk your life again by keeping you here longer than I should."

He turned my words over in his head. "But you're staying?"

"Kate's—she's gotten herself tangled up with a not-so-great crowd. I have to stay to stop them. I can't let her hurt any more people the way she's hurt you."

Another pause settled between us. "What do I tell people at school? What do I say to Brenna and Nick?"

Something in my gut, heart, and head told me that I wasn't going to return home anytime soon. "Find my grandma. She knows about everything, and she'll know what to do—what to say."

He stood, but seemed reluctant to close the distance between us. As painful as the truth had been for me to reveal, it seemed to do him a great deal of good. He didn't appear to look as slouchy, and his eyes no longer weighed with as much depression. Sadness still lurked, but it was different, as though he was finally coming to terms with the death of his friend.

"If you want to forget about all this, I can wipe it all from your memory," I offered.

He shook his head. "No. I'm glad I know, and I'm glad you told me."

I pulled him to me and clung tight. "I wish none of this had happened to you." He inhaled deeply and pressed me into him tighter.

Though our common paths had finally come to a fork in the road, we both seemed to wonder what would have happened had they never split in different directions. The Hunter and Myra reentered the tent, and with Myra's patient instruction, the

Hunter created a portal to send Connor back to his world. He raised a hand and gave a curt wave before he turned, walked through the doorway, and faded into the air.

Myra collapsed on the bed. I was grateful she didn't mention the conversation between Connor and me. "After these last few days, all my hair is going to turn white."

I still stared where Connor had once stood. All that remained was his image in my mind.

"Your hair *is* practically white," I replied. Her bleached-blonde hair did look white in some light, which made her youthful and round face seem out of place.

She tossed me a sideways sneer. "Come. Kyraine's been waiting to see you."

I followed Myra from the tent, and a wave of familiarity hit me. I wound my way through the sea of tents again, and, unlike my first time navigating through them, I was filled with ease and comfort. It was strange, but I felt like I was home among them. Some of the leaves bristled as though they were asking me why I ever left.

I thought back to that day when I had faced Kate in the cold throne room of Azlaya's castle. After she and Azlaya had escaped, my father, whom I'd reunited with briefly, forced me to return home. I had tried to convince him to come with me, but now I understood why he couldn't. Since Connor couldn't be in Alagia for long, surely the same principle applied to my father. It wasn't until I was back in the forest in the middle of the bustle of the Hunters' camp that I realized how much I really missed Alagia. I should have fought harder to stay.

As I walked in step behind Myra, I was greeted by various Hunters, each bowing respectfully as I passed. They smelled of the forest that surrounded them. It was comforting to be swept up by the smoke, the flowers, the herbs, and the grass that coalesced into a single fragrance of the outdoors. Even when I was in Europe, I preferred the days I spent in the countryside to the urban settings.

Fond memories of sitting around the campfire listening to the Hunters' stories of far away lands and legendary battles floated through my head. A few of the warriors that I had gotten to know better during my last visit detained me for a few minutes, asking all sorts of questions and telling me how they had kept busy while I'd been away. I wished I could have spoken with them longer, but the impatience in Myra's eyes forced us to part ways prematurely. I quickly disengaged myself from them, but not before promising to catch up with them later.

I ducked out of the way of four Hunters carrying an oversized chest above their heads. They weren't the only ones transporting cargo. It seemed everyone in the camp was carrying a bow to be restrung, a sword to be sharpened, or a saddle to be mended. It was the most chaotic I'd ever seen the camp.

"It's so busy," I called to Myra.

Myra looked over her shoulder. "They're stocking up and getting ready," she replied, but her voice was drowned in the commotion.

I half expected a Sagen raid to suddenly come rushing out from the trees. Myra waved me forward as she held open the flap to the tent used for planning attacks and tactics. I ducked inside.

The shape of the tent was rectangular and fifty people could have comfortably fit inside. Tied up with thread and hanging along the sides were maps of Alagia, the Hunters' territory, the Huntsmen's territory, and a map of each of the four kingdoms. My eyes lingered on the map of the Huntsmen's land, which was a grassy expanse rolling with hills. Several blue shapes speckled their lands, which I assumed were lakes. Thoughts of my father crossed my mind, and I wondered if that was where he was at the moment.

Deeper into the tent, I spotted Kyraine speaking to two Hunters. They wore their usual garb of forest green tunics, dark riding boots, and a cloak with gold, braided embroidery on the edges. Around their waists were brown leather belts holding weapons such as daggers, hunting knives, or small axes, depending on their personality and style. Slung across their backs were their bows, arrows, and one Hunter even wore what looked like a hunting pouch for small game.

Kyraine handed one of the Hunters a rolled scroll and sent them on their way. As they passed me, their gazes fell on my face. It took them each a second to recognize me, but when they did, they lit up and bowed their heads respectfully. I nodded my head in reply, as they exited.

When I looked up again, Kyraine stood before me with the most relieved look on her face. "Thank the heavens you're safe," she breathed, grasping my shoulders warmly.

Someone else had entered the tent. Kyraine smiled, so I twisted around to see who it was. Gwendolyn Stone, the Hunter next in line to take over Kyraine's position, placed a firm, but warm, hand on my shoulder. She was several inches taller than I, and her red hair was twisted into a long braid down her back.

"I had to make sure the rumors were true. It's good to see you again, and so soon," Gwen said, giving my shoulder a squeeze. She dropped her hand and I caught a glimpse of her fingers, which were lined with dirt, a Hunter's nail polish.

My eyebrows pinched together as Kyraine directed us over to a long wooden table. We all took our seats towards one end, and Kyraine asked a servant to bring us refreshments.

"So soon?" I finally asked after trying, and failing, to understand what Gwen meant. "I've been away for almost half a year in my world. That has to be years here, at least," I said nervously, as my words settled in. Did this mean that Kate was several years my senior now, instead of several minutes? I brought my eyes to meet Myra's, and, staying true to character, she was as calm and composed as ever.

"You haven't been gone for years," Myra began to say. "It hasn't even been a year in fact." I opened my mouth to argue, but Kyraine cut me off.

"It's only been five months, two weeks, and three days since you left." I felt the skepticism grow on my face, but as I ran the numbers through my head, they added up.

"But that makes no sense. Last time, I was here for weeks, and it only amounted to a couple of days back in my world." We were all perplexed.

Our thoughts were interrupted when a servant boy, his olive-toned skin darkened by the sun, rushed into the tent and set down a platter of fruit, shaved meat, a basket of bread, and glasses of water. He looked no older than twelve. His hair was black, and he wore a navy blue cap that resembled a beanie. His clothes were loose-fitting, but I could tell he was strong and healthy by the way he carried himself. Kyraine thanked him, and as he was turning to leave, his eyes washed over my face. I sucked in a sharp breath as familiarity hit me. The boy left the tent before I could say anything to him.

"He looked like—" I stopped myself, a little hesitant to say the name since I didn't know how she was perceived anymore.

"Veronica," Kyraine added. I nodded. "We took her brother and sister in after she died. He works with the kitchen staff and her sister is a stable hand. They've been of great help." I couldn't stop the smile from creeping onto my face. Knowing that the Hunters decided to bring in the siblings of a fellow Hunter that betrayed them only confirmed further that I had chosen the right group to fight with. At the mention of Veronica, my mind wandered to Azlaya, and then Kate.

"Have you found them? Is that why you sent Brennon to get me?"

Myra shifted in her seat. "Not quite. We got a tip from a source of mine that the Sagen were coming for your necklace, so we sent Brennon to bring you back before they found you, but..." She stopped herself short.

"I didn't think you could make portals between our worlds without the necklace." I saw a flicker of sadness in Myra's eyes, but it was too easy to see how exhausted she appeared. She always sat with perfect posture, all her features perked to assess any and all information coming her way. But now she sat slumped, with an arm propped on the table to hold her head up.

"You can do it, but it drains you immensely. I don't think I'll be able to do anything other than make a flower bloom for at least a couple of weeks," she admitted.

I finally understood why she was having one of her students heal Connor and me, and why she looked disheartened. She was a nymph, so her powers were an integral part of her. Knowing that they were suddenly unusable would dampen the spirits of anyone who shared her abilities. While I didn't use my powers every day like Myra did, knowing that they were there to be used if I needed them was comforting. She must have sensed my concern over her, so she gave me a meek smile. "I'll be fine, Casey."

"We still have no idea where they are?"

Kyraine gave Myra a break from explaining, for which she looked grateful. "It's most likely that they've gone to the Shadowlands to oversee Azlaya's army. As you can imagine, there is no way to confirm that without going there, and going there would get you killed, which is why I haven't sent any scouts that far north."

I nodded, turning over the dilemma in my head.

"We also have reason to believe that they are in Eileen."

"The kingdom?"

Kyraine nodded. "We've heard whispers that Azlaya has been spotted in Eileen with Queen Gisele—"

Brennon walked swiftly into the tent, cutting Kyraine off. "Kyraine. Gwen. Casey." He greeted us before pausing. "Myra," he said slowly. He lowered himself into a chair and snatched a roll of bread from the basket. "Next time you send me through a portal, can you make sure I *don't* almost die on the other side?" His tone was light, but his eyes conveyed how serious he was.

She rolled her eyes, already bored with the conversation. "You lived."

"Barely."

"Brennon," Kyraine interjected, "we were just about to explain our plan to Casey," Kyraine interjected, before he could take another crack at Myra. He waved his roll at her to let her continue. "What we need to do," Kyraine started, bringing my attention back to her, "is bring Eileen into this war."

"They wouldn't join to begin with?"

Brennon laughed tersely. "Queen Gisele refuses to be a part of the conflict. She made a deal with Azlaya saying that she will keep her kingdom and resources out of the war. Supposedly, it's recorded on a document."

"Why would she make a deal with Azlaya?"

Brennon replied, "We assume it's in exchange for her protection."

"Why is it so important that they are involved?" I questioned.

"Eileen is known for its military, which is, unfortunately, far superior to any other kingdom's. Major wars in the past were not won without the help of Eileen. Consequently, without their support, I doubt the other kingdoms will join our efforts, either." Kyraine picked up where Brennon left off. She wasn't paying any attention to her food anymore. No one was.

I only nodded my understanding. Of course the queen with the largest and most powerful military wanted to stay as far away from the battlefield as possible. "How do we bring Eileen into the war?"

I couldn't have been conscious in this land for more than an hour, and, just like that, I had gotten tangled in the web that was Alagia.

"Dissolve whatever agreement Queen Gisele made with Azlaya," Gwen said flatly, as though it was the most obvious thing in the world.

"How?" I asked, not directing the question at anyone in particular.

Brennon and Kyraine exchanged glances from across the table. Their gazes were tense, as though they didn't agree on something. Kyraine blinked first and looked away, so Brennon spoke.

"We need to recruit Kyraine's brother, Aiden. He works for the Queen of Calem."

I remembered talking about Aiden once with a merchant from Calem who had sold me Adalia. He'd, incorrectly, told me Aiden was Kyraine's seventeen-year-old brother (he was actually twenty years old when he became a half-immortal) who worked in Calem for the queen. The merchant had been very vague about what it was Aiden did. He called him a spy; said he stole information; but his occupational description sounded more like a thief's work than a spy's. But if the merchant was vague about Aiden's job, he was even vaguer about Aiden and Kyraine's relationship. Looking at Kyraine now, I didn't really get a better understanding. A mix of what looked like irritation, admiration, guilt, anger, and sadness were all somehow wound up in her eyes. She was excellent at not letting her face give away her thoughts, but now her eyes put everything on display.

"He knows Eileen well. It's where he trained and worked for several years." Kyraine's voice was tight, as though it pained her to speak. "If there really is a document, he'll know where to look."

"Meanwhile, we need to replenish the Hunters' weapons. With Eileen denying aid to everyone, our weapons stock is suffering, because Eileen specializes in blacksmithing and weaponry," Gwen said.

Nothing about Kyraine showed how overwhelmed she was, except for her eyes. They were the only part of her that had not adopted the hardness required of Hunters. Even in her most dangerous moments, her eyes remained windows to her inner thoughts. Seeing her drowning in her plight made me speak up.

"Let me help. I can convince Aiden to help us."

"Casey, you just arrived. I can hardly—"

"Kyraine, let me help. I won't be of much use here." She still wasn't convinced. "Who were you planning on sending?"

Brennon jumped into the conversation. "Me and my skills of diplomacy." Another silent, but tense exchange shot between him and Kyraine. "But I'd be happy to have another travel companion."

Kyraine's face wavered. It wasn't until Gwen started to consider it that Kyraine's face relaxed into submission.

"Casey, you are in no condition to travel," Myra added.

"I'll take some time to rest, and then I'll set out with Brennon. Do I have your permission?"

Kyraine turned my proposition over. "You do."

Gwen said, "I'll start to gather Hunters to travel with you—"

"No," Kyraine cut in. "They shouldn't travel with a caravan. This mission needs to be carried out with the utmost secrecy. A caravan of Hunters would threaten that."

"I can get us to Calem safely," Brennon added.

"All right. Are we all in agreement?" Kyraine asked around. Everyone present nodded.

In the midst of all this conversation, I'd completely forgotten about something that had been nagging at me since I glanced at the map of the Huntsmen's land. "Where's my dad?" I asked. My use of the word 'dad,' rather than 'father,' as I usually referred to him, only proved more to me how much I truly wanted to see him.

"He returned to the Huntsmen shortly after you left," Myra replied. It seemed like she was trying impossibly hard to keep her eyes from drooping.

"Oh." I wasn't going to see him right away like I'd wanted. In a dark place in my mind, I thought of hugging him in the middle of a battle, and how that may have been the last time I would ever see him.

"Casey, he's fine," Myra reassured me. I shook my head and shot her an apologetic look.

All the information was a lot to consume. I had a mission, and it started in Calem. I was actually looking forward to going to Calem, because I heard so many great things about it from the Hunters who had lived there. While I was a little disheartened about splitting from the Hunters again, I had gotten what I wanted. I got to return to Alagia, and true to its form, it kept on moving regardless of who was a part of it and who wasn't. I'd stepped back onto the rollercoaster, and probably right at the bottom of a steep hill.

But I was home, and this time it felt right to say it.

Chapter 6: Brennon

FIVE MONTHS AGO, shortly after Casey had returned to her world, Kyraine sent me back to the Huntsmen. I was eager to return to my brothers, but I was also reluctant to leave the Hunters. More specifically, I was reluctant to leave Kyraine.

The day I was to leave the Hunters' camp, I had all my things packed and slung over the back of a horse. Kyraine had insisted that I travel with escorts, but with the battle between the Hunters and the Sagen having ended just a few days earlier, I refused to take any of her warriors from her. I was adjusting the saddle when I heard her voice and spun around. She'd always been light on her feet and nearly impossible to hear coming—surely terrifying knowledge if you were her target.

"I can stay longer, and help where I can," I offered.

She tossed me a quick smile. Her dark hair was pulled back into a low ponytail, but so many random strands were falling out I wondered why she even bothered to tie it back at all. Under her eyes, dark circles were forming. The deep gash she'd gotten across her forehead was finally healing. One hand rested on the hilt of her dagger in her belt, and the other hovered near her sword. She hated being caught off guard.

"No, you should go. I've kept you from Cade for too long."

I held in my sigh, not wanting to let her see any disappointment. During those weeks with the Hunters, it had been difficult to gauge where Kyraine was emotionally. She had been busy with training and devising strategies for attack, so I couldn't blame her. But before leaving for an indefinite amount of time, I wanted to test her for myself.

I approached her and swiftly grabbed the hand that was near her sword. I pulled it towards me and lightly brushed my lips over it. I felt her tense as soon as I did it, but when I stole a look at her face, I could already see her cheeks changing color.

I smiled inwardly. "Until next time," I whispered and dropped her hand, which floated slowly back down to her side.

I jumped onto the horse and nudged him into a canter, so I wouldn't have to hear a hurried excuse for her reaction. I glanced back one time, and I swear I saw the face of the young woman I'd known years ago replace the face of the Mistress of the Hunt, if only for a second.

Who knew we'd see each other in only a few months? I had actually come back to the Hunters on assignment. Cade had sent me, along with a group of Huntsmen, to take inventory of what the Hunters needed in preparation for the war, and I was to tell Kyraine what the Huntsmen needed. We had been planning on uniting the groups in a few weeks to form a stronger force to face Azlaya and her army. Sharing our weaponry stocks was necessary, since Eileen was withholding its arms.

When we arrived, we were greeted with the usual feast reserved for esteemed guests, and tents to call our own, for the duration of our stay. The next day, Kyraine and Gwen were explaining their plan for bringing Eileen into the war; a few days later I was being thrown into a portal to bring Casey back before the Sagen stole her necklace. Myra had apparently received a warning from an informant. All my suspicions about this warning disappeared when Casey and I found the Sagen in her house.

I understood why Myra couldn't go to Casey's rescue, because her sorcery didn't work in Casey's world. Risking the Mistress of the Hunt's life wasn't an option either. But still, a different Hunter could have been whisked away, and yet I was the one getting shoved through. Wrong place at the wrong time, I supposed.

It had been five days since Casey's return. One of the Hunters' physicians finally decided that she was well enough to travel, so we were to head out the next morning. Though I wouldn't admit it, I was grateful for the extra time to rest, because whenever I went to sit up, my ribs protested. Casey had healed them completely, according to Myra, but they were still sore, and a dull pain lurked in my chest. After five days of rest, though, it had finally started to subside.

In celebration of the commencement of our mission, Kyraine decided to hold a feast that night. I caught a whiff of baking ham as I reclined on my bed. My arm slid away from over my face, and my stomach growled. I hadn't eaten since breakfast, and that had only been a boiled egg and some berries. The smell of the cooking food kept wafting into my tent, and I wanted nothing more than to go and sample the food as it came from the cooking tent.

I was about to go invade the kitchen when Casey stepped into my tent. She wore a tunic, leggings, and moccasins. Her brown hair fell around her shoulders and I saw a silver chain around her neck. I realized it must have been her necklace. She gave me a demure look as she lowered herself onto a chest near the bed and offered me what she brought.

"I practically heard your stomach from across camp," she told me with a chuckle. I gratefully took the bread rolls she must have swiped from the kitchen tent. I said my thanks in between bites. "Drink this, too," she said as she held out a silver goblet. "Myra says it'll help with the soreness."

I took the cup from her and gingerly held it to my lips. She saw my hesitation and tipped the cup back so its contents slipped into my mouth. "I was getting there," I laughed, as she pulled the cup away from my mouth. I felt the liquid slide down my throat and immediately a chill ran through me. A few seconds later, I felt my insides become cool, as though they were on ice. The strange temperature change began to fade, but my body still felt colder than before. I straightened without any whining from my ribcage and came face to face with Casey.

"You do know your stuff." Her mouth tugged at one corner as though to say, *of course I do*. My eyes flitted to my tent flap. "How are you feeling?"

"I'll be ready to travel tomorrow." I matched her gaze. She was clearly impatient to leave and tired of being fretted over by sorcerers. I flashed my eyes, showing her I understood.

"How much longer?" I asked, referring to dinner.

Casey stole a glance, too. "It shouldn't be too long now. I passed a baked chicken on my way over." I felt my mouth water. "Where do you think we should start looking for Aiden?" she asked.

"The obvious answer would be the queen's castle, since she employs him," I started to say as I stood. I rummaged through a knapsack and pulled out a thicker shirt with a warmer lining. Even though Casey's drink did soothe my ribs, it left me chilled from the inside, too. "But the practical answer would be a tavern or brothel." I pulled the light gray shirt over my head, and, having exposed my skin for a couple of seconds, a shiver raced through my body. I quickly slipped into the heavier, wool shirt and turned back to Casey.

She had cast a skeptical expression my way. "Why would he be there?"

"If there's one thing you should know about Aiden, it's that he and his sister are very different. He pursues certain—entertainments—that Kyraine doesn't quite approve of." Casey's face showed that she didn't really understand what I meant. "I would try to explain him to you, but he'll do a better job of that once you meet him."

That was honestly the best preamble I could formulate for Aiden's introduction. He was the opposite of Kyraine, but, then again, that wasn't entirely true. They both had good intentions, some of the time; and they both worked to help others, though Aiden's work was more lucrative. The men of the court and officials referred to him as a spy, because technically that's what he was. However, it was his other skill set that earned him notoriety in all the kingdoms.

"Can we discuss this later? I'm starving." I tugged her out of the tent with me.

We meandered through the campsite until we reached the center, a huge clearing reserved for eating meals and mass debriefings. There were hundreds of tree stumps and moveable logs for seating. Lit lanterns encircled the space, casting random shadows across everything. Several huge basin-like pots were suspended over a fire, and next to it was a long table with all kinds of meat, fruit, cheese, and bread spread across it. Another table adjacent to it supported ten wide bowls filled to their brim with wine and other libations. The Hunters did know how to throw a feast.

Hunters were flooding into the clearing from all directions, closely tailed by the wolves. I spotted Adalia among them. Casey and I took our places on a log near the edge of the clearing, so I could warm my body with the heat emanating from the lantern. I was telling Casey what she should pack before we set out tomorrow, when a Hunter sat on a stump, inches from us. We cut off our conversation and greeted her politely. She looked vaguely familiar, but, then again, they all did to some extent.

She had dark skin and even darker hair that had been twisted into a bun at the nape of her neck. The way she shifted in her seat told me she was either nervous or just fidgety. Her smile was wide—overeager. I noticed that her bow was shorter than usual, so she couldn't shoot objects at a very far range. Her sword was also thinner than it should have been. I studied her face again. The smile hadn't dissipated. She had probably joined the Hunters recently, what with her novice training weapons and far-too-eager expression.

"You're Brennon. Brennon Harrow, right?" she asked.

I nodded once. "I am." I extended my hand out to her. "And you are?"

"Mel Basemeth. I joined a couple months ago." She gave my hand a firm shake before tucking her own hand into her lap. I shot her a congratulatory smile, and she leaned forward. "The reason I'm over here, is that I wanted a Huntsman's perspective on what's going on," she said in a low voice. "I heard that after the attack on Azlaya's castle, our weapons stock was low, and now with Eileen refusing to sell its arms, it seems like our situation is dire. Are the Huntsmen experiencing the same problems?" Her question caught me off-guard, and my expression must have shown it, as she added, "I'm only asking you because no one really tells us new kids what's going on. My superiors just make it seem like everything is fine."

I cleared my throat, understanding the frustration of being told diluted information. "Well, the Huntsmen's stock isn't as low, but it isn't battle ready either. So, we've resorted to hiring local blacksmiths to produce our armor and weapons, but their production is nothing like Eileen's, I'll admit. That's not to say the situation is *dire*, but it's putting the Master and Mistress of the Hunt in a tough spot," I told her evenly.

She turned my words over thoughtfully as three plates of food were passed our way. Casey and Mel waved aside the person serving wine, but I gladly accepted a glass. As I was cutting into a sizeable piece of lamb, Mel asked me what it was like to be a Huntsman. She was so curious and intent on listening to me that she seemed to completely forget that Casey was there, too. She must have assumed Casey was just another Hunter. After several minutes of vetting Mel's questions and trying to snatch bites in between them, the questioning stopped when Kyraine stepped into the center of the clearing. Conversations drifted into silence, and the sound of forks and knives clinking on plates ceased.

"Good evening, everyone," she greeted. "It's not very often we get to dine like this, so please appreciate this time." A couple of excited hollers sounded, as well as some short applause. "I want you all to know that this feast is meant to celebrate the return of Casey Coles. She has agreed to help us negotiate with Eileen to lift the trade embargo, so that we can acquire the necessary arms to fight Azlaya and her army. Casey," Kyraine announced as she motioned for Casey to stand.

The reluctance on Casey's face was undeniable, but she slowly rose to her feet. A thunderous applause followed, and even in the dim light I could see her cheeks blush. She acknowledged Kyraine with a silent "thank you."

"And we can't forget our good friend from the Huntsmen who will join her on this assignment, Brennon Harrow."

I didn't wait for my queue and stood instantly. I smiled and nodded in each direction. Then, I turned back to Kyraine and bowed respectfully. The Hunters went wild again. When I straightened, Kyraine was giving me one of her heartbreaking smiles—a restrained one on her lips, but hid the real one beneath.

"Please, enjoy your meal. Squadron leaders, there will be a brief meeting after dinner," Kyraine called over the noise, which was dying down.

Casey and I sat back down. I glanced over at Mel's face, which held all the shock in the world. "You're Cassia Coles?" she asked in disbelief. Casey laughed nervously. Mel leaned away from me and towards Casey. "You're the reason I joined the Hunters in the first place. Oh my god, I'm so sorry I didn't say anything before. I had no idea who you were." I could tell that Mel was about to launch into another story, so I took that as my signal to leave.

"Ladies, if you'll excuse me." I placed a warm hand on each of their shoulders, gave Casey's an encouraging squeeze, and then left her to handle the zealous Mel.

My eyes hadn't stopped following Kyraine as she wove her way to the outside of the circular clearing and headed back to the strategy tent. I skirted my way to the outside of the clearing, darted around some trees, and passed some straggling Hunters, so that I could intercept her. I ran, and waited a couple minutes in my hiding spot. When I could just hear the nearly inaudible crunch of her feet, I grabbed her wrist as she passed and yanked her behind the tree with me.

My hand flew over hers, which was already unhinging her dagger from her belt. "Relax," I whispered. "It's just me." I felt her muscles ease, but her face remained tense. I began pulling her forward with me.

"I have notes to review before my meeting," she protested, but I didn't drop her arm.

"They can wait."

When the loud voices and excitement from the feast had all but disappeared into a faint hum, I stopped tugging her along and let go of her wrist. I spun to face her. When her eyes caught a certain light, they had a fierce intensity about them that reminded me of a wounded mountain lion protecting its den.

"Brennon, I don't want to have this argument again."

For the past several days, Kyraine and I had tried to think of ways to bring Eileen into the war without involving her brother. It wasn't his safety that we were concerned with, but rather our obligations to the Hunters and Huntsmen. Aiden Redding was a deserter of the Huntsmen, after all, and as loyal members of our respective groups, we technically had the responsibility to bring him in to answer for his crimes. Kyraine knew this when she asked me to recruit him for this mission, and even though she understood the dilemma I was faced with, she asked anyway.

I had told her, "By working with him, I jeopardize my oath, my brotherhood, and my life. He is a fugitive in the Huntsmen's eyes. What will they think when they discover we're working together?"

"Brennon, please. Let me worry about Cade. I'll take all the blame. Without Aiden, we don't stand a chance. I agree that he should be punished for his desertion, but let him do that after we improve our chances to win this war."

It was tough logic to ignore. Aiden had trained and worked in Eileen for years. If anyone could find out where this rumored document was, it was he. Duty aside, Aiden was our one hope.

"I know. I didn't bring you out here to talk about that."

She had crossed her arms in front of her as if they were a shield. I sighed heavily. I had turned these words over in my head for so long, but this was the first time they were passing my lips.

"Kyraine, we're about to go to war…one that you and I both know we are utterly unprepared for. We're going up against dark spells with swords and arrows." I paused to let my words settle. "But I don't care about that, and I will die fighting for a better world; I will. But I want you to know—"

"Stop," she breathed. "Don't do this."

I couldn't hide the hurt on my face. My chest tightened. "Don't do what?" She bit her lip to keep it from quivering. "Don't tell you how much I care about you?"

She sucked in a sharp breath. "I took an oath. I knew all the terms, and I agreed to them," she said shakily.

My pain was turning into frustration. "Screw the damn oath! You're asking me to ignore mine. Kyraine, listen to me." I rushed at her and grabbed her shoulders, forcing her to look at me. "Really listen to me. I will fight to the death in this war, but I don't *want* to die. I want to live, and I want someone to live for." I paused to see how she was grasping my words. Her eyes melted into orbs of confusion, and her lips were parted to say something, but not even a whisper came out. "*You*, Kyraine. I want to live through this war for *you*. Give me a reason to live through it!"

"You know why I can't." Her voice wavered, and her words were choppy. I heard the uncertainty in her voice, but she was still adamant about upholding her duty as Mistress of the Hunt.

I pulled away from her. We hadn't had this argument in years. It had rested dormant inside me until now, and it wasn't going to seep out slowly, like in the past. No, it was going to erupt uncontrollably, hot, and overflowing with passion.

"Unbelievable. I *know* you, Kyraine, and somewhere underneath that Mistress of the Hunt façade you put up all the time, there's the real you—the woman I fell in love with."

"Brennon—"

"And I know how you feel about me. I know there's a part of you that still loves me. I don't care how deep you've buried it. I know it's there." A stunned silence spread between us. A mix of sadness, pain, hope, and relief swirled in her eyes. I let out an exasperated sigh and ran a hand through my hair. "Look, I'm not asking you choose between the Hunters and me—especially not now. But if we survive this war, would you step down as Mistress of the Hunt? We'll both step down, end our services, and we can start a life together—a real life together. Come on, Kyraine, what do you say?" My voice had lowered back to an encouraging whisper.

Kyraine's lips were pursed, and she seemed to be hugging herself even tighter. She turned her ear back towards the commotion of the campsite, and all her conflicting emotions swam in her eyes. I was asking her to choose between two lives that could not coexist with each other. We had resigned ourselves to that fact when she was appointed the leader of the Hunters, but while I never lost sight of having a life together, it was clear that she had forced herself to forget it a long time ago.

Her mouth finally parted, and I waited for a sound, but still nothing. She was too stunned to make coherent words. I breathed outwards with disappointment at not receiving the answer I wanted right away—or any answer at that point. I approached her slowly, as you would a wounded animal. When I was inches from her, I took one of her clenched hands, eased it open, and placed a small pastry inside it.

"Here, I know they're your favorite." I brushed her cheek with a restrained kiss before stepping around her and heading back to the camp.

The first time I'd met Kyraine had been at a festival one summer when the Hunters and Huntsmen united for several weeks to enjoy peacetime. The Hunters had come to our campsite, so the number of tents doubled and the lake was always crowded with people, whether they were swimming, canoeing, or just playing around. That night, however, a famous magician had graced the festival with his presence, so everyone had crowded around the stage to watch his routine. I stole Kyraine away with me to the lake, and for the first time in days, it was completely still with no one to disturb the water's surface. The moon peeked in and out of clouds, but when its reflection was caught in the lake, Kyraine's eyes seemed to absorb it. The sight left me breathless.

We sat on the bank, hearing the crazed 'ooos' and 'ahhs' coming from across the lake, where we could just see the stage over the masses of tents. The night wasn't cold at all. If anything it was hot, but Kyraine still snuggled up close to me as though it were winter.

"I brought something for you," I had whispered to her through her hair. She sat up and her doe eyes fell on me.

I revealed a pastry that resembled a miniature pie. It had thinly sliced peaches arranged in a circle and cinnamon sugar sprinkled generously over it. Kyraine's face lit up at the sight. "I overheard you telling your friend that you made these all the time when you were younger." I offered it to her.

She held it up to her nose, and her face relaxed into a state of nostalgia. Then, she resurfaced, and sat back from me. "Were you eavesdropping on me when I was talking to Azlaya?"

"No, I said I overheard." I couldn't keep the smile off my face. "Go on. Is it as good as you remember?"

She bit into the pie gingerly and grinned the whole time she chewed it. "Do you want some?"

She held it out to me, but my gaze wouldn't leave her face. Her smell invaded my nose, and her touch was intoxicating. My body was leaning towards her before I could even stop myself.

"No. I want you."

I had pulled her into me and pressed my lips to hers. I could still taste the sugar crystals on her lips. I wondered if this memory was what came to Kyraine's mind when I handed her the pastry, because, heaven knows, it was all I could think about.

I only wanted her then, and I only wanted her now. She was all I'd ever want. It was a heartbreaking truth that locked us in an endless cycle of longing and misery.

Chapter 7: Casey

I STILL COULDN'T entirely believe that I was back in the Hunters' camp. I eased comfortably back into their routine after only a couple of hours. When evening training had wrapped up, Hunters returned to their tents to change tunics or put on more layers, and then everyone piled into the clearing for dinner. Much like how cities really come alive at night, the Hunters' camp hummed with energy as the lanterns were lit. Conversations buzzed everywhere, and unlike before, they weren't fixated on the war, or Azlaya, or my sister. The Hunters were warriors, no question about it, but they gossiped and chatted like any group of young women would do. It was hard to imagine any of them as ferocious fighters on the battlefield, save for the multitude of lethal weapons each kept an arm's length away.

The night felt familiar. I ate dinner with the Hunters, surrounded by trees, campfires, and tents. I overheard them telling stories to try to rival the ones before, making for a long competition of who could tell the most thrilling tale. Laughter electrified the cool, night air. In the depth of the revelry, I noticed some familiar faces were missing from the group. My mood shifted, but I hid my inner thoughts behind a guarded smile and blank eyes. In the distance, I could hear low voices begin to hum and sing tunes. I recognized a few of them, but most of them just floated through me, aimlessly soothing me. I'd always cherished my time sitting and listening to them talk about their lives before joining, or the latest news from their hometowns. But that night, the enthusiastic Mel held me hostage.

Since Brennon had ditched me, she hadn't stopped talking about why she had joined the Hunters and how excited she was to be part of such an esteemed group. I was only half-listening, and my eyes kept skimming the crowd in desperate search of Brennon, or Kyraine, or Gwen, or anyone that could pull me away from this one-sided conversation.

"He's pretty cute, right?" Mel asked. I returned my attention to her. She still had that wide smile stapled to her face. I turned her words over, trying to figure out whom she was talking about.

I quickly scanned the area to see if I was missing the guy she was talking about. "Who?"

"Brennon," she exclaimed. "You're so lucky you get to travel with him." I smiled weakly and tapped an impatient finger on my leg. "You two seem to know each other well." I sensed an unasked question behind her guarded smile. "Are you two—?"

"What? No, no; of course not," I said in a hushed tone, not wanting others around us to find interest in what we were talking about and start spreading rumors. "He's my friend." Mel's expression changed from one of inquiry to one of pure hope. My throat tightened with dread, because I didn't want to give her any ideas. Brennon already belonged to someone, and I felt like I needed to make that clear. Mel's personality seemed to reveal that she could march right up to a random man, plant a kiss on him, and declare her love. "He's seeing someone," I added hastily.

Her face melted. A question lingered on her lips, and just as she was about to press me for more information about this "someone," she closed her mouth and jumped to attention. I looked over my shoulder, and, as though I had summoned her, Kyraine stood waiting.

"My Lady."

Mel saluted Kyraine with a low bow. She started to ramble on about how great the meal was, before Kyraine cut her off and asked to steal me away. I was already standing before Mel nodded and went to go catch up with another group of Hunters close by.

"Thank you," I breathed gratefully.

I studied Kyraine's face. Her mouth was pulled tight and her expression was hollow. I followed her away from the noise, but it didn't look like she was registering anything around her. If a Sagen attack came right now, it seemed like she would look their way languidly and return to ignoring them. She took me outside the ring of lanterns circling the clearing, so the dancing light barely reached our faces. Her shoulders slumped, and her usually confident walk had become slow, almost delayed, as if she had to think about each step she took. When she stopped and turned to face me, I noticed that her eyes shimmered. I wondered why on earth she would be holding back tears. She blinked them away and cleared her throat.

"I wanted to talk to you about Aiden before you leave," she began. I waited patiently for her to continue. I could plainly sense the conflict that tumbled in her thoughts now. "He probably won't want to help you at first, especially since the request is coming from me." My face showed the puzzlement I felt. "My brother and I are not, and haven't been, on the best of terms for years. So, don't be surprised when he's reluctant." She paused and wet her lips. "He's motivated by money—" Kyraine stopped short. "Tell him to name his price. I'll send some money with you to get him interested, but tell him he can collect the rest of his reward after it's over."

"Wouldn't he do this as a favor for his sister?"

Kyraine chuckled darkly. "You don't know my brother."

My mouth twisted at one corner, but I decided not to question her. "I'll let him know."

My gaze lowered from Kyraine's face to her hand, in which she cupped something. Following my eyes, she opened her hand, bringing a pie pastry into the light. The more she looked at it, the more her hollow expression returned. She snapped out of her stupor and tilted her chin back towards the camp.

"You should go pack and turn in for the night. You have a long journey ahead of you."

Before I turned to leave I asked, "Have you seen Brennon by any chance? He just left me earlier and I didn't know where he disappeared to."

A look of sadness deepened on her face, and then it struck me that maybe this was why her eyes glistened. Had she and Brennon had an emotional farewell before splitting up again, for who knew how long? But it didn't seem like Kyraine to cry over goodbyes that happened so frequently between her and Brennon. I caught her staring at the pastry in her hand again.

"I think he turned in, too," she replied distantly.

A heavy pause spread between us. "They're good, you know. I tried one and really liked it," I said, pointing to the pastry. I'd never seen someone so hesitant about eating a dessert before.

She shook her head rigidly. "I know—they're my favorite." Remnants of a smile jaggedly formed on her lips, but she ushered me away before the whole thing solidified.

The next morning, I woke up before the sunrise painted the sky. I pulled on black leggings, a long-sleeved shirt, a cloak, and heavy riding boots. Brennon and I would be traveling beyond the Hunters' protective borders, so I figured wearing dark colors would prevent drawing any unwanted attention. I pinned my hair into a bun and splashed water on my face to wake up.

I shuffled around my tent. I made my bed and pushed all the spell books back under it. I had pulled out a few last night to refresh my memory of the ones I hadn't performed in a while. I peeked outside. The sun still hadn't risen all the way yet. Maybe it was nerves from knowing I was embarking on my first journey away from the Hunters' camp that made me rise so early. I distracted myself with folding the clothes I had thrown haphazardly into the chest. Something that had always puzzled Brennon was why I didn't use magic for everything, when I easily could. True, it would have been easier to snap my fingers and have my homework done for me, or with a flick of my wrist have my room picked up, but oftentimes the physical work allowed my thoughts to escape from other worries. At least that was how I felt as I went through my tent again, organizing and then reorganizing it.

My eyes fell on a dark book with silver letters spelling out two words that still sent small shivers up my spine: Dark Magic.

I wondered how many of these books Kate was scouring through each day as she readied to face me again.

Kate. I hadn't *really* thought about seeing her again until now. The last time I saw her, her hate for me had all but consumed her entire being. She seethed with anger that seemed to have no source other than the blatant lies Azlaya had been feeding her. It still unnerved me to think of how cold she had turned towards me, and I wondered all the time if she'd ever be able to release herself from Azlaya's grip and think logically like the Kate I knew.

I quickly swallowed a roll from last night and headed off towards the stream. Due to recent rains, the usually calm stream had turned into a rambunctious river in a matter of days. I tossed a stick into the currents to test how rapidly the water was moving. The stick was swept downstream before I had the chance to straighten from my crouch.

I stretched an open hand over the river and felt the pure energy of running water. An interesting thought crossed my mind, and I placed my hand into the water, the swirling chaos underneath rejuvenating me. I closed my eyes, breathed deeply, and then flexed my fingers. I moved my hand very slowly against the current, and just as slowly, the water began to calm until it stood still. I held the water at bay for a couple of minutes before its power wore me thin enough to let it go and return back to its untamed state. It bubbled again noisily as it rushed over the stones and sand underneath.

Though I had exercised my powers daily while abroad, it had never been for combat. For that reason, I'd felt rusty during my close encounter with the Sagen, so I made a mental note to fit the drills into an everyday routine. I sunk into the grass to catch my breath. It was the first time I registered the orchestra of birds whistling and trees chattering. It was a sweet sound that I had missed while abroad. In the serenity, I heard the slightest rustle of grass, and I snapped my head around. I twisted my torso and raised a hand in warning. It began to glow with the spell aimed to fire.

"Please, don't torch me on our first day," Brennon said as he walked out from behind a tree, his hands raised in surrender. A huge grin spread on his face. I let out a breath I didn't know I was holding in and lowered my hand. "Are you ready to leave?"

I stood in response and motioned back to the camp. As we reentered the center of camp, Hunters that had stood watch along its borders during the night were being replaced with the day shift. Their eyes dragged with weariness and several couldn't stifle yawns as they gratefully headed back into camp to grab breakfast, and then head off to sleep. Smells of smoking meat and freshly baked bread were spreading through the air. I noticed some wolves were darting in the direction of the kitchen tent to get any scraps they could find.

Brennon and I crossed the camp to the northeast end where the Hunters' stables housed their horses. When we arrived, a group of stable hands was saddling our horses and securing our packs.

I singled out Veronica's younger sister immediately. Her long, dark hair fell down to the middle of her back, and she had a scarf wrapped around her hairline to keep hair out of her face. She wore a plain, brown dress that was a little darker than her sun-kissed skin. Her features were delicate: small nose, small mouth, and small eyes. She was gently coaxing the horses to eat oats from a pail she held up to their muzzles. I smiled inwardly and felt my heart tugging me forward to offer my condolences for her older sister, but her purely joy-filled expression stopped me. Who was I to ruin her mood with such horrible memories? I wondered if she and her brother knew the whole story of how and why their sister had died.

My thoughts were interrupted when I felt a light hand on my shoulder. I turned to face Myra, who still fought exhaustion. Her eyes were weary, but she still managed to put a smile on her face, however strained it appeared. She had a flower headband arching from ear to ear and wore a dress made entirely of yellow flower petals. I was instantly reminded of some of the fashion I'd seen on the streets in Paris. Myra would have made a good designer.

"Are you feeling any better?" I asked her.

"Marginally," she whispered faintly. She eyed Brennon, who was helping one of the stable hands tie a pack onto the back of his horse. "You two understand the plan and what you need to do?"

"Travel to Calem, track down Kyraine's brother, and convince him to help us; travel to Eileen, break the alliance between Queen Gisele and Azlaya; and return to the Hunters, all without getting killed. Did I leave anything out?" Despite her weariness, she still managed to level my sarcasm with a reproachful glance.

"We'll keep in touch through postage. Brennon will know how," Myra explained softly. I had to lean towards her a little so I could hear her clearly.

I felt something wet and slimy push into my hand. Adalia had found me and nudged me impatiently, her eyes yearning. I knelt down so I was eye level with her and rubbed her ears. "I can't bring her with me, can I?" Myra shook her head.

I glanced at Brennon. I guessed Danzinar was definitely out of the question, then. That was when I realized that Brennon had yet to mention his pet dragon, nor had I seen him since my return. Adalia distracted me with shrill whines, as though she already knew the verdict about coming with me. I silently hushed her and told her that she would have to stay behind. She understood every word, and her head drooped. I rose as Kyraine approached. The farewell party was slowly accumulating more members. We exchanged nods. Out of the corner of my eye, I saw the strangest reaction from Brennon. He stiffened. I had to do a double take, but he remained tense.

"Ready to go?" Kyraine asked me.

Her eyes were clearly avoiding Brennon. I thought back to her shimmering eyes the night before. A small entourage of Hunters had accompanied her, and wished us luck and speed. Mel was with the group, and she had wandered over to Brennon.

"Just getting our last things together."

Kyraine moved closer to me and held out a pouch the size of a grapefruit, stuffed with what I could only assume was Aiden's bribe. She didn't need to explain herself as I quickly stowed it in a leather bag slung across my body.

"Remember to tell him the rest of it is his when you return."

I still had trouble believing that Kyraine had to pay her brother to get him to help, but, then again, I didn't really have grounds to judge their relationship when my own sister and I were in a far worse place. I reassured her that I would get him the money and let her know as soon as we left for Eileen.

I exchanged a few more goodbyes, gave Myra a hug, warmly grasped hands with Kyraine and Gwen, and then mounted my horse. Brennon lingered on the ground, as though he was debating getting on his horse just yet. He decided against it, approached Kyraine, and drew her hand up to his lips. As he placed a soft kiss on it, even from where I sat several feet away, I could see the rapid exchange of silent words through their eyes. It ended quickly, and Brennon swung onto his horse.

"Farewell, Hunters. Until next time," he called to them as he turned his horse and started cantering away. My horse followed after the leader, and, just like that, we were off. Rather than cutting back through the camp, which was the direction towards Calem, Brennon directed the horses around the outskirts, so that we could avoid the traffic contained within. After what felt like an hour, a pathway appeared, and the thick forest began to thin.

The wind whistled past my ears, and my hair bumped rhythmically against my neck. Winding through the trees brought me back to the night I had slipped out from the Hunters' camp to rescue Irene, the village girl whom Azlaya had taken captive. I had asked Gwen about Irene when I passed her at dinner last night, and she told me that she had gone to Canabar with a family from the village. I was relieved to know that a family had adopted her after her parents were killed in a Sagen raid, leaving her to beg on the streets.

As I rode behind Brennon, I realized that his shoulders still looked stiff from his encounter with Kyraine. It had not appeared to be an awkward encounter, unless something had happened that I didn't know about. I thought about asking him what really happened and decided that it was best not to ask while we were riding. Knowing him, he would take out his frustration on the horse, pushing it to go faster, and then possibly leaving us with incapacitated horses for the rest of our weeklong journey. I left him in his silence and enjoyed the otherwise-peaceful ride through the trees.

Hours later, after stopping twice to rest the horses and stretch our legs, and once for lunch, the horses were dragging their hooves, so we decided to call it a day. The sun hadn't set, but it was going to start its surrender to night. We stopped along the twisting path that we had been following.

Brennon explained that we were following one of the major trade routes that crisscrossed over the land. As we made our way towards Calem, we would pass through Emberrun, one of the largest trading posts in Alagia, which was nestled at the edge of the Hunters' lands. I hadn't traveled that far west during my last time in Alagia, but the Hunters had told me it was much larger than the small village where I'd first met Irene. The other trading post that matched Emberrun in size was Bronzeshore, a busy port that sat at one end of Bronze Lake. Brennon told me that many ships from the Western Sea docked at Bronzeshore, bringing with them treasures from their travels. Just as in his youth, it was still his favorite trading post.

We set up a makeshift camp for the night. I threw together a small fire and Brennon pitched a tent, which was really just a long sheet tossed over a tree branch. Brennon retrieved two fish he had speared in a river we had passed, cleaned, and gutted them, then skewered them and placed them over the fire. While he cooked the fish, I busied myself with refilling our canteens with water I gathered from nearby plants. A few minutes later, dinner was ready. Brennon added some cedar wood and sage leaves to the fire, which acted as bug repellent. We huddled close to the flames as the temperature gradually dropped.

Other than my geographical lesson of Alagia, Brennon and I hadn't spoken much, but that didn't make the atmosphere any more awkward than if we had spoken constantly. As I faced him in the flickering light, I realized just how distracted he was. He wasn't amusing himself like he usually did. Instead, he stared at something for a couple minutes, sighed, readjusted his gaze, and repeated the whole thing. I allowed this to happen several times before I interrupted his thoughts.

"Do you want to talk about it?" I offered. My tone was firm, meaning that even if he didn't, we were still going to.

"I don't think there's anything to talk about," he tried to say lightly, but it just sounded depressing.

I turned away from the fire and faced him front-on. "Did you and Kyraine get into a fight?"

I'd had this conversation many times before. Instead of being in the forest camping, though, it would have been on my bed with Kate sitting across from me. She'd come into my room utterly broken up about something, tears welling in her eyes. I'd wait patiently for her to explain what had happened, through the tears, hiccups, and everything. Then, I would talk her through the various scenarios of staying in the particular relationship or ending it. It was almost like explaining a diagram: *if you choose path A, this is where you'll end up, but path B brings you another way.* Afterwards, I dragged her into the kitchen to cook. That was the one thing that she could always distract herself with, and I was left with a delicious midnight snack.

"I think in order for it to be a fight, two people need to be involved," Brennon replied bitterly. I waited for him to continue.

"She just can't picture her life not being a Hunter. She can't see any way to live other than how she is right now."

"You want her to abandon her livelihood?"

"Do you have to put it that way?" His lips twisted and guilt spilled onto his face. It was as though talking through this with me was making him see Kyraine's point of view more clearly. "I know it sounds like an insane request, but I would step away from the Huntsmen, too."

This was news to me. I knew how deep Brennon's love for Kyraine was, but I didn't realize his plan was for them to quit being members of their respective groups. It did make sense. The only way for them to really be together was for them to abandon the life they had both lived for so long. That way they could begin a new one as a couple, and do all the things the Hunters and Huntsmen were forbidden to do.

In my silence, Brennon continued. "Maybe she's right. Maybe *that* life is just too far-gone. We left it in the past; maybe it should just stay there."

I sympathized with him. His torment over what he wanted his life to turn into and where it seemed to be heading was clear on his face. Unlike Kyraine, whose emotion was nestled in her eyes, Brennon's was visible on his face.

"Hey." I nudged him. "She'll come around."

He turned towards me, and his face revealed all the passion he felt for one woman since the moment he laid eyes on her. It took my breath away. I struggled to understand how Kyraine didn't succumb to that gaze and give up her position on the spot. Perhaps she had grown so used to ignoring it, for the sake of her oath, that she had become immune to its effects. Or maybe she was just stronger than most.

After Brennon and I finished dinner, we laid out two mats, side-by-side, and collapsed onto them. I was grateful to get my butt out of the saddle and couldn't help sighing in relief. Brennon used one of his packs as a pillow, and I tucked my arm under my head for support. I could hear the horses a couple feet away, breathing deeply and shifting their weight as they, too, relaxed from a long day of traveling. My feet were close to the fire, and they soaked in the last bit of warmth before it died.

"Imagine how fast we could get to Calem on Danzinar." I hoped the mention of his dragon would brighten his mood. I saw the first genuine grin spread on his face. "Where is he?"

"With the Huntsmen, wreaking all sorts of havoc, I'm sure."

"Good. I wouldn't expect anything less."

I laughed lightly. My eyelids were heavy, and I felt another question hanging on my lips, but my weariness got the better of me, and I drifted off to sleep.

Chapter 8: Aiden

I'M NOT A good person. Let me say it again, just in case you get confused later on. I'm not a good person. Take one look at my past and anyone would agree with me. It was darker in some places than others, and I was trying to climb out of a tunnel that, for years, had threatened to swallow me. I may not have been out, but I could finally see a dim light in the distance.

Years ago I worked for a group, the Night's Guild, that operated on the basis of how much money they would make, not necessarily caring what impact, positive or negative, their actions may have had. Leaving them was like escaping from shackles. While my work still consisted of things I had learned in those years, on very rare occasions, I worked jobs that had no monetary incentive.

That was why I ran through the humidity blanketing a village towards the edge of Calem that night. I wore tight, black pants and boots with soft soles on my feet. Over a snug, black shirt I wore a protective plate that covered my chest and back. Leather pads covered my shoulders, and a short cape that just covered my shoulder blades was fastened with a silver pin on my left shoulder. Long, black gloves that stopped at my knuckles and left my fingers bare, extended up to my elbows where I had another pad laced firmly on that joint. I was trained to always travel with concealed weapons, but that night I wanted my target to see them. I wanted to see his fear. I had a dagger strapped to my bicep, another on my right thigh, two more on the belt around my waist, and one on the side of each boot.

I had a certain talent when it came to daggers, and my reputation preceded me enough that oftentimes it did most of the work for me. Fear was my best companion when on assignment. It definitely made interrogations easier and faster. I remember being on a mission once with some other members of the Night's Guild in Eileen. We had stopped under an overhang to escape the sleet for a few minutes when one of my men, Bron, spoke up. He had been trying to undermine my authority since the first day of my appointment as the leader of our small, elite band.

"We should have approached from the north side. It was the easiest access route. This route will increase this mission by at least an hour. We'll be racing the clock to get to the rendezvous spot and deliver a report to the Commander," Bron had complained. "I don't know if I feel comfortable following someone whose head isn't in the right place."

I had shot him a look of warning. The other Guild members with us had shied away from the encounter that had been weeks in the making. "What's that supposed to mean?"

"We all know you have been hiding a family somewhere. The Commander warned us from the start not to have emotional ties to people. It's a distraction, and being led by someone who is distracted is like being on a suicide mission."

"Hmm," I thought.

I had swiftly drawn a dagger from my belt and flung it towards Bron. Before anyone could even make a sound of surprise, the knife lodged into the wall an inch above Bron's head. The fear on his face was plain to see.

"I guess you're right," I had mused. "I must be distracted, because if I weren't, that would have landed right here." I placed two fingers in between my eyebrows. Bron had been too shocked to say anything, and the others just stared, wide-eyed. "Are there any other concerns that need to be voiced? Good. We're not getting paid to kill each other."

I made a sharp gesture with my hands to move forward and took off, closely followed by the rest. Bron had taken up the rear and tried to regain his composure. He couldn't though and remained shaken for the rest of that mission. In hindsight, I probably shouldn't have silenced him the way I did, however effective it had been. My knife was typically the last thing my targets saw. I didn't get the nickname Silverslinger for nothing. I knew, and Bron knew, that I only missed when I wanted to.

As I raced along rooftops littered with vines from the jungle, I undid the bandana that hid my nose and mouth from view. I breathed in deeply and quickly, letting the humid air fill my lungs. I saw Queen Amelia's castle in the distance (it'd take three hours to get there if I could maintain my pace) sitting on a hill overlooking her kingdom—or at least the part of the kingdom that could be seen. There was about a two-mile radius around the castle where you could see houses and buildings, but beyond that, the jungle swallowed everything else from view. I grew up so far from the castle that for many years I was skeptical we even had a queen. We were only minutes from a white, sandy beach. I'd spent hours getting burnt in the sun, playing with my sister, and later entertaining my brother. I dismissed those memories. It was dangerous to let them resurface when I had to focus.

I noticed a gap between the roofs ahead and picked up speed. I launched myself through the air, rolled and kept going. I darted across three more rooftops before jumping again. That time, though, I fell below the roof of the building and effortlessly latched onto a balcony three stories from the ground. I swung to a windowsill and hung that way for a few moments to make sure the street was still silent. My fingers were strong, but after several minutes, they too protested. When I was sure no one had heard me, I climbed down the building faster than it would take someone to stifle a yawn.

The castle fell from view, and candlelight flickered from lanterns that lined the dirt road. The buildings were wooden and vines snaked along all of them. A few of them had vibrant flowers sprouting from the thinner vines. From below, the city lost the uneven topography that was perceived from above. On the ground, all the buildings, streets, and alleyways looked the same, unless you had them committed to memory, like I did.

That deep into the jungle, it was hard to see much in any direction, and as I had learned the hard way as a child, the shuffling sound in the bushes could be your friend hiding from you just as easily as it could be a jungle cat. I had the scar to prove that one. Though, the worst part of that day had been when Kyraine found me. I thought she was going to finish what the cat had started. When she finished her diatribe about my recklessness, she dragged me home to our mother, whose face went white when she saw the gashes across my arms and chest.

It was a wonder I hadn't been killed that day, and that motif had persisted throughout my life.

I rounded a corner into a dark alleyway. A stack of neglected crates sat at the end, and I made a mental note of them before approaching a red, wooden door. I could hear the sound of muted conversations through it, as well as stools scraping against the floor. I'd thought about making a surprise entrance from the rooftop door, but surprise entrances are no fun when you're expected.

I rapped twice on the door and readjusted the cloth over my nose and mouth so that only my eyes were visible. A small door slid open, and two bloodshot eyes peered through. "Who is it?"

"Redding to see Thatch."

More muted conversation permeated the door before I heard a series of clicks and it swung open. The familiar smell of local tobacco smoke and cheap alcohol enveloped me as I entered. Lanterns lit the space, giving it an orange glow with dark shadows in the corners. In the middle of the room stood a high table with tall stools around it, each occupied by a member of the Boas. I'd liken them to pirates, but that would be an insult to pirates. Pirates had a code. The Boas were merchant thieves who stole from anyone, and their operations were sloppy. Someone was always getting caught and turned over to the authorities. It surprised me that their group hadn't been eradicated yet. I suspected that someone was being paid off somewhere.

Three women and two men with stringy, oily hair sat on the stools at the table. Their teeth were yellowed and their eyes looked strained and red. Who knew what kind of substances coursed through their veins? Each of them lazily flicked a pipe around their lips and kept their bulging eyes on me. Though they tried to hide it, I could sense their unease at my presence. Two men guarded the door through which I'd entered, and another two stood on either side of the man I had come to see. Thatch.

He was bald and had black, beady eyes—that was all I cared to notice.

"Ah, it seems the Silverslinger has come out of hiding." His voice corroded the air. I remained still and silent. He was clearly trying to put on a cool front, even though his anxiety was etched into his expression. "I imagine you're here about the offer we put out?"

I had to refrain from rolling my eyes, since they were the only part of my face left uncovered. The offer to which he referred was a typical scheme of the Boas. Somehow they had gotten word that a rich lord's caravan was passing through Calem on its way to another castle, and the Boas wanted to intercept it while on its route. However, they didn't revolve in the necessary social circles to acquire such information, so they put out an offer that said they would give a percentage of what they would steal to whomever could find out the route of the caravan. Only the Boas would ask something so trivial. Regardless, I had to make Thatch and the others believe that I had the information they wanted in order to even get a somewhat-welcoming audience with them.

"Yes, I have the information you want," I finally replied. Thatch smiled greedily and wrung his hands. "But first, we need to discuss something else."

Before Thatch's expression had time to change, I had already jammed my foot into the guts of one of the men guarding the door. My hand whipped out and cut off the airway of the other man who doubled over on top of his partner. The men and women at the table were jerked out of their stupor and jumped up to attack me. The first woman swung out with a lazy fist, and I connected hard with her elbow, dislocating it with a single blow. Two of the men rushed me and as I blocked the punch of the shorter one, the stouter one landed a glancing punch to my shoulder. I spun away, grabbed a stool, and cracked it over the head of the shorter man. The stout man rushed me again, so to slow him down I thrust the stool in his direction and slid under the table so that it created a barrier between us.

The two men guarding Thatch finally stepped forward to apprehend me. I dislodged two daggers from my belt and launched them across the room. Their screams melted into the amalgam of chaos as the daggers plunged through each of their hands and into the walls behind them. The other woman wisely backed off and raised her hands in surrender in the corner, while the last man poorly threw a kitchen knife in my direction. I didn't even move since it missed me by two feet. I made an unimpressed face. He started to rush me by coming around the long table, but as he did I jumped over the table, kicked out at him, and watched as he lost his balance and tumbled. As he was trying to regain his footing, I stabbed a long, serrated knife through his foot. He bellowed angrily, but stayed down.

I shot a cordial smile at the woman still hovering in the corner and approached Thatch. He was reaching frantically for something behind his chair. I was feet from him when he pulled out a cross bow and fired it haphazardly. Once again, I was left unscathed. As he was preparing to fire the weapon again, I already had a firm hand on it and ripped it from his grasp. My other hand closed around his throat, cutting off his airway.

Thatch clawed at my hands and tried to kick me. I grabbed another dagger from the side of my boot and pressed it into his neck, at which point he stopped struggling immediately.

"All right, all right, enough. What is this about?" he wheezed out, fear evident in his voice.

"Two days ago your men stole a chest from a village home. Where is it?"

"You did all this for *that* small thing? They were just random villagers." He scoffed, but I held the dagger firm.

"The chest," I repeated. Thatch's eyes darted sideways. I stepped away from him as he slowly rose from the chair and went over to a wall. I heard a series of clicks and the wall swung open revealing several shelves filled with stolen objects. He pulled out a small box that was no bigger than a loaf of bread. He gruffly handed it over to me. Though he tried to act cool, I noticed that his hands trembled.

"If I ever hear that you go near them again, I'll make this look like a friendly gathering," I cast a fleeting gaze on all his henchmen writhing in pain around him.

"I didn't realize the great Silverslinger was a philanthropist," Thatch said through gritted teeth. When my eyes locked with his, he immediately shied away.

"I'm not. Striking fear into people's hearts is just a hobby." My crooked grin made him sweat. I concealed the dagger again and could see Thatch's muscles visibly relax. I reached into my breast pocket and placed the wrinkled paper that was inside on the table. "The caravan route. Try to keep your petty thievery restrained to those who won't notice when their diamonds go missing. Leave my share in the well out back."

I turned and left to the sound of Thatch unfolding the paper to start drawing up plans to intercept the caravan. He was already berating his henchmen as I climbed the stack of abandoned crates at the alley's end and disappeared into the night.

The muffled clinking of coins in the chest was the only sound that melted into the cacophony around me as I stepped over rooftops. Bugs chirped excitedly tonight, and in the distance, I could just hear the growls of a jungle cat. Every now and then, coos of a group of monkeys split the night air, too. I came to a poorer district where the overgrowth was worse and the buildings less stable. Wooden boards creaked as I ran over them and many of them were uneven. I ran across a thick vine that spanned the distance of two buildings and arrived at the house.

I reached over the side of the building and tapped a couple times on the window that faced the dark street. A few minutes later, a boy, no older than twelve, crawled out and met me on the roof. He rubbed sleep away from his eyes and looked up at me in wonder.

The other day he had been walking around the village begging anyone who would listen to tell him where he could find Silverslinger. The Boas had stolen all the money he and his mother had and they would be evicted from their home soon if no one helped them. Word of his story had reached my ears, so I went to him that night to ask him how I could help. He explained that I was the most dangerous person he knew of, so if anyone could scare the Boas into leaving him and his mother alone, it was I. I had agreed to help him only a few hours prior to our second meeting. I held the chest out to him.

"You got it," he breathed in amazement.

"They aren't going to bother you and your mother anymore." The boy opened the chest and started to pick out coins to pay me. I held my hands up. "Don't worry about it. Go back inside. You can tell your mother in the morning."

I turned to leave when he called out. "I don't care what everyone says about you, or how awful the stories are. You're a good person in my eyes," he said innocently.

The stories to which he referred were exaggerated, or just plain made-up, tales about my past missions. The worst ones in circulation detailed a mission when I murdered infant sons in their cradles; a mission when I ripped a screaming child from its mother's arms and drowned it in the river; and a mission when I flayed a man because I was bored. I'd also heard a story about me that said that every woman I took to bed I then killed the next day. None of them were true, but they could have been. That was what perturbed me. Sometimes the real and fake accounts of my past were so close that I wondered why I tried to draw a line between my real and fake self in my mind.

I half-turned to acknowledge what he said before disappearing into the night. I knew then why I had agreed to help him. There was something about him that reminded me so much of my brother that I couldn't say no. It wasn't his appearance or his voice. It was his character; his pure belief that the world was a good place, full of good people who just made bad decisions from time to time. My brother's attitude was one that I had admired, but came to despise with time. He liked to see the good in everyone, despite their past mistakes. I wondered all the time if he would still think as highly of me if he could judge me today. It would always haunt me—the encounter that could never happen.

Chapter 9: Casey

THE NEXT MORNING we had fruit, nuts, rolls, and some water that I had collected from a stream nearby. Living on the road wasn't very different from living in the Hunters' camp. We ate the same food, spent the day outside, and slept in a tent. The biggest difference was that we had to hunt and gather our own food now. Not seeing a tent in every direction was a little strange at times, and I couldn't judge how far we had traveled in the unmarked maze of trees, but Brennon led the way confidently.

For lunch, he caught three fish in a small river we had passed. He cleaned and gutted them and then wrapped up some of them for dinner that night. The heat of the day made my shirt stick to my sweaty back. Even Brennon, who always sported a cloak, removed it to get some reprieve from the sun. By late afternoon, our rears were numb from sitting in the rigid saddles for hours, so we dismounted the horses and walked beside them until our blood circulation regulated itself again.

As we neared Emberrun, we passed more groups of travelers, with whom we traded food and supplies. When we finally broke through the dense forest and arrived in Emberrun, I was immediately reminded of the village by the Hunters' camp. It had similar, medieval-looking buildings that were of various heights and sizes, but they were sturdy and didn't bear the signs of fire damage or a recent Sagen attack. The streets bustled with people and cart traffic, and we couldn't walk more than several feet without passing a merchant with furs to sell. Brennon and the Hunters weren't lying when they said Emberrun was large, though. It was the largest settlement I'd seen in Alagia, and Brennon later told me that the population was around two thousand people, when trade was slow.

We bought food that would last us the remainder of our journey, Brennon got another hunting knife, and I got us two beaver pelts with which to cushion our saddles. After nearly half a day spent in Emberrun, we finally set out on the road again, towards Calem. Brennon led us away from the beaten path and towards a smaller and less-traveled road. He explained that following the major trading routes all the time wasn't always efficient, and that we would take smaller paths not seen on maps for the rest of the way to Calem.

The rest of our days were spent in the dull routine of waking up, eating, packing up camp, setting out, taking a few breaks, setting up camp, sleeping, and starting over. Brennon and I passed the time by telling stories to each other. Brennon did most of the talking though, because I picked his brains about the kingdom of Calem. Like Kyraine, Brennon was born and raised in Calem. He lived in the city, close to the castle, so he knew how to navigate the traffic that came with hundreds of thousands living in a congested area. His favorite tales were about his school days and the childhood he spent wreaking havoc wherever he went.

"You delayed the King's birthday parade?" I asked in bewilderment in the middle of one of his anecdotes.

He chuckled lightly. The sun was warm on our backs as the horses walked along a beaten path. As we neared the kingdom's walls, the pathways had become more distinct.

"Yeah, I was playing fetch with Bruno, my dog. I threw the ball too hard, and it bounced off a wall and rolled down a sloped alleyway and right into the middle of the procession. Bruno took off after it, and I tried to stop him, but I was too late. The next thing I know, I'm in front of twenty horses leading the King's carriage down the street."

I laughed at the thought of a young Brennon staring up in surprise at the King's procession as he tried to retrieve his dog. "That was Queen Amelia's father?"

Brennon nodded. "There were rumors that he found the whole mishap very amusing, so as a result I became the most popular kid around." He winked at me.

The horses walked a few more paces, when I finally asked the question that I had been avoiding for days. I didn't want to bring up Kyraine after hearing about Brennon's most recent encounter with her, but I needed to know more about her brother and how I was going to convince him to help Brennon and me.

"How long have Kyraine and Aiden been on not-so-great terms?"

Brennon's lips twitched. "I'm not sure that the source of their conflicts can be isolated to one event. Their father left them shortly after Greyson was born, and when they were both getting pretty involved in their own professions, their mother died, so Greyson's care fell on them. Aiden's desertion of the Huntsmen didn't help. Then he joined the Night's Guild, but most of their communication stopped after Greyson died in that raid. It had escalated over the years, but Greyson was their breaking point," Brennon explained.

"Kyraine meant it when she said Aiden wouldn't help us out of the goodness of his heart?"

Brennon laughed darkly. "Aiden's always pursued lucrative work. It doesn't matter who's paying him, as long as he gets paid. He's always been that way."

I was going to ask more when the trees overhead started thinning out enough to see farther than ten feet ahead.

"There it is," Brennon said proudly.

Finally, on the last day of our journey, we had reached the city walls, though the word "walls" didn't give the sight justice. They stood at least two hundred feet tall and stretched for miles in each direction around the city of Calem that circled the queen's castle. I wondered how long it had taken to build such impressive fortifications that bore many resemblances to the Great Wall of China.

"My God, what are they trying to keep out?" I mused.

"Well, hundreds of years ago, it would have been barbarians, wild tribes from the south, and dark sorcerers from the north. All the kingdoms erected walls to defend against them." We exchanged glances. "Those were darker times. As Alagia became safer, people started venturing outside the walls to live. Now it just serves as a reminder of our resilient spirit to survive, I suppose." Brennon had a way of ending every story as though he was packaging it up neatly.

I caught myself staring at it for a moment too long, as Brennon called me back to attention. He said we still had several miles to go before reaching the gates to the city, so we stopped at a quaint pub just ahead. I was grateful to take a break and refresh before heading into the commotion beyond the walls.

Once we tied the horses by a watering post, we entered the small building. The smell of alcohol was immediate and overwhelming. Smashed bottles were scattered all over the floor and men and women crowded the tables, drinking. A few questioning looks were cast our direction. It looked as though last night's party was still carrying on.

I felt my body hesitate at the sight, but Brennon guided me over to the bar, making sure his body language suggested that he would protect me. He pushed me onto a stool and waved a bartender over.

"I'm going to go get the horses some water and oats," he said softly to me. "Order me a rum and get what you want." He slipped away, but not before stealing a jar of sugar cubes from behind the counter, as a treat for the horses.

A young, red-haired girl came up to me with a look of interest on her face, her eyes following where Brennon had gone. "Can I help you?" she asked. Her eyes still hadn't peeled from the door.

"Rum for my friend, please—" The bartender tore away from me before I ordered for myself. She quickly returned with Brennon's drink in hand.

"And for you?"

"Just water, thank you," I replied choppily. She placed a glass in front of me and poured the water into it.

Her eyes were fixed on something behind me again. "The guy you're traveling with—your brother?"

I shook my head. "No."

"Husband?" I halted mid-sip. My expression made her guess again. "Lover?" I nearly choked that time.

She looked as though she was staring at a pot of gold. I knew by the gleam in her eyes and the seductive tug at her lips that Brennan had returned.

"Everything all right, ladies?" Brennon's smile seemed to knock the breath out of the bartender. She smiled widely back at him.

She pushed Brennon's drink closer to him. "Finished distilling that yesterday. I like a man who can handle his rum."

I felt my body tighten, but Brennon just made a face as though he was reasoning with a toddler. He smiled wanly, before planting a solid kiss on my cheek. He did it so slowly and deliberately that I was too shocked to move away from him. It did, however, have the desired effect on the bartender. She spun on her heel to hide her red cheeks and hurried away.

"Has she gone?" he whispered. I made a noise in my throat, and Brennon pulled back and sat next to me. "Don't give me that face. It worked."

"You're lucky it only took a peck on the cheek." He chuckled. Even from across the room, the bartender kept tossing glances in Brennon's direction. "I'm not going to bars with you any more if this is the type of reaction other women are going to have," I told him scornfully. He smiled knowingly, trying to cushion his ego with a humble smile.

The smell of body odor, mixed with the alcohol and smoke, made any hunger I may have had vanish. Everything about this place made me feel dirty, like a public restroom at a state fair. Brennon didn't even seem affected. I remembered him telling me that Aiden typically hung out in places like this. Everything I had been learning about Aiden only made me less anxious to finally meet him. I could handle scouring bars and taverns looking for him, but I drew the line at the brothels. I constantly wondered about his credibility if he really did live up to the reputation I'd been told about.

Brennon nursed his rum while I drained my water. My stomach still felt uneasy from the mix of smells. When we felt rested enough to resume our journey, Brennon left a couple of coins on the counter, and we rose to leave. I caught one last look of the bartender longingly watching Brennon as he walked out ahead of me. It was a wonder to me that, with all the attention Brennon could get from young, pretty women, he still never strayed from Kyraine. She had to know how much he loved her, which is why I couldn't wrap my head around the fact that she was still reluctant to believe that a future with him was possible.

We re-saddled the horses and kept making our way to the wall of Calem. The structure was even more intimidating as we drew closer. It was made of massive sandstone bricks that seemed to absorb the sweltering sun. Every quarter mile along it there were crenelated battlements, and even from way down below, I could still see guards pacing, watching over everyone. The closer I got, the more anxious I felt to be inside. This was, after all, the first time I was seeing a real city of Alagia. Brennon couldn't help but grin at my reaction.

We approached the largest doorway—easily standing one hundred feet high—I'd ever seen. At the gate into the city, there was a line of people waiting to enter. I could only describe it as border control, as guards scanned over items that people were bringing into the city. People held baskets, blankets, vessels, and even livestock as they waited. As we neared the line, Brennon's horse sped up into a trot. My horse followed closely behind, but I couldn't help but wonder why we weren't heading to the back of the line. Brennon approached the soldiers acting as security guards. He jumped down from his horse, and the guards gave him their full attention. They examined Brennon, and then me, suspiciously. I couldn't hear what Brennon said to them over the ruckus, but when I saw him readjusting his sleeve, I knew he must have shown the guards his Huntsmen branding. Brennon nodded stiffly in thanks, handed the reins of his horse over to another guard, and signaled for me to follow. I slid down from my horse, gave him a quick pat, and followed Brennon through the gateway.

The inner city unfolded before me, and I felt my eyes grow larger, trying to take in all the commotion, the variety of structures, signs, and people populating the area. The buildings were wooden, some standing on stilts. They were all piled on top of each other in a chaotic, unplanned heap. Thick, green jungle vines spiraled around the buildings' stilts and across walls. Colorful flowers sprung from them in a way that made the whole city beam with color. The street was paved stone similar to that which made the wall, and large, luscious trees lined streets and hugged buildings. Everything was packed together tightly, but in way that didn't make the crowding unappealing. The outer wall extended endlessly for miles around a hustling, bustling community. Children ran through the streets and bakers stood along the sides of the streets, handing out samples of their finest breads and pastries. Dogs ran around barking, women chased and chastised their children, men traded, and carts and horses rattled in the streets. I felt like I had stepped back in time to a jungle kingdom, but the liveliness that emanated from everyone was the same feeling I got while standing on the streets of any metropolitan area back home. Once again, I was amazed by how different Alagia was, and yet it felt as familiar as places from my own world.

Brennon caught my gaze and sighed, "It's something else, isn't it?" I nodded.

He gently tugged my elbow and led me down the street past a bakery. The smells floating from the open doorway made my mouth water. A plump man with a red face approached us with a tray of what smelled like coconut cake.

"Only the finest cake, for Calem's finest ladies. Surely a weary traveler like yourself would like some desserts hot out of the oven." My stomach answered for me.

"Maybe later," Brennon interjected before I could answer. I flashed a disapproving face at him, which he impassively waved off. I reluctantly ignored all the vendors and traders bordering the crowded streets, though so many rich smells were wafting to my nose.

Brennon calmly led us through the masses and down several streets until we were far away from the gate through which we had entered. The commotion had calmed and the streets weren't nearly as busy in this section of the city. He made a couple more turns before he led me into a small store that occupied the lowest level of a three-story building. Immediately I could tell that it belonged to a seamstress, after seeing beautiful dresses on mannequins. The walls seemed to be made of a green bamboo, and behind a small counter there were rolls of bright fabric.

A buxom, old lady behind a counter and looked up at me through her spectacles. She had dark, glossy hair that was piled on her head and held in place with two sticks of jade. She wore an airy, beige dress that was fastened with a brown rope.

"How may I help you?" she chimed, more in Brennon's direction than mine.

"I know this is last minute, but we're dining with Queen Amelia tonight, and she needs a dress for the evening," Brennon explained, and stood back to let the woman inspect me.

"Tonight? She'll have to wear something that's not custom-made," she exclaimed.

"Anything other than what she's wearing will do." Brennon flicked his gaze towards the mannequins. She looked at the dresses fondly, then back at me. She was clearly unimpressed with the clothes I wore, but her expression made me think there was hope for me yet.

"All right, I can work with this. Come with me," she beckoned, and I followed her into a back room.

She motioned for me to stand on a podium as she examined my body. She instructed me to strip to my undergarments. She pulled at my clothes, poked at my sides, and wrapped a rope around various parts of my body to measure them. When she was done gathering her measurements, she stepped back, rested a wrinkled finger on her lip, and tapped it in a rhythmic beat.

"I'll be back in a moment." She waddled out.

I looked around the room. It was plain, other than the rolls upon rolls of fabric on the walls, and the thread that was everywhere.

"You really brought me here to get a dress?" I called out to Brennon in the other room.

"I'm not so sure Queen Amelia would appreciate her guests eating in—" he stuck his around the corner, "that."

"And what about you? Shouldn't you be getting fitted for something?"

He busied himself with counting coins he had taken out of a small pouch. "My dress clothes are at the castle." I shot him a questioning look.

"I've got it," the woman bustled in, quieting me before I could ask Brennon to clarify.

The woman held a dress up in front of me. It was white with gold detailing. The bodice was form-fitting with gold, vine-looking designs snaking around the bust and across the stomach. There were more of the gold designs on the shoulders, making it look like armor. The skirt was a lightweight fabric that became sheerer towards the bottom.

"It's from last season, but I believe it will suit you. Let's try it on, shall we?" she said. The woman turned to Brennon and before a single word could pass her lips, he ducked into the other room. She helped slip the garment over my head. It hugged my hips tighter than I preferred and hung loosely at my chest. But when I turned to look at myself in the mirror, I sucked in a sharp breath. The fit issues fell away as I became enamored with the gown. The skirt flowed like water and the gold detailing would easily draw envious eyes at a school dance.

Brennon stuck his head around the corner again, and I caught his reflection smiling with approval.

"It's beautiful," I gasped, twisting around to get a look at the garment from every angle.

"It's perfect, Madam," Brennon interjected.

The woman motioned for him to follow her back out to the main room. I stared at my reflection for a couple more moments, wondering what words of encouragement Kate would be saying to me now if we had been shopping at home. I wondered if my mother would say I looked like her when she was younger, or if my grandmother would start listing accessories to wear with the dress.

I swallowed these thoughts and slipped the dress off my body. I pulled the black shirt and riding pants back on and met the woman and Brennon in the main area. The woman stood behind the counter again, and she and Brennon were conversing. I handed her the rumpled dress, and she expertly folded it into an immaculate package. She wrapped it in scrap fabric and tied a bow.

"Could you please have this sent to the castle for Brennon Harrow, guest of the queen?" Brennon said as he handed her the last of the coins.

A look of unease tinted her face. "I don't normally ship my dresses—"

Abruptly, she stopped talking. Her eyes were fixed on my neck, and as I moved my hand there, I realized what she was staring at. She couldn't take her eyes off my necklace.

"You—you're her," she said in a choppy breath.

I looked down at the pendant, and then met her gaze again. She came around the counter that separated us and clasped my hands into her own. They were warm and calloused, and she brought my hands to her lips and brushed my knuckles with a light kiss. As I watched her, she lowered our hands, but held a firm grip.

"I didn't think I'd live to see this day," she whispered.

She let my hands fall back to my sides. We held each other's gaze for a moment, and then she shuffled back around the counter. I could sense more prayers of thankfulness tumbling around in her head, but her lips stayed sealed.

"I'll send a messenger to the castle with the dress, Mr. Harrow," she said as she fastened the last strings of the package.

Brennon nodded his thanks and, with a hand on my back, directed me out of the store. We exited the shop and found ourselves back in the crowded street.

"How did she know who I was?" I asked Brennon.

"The intertwined circles." Brennon brushed his fingers over my necklace. "It's the symbol of the prophecy. Every man, woman, and child would be able to recognize you just from that necklace." He swiftly tucked it into my shirt. "So let's not give them the chance."

I nodded. "Where to next?"

Brennon looked up at the sun. "We have a little time to kill. Did you see anything—"

"The bakery," I said instantaneously.

Brennon gave in to my wish and led us back to the bakery we had passed. We went inside, and the warmth of the store enveloped me. Woven baskets of various breads and pastries hung on the back wall behind the counter. After going back and forth over what to get, Brennon and I finally decided to split an herbs and cheese loaf, to save our appetite for Queen Amelia's feast.

Out on the street again, I lost all sense of direction as I blindly followed Brennon. The only thing that kept me somewhat oriented was the sandstone wall looming somewhere off in the distance. We came upon a square in the city where a fountain with an elephant statue stood regally over everything. Lilly pads and other tropical vegetation floated in the water, and children dipped their fingers in to mess with the fish that swam below. Brennon and I sat on the edge of the fountain, and I tried to absorb everything around us. The square was cozy and full of food stands and stores with open, inviting doors. Odors of baking breads and roasting beef filled the air.

"How often did you come here after you joined the Huntsmen?" I asked Brennon.

"When there wasn't a conflict to be dealt with, we always came here," he responded. "There's much more to do here than out in a field. I think the Hunters would agree. In times of peace, we were usually allowed summer trips to the kingdoms."

I'd seen enough maps of Alagia to know that Calem and Eileen were in opposite corners of the four-kingdom land. "What's Eileen like?"

"Cold—the people, and the weather. You'll see once we get there."

"Remind me—why does Aiden knows Eileen so well?"

"After he deserted the Huntsmen, he went to Eileen to train as a spy." I noticed Brennon's voiced faltered a bit, as though the word *spy* wasn't genuine. "Between training and working in the kingdom for several years, Aiden knows its nooks and crannies better than anyone. If there really is a document with Queen Gisele and Azlaya's agreement on it, he'll know where best to look."

"That's if he agrees to Kyraine's offer," I said, remembering my parting conversation with Aiden's sister.

"Yes, if he agrees," Brennon repeated. He checked the sky again. In the comforting environment of the square, I had forgotten that Brennon had sent ahead a letter of our arrival in Calem, so Queen Amelia was expecting us. "We should get a move on. Best not to be late to the queen's feast."

Chapter 10: Brennon

WITH A LENGTHY walk to Queen Amelia's castle, Casey and I had to hurry if we planned to make it to dinner in a timely manner. Although it probably didn't seem like it to Casey, the streets were fairly empty compared to a real market day. Shadowed memories slid into my head of years ago when I had come here with my fellow Huntsmen. I remembered when one of my good friends, Alexander, and I stole a bag of apples for some hungry children. Myra's deceased lover was still one the greatest friends I'd made while being part of the Huntsmen.

"Look at them. They're starving," Alexander had said to me after we heard the children ask the apple vendor to spare some of his rotten crop. With a broom, he angrily chased them away from his stand.

Across the street, the cart full of apples dared us to do something that neither of us realized we were thinking, until we made eye contact. Like dogs called to a hunt, we jumped into action. I nudged Alexander, and we walked over to the vender. Alexander approached and gave him a wry grin. They struck up a conversation while I ducked out of sight.

The man was confused for a moment, but he regained his composure and agreed with whatever Alexander had said to him. Alexander had a unique gift for being able to talk to anyone, and made it seem that he agreed with whatever anyone said, making it that much easier for people to converse with him.

I half-listened to Alexander and the vendor, while I slyly grabbed apples off the cart and dropped them in the hunting bag hooked on my belt. I made eye contact with Alexander for a split second, and then took off.

Alexander quickly wrapped up his rather one-sided conversation, and departed the scene. He was half a block away when he heard the vendor's angry cries about missing apples. Alexander and I rendezvoused in an alley and went to search for the hungry children. When we tried to hand over the bag of apples, they were terrified at first, but hunger won them over.

Casey had asked what Eileen was like. In all honesty, it had many things in common with Calem, except that no one would have stopped to give starving children apples, or any food, for that matter. The children would not have received even a second glance as people passed by. That was the biggest difference, and it was reflected greatly in the queens that ruled the kingdoms.

Casey and I weaved our way through everyone and made it to the castle gates just as the sun was starting to dip lower into the sky. We walked through towering gold gates into a vast courtyard with a white pathway leading up the castle's main entrance. On either side of the path there were long pools of pristine water littered with lotus flowers, and beyond them were blooming gardens. Casey's eyes were darting everywhere as the castle's outer courtyard unfolded before her. We approached the guard who was monitoring entries into the castle.

"Huntsman Brennon Harrow. Ambassador to Queen Amelia and guest for the evening," I said.

I pulled up the sleeve of my shirt. Inked onto my skin on the underside of my wrist was a hawk in midflight. The same symbol, but of an owl, could be found on any Hunters' wrist. The guard curtly nodded and allowed us through.

"Ambassador?"

"The Huntsmen's ambassador to Calem, my official title." Casey was about to say something when the full view of the castle stole her attention.

"It looks like the palace from *Aladdin*," Casey exclaimed to herself. I thought it best not to question whatever comparison she had just made.

The castle had large towers and turrets, many of which ended in domed roofs with a series of windows. It was a pale, yellow color, like some of the cottages in the village. The inner courtyard overflowed with flowers, trees, butterflies, and bees. The floral scents seemed to please Casey, but I rushed us through because the pollen overwhelmed me. There was a circular path in front of the castle to allow for easier traffic flow when the queen hosted a party. Tonight was one of those nights, and horse drawn carriages filled the pathway as members of the court exited from them and entered the castle doors. As each decorated couple stepped from their carriage, they were led up a wide staircase, their arrival was announced, and then the next couple repeated the process. It was an orchestrated chaos if I'd ever seen one. It was quite a sight if you weren't used to seeing it, and of course I had to shuttle the one person who'd never witnessed anything like it before in her life.

I managed to pull Casey around to the side of the castle, and we entered through a side door I often used while in Calem. Rather than go through the main door and deal with a formal introduction by the herald, I always took an alternate route that lead into the kitchen. We were overrun with cooks and kitchen staff hustling around trying to get the last dishes finalized for the night's event. Food went one direction, kitchen servants ran another, and all while cooks barked orders to keep the flow moving as best they could. In the commotion, we weren't given a second thought.

The heat was oppressive. I thought of what the kitchen looked like when dinner was more than just a casual gathering of the queen and her court. Casey and I scooted over to a door that led into a back hallway. She trailed me as I confidently wound my way around the castle. We raced up a staircase and burst out onto the floor where all the guest bedchambers were. Maids rushed around getting rooms ready for the guests. When I'd written to Queen Amelia telling her about our arrival, I requested one of the best guest rooms for Casey.

"Do you know where we are going?" Casey questioned, casting a wary look at the disarray around us.

"To your room." We finally came to a stop and pushed open a pair of double doors.

When my eyes fell upon the room, I saw that nothing had changed from when Cade had stayed there. For the second time that day, I heard Casey gasp.

The walls were a cream color with sprawling, leaf-like patterns. There was an elongated sofa and coffee table with a bowl of apples, pears, and figs next to it. On the other side of the couch sat a mahogany case holding various bottles of what appeared to be wine.

Three people could comfortably sleep in the bed, and the multitude of pillows could be used to make a second bed on the floor. The pillows were square, round, long, short, flat, plump, and all piled on top of one another in a heaping mountain. The golden hue from the setting sun lit Casey's face.

"This can't be my room," she exclaimed.

"It is, but you don't have time to stare. You'll have to dress quickly. The bath is through that door and there's a cabinet on the wall with soaps and oils." I looked over and saw the packaged dress resting on the bed. "Your dress is on the bed. I'll call some servants to help you."

All thoughts of speech abandoned her, so she just nodded her head. I left her marveling at the room, but not before calling out to her to get ready.

"We have less than an hour!" I added as I closed the door.

On my way to my room, I alerted a group of housemaids that Casey was ready for their assistance. Golden candelabras lined the walls and swooping arches wrapped around the upper-level railing over the main foyer. I quickly regained my familiarity with the castle and found the room I always stayed in when I came. As an ambassador to Calem, my trips' purposes had been to update Queen Amelia on the Huntsmen's affairs. Typically, I came with mundane reports about our membership numbers and the status of our livestock. Thus far, battle plans and war tactics hadn't been a part of my briefings. I had a feeling that was going to change very soon.

When my door came into view, fond memories filled my mind. I could see my name written on it, because Kyraine had etched it into the door as a joke. The Hunters and Huntsmen had met in Calem that year for a summit. It was before Kyraine had become Mistress of the Hunt, and we could spend long nights together without fears of breaking any vows or oaths. It was a time when we could afford to be reckless. I traced my fingers over the scrawled letters before going in. It was the same as always, except that the bed was made and the desktop visible.

A detailed map of Alagia and its kingdoms hung on one wall, and a bookcase stood against another. The bed was big enough for two people and was made neatly with fresh linens. I remember leaving the room in a disheveled mess the last time I'd been there, which must been over a year ago.

I sat at the desk, grabbed a quill, and began penning a letter. I tied it with a string, walked over to the window, and pushed it open. I whistled into the young night. Within minutes, a black hawk sat perched on the windowsill. It squawked its hello to me, as I tied the other end of the string to one of his talons. I watched as my message to an old friend and former Huntsman took flight.

Chapter 11: Casey

I HAD NEVER seen such a beautiful room. The high, golden ceiling, the king size bed, the sheer drapes fluttering in the wind, it all overwhelmed me. To think the room was mine for the night made me gaze in wonder. It was like I had walked into the Taj Mahal and became royalty.

A gentle ocean breeze from the open balcony doors beckoned me to come and take in the beauty around me. The smell of the sea was distinct, even this high up. It was a soft whisper that filled me with endless longing. I stepped out onto the balcony, my eyes widening at what I saw. Thinking back to my eighth-grade mythology class, I immediately thought that this was what Zeus must have seen when he looked over the world from Olympus. The clouds seemed close enough to touch.

Hundreds of feet below me, I could see the deep, blue ocean that licked at the white cliffs. The sun sparkled off the water and seabirds dipped in and out of the tide. Queen Amelia's personal vessel, with golden sails, and was docked near the cliffs. Further up the coastline, I could see more harbors, the royal fleet, and fishing communities. I wished I could freeze that moment of pure serenity and live in it forever. Another wind gathered the loose hair around my face and whipped it around in my eyes. I brushed my fingertips over my face to clear the wild strands, and then I just let my chin collapse into the cup of my hand. A contented sigh played inside me, but I held it in, wanting to keep this happiness to myself and let it remain in my chest forever.

Several maids filed into the room, each carrying something for my bath. I turned to greet them, but they had already marched into the bathroom, without any orders. I heard the sound of water and chills raced through my body at the thought of sitting in a hot tub. When I walked into the bathroom, the bath was already foaming with bubbles, and the scents made me think of Kate's room when she tried to figure out which perfume drew the best kind of attention.

The maids stood to the side, as if waiting for me to say something. One stepped forward and said, "We are here to wait on you."

They descended on me, and before I could say anything to stop them, they were pulling my cloak from my neck, and then removing my shoes, then my shirt, and my pants. Before I knew it, I was showing bare skin in front of strangers. They didn't seem uncomfortable, despite my clear discomfort, and led me over to the tub.

Steam curled and danced on the water's surface, and the bubbles bobbed like buoys. One maid clutched my elbow, and I stepped into the hot water. My toes curled in protest at the sudden change in temperature, and I lowered myself into the scalding water, wanting to cover my body with bubbles. At first the water was painful, and then it started to numb my body until I could only feel its warmth and not its sting. The maids still hadn't left. They began retrieving soap from surrounding cupboards. I absentmindedly wondered how dirty I must have looked to them.

"Oh no, I can wash myself—"

"No, no. We have specific instructions from Queen Amelia to attend to you properly," explained the one who seemed to be in charge.

I breathed outwardly in defeat. "Remind me to thank her," I muttered to myself.

It seemed there was no escaping them. At my surrender, the three girls resumed their duty and began scrubbing my arms and legs until they were red. As one girl pulled my leg up, another snatched at my arm. A couple times, I slipped on the smooth surface of the bottom of the tub and almost dipped under the water. Small whimpers and sharp sounds of protest kept jumping from me, but they were flicked away like pesky mosquitoes in summer.

After my body felt cleaner than it had ever felt before, they started in on my hair. I didn't have a sensitive head, but that didn't mean I enjoyed having others pulling combs through nasty knots. First, they dunked my head under and began pouring soaps onto my scalp. I closed my eyes and tried to imagine I was at the salon with Kate next to—

No. Someone was massaging my head. *You can't think like that.* Fingers ran through my now stringy, wet hair. *Not any more.* They picked their way through a never-ending maze of knots. *She is gone.* A stab of pain jolted through me. Whether it was from the girls pulling too hard on my knotted hair, or from my own thoughts, I didn't know.

I was so busy having a conversation with myself behind my closed eyes that I didn't hear one of the girls tell me to stand up. She repeated herself, and my eyes flashed open, and I saw that one was holding a towel. I clutched the sides of the tub and lifted myself up and over the sides, careful not to slip. The slimy soap on the already slippery tub made standing twice as dangerous.

I gratefully wrapped the towel around myself. My hair was a drenched blanket on my back until one of the girls wrapped it in a towel, drying it thoroughly. As the tub was draining, I walked back into the bedroom, still accompanied by my posse. They had already stripped me down naked; of course they wanted to redress me too. I felt like the dolls I used to play with as a child.

I finally took the time to look at them. They wore dark shirts that exposed their stomachs, and baggy pants that cinched around their ankles. They had their hair pulled back in tight, but elaborate, braids. When I was done studying their features, I noticed that they were all adolescents. They couldn't have been older than me, except for the one in charge. I was about to try to dismiss them again when I felt a tug at my towel, and the whole process started again.

First, they slipped undergarments on to me that consisted of satiny underwear and a bandeau around my chest. I heard the girls untying the package and turned to see the white dress before me. It would have taken my breath away all over again, but I hardly had any breath as it was. I gave a slight nod, and the dress descended on me. One servant dried my hair while another made sure the dress lay properly on my hips. Between my dress and the servants' uniforms, I realized how free flowing the clothing in Calem seemed to be. I was sure it had to do with the tropical heat.

With the last of the strings tied, I lifted my head to see myself in the mirror, and for once, I didn't see a scared, nervous girl. I saw a young woman—a beautiful young woman who stood solidly, readily waiting to confront her next challenge.

My feet were guided into gold sandals that laced up my calves. I took a couple steps to test them. I nodded approvingly and smiled warmly at the maids. On the outside I may have appeared ready to face whatever awaited downstairs, but on the inside, I was suddenly nervous. What if Queen Amelia knew that I had run back to my world, leaving her and Alagia to endure Azlaya, Kate and the Sagen in my absence? The idea of her harboring bitterness towards me didn't seem that far-fetched. I caught another glimpse of myself in the mirror. Whatever had happened, had happened. I was here now, and I was ready to start devising solutions to the problems my sister was causing.

The maids led me from the room. On one side of the hallway there was a wall lined with candelabras and on the other side there were arches that opened into a large space where the staircase spiraled down to levels below it. At every corner we turned, I kept an eager eye out for Brennon. We rounded the final corner that fed right into the grand staircase, which I assumed spilled into the main ballroom. I leaned over the marble bannister and was peering downstairs when I felt a hand on my shoulder.

I spun, tangling my feet in the abundant skirt of the dress. Brennon steadied me and suppressed a chuckle as I straightened back up.

"Calm down. It's only me," he said, still trying not to laugh. He wore a dark blue shirt and loose-fitting pants with tight ankles.

"I miss my riding boots."

"I don't miss that saddle. Come on, the feast is beginning."

Brennon hooked my arm in his. I wondered who waited for us at the bottom of the stairs. Then, I recalled all the carriages dropping off people at the castle gates when Brennon and I had arrived. He escorted me to the top of the stairs, and my breathing accelerated. Brennon nudged me for reassurance. We began our slow descent down the grand staircase.

Left. Click. Right. Click.

A slow wave of music traveled to my ears. String and flute-like sounds drifted through the humid air with such delicacy that a wrong note would have shattered their enchanting spell. With every step, my shoes clicked, as a preamble to our entrance.

Left. Click. Right. Click.

Sheer drapes flowed in the wind, slipping in through the open windows. I blinked and suddenly stained glass windows wrapped around the walls. Dragons consumed the room in fire. An imperial chair sat atop a raised platform. Long tables filled with Sagen exchanged information about Hunter casualties. Everything was suddenly eerie and distant, while at the same time real and near. Then, I was suffocating.

Suddenly, I couldn't move my feet, and the clicking of the shoes stopped. The stairs twisted on the way down, and Brennon had brought us to a halt right at the curve. From where we stood, out of sight, we weren't any more than ghosts to people in the ballroom. His eyes, warm as honey, slid over my face. It was as though he knew what I saw—what had come over me. He could feel it in the hand that gripped his bicep, probably leaving indentations from my fingernails. First worry, then guilt, and finally sympathy, flashed across his face like a slideshow. It had been months since I was in the depths of Azlaya's castle, and I thought the horrors that occurred that day had died somewhere within me. Yet, as I walked through Queen Amelia's castle, I could see Azlaya's as clearly as if I were in it again. My lips parted, but Brennon filled them with words.

"Don't think about that," he said lightly. I tried to steady breathing as I stared blankly in front of me. I wondered if this brief relapse was one of Kate's tricks. I wouldn't put it past her. "You're safe here," he coaxed softly, trying to bring me back to *me.*

I shut my eyes and tried to erase any and all images of Azlaya's castle from my thoughts. The aroma of grilled meat, roasted vegetables, and breads tickled my nose, but my stomach wanted nothing.

His words replayed in my head, insistently. *You're safe here.*

When I was out of the country, far removed from my old life and everything that reminded me of Kate, I felt uneasy, but never unsafe. But, now that I was back in Alagia, I couldn't help but to harbor a little fear—this had become Kate's turf in my absence. I inhaled and exhaled deeply. "I'm all right," I answered shakily. I was hoping that walking down the grand staircase would be the hardest challenge of the night.

Brennon pulled me closer to him, and we continued forward. "They're only ladies and lords of the court, Casey. Hardly anything, compared to what you've faced before." I nodded numbly. I didn't remember the rest of the stairs passing under my feet. I only recalled finally getting to the foot of them. To our relief, we had arrived late enough that the herald no longer called out arrivals, so we glided into the room without a grand introduction.

As I predicted, the staircase spilled into the ballroom, which was gorgeous. Tall pillars lined the round room with long, gold drapery hanging between them. Beautiful vines with a multitude of colored flowers spiraled up the columns, and in the middle of the room there was a towering fountain with a peacock spouting water from its beak. On one side of the room there was a square mat where a group of musicians sat playing a mix of string, wind, and brass instruments, all twisting together making mesmerizing and entangled sounds.

Tall round tables were spread around the perimeter of the room, where people took their small plates of food and chatted with others. The whole scene was an elegant spectacle. The men wore long-sleeved shirts and baggy pants fastened with gold belts. The women wore dresses much like my own, but most had beaded shawls thrown over their shoulders. The mix of colors in the room was breathtaking.

"Where is she?" I whispered into Brennon's ear. His eyes scanned the room as well, keeping a keen eye out for the queen.

"Ambassador Harrow?" a sharp voice chimed.

We turned in unison. A tall, lean woman with dark, olive skin and jet-black hair approached us. She had wide, brown eyes, and lips the color of ripe strawberries. Her eyelids glittered with gold dust, and she wore a piercing blue jewel on her hairline that was held in place by gold chains twisted into her hair. Her dress was a striking sapphire blue, covered in jewel embellishments. The sleeves of the dress were covered in feathers, and she wore a beautiful peacock feather cape that fanned out behind her. The way she walked made it look like she floated on water, and everyone's eyes were glued to her.

"Your Grace, you look lovely as ever," Brennon complimented her sincerely. I released my grip on him, and we bowed together. Brennon straightened and presented me to Queen Amelia. "This is Layna Coles' daughter, Cassia Coles."

Her brown eyes washed over me, and her lips tugged at the edges. "Of course," Queen Amelia breathed. "Welcome to Calem."

"Thank you." My words were mouthed more than spoken.

"Your Grace, as I said in my letter, we have come to ask a favor," Brennon began.

Queen Amelia's dark eyebrows piqued with interest, but she saw that Brennan was reluctant to continue. She turned and waved her lingering guards off.

"I'm sorry," Brennon continued. "We don't need the whole city to know. It's about Aiden Redding."

Queen Amelia nodded thoughtfully. A few onlookers tried to appear as inconspicuous as possible, but the allure of a private conversation with the queen was tempting for eavesdroppers. She shot a reassuring smile in their direction, before turning back to Brennon.

"Let's talk later tonight," Queen Amelia whispered as she placed a hand on Brennon's arm. I noticed for the first time that she had spiraling, Henna-like designs covering her hands. Brennon nodded, and we bowed again before the queen turned to converse with another couple.

Throughout the rest of the dinner, Brennon and I waited in anticipation for it to end so that we could have our private audience with Queen Amelia. We spent our time sampling dishes; making small talk with other people, with Brennon doing most of the talking; and listening to the music, as we nursed nectar drinks. Soon, desserts appeared and before long, the number of people in the ballroom began to dwindle. Brennon explained that the night was just a casual feast for the queen's court. He said it happened at least once a month, but if I wanted to see a real spectacle, we would have to come back for a dinner meant only for the royal family.

As the last few groups of people were collecting themselves to go, palace guards escorted Brennon and me through a series of doorways until we arrived at a sitting room. We lowered ourselves onto the pearly couches and waited. A few minutes later, Queen Amelia entered the room. Guards closed the door and left the three of us in privacy.

She skipped the pleasantries and jumped right in. "I'm listening," she said as she sank onto a couch.

Brennon and I exchanged glances. "We've come, on the orders of the Mistress of the Hunt, to ask for the exclusive use of your spymaster, for a mission," Brennon said.

"Forgive me, Brennon, but when a Huntsman turns up asking after a deserter, who happens to be my best spy, I can't help but be suspicious."

Brennon nodded. "I understand, but believe me when I say that this is larger than broken oaths between Aiden and the Huntsmen. I'm not here to bring him back to stand trial. You have my word, Your Grace."

"What it is you plan to use him for?"

"We need his help to navigate Eileen and learn more about the agreement between Queen Gisele and Azlaya that prevents

Eileen from allying with the other kingdoms in times of war. We mean to destroy their arrangement. Both the Master and Mistress of the Hunt recognize that without Eileen's military power, the battle may be lost before it's begun." While Brennon spoke, Queen Amelia's face remained blank; she was quite adept at keeping her true emotions from showing.

"I see," she finally said. "Well, he's currently not on any assignments for me, but you should know, this isn't be the first time he's been asked to do this."

"What do you mean?" I asked.

"I've known about the alliance between Queen Gisele and Azlaya for years now. I asked Aiden to pursue it and find a way to dissolve it. He refused. He won't go to Eileen. He hasn't returned since his last mission there."

"Why not?" I asked.

"The servants say nightmares. I say stubbornness," the queen replied nonchalantly.

"What if we are able to convince him?" I asked.

"I'll be glad for it. My advisors have made it clear that this war is imminent. I know Queen Gisele's alliance threatens our survival, and it must not stand anymore. I grant you permission to request Aiden's help, and, if he agrees, tell him he has the same mission I proposed to him years ago. He'll understand what that means."

Queen Amelia rose, and Brennon and I stood in response. "I trust in both of your capabilities. I wish you speed and good fortune."

"Thank you, Your Grace," Brennon said. Again, we bowed as Queen Amelia dipped her head in acknowledgement.

Palace guards escorted us back to our rooms. I waved a goodnight to Brennon before I disappeared into my chambers. Inside, the maids that had helped dress me before dinner were waiting to undo their work. This time, I didn't protest as they unfastened my dress, pulled pins from my hair, and wiped makeup from my face. I was left wearing a nightdress and shawl. The maids whispered their farewells as they filed out the door and left me alone.

I went to the balcony, pushed the sheer curtains aside, and stepped into the night air. I brushed my hands along the cool, marble railing. Below, the ocean was calmly lapping at the cliff on which the palace sat, and white birds dipped in and out of the water, doing their nightly hunting. In the serenity, I found myself wondering again about Kate's whereabouts.

This had been the longest time we had gone without seeing each other, and a part of me missed the old Kate. It always would. I imagined how much more enchanting Alagia would be if we had gotten the chance to share it together. I turned away from the ocean and went back to my bed. I blew out the candles, draped my shawl over a chair, and crawled under the covers.

As I tried to sleep, I wondered why Aiden had refused Queen Amelia's order to go to Eileen. I wondered why he wouldn't return to Eileen. Most of all, I wondered how I was going to convince Aiden, as I told Kyraine I would, to help us, when he'd already said no to a queen. Who says no to a queen?

Chapter 12: Kate

"DISRUMPO!"

I DOVE to the side, and the spell went barreling into the wall behind me. I stole a glance at the wall and saw that a large chunk of it was missing. The jagged edges glowed faintly with the remnants of the spell. I crouched low and peered out from behind a thick pillar. I moved out of the way quick enough to miss getting hit by another spell. Dust from the wall sprayed over me. I heard footsteps approaching. I slowly rounded the pillar as the other sorcerer tried to corner me. I jumped out from behind the pillar and caught him off guard. My hand found the back of his neck and shoved his head against a wall.

I tried to restrain his arms when he swung out at me with his elbow. I muttered a spell that froze him where he stood, mid attack. His face was contorted into an angry scowl. "Let go of me," he growled.

I brushed my hands against each other to rid them of the dirt that was on them. "I'm about to." I touched my tattoo and waited for a Sagen to appear. My attacker was a scruffy guy. His hair was thick and long, and it swallowed up his dark, narrow face. His clothes were tattered, and I think one of his shoes had a hole in the toe.

"Who are you?" he spat.

"Kaitlin Coles. The girl from the prophecy. Azlaya's bloodhound." I bowed in a mocking manner. I let him figure out what that meant, but I think he pieced it together very quickly. Fear began to creep onto his face. When the Sagen warrior appeared, he was terrified.

"Azlaya requests your presence back in the Shadowlands," the Sagen informed me. I gestured for it to gather the sorcerer, and then the Sagen transported all three of us back to the black dust bowl.

When we were firmly in the Shadowlands, and no longer in the in-between state of transportation, I stepped away from the Sagen's iron grip on my shoulder. Azlaya was waiting for us. She wore a black dress that exposed her knees, and a grey, fur vest. Her hair was pulled back in a curly bun, and her makeup was as dark as the horizon. She glanced at the captured sorcerer for a brief second.

"You called?" I asked her.

"Yes. Come."

She motioned for me to follow. I trailed behind her and the Sagen as they led the way to a distant area I had not seen before. We scaled a steep hill that had always seemed like the side of the bowl in which I had lived. When we reached the top, my eyes were overwhelmed.

Hoards of Sagen floated around in the vast expanse below. I'd never seen so many in my life. Their masses made them look like thousands of reapers, gathered to celebrate the apocalypse. We descended the hill, and the strangled hissing sound that came from a single Sagen was multiplied exponentially. The eerie sound made it hard not to cringe. At the bottom of the hill, the masses of Sagen began to take notice of us. The Sagen we traveled with still restrained the terrified sorcerer, who struggled to free himself. He was begging Azlaya, the Sagen, and even me to release him.

Azlaya called out into the crowd. I cast her a sideways look; if she was calm, I would be too. Sagen started to float our way. I had been around them enough to withstand their approach, but seeing them in such numbers did have an unusually creepy effect on me.

The Sagen holding the sorcerer held him out to another Sagen, who was making shrill sounds. The warrior reached out a skeletal hand and placed it on the sorcerer's chest. The man's eyes widened with fear, and his lips pulled tightly over his teeth. Suddenly, his agonized scream split the air. My chest tightened at the sound, but more so at the sight, as, slowly, his body aged before my eyes. His skin started to turn a sickly, grey color and hang loosely on his bones. His cheeks became sunken, and his limbs shriveled. Unintentionally, I started to move away from the grotesque scene. Azlaya saw this and snatched my elbow to steady me.

"*This* is how you will get to reunite with your mother. You need their help, and they need sorcery in order to help us," she said with a tight jaw. A few more seconds passed, and then the Sagen that had been holding the sorcerer let go. What was left of the man crumpled to the ground, and he instantly disintegrated into black ash.

I couldn't hide my distaste. My gaze slowly dropped to my ash-covered boots. I felt Azlaya's hand on my shoulder, directing me away from the scene. I twisted my head to see other Sagen surrounding the one who had acquired the sorcerer's powers, asking for a share of its new Dark Magic. Azlaya pushed me all the way into her chambers where she pointed at a chair for me to sit. I stared ahead of me, my thoughts in a distant place.

"I wasn't expecting that," I said absentmindedly.

"The more sorcerers the Sagen get, the more powerful our army becomes." I nodded my understanding, but my state of mind hadn't changed.

"Was that why you wanted me to come back?" I asked.

"No. I wanted to show you this." Azlaya handed me a book. It read, *Accords and Dark Sorcery, by Mikhail.* A page towards the end had been marked, so I flipped the book open.

I blinked quickly to clear my thoughts. "What is it?"

"That is the spell that will enable you to resurrect your mother. You must bind yourself to the Sagen's energy. Doing so will give you the ability to raise the dead."

"What does binding myself entail, exactly?"

"You and the Sagen will become connected to one another through Dark Magic. They will feed off your power, and you off theirs."

"This is how I save my mother?" I asked again, wanting to clarify every part of her plans.

"Once you do this, making the dead rise again will be a small part of a new arsenal."

That was when I realized the strangeness of Azlaya's request of me. Why was she pushing so hard for me to gain power that seemed would surpass her own? "Why haven't you done it?" I asked.

"I'm missing a key component."

I dropped my gaze to the book. Illustrations of three hearts, dripping with blood, headed the page. The symbols on the page looked foreign. There were diamond, circle, and star-like characters that tangled together to make a language I'd never seen before. I blinked in alarm, because suddenly my mind was connecting the symbols with words. Azlaya made an impatient sound, so I ignored the strange markings and glanced at what she had written in the margins. Though her writing was much easier to understand, I couldn't completely look away from the other symbols.

I skimmed Azlaya's translation. In order to perform the spell, the sorcerer needed three things: the heart of a bloodline, the heart of a person he or she loved, and, finally, his or her own heart. I lifted my head.

"What are these symbols?"

"It's Aelonian, an ancient language used by the first sorcerers. It's long since died out."

"But you—you can read it?" I gestured to her translations.

"No. It took years to track down other books that helped me translate that spell. No one can understand it anymore."

I suppressed my thoughts, keeping my discovery to myself. I glanced at the spell again and realized that the component Azlaya was missing was the heart of a bloodline, since her family had died a long time ago. I supposed a candidate existed for the "heart of someone he or she loved" portion of the spell, but I didn't ask.

"So is this literally or figuratively?" Azlaya's face twisted into a dark look of condescension. I pressed my lips together. "Oh. What do I do with the hearts once I have them?"

"Bring them to the head Sagen." I thought of the Sagen mentor with the silver medallion around its neck. "It will help you perform the spell."

I looked doubtful. "And you're sure this is the only way to bring my mother back?"

"I'm not an amateur when it comes to dark spells such as this. Do this successfully, and even the greatest sorcerers in the land will pale in comparison. This is your ultimate goal. For now, return to Eileen and keep gathering sorcerers. We must keep building our army in the meantime."

I nodded and rose to leave.

"You already have one of the components for the spell." Azlaya pointed to my chest.

"I really need to prepare to have my heart ripped out of my chest?" I said derisively, to try to lighten the heavy conversation.

"Yes, so guard it well."

I paused for a second. Azlaya's gaze was hard. Her was mouth unwavering, her eyes unyielding. I bowed my head and rushed from her chambers. My heart was beating faster than when I'd entered—from anticipation or fear, I wasn't sure which.

During the time I'd transported back to Eileen, I couldn't stop thinking about what Azlaya had said about that spell book. What was Aelonian? Who were these sorcerers she had mentioned? And, most importantly, why was I able to understand their dead language?

My mind was spinning in circles around these newly forming questions, when my powers sensed a sorceress nearby. My inquiries about Azlaya's mysterious books and plans would have to wait. Another hunt had begun.

Chapter 13: Brennon

I HELD MY sword in one hand and the sharpener in the other. They slid against each other until the blade could easily slice through skin and bone. As I worked my sword sharper and sharper, I heard a rustle at the window. I stood and pushed the window open, and a black hawk swept in. Tied to one of his talons was a small piece of parchment. I untied it and held it up to the candlelight.

Once I had skimmed over the note, I shoved it into a hidden pocket on the inside of my shirt. I tore a small piece of bread from a roll on my nightstand and fed it to the bird. Then, I clicked twice at the hawk. "Go on."

I opened a drawer where I kept my extra clothes. I slipped into a lightweight shirt with loose sleeves, fitted pants, and my riding boots. I went over to my bed and fastened a blue cloak around my shoulders. The thick belt tied around my waist held my sword in its sheath.

The sun was peaking over the housetops, casting long shadows over the palace grounds as I left my room. I made my way silently down the corridors. I'd spent so many nights navigating these halls when I came to discuss Huntsmen business with Queen Amelia and her advisors that my feet brought me to Casey's room effortlessly.

I was about to rap on the door when it simultaneously opened. Casey was startled to see me waiting, hand poised to knock. Her clothes mirrored mine: shirt with loose sleeves, fitted pants, boots, and a cloak. Her hair was wavier than usual from the various twists tied into it the night before, and she had pulled it back into a ponytail.

"Are you ready?" She nodded and followed me down the long corridors to where Queen Amelia would be waiting. We walked towards the grand staircase, where a man was waiting for us. His ornate robes and the royal emblem on his belt told me he was one of Queen Amelia's advisors.

"The queen was unable to see you off this morning. She had other things that required her attention," the man said.

"Of course," I said understandingly.

"Here," Queen Amelia's advisor said as he handed me a paper. I unfolded it as he continued to speak. "I have written the names of the businesses Spymaster Redding frequents. Hopefully this will be of use."

I was nodding my head. "It will. Thank you. Please, tell the queen that she has our deepest gratitude," I replied, and the advisor nodded.

The city was just beginning to wake up as Casey and I exited the palace grounds. Slowly the crowds grew in number as more people spilled onto the streets. Children stopped by fruit carts to grab breakfast before classes. Shops began opening their windows to invite customers in. Casey and I wound our way through the bustle as I led us to a stand on the side of the road. I pushed some coins into Casey's hand.

"Go buy us some mango juice." I nudged her to go stand in line before leaving her side.

Across from the stand was the postal building. I wove through a group of schoolboys and pushed my way inside. The smell of paper and ink invaded my nose. A couple desks filled the room, each with a stack of paper, and pens for people to write letters. I pulled a piece of paper from the pad and retrieved a special quill from my pocket.

We arrived safely in Calem. Queen Amelia has agreed to let us request Aiden's help. Casey and I are going to search for him today. I'll let you know what he decides. Brennon.

I blew on the note, and the words began to fade until they disappeared. That way, if the note ended up in the wrong hands, no one would be able to read my message. No one except Kyraine, that is. She had the brother to my quill, which meant that she once she brushed it over the note, my message would reveal itself. It was a smart trick that the Hunters and Huntsmen used for all our correspondents. I rolled the note and approached the counter. An old, stout man stood behind it.

I handed him my note, which he tied with twine. I was looking past the man when he asked, "Where is this going?"

"To the Hunters," I responded.

"Ah, yes. One of their owls flew in a couple nights ago." I searched the wall of cubbyholes for the owl. The wall was open so that the messenger birds could come and go as they pleased. My eyes finally fell on Kyraine's white owl, Izona. Her back was turned to us as she dozed in a corner.

"There she is," I pointed. "Izona." Slowly, the owl lifted her head and turned it all the way around to peer at me. Her eyes matched the fierce intensity of her owner's. "Break's over."

She flew over to the counter. The man carefully tied the letter to her talon. He gave Izona an affectionate pat before she made her departure. I thanked the man and left the building.

Casey was just being handed the two cups of rich mango juice. She came over to me and held one out. "What were you doing?" she questioned.

"Sending a post to Kyraine."

Casey nodded and took a sip of her juice. We began to stroll down the street. "Where should we start?" Casey asked in between sips.

A horse-drawn cart full of freshly caught fish came rushing around the corner, and I yanked Casey out of its path. "I have a friend here, and he may know where Aiden will be tonight," I told her.

Casey looked at me puzzled. "How?"

I pulled out the letter the hawk delivered that morning. "He says that there is a huge card game tonight at the Pearl Tavern—Aiden's scene. In the meantime, we should still check these other places," I explained as we glanced over the list Queen Amelia' advisor had provided.

For hours, Casey and I traveled to over a dozen taverns, several pawn shops, and a few brothels, none of which Casey would enter. Every place we went, Aiden's name rang bells, but no one knew him enough to pinpoint his location. He visited these establishments enough to be a familiar face, but not an expected one. His untraceable movement didn't surprise me though. If he were easy to find, he wouldn't have been the queen's spymaster.

In late afternoon, Casey and I headed west towards the shipyard district. This part of town had a more industrial culture. Ships were being repaired, goods from the other kingdoms were loaded onto carts, and Calem Royal Fleet soldiers marched through it all as they brandished dazzling armor and spears. There was a constant movement of men and materials.

We rounded a corner and moved through the congestion. Finally, we came to a clearing in the streets. It was not as grand as the elephant fountain square near the castle, but the area was just as good at serving its purpose: it offered some relief from the densely packed streets.

There were shops surrounding the square, and Casey and I entered one tucked in the corner. It was hot inside. Knives, swords, shields, axes, spears and armor hung on the walls. At the back of the room stood a counter with more weapons in glass display cases.

The apprehension on Casey's face made me regret not explaining to her what we were doing there, but someone walking through the archway behind the counter stole my attention. He was about my height, a couple heads taller than Casey, and he had dark skin, from working out at sea for years. I noticed wrinkles at the edges of his eyes; he wasn't as young as I remembered. He wore a heavy apron and large gloves on his hands, and he was wet with sweat. He rested his eyes on me for a minute before they lit up as he realized who I was.

"Roth?"

"Harrow?" he exclaimed.

I broke away from Casey and shook hands with the man, then turned to introduce him. "Casey, this is my friend, Ashton Roth."

She stepped forward and took his hand. "Nice to meet you," she greeted him.

"Likewise," he replied warmly. He stepped back and crossed his arms over his chest as he glanced between Casey and me. "I hear you're in pursuit of the notorious spymaster."

Chapter 14: Casey

ASH INVITED BRENNON and me back to his home, which was through the archway on the other side of the shop. Ash posted a "Closed" sign on the door, and then joined us.

He had a fireplace on one wall and a sitting area with books about weaponry next to it. Across the room there was a kitchen, fitted with a wood-fired oven. In the corner I saw a winding staircase leading to the upper level. It was a softer, quaint space that didn't fit with the store on the other side of the wall.

I was dying to rest my feet. Ash must have seen the yearning on my face, and offered, "Please, sit."

I gratefully fell onto the couch and let out a satisfied sigh. I was about to thank him when my words caught in my throat. I suddenly realized that in place of one of his legs, Ash had a wooden peg, starting at his knee. I knew it was rude, but I couldn't stop staring, and my first thought was that he was a pirate. We were in the shipyard district, and the room of knives and swords would make sense. But something about the cozy room I sat in wouldn't let me accept the fantasy that had run rampantly through my head.

"I'm sorry, I—"

"It's nothing," Ash interrupted me. I met his gaze as he sat across from me. Brennon dropped next to me.

"What happened?" I asked, not sure if I wanted to hear the answer.

Ash spoke of it freely, as if the memory didn't cause him pain anymore. "My leg was cut during a tribal attack and got infected, so much so, that I had to get rid of it or die." He trailed off, letting me conclude the outcome.

"Tribal raid?"

"There are tribes in the south that attack the Huntsmen from time to time, to get supplies. They don't pledge allegiance to any kingdom, and attack other groups to get what they need to survive."

"I had no idea. I just thought if you weren't a Hunter or Huntsmen, you belonged in one of the kingdoms."

Ash shook his head. "No. There are many tribes and groups of people that live outside the laws of the kingdoms. Old nomadic tribes that never assimilated."

I nodded. I looked between Ash and Brennon. "That's how you know each other. You're a Huntsman?"

"*Was* a Huntsman. After this, I couldn't fight anymore," he said, tapping on his wooden leg. So I came back here to work as a blacksmith."

"And he makes the finest weapons around," Brennon praised Ash. "I still come to him when I need a new sword forged," Brennon said to me.

Brennon rose to his feet and went to the kitchen area. "Do you have anything to eat? I'm starving," he called to Ash.

"Look in that basket. Ara made bread this morning," Ash answered.

"Did you know my father?" I asked him when he turned back to me.

"Everyone knew Aaron Coles," he started. "Excellent swordsman. Damn good man. I was so happy to hear that he was alive," Ash said.

I smiled, hoping that sometime on this journey, I'd get to see the father I had to leave behind on my last visit. Brennon rejoined us, bread in hand. He ripped chunks from the loaf and handed them to Ash and me.

"Like I said in my post, Brennon, if you haven't heard from Aiden by now, I guarantee he'll be at the Pearl Tavern. There is a game tonight that people 'round here have been talking about for weeks. The stakes are high and the pay is rich."

"What game?" I questioned.

"They call it Judge, Jury, and Executioner. I don't know how it's played. You'd have to ask my wife."

"You're married?" I asked, stealing a quick look at Brennon's face. Here was living proof that his plans for himself and Kyraine could work.

"Since I couldn't serve as a Huntsman anymore, I annulled all the vows I had made and relinquished my duties. I would age again, and I could love again," he explained. I looked at his face, and for the first time, I saw how much older than Brennon he looked. The creases in his forehead and wrinkles at the corners of his eyes gave it away. "You two look tired. You're more than welcome to stay for dinner. You can head to the Pearl Tavern afterwards."

Brennon thank him cordially and I nodded in agreement. Ash showed Brennon to a washbasin out back and then led me upstairs to a guest room. The room was bare, save for the bed, dresser, and basin. Ash pointed to the dresser, saying the soaps and washcloths were inside. I thanked him before he went back downstairs.

I could see the sun dipping just above the rooftops of the houses and buildings out the window. I stripped to my undergarments before retrieving washcloths from the dresser. After I'd given myself a sponge bath, I dripped one of the fragrances in the dresser onto my clothes to mask the scent of sweat and dirt. I combed my hair out with my fingers and pulled it away from my face again. Satisfied, I left the room and went downstairs. I heard laughter below. When I turned the corner, I saw Brennon and Ash nursing glasses of wine and a woman cooking over an open flame.

She had silky hair that fell to her waist, and caramel-tone skin. When she saw me, awe seemed to overcome her. "Is this her?" She abandoned the food she had been preparing and closed the distance between us. I smiled shyly. "May I—see your—" Her fingers brushed a necklace that hung around her neck. I revealed my own and her eyes doubled in size. "You *are* her," she said breathlessly. "A daughter of the prophecy, in my home. I'm Ara, Ashton's wife. You are welcome here anytime."

"Thank you," I said. "Please, call me Casey."

"Do you like fish, Casey?" I nodded eagerly, because my belly was rumbling. I figured she must have had hundreds of ways to cook a fish, since she and Ash lived in a fishing community on the edge of the sea. Ara returned to the open flame, where she cooked the fish. I went over to Brennon and

Ash, who were in the middle of reminiscing about one of their biggest misadventures with the Huntsmen. I stepped over Brennon's legs and sat next to him.

"We were just talking about the time when we took Cade's new horse out for a ride. It was this magnificent black stallion that was envied across the land," Brennon said.

Cade Seto, the Master of the Hunt, had rescued me from Sagen the first time I came to Alagia. I would never forget how he risked his life for me, and was prepared to die before he would watch me be hauled off to Azlaya.

"And then it ran away from us," Ash laughed.

Ara set the cooked fish on the table as she added, "And he had you all search for the horse for two days straight, until you found out that it had returned to the stables all on its own. Some Huntsmen you two were."

I joined in the laughing until Ash continued. "But the worst part was after we found the horse. We took it to Cade—Brennon, the three other guys who had been with us, and I. He told us to strip and jump in the lake."

I burst out laughing. "What did you do?"

"We took our clothes off and jumped in the lake. For two days we had to stay there. I smelled like lake water for a month," Brennon concluded.

We all laughed and joined Ara at the table. She had grilled fish and cooked rice. We sang our praises and dug in. While we ate, I listened to more stories. Ash and Ara wanted to hear about my world. I told them about my life back home and how I'd discovered Alagia. It was nice, for a change, to be answering the questions rather than asking them. Soon the conversation turned towards the purpose of our mission. Brennon explained the plight of the Hunters and Huntsmen, and, immediately, Ash pledged his blacksmithing services to them.

It was getting late, and Brennon and I had to get going. While Brennon and I were getting ready to leave, we thanked Ash and Ara for their hospitality. We were led to the back door of the house and said our final goodbyes before departing to find Aiden.

The streets were substantially less crowded at night. Vendors no longer called out as we passed; children had all gone to bed; and carts didn't race past. After walking several blocks, we turned the corner and saw the Pearl Tavern. It was a short cottage. Two lamps lighted the outside of it, and it sat back from the street, mostly hidden from view. A few men hung around outside, talking and toasting. Instinctively, Brennon walked closer to me as we passed them and entered through the door.

I could smell the ale and rum before I got inside. Gas lamps dimly lit the room, which was filled with tables, and a bar against one wall. Through a doorway I could see men already engaged in several games of cards, and gambling with oddly shaped dice. Every now and then, excited hoots and hollers came from their direction.

Brennon directed me to a high table at the edge of the room. We pulled up two stools and a waitress came over. "What can I get for you?"

"Two ales," Brennon ordered, while I scanned the room for someone who looked like Kyraine. By the time the waitress had returned, I still hadn't see anyone who resembled Kyraine enough for me to think it was her brother. "Patience," Brennon soothed me, as he sipped his drink. As if on cue, the door creaked open, and in walked someone with familiar features.

His boots thumped when he walked, and his cloak dragged on the ground. He pulled the hood down and casually took a seat at one of the tables. He had dark, brown hair that hung around his eyes, and I'd say he was about as tall as Brennon. His eyes were deep brown, and his nose was straight, like his sister's. He wore fitted brown pants, and a green shirt with loose sleeves.

A waitress went over and asked for his order. I watched him strike up a small conversation with her. He was clearly flirting and handing out suggestive compliments. After watching him for only minutes, I could tell he had an arrogance about him that said, " I'm attractive and I know it." My eyes narrowed in annoyance.

"That's him," Brennon breathed.

I studied the young man. I could see his and Kyraine's similarities, as well as their differences. For one, his skin was slightly lighter than hers, since she spent all day in the sun running drills. However, their eyes were the same. His were calm, but alert to everything in the room. He took a swig of his drink and gazed into the rambunctious, gambling room. He set the drink down and began to fumble with a pouch on his belt. I saw my opportunity and pounced.

I slid from the stool, weaved between waiters, and planted myself in the chair across from Aiden. He slowly twisted his head and straightened his body. His eyes narrowed slightly as they slid over me. He dipped his chin, and a faint smile wavered on his face.

"Hello." He exaggerated the vowels as though to invite me in.

I felt the sudden urge to bar myself against his advances, so I crossed my arms and legs and sat back in the chair. This piqued his interest more.

"Aiden Redding?"

The curiosity he had shown before vanished, and suspicion settled in. "You don't look like a Hunter." His response caught me off guard. "You're not carrying any weapons; you're not searching for one now; no branding; not to mention you smell like—" he sniffed the air, "coconut extract. Yet, your friend is clearly a Huntsman. Even disguised, I could spot him a mile away."

My mouth hung frozen on a word, because his deduction skills had stunned me into silence.

"I've known you were coming for hours. Information from the palace travels quickly. Though it seems it wasn't accurate, since you are no Hunter. So," he paused and leaned forward, "who are you?"

I blinked from my trance. I knew that my name was something that drew attention, and attention was dangerous. Not having an identity, especially in a place like this, kept me in the dark, and I wanted it to stay that way.

"I'm," I stammered, "a friend of your sister's. She sent me."

His smug smirk dropped to the floor. He leaned away as though I repulsed him. "No. Whatever it is. No. I don't take orders from my sister, no matter how pretty her friends are," he said defiantly. He had pushed his chair back to leave when I felt Brennon behind me.

Aiden suddenly looked concerned. "Harrow—I knew I recognized you."

"Relax. I'm not here to turn you in to the Huntsmen." Aiden's gaze shifted from the exit back to Brennon. "We need your help. Trust me, I wouldn't be here if this weren't important. Listen to what she has to say."

Aiden's chin rested on his hand and his thumb stroked his jawline as he studied us suspiciously. His gaze could have leveled a building, and it made my skin crawl. He exaggerated a sigh. "Pray tell what errand my sister has sent you two on."

"We need you to help us find something," I told him plainly.

"*Find?* Am I a hound?"

"Well—and steal, if necessary."

He flashed a quick smirk. "That sounds more like it. It seems my sister has finally loosened the moral noose around her neck." He took a swig of his drink. "And this *thing*—what is it to her?"

"It has a great deal of importance, which I'd be willing to discuss somewhere more private," Brennon added. His tone matched the playful seriousness of Aiden's.

Aiden ducked his chin and lifted an eyebrow. It seemed to be his face's natural expression. "Does my sister know that I don't work for free?"

Brennon looked to me, knowing Kyraine had told me what to say when this topic arose. "Kyraine said to name your price, and she'll pay it if we're successful," I said, slowly, so he could pick up every word. I could tell this caught his attention.

"She said this?" Aiden asked skeptically.

I nodded. "We've already spoken with Queen Amelia, and she has agreed to let you work with us. She also mentioned that her old proposal is still on the table—she said you would know what that meant," I added.

Aiden appraised us silently as he thought. "And who did you say you were, again?"

"A friend of Kyraine's," I answered.

"Can I have a name 'friend of Kyraine's,'" he pressed.

"Not knowing who I am is better. It's safer," I said. Brennon watched us silently now.

"You're worried about my safety?" Aiden scoffed incredulously. His eyes flicked to Brennon to make sure it wasn't a joke.

"I'm worried about the attention my name will bring," I shot back. Aiden didn't budge. So he and Kyraine were both stubborn to the core. A deep sigh fell off my lips. "I'll tell you," I glanced around, "but not here. Somewhere private."

Aiden was looking past me into the gambling room again; his interest in us was waning. When he spoke, he still looked past me. "All right, let's meet later tonight, and then you can explain. With luck, I'll be treating."

"There's an inn with dark green shutters a few blocks from here. We'll stay there for the night. You can meet us there." Brennon told him.

"I know the one," Aiden replied before briskly rising and walking away. I turned in my chair to watch him go. When he walked into the gambling room, a roar of approval erupted. I almost wanted to go watch, but Brennon tugged my elbow to leave. I stole one last glance at the young man who was ultimately going to help us win or lose this war.

Chapter 15: Brennon

THE INN WAS a short walk from the Pearl Tavern. It was a large cottage that had about twenty rooms for travelers. I got a room for Casey and me, and we went to drop our travel things there. The square space was lit with flickering candles scattered about the room. There were two beds, a trunk for clothing and storage, and a window. Tucked in the corner near the door sat a small dining area with a short table and stools—nothing like the guest rooms at Queen Amelia's palace.

Casey set down her saddlebag, discarded her cloak, and collapsed onto the bed with a contented sigh. I busied myself with wiping wet mud from my boots. We stored our meager travel things and freshened up before heading downstairs to wait for Aiden.

The bottom of the staircase faced the front desk area, where a large jaguar pelt hung behind the desk. The innkeeper, a stern looking woman with a headscarf holding her stringy brown hair back, perched at the desk. Her face was red and her breathing was heavy as she bent over some papers and scribbled furiously. She took notice of us as Casey and I escaped into the next room. On the other side of the wall there was a small pub, much like the one we had just left.

Casey found us a table, while I ordered bread and drinks. I joined her at the table she'd picked at the edge of the room, which offered some privacy. The inn wasn't nearly as lively as the Pearl Tavern, but enough people talked to create a constant buzz of conversation. The cook, a round man with a food-smeared apron, delivered our bread and ale. Neither of us was that hungry, but we picked at the food as we waited in bated silence and watched everyone around us.

It was strange being in the city and not playing a game or drinking heavily, as most of the others were. Years spent routinely searching out the best gambling hubs goaded me on the inside, but then I caught a glimpse of Casey. Her curious expression was evidence that she wasn't used to environments like this, so getting involved in them would be reckless. Now it was my business to stay as far away from it as possible.

Time passed. We were both nursing our second drinks. Though her cheeks flushed, Casey didn't seem to mind the ale. I imagined her tolerance would increase as our travels continued. Casey's eyes were floating over every living soul in the room. She reminded me of Aiden in that way, always keeping her senses tuned in to what was around her.

"What was that?"

"What was what?" she asked through another yawn.

"The night's still young, Casey. Don't tell me you're tired." I bumped her arm.

"It's been a long day," she protested without much commitment.

I looked over her shoulder as Aiden entered the room. "You better wake up," I said, pointing at Aiden. She whipped around as he approached. "That game was shorter than I expected," I said as he sat down.

"They ran out of interesting things to play for," Aiden said indifferently, though his pockets jingled happily with his winnings. His default manner of speaking was in this uninterested way. "So," he turned to Casey who was wide-awake now. "I believe we left off at your name?"

Casey had opened her mouth to answer when a bald man with wide shoulders and bulging arms interrupted. His thick mustache made his face seem off balance because his head was so small.

"Redding?" he asked gruffly. Casey stole one look at the stranger and clamped her mouth shut. We exchanged curious glances. My hand already gripped the hilt of my sword.

Aiden faced the man and wasn't even dismayed. Casey and I exchanged glances. "Who's asking?"

"The man you cheated out of forty silver pieces with your loaded dice," he spat. I had a sinking feeling about where this was headed.

Aiden's face pinched as if he were trying to recall something. "Evan? No—Roger—Samuel—give me a minute; I'm going to get this—"

"I'm out a lot of money because of you, you worthless piece of shit!" he bellowed.

"Now that's a little harsh," Aiden said dismissively, as though he spoke to a child.

Suddenly, the man swung out at Aiden, who ducked and managed to slip away. He dashed through a few tables. Aiden moved with the speed of a lizard but had the footing of a cat. He landed two blows to the man's side before getting jumped on by one of the man's friends. Despite the small number of people in the bar, one would think it was packed, judging by how loud the hooting and hollering was. Aiden had managed to get punched in the jaw, and as he rubbed it, the playful glint in his eyes was being replaced by irritation. He delivered a violent kick to yet another man who had joined the fight, before engaging with two others. Swings, punches, and kicks were being thrown haphazardly. My hand had stayed frozen on my sword in the handful of seconds it took for the madness to erupt. Casey's trance ended before mine, and she shoved her way through the crowd.

"Stop!" she screamed. "*Duratus!*" She froze two of the man's friends in mid-attack with a spell, just as Aiden had pinned the burly man against a wall. Though concealed, I knew Aiden held a knife to his stomach. Everyone who was watching fell silent.

"I'm not going to kill you, but I want you to know that I could." He pressed the knife deeper. "You would do well *not* to forget that."

Aiden withdrew the knife and hid it in his clothing again. When he saw the two men frozen behind him and Casey's faintly glowing hand, he didn't seem the least bit surprised. Casey dropped her spell and the three scrambled to get out of the inn. The spectators dispersed. Aiden approached us, rubbing his already swelling jaw. "We should go to your room before the old hag chases us out. Wouldn't want to cross knives with her."

In an instant, the lethal instincts were replaced with playfulness. It was a complicated balance that Aiden had maintained for as long as I had known him. Though he tried to appear unimpressed, the way his eyes furtively studied Casey said otherwise. A dark part of me was eager to see how Aiden and Casey's personalities would clash if Aiden did agree to help us.

"Here," Casey offered. She handed Aiden a block of ice that she'd frozen once we were back in our room.

"Now that we have the sorceress part out of the way, are you going to tell me who you are?"

Aiden and I sat on the stools at the table and faced Casey, who sat on the bed. "My name is Casey Coles."

Aiden peered at her. He had his head cocked as he gazed upon her, and as if someone hit him, the realization set in. "The girl from the prophecy," he concluded. I nodded. Then Aiden looked at me as if trying to put two and two together. "How are you connected to her?"

I explained to Aiden how I had volunteered to train Casey in swordsmanship. Then I told him about coming to find him, as a favor for his sister. His expression instinctively darkened at the mention of Kyraine's name. Given my last conversation with her, my face may have been doing the same thing without my knowledge.

"Tell me more about this mission my sister has sent you two on."

"We need to find a way to bring Eileen into the war, and to do that, we need to dissolve the alliance between Queen Gisele and Azlaya," I said.

Casey continued. "Rumor is that their agreement is recorded on a document. That's what we need your help finding, if it exists."

Aiden didn't move. His limbs seemed to have frozen as though he was under one of Casey's spells, but I could see in his face that he knew what we were talking about.

"Kyraine sent us to find you, because you know Eileen well, since you trained and worked there for years."

Casey's voice trailed when Aiden didn't reply immediately. He just gazed at Casey blankly as if he were replaying her words in his head. I didn't know Aiden that well, but well enough to know that few things ever caught him off guard. And strangely, this seemed to be one of those things.

"What does Kyraine know about their agreement?" All the apathy from before had dropped from his voice, and he used a tone that drew my eyes to his face. It almost sounded like he was apprehensive.

I spoke up. "Not much. Only that it threatens the effort to unite all the kingdoms against Azlaya's army."

"She doesn't know how it—came to be?" Aiden pressed.

"No," I answered. "I don't know that anyone does. We've all just assumed that Queen Gisele wanted protection, and Azlaya offered it." The unusual expression I'd seen on Aiden face only a few moments before disappeared. "Aiden, Kyraine asked us to find you because you know the inner workings of that city unlike anyone else. And I think you, of all people, can understand when I say that she is desperate if she's seeking your help."

Aiden appraised my efforts to convince him. "You want me to help you pull a queen into a war she wants nothing to do with?"

Casey's face faltered, hearing our plan put in different terms. "Without Eileen, the other kingdoms won't join the Hunters and Huntsmen. Without Eileen, we lose." Casey's voice was small, but her words were powerful. We waited with bated breath as Aiden considered our plan.

"Give me a couple days to think on it."

When Aiden left, Casey and I were unsure of whether or not we had convinced him. By the look on his face, it seemed like we were asking him to walk a tightrope between the towers of the palace while balancing an elephant on his shoulders. Not only an absurd request, but one that scared the piss out of him. Why our plan received this kind of response from him, though, I had no clue.

Chapter 16: Aiden

MY HEART THUMPED in my throat when I left Casey and Brennon. I raced out of the city on horseback that I night. Was Brennon telling the truth? Did Kyraine really not know the history behind Gisele and Azlaya's agreement? Was this a twisted trap? Would Brennon really honor whatever deal he made with my sister and not turn me over to the Huntsmen?

Uncertainty cloaked me like a shroud. I had been planning to hear what the Hunter and Huntsmen looking for me had to say before sending them on their way. But I was thrown off when one of them wasn't even a Hunter, and then again when they explained their reason for seeking me out.

No one knows, I thought.

Not yet, they don't, a dark voice in my head responded.

My thoughts reeled; the only distraction was staying rooted to the horse that galloped beneath me. My heart didn't stop thudding against my chest until I reached Goldtree Castle, my reward from Queen Amelia, given after I had buried a scandal about her. It was after my successful completion of that test mission that she hired me to conduct classified operations in

Eileen. Once a beautiful oasis in the jungle, Goldtree Castle had fallen into ruin and was left abandoned in the jungle's depths. It was the perfect place to get away from the city and an even better hiding place for Lysander. Since his youth, it had become his playground, his classroom, and his home far away from curious and prying eyes.

The horse furiously protested my kicks as I nudged him up to the front courtyard. Stable hands and servants rushed out to attend to the horse and me. I finally rolled off its back and hit the ground, my legs shaky from the journey. The sun had risen a few hours ago. Sweat ran down my back, and I breathed as laboriously as the horse.

The steward got to me first. "Spymaster Redding, are you—"

"Fine. I need to speak with Blakemore and Lysander," I said as I tried to catch my breath. "Now!" I shouted, when he didn't move.

A few minutes later I burst into Blakemore's study. It was circular and long windows stretched the height of the walls; though none had panes, so overgrown vines overtook the space. Blakemore never seemed to mind. When his aged eyes fell on my disheveled state, he put down his tea and the scroll he was reading.

I opened my mouth to speak, but I wasn't sure where to begin. So, I paced. Like a confused dog, I walked in circles. Blakemore watched sympathetically, but without concern.

"What's happened, Aiden? I wasn't expecting you for several more months."

I kept circling. "My sister wants me to go after it. She's sent people after it—the agreement between Gisele and Azlaya."

I paced for several more seconds while Blakemore turned my words over. He stroked his grey beard as he thought. "What do they mean to do with it?"

"Destroy it, so that Eileen can ally with the Hunters and Huntsmen and convince the other kingdoms to join their war effort."

He watched me for several more seconds before he added, "You're afraid that if they search long enough, they'll uncover everything you've tried to keep buried." I halted and matched his even gaze. Blakemore's intuition was still as sharp as the day I met him. When he spoke again, he didn't seem pleased with what he was saying, but he knew I needed to hear it. "Why don't you go with them? Accompany them to Eileen."

"I said I wouldn't return until—"

"Until Lysander was ready to assume the throne. He's ready, Aiden." The reassurance in his eyes quieted my anxieties. "If you don't want the truth about what happened to come out, then don't let it. While I don't agree with this, you can control the narrative if you're with them."

Blakemore had the unique gift of being able to say exactly what one needed to hear in exactly the right tone. The tone he used with me was supportive, but firm. He was one of the only people that knew the details of my last mission in Eileen. Not even Amelia knew what he knew—and she had commissioned it.

I hadn't realized I was nodding at his words, when Lysander charged into the study. His warm, olive-tone skin stood out against his loose-fitting white clothes. The black hair that typically fell around his shoulders was tied at the nape of his neck. He had been riding. Lysander had the hard jaw of his father, but the warm eyes of his mother. He had the dangerous fighting skills of his brothers, but the gentleness of his nanny. He walked with the grace of a king, had the face of a prince, and the mind of a scholar. When he saw me, he grinned widely, despite the tumult of emotions battling on my face.

"Aiden! You damn near killed that horse out front." He greeted me with a warm handshake. "I was called in early from my ride. What's happened?"

"It's time, Lys." I said gravely. Lysander's smile dropped to the floor as he looked from Blakemore to me. "I'm going to bring Eileen into this war, and you're going to be crowned its king when I do."

Lysander let his arm fall back to his side as he collapsed onto a tree root that acted as a bench. "I thought I had at least two more years," he said. I had originally planned to set my scheme in motion in the year of his twenty-fifth birthday.

"I know this is unexpected, but Lys, Blakemore is right. You're ready." His bright green eyes met mine. "Eileen needs a king like you right about now."

"Good thing I had my crown polished up yesterday," Lysander said lightly, though his face conveyed his consternation.

I grinned crookedly at him and clapped him reassuringly on the shoulder. Since he was a child, I could never picture him wearing a crown, surrounded by royal subjects in a throne room. He was always playing tricks on his nanny, climbing waterfalls, wrestling with the servant boys his age, and riding until his limbs were rigid. I always wondered how someone so boyish would grow up to be the king I wanted him to be—the king I needed him to be, especially after the pain Gisele had caused. Though, as Lysander joked about his imaginary crown, I could picture it, and nothing seemed more fitting.

The three of us spent the next couple hours talking about how Lysander would prove his legitimacy to the Eileenian throne. Blakemore produced the documents that identified Lysander as the only living son of the Tennenbay family: his birth records, the family insignia papers, and the documents claiming him as a member of the noble House Morecolt. I told them that if I was unable to accompany them, they should seek Queen Amelia's help in proving his legitimacy. She trusted me, and though she wouldn't be happy about it, she would honor his claim. Once we had reviewed all the details of how we hoped the next several weeks would unfold, I breathed a sigh of relief.

The next morning, as I waited for the stable hands to saddle my horse, Lysander finally said what he'd been keeping to himself for hours. "I never thanked you."

I rejected his gratitude with a cruel chuckle. "I'm hardly someone you should be thanking."

"I understand why you did it—why you did everything. I've understood for years, and I mean to repay you in how I rule."

"That's all I can ask for, Lys."

We hugged each other, as brothers would. When we stepped back, something flickered in his eyes. It was fear. Not for his future, but for mine. He worried that this was the last time we would see each other. I wanted to quell his fears, but I couldn't. I had promised him years ago, when he asked about how his family had died, that I would never lie to him. In the twenty years I'd known him, I'd kept that promise.

"Aiden?" Lysander's voice was suddenly low. "This means you're going to see the queen again. Are you ready for that?"

A younger, more naïve me had joined the Huntsmen to make the world a better place. After five years of initial training and taking their oath, I deserted, feeling that my will was not my own. It wasn't until I started working for the Night's Guild that I understood what it truly meant to have no control over one-self. It was then I became disillusioned and committed my worst acts. Greyson had always been able to pull me back from the abyss that invited death more times than I could count. After he died, it was even more inviting. Then Lysander came along, and through the twisted and bloody plots, a scheme was born. With it, the naïve self that had joined the Huntsmen was reborn inside me, however small and weak it was. Miraculously, it lived inside me, and I felt it surge with hope when I looked at Lysander now.

"I will be, knowing that you'll sit on Eileen's throne when I've finished with her."

Chapter 17: Kate

"DO WE HAVE a deal?"

Tano, the leader of the Muskoxen rubbed her thumb along her bottom lip as she peered at me. She sported a blonde pixie cut and had a scar from her temple to her jaw. Tattoos twisted around her neck, disappearing into her collar. Around her shoulders she wore a long cloak, made, I imagined, of thick, stringy muskox hair.

"And after your Sagen overrun the kingdoms, what will happen to us?"

"You'll be rewarded for helping me. All of you will live like royalty." Another pause. I was starting to get impatient, and I think Tano could sense it.

I pulled a full pouch from my coat pocket and held it out to Tano. She took it and looked inside to inspect the contents. "Five-hundred silver pieces, to show that I'm serious. Think of it as a commission." She must have been pleased with the money, because she put out her hand. We gave each other a firm shake before pulling away. "Remember, once you've found a sorcerer, alert the Sagen. They will be roaming the streets waiting for a signal. Use the bands I gave you. There is a Summoning spell on the metal embellishment, so when you touch it, a Sagen will be called to you. Understand?" Tano and the other members of the Muskoxen present all nodded. "Good. Do this right, and none of you will have to worry about anything when this is all over."

I spun on my heel to leave. When I had explained my plan to Azlaya, she was overwhelmingly skeptical. I had wanted to accomplish my task on my own, but the more I thought about it, the more I realized that one person could not possibly uncover all the sorcerers in one kingdom. So, I decided to seek the help of a group who knew the intricacies of the kingdom of Eileen. This brought me to the Muskoxen's door. They were one of four mercenary groups that worked in Alagia. The other three operated in the other kingdoms: the Boas in Calem, the Falcons in Aerilon, and the Scorpions in Canabar. Each consisted mostly of brutes and thieves and would do anything for money, even if that meant working with the Sagen. By hiring the Muskoxen, I was increasing our efficiency and effectiveness for finding sorcerers, and thus, decreasing the amount of time it would take to build a strong army of Dark Magic-wielding Sagen.

I exited the Muskoxen headquarters, which was a small tavern located in a busy market with stalls and stands, and walked onto the street. Snow fell from above lazily, swirling and spiraling on its way down. I tugged my fur-lined coat closer around my body and pulled the hood over my head just as another gust of wind attacked me from behind. Eileen was drastically colder than the Shadowlands, which was strange, considering only a mountain range stood between the two. The people on the streets with me didn't seem to notice the cold, however, and went on with their business without a fuss.

I ducked down a street I had passed earlier that night. I felt a hum of energy emanating from the street; a feeling Azlaya told me I would get when other sorcerers were near. I had used a simple enough charm to heighten my awareness to such sensations. I began to take notice of the village through which I walked. The buildings looked medieval in structure and design, and the street was paved in what I guessed was cobblestone. Lanterns flickered with firelight along the road. The handful of people that were out in the wintry weather hardly took notice of my presence as they passed. We were all ghosts, anonymous to each other.

The freedom to walk the streets without a care in the world, and without others questioning my identity, was so liberating. I reveled in the chance to burn my throat with cold air, instead of ashy air as I did in the Shadowlands. I could go where I wanted without alerting a Sagen first. I could exist without someone hovering to tell me what, when, or how, to do something. Despite this newfound freedom, I still felt a presence watching me. Perhaps Azlaya had a Sagen shadowing me in the darkness, out of sight. Or perhaps it was Azlaya herself. I would come to find out that neither of those was true. I was being trailed by a new kind of beast, and one I'd never encountered before.

I spotted a high-rise building at the end of the street and found that there was an escape ladder leading to the top. I climbed it and looked out over the scene before me. Thousands of stone buildings spread across the land. Small lanterns provided minimal light on the hundreds of crisscrossing streets. In the distance, I saw Queen Gisele's castle looming over its domain.

One day all of this will be ours, a voice in my head said.

I imagined the formidable force Azlaya, my mother, and I would be as rulers of Alagia. Soon, the sorcerers hiding within Eileen's kingdom would be uncovered, and our army would be built. And then, I would be reunited with my mother. I gazed out over my hunting ground, sucked in the fresh air, and slipped into the night.

\

Chapter 18: Casey

"YOU WILL?" I exclaimed after Aiden agreed to help Brennon and me. My insides lit up, but I maintained control of my face. After Aiden had left the inn a couple days prior, Brennon and I were doubtful he was going to agree.

Though it seemed part of what swayed Aiden to help us was thinking about the bags of money that would follow the first one I'd handed over, I didn't care. I wasn't going to criticize his motives. Not yet, anyway. Relief flooded me, knowing that we were one step closer to winning the war.

"We'll leave tomorrow," Aiden said to Brennon and me as we huddled around the small table in our room. We nodded. Aiden stood and moved towards the door. "I'll see you two in the morning. I have some things I need to take care of."

"Wait a minute." I shot to my feet. Aiden cradled the pouch of money as though he had plans for it. "I just pulled you out of a fight the other day. Don't tell me you're going to go get yourself in another one. Can't you just turn in for the night?"

Aiden smiled arrogantly. "Don't wait up for me."

And he was gone. I made a sound of disbelief and stared at the door with my mouth agape.

"Leave him, Casey. He's like that," Brennon said calmly as he finished getting ready for bed. Brennon's indifference towards Aiden's suspicious business in the city made me even more anxious. One of us had to worry about Aiden.

No matter how hard I tried, I couldn't convince my body to sleep. My mind hummed with worries about Aiden and what trouble he might be in. He was our only hope of finding a way to bring Eileen into the war, and yet, all he seemed to care about was getting into brawls and gambling the night away. Hadn't we made our desperation clear? My stomach churned with irritation. For the next few hours, I lay restlessly awake.

It was the early hours of the morning when Aiden finally slinked back into our room. I had my back to the door and quickly closed my eyes to make it appear as though I'd been asleep. I heard him cross the floor to relight a candle. His back was to me, and I still don't know how, but he knew I was awake.

"I told you not to wait up for me."

I was tempted to lie still and pretend that I was sound asleep, but my curiosity in his acute senses caused me to slowly sit up. I crossed my legs and studied him as he began to take his shoes off. "How did you know I was awake?"

The corner of his mouth tugged. "My observation skills are impeccable," he said softly, so as not to wake Brennon.

"What were you doing?"

"If I told you, I'd have to kill you," he said as he threw his cloak over a stool. "And that'd be unfortunate. We just met."

I rolled my eyes. I wasn't going beg for a real answer. As Aiden was undoing his shirt, I could only stare at him and wonder how this was Kyraine's brother. Between the smugness and arrogant wit, I couldn't picture them growing up together without constantly fighting. Beyond some of their physical attributes, I would never guess they were related. Kyraine was so noble and dutiful in everything she did. Her brother, on the other hand, seemed to float around without much commitment or interest in anything.

Aiden pulled the shirt over his head, and the candlelight illuminated his body. I couldn't stop a sharp gasp from escaping my lips. Scars littered his shoulder blades and back. They criss-crossed all over his skin in so many directions that it was like looking at a map of converging streets. They were a darker shade than his skin, so I knew they couldn't be new. Still, I was taken aback.

Aiden immediately knew what had caused my reaction. "Never seen a scar before?" he asked me as he tossed his shirt on top of his cloak.

Some of the wounds stretching across his back and shoulder blades were as long as my arm. "I've never seen so many," I replied unevenly.

He shrugged. "It was a long time ago." I shifted uncomfortably on the bed and stayed silent, not wanting to delve into whatever he was talking about. He turned so that his bare chest faced me. "This one's my favorite." He gestured to a thicker scar under his collarbone. "Missed my heart by an inch."

Then he continued to silently maneuver around the room. I had no idea how to react to his attitude, nor to what he said. He seemed so nonchalant about the fact that his backed looked like a bear had mauled it. Clearly, someone was responsible for the lashes, but he appeared to be indifferent about it. I wondered if he had deserved them, or if Aiden was mentally sound, but decided not to concern myself with it tonight. I was tired, and he was safe. That was all I cared about, so that our mission could continue.

I only had a couple hours of sleep before my internal clock woke me again. I pushed the blankets aside and carefully picked my way across the floor and peered out the window. The sky above me was deep blue, with purple and pink clouds transitioning to reds and oranges as the sun began to rise. I went back over to Brennon's bed. One arm was folded up by his face, and one was tucked under his head. I gently shook his shoulder. He groggily raised his head and combed his fingers through his hair.

I went to awaken Aiden, wherever it was he had decided to curl up to sleep. "I'm awake," he said to me. Startled, I jumped. He sat at the table picking at a piece of bread. "I got us some breakfast."

I crossed my arms. "Do you ever sleep?" He was fully dressed again, with his cloak fastened around his shoulders. I looked at his face, but there were no signs of drowsiness.

He cocked his head, crossed his arms, and eyed me before replying. "Someone has to watch the door for burglars."

I was about to retort when Brennon interrupted us. He trudged over, saying how hungry he was. I held my tongue and turned my back on them while I started to dress. When I turned back to them, I wore a baggy shirt and riding pants. Then I drew up my riding boots and laced them. I twisted my brown, wavy hair into a braid, and tied my cloak.

Brennon finished eating and quickly dressed while I sat at the table to eat. Afterwards, we all gathered our things, stowed them in the saddlebags, and made our way downstairs. Brennon fetched fresh horses from the stable hand. We slung the bags over their backs and took off down the road.

We meandered through the streets easily, since only small groups of people were awake and no carts crowded the road yet. It took us several hours to cross through the city and reach the East Gate of the wall. Guards admitted us through, and I no longer felt claustrophobic as we directed the horses onto the open path towards the jungle. My horse fell in line behind Brennon's, and Aiden's took up the rear.

Soon, we passed the tavern where Brennon and I had stopped on our way to the city. I glanced back at Aiden, who was looking longingly at the little building. It seemed like he was deciding if he should stop for one more drink. As he was turning to face forward, I quickly turned away from him and pretended to study the rainforest around me. Towering trees created constant shade, and vines became tripping hazards for the horses. I passed leaves big enough to wrap myself in, and, in the distance, it sounded like monkeys called to one another. This forest was much more vibrant, bursting with bright colors, than the forest where the Hunters lived.

Hours later, the horses finally began to show signs of fatigue, so we slowed them to a labored walk. Aiden's horse pulled up next to mine. I shifted in my saddle to stretch my rigid limbs. I was straightening when Aiden broke our silence.

"So, Brennon, when did my sister loosen up enough to seek my help?"

I knew that comment, whether or not Aiden knew it, had to strike a nerve in Brennon, especially after their last parting. I spoke up, so as to spare Brennon. "When she realized you were her only hope."

He stole a look from my face. "What? Do you expect me to say I'm *honored?*"

I stammered, trying to think of what to say.

"I understand my sister's desperation, because by asking for my help, she's doing something she's never done before—going against her oath to the Hunters."

I was confused. "What?"

"Brennon didn't tell you?" I glanced between the two of them. "She's committing treason by asking for my help. Brennon's committing treason for working with me, a fact I'm sure the Master of the Hunt doesn't know." Brennon was stiff, though he tried to appear untouched by Aiden's harsh words. "And I might as well throw myself into the mix, because I committed treason—but that was ages ago."

"Brennon?" I suddenly needed to see his face. "Is that why you two are—"

He angled his body so that I could see the side of his profile. "We argued about a couple things, this mission being one of them," he tried to say in a cavalier manner.

"Why didn't anyone tell me?"

"Casey, Kyraine and I talked about it long before you arrived. I agreed to this of my own volition, and she asked me of her own. No one is doing this against his or her own will."

"My *honorable* sister is finally tarnishing her vows. It's about time," Aiden marveled.

I cut my eyes at Aiden. "What's the punishment for treason, Brennon?"

"Death," Aiden replied. "Well, first there's a trial, but that's typically followed by death."

"Why are you acting like you're above this?" I hissed at Aiden. That arrogant smirk was wearing my temper thin.

"I deserted the Huntsmen over twenty years ago. They haven't caught me yet, and I very much doubt that they'll catch me now, though being in the company of one does put a mark in my record."

I ignored Aiden and called out to Brennon. "I'm sure Kyraine will handle this. She wouldn't ask you to do this if she didn't have a plan." Brennon tossed an unconvincing smile back at me.

Aiden grumbled. "You give her too much credit just because she's trying to *save the world*," he jeered. "She's always been too idealistic for her own good. Now, it seems, it will be her undoing."

"She's devoted her life to helping people, and you—it seems you've devoted yours to helping yourself," I replied icily.

His expression wavered between offense and amusement, as though he'd been trying to draw this fight out of me the whole time. His voice darkened, but his eyes weren't consumed by its sudden menace.

"I'm glad you can see how incredibly different my sister and I really are."

Chapter 19: Brennon

ALMOST A WEEK had passed when we finally reached Bronzeshore, the trading post on the banks of Bronze Lake. The buildings were similar to the ones in Calem. Most of them were constructed from bamboo, had thatch roofs, sat on stilts, and were covered in colorful vegetation. I'd spent many hours running through the port as a boy. Pirates from the Western Sea would come to exhibit their treasures; merchants pushed around carts full of strange fruit; and sometimes other young children had small wrestling tournaments in the back alleys. It was also in Bronzeshore that I had first encountered the Huntsmen.

I'd been watching a magician twirl flaming batons when I heard a woman scream that someone had stolen her satchel. Without hesitation, I raced after the thief, bearing no weapons of my own. Thinking fast, I threw the apple I held at his head. It surprised him just enough that two muscular men, stock-full of weapons, were able to apprehend him within seconds and return the woman's bag to her. After slinging several threats at the thief, they let him scamper away. One of the Huntsmen spotted me watching them and approached me. He smiled warmly and handed me a fresh apple from his own bag.

"You're a great shot," he had said, thumping me on the shoulder. "I'd hate to fight you when you get some meat on those bones."

Years later, when I did finally become a Huntsman, I faced the same guy in a combat session during a training exercise. Afterwards, all he said was that he had been right about not wanting to fight me.

Aiden yanked me from my moment of revelry, elbowing me in my side. He had his hood up to conceal his face. "Hey! We aren't exactly in friendly territory right now—quick, face this way!" He jerked my body, his keen eyes on something over my shoulder. He had tried to convince Casey and me that we should avoid Bronzeshore altogether, but we needed to resupply, so we had to go pass through it.

"What is it?" I asked, thinking Casey was in trouble, but she was bargaining for camping supplies with a vendor a few carts away.

"I think a few of your friends spotted you," he muttered, his hands resting on his concealed weapons.

Bronzeshore was a popular destination for Huntsmen when they weren't on duty or were traveling in the area—the same Huntsmen that would be thrilled to find Aiden Redding in their midst, so they could capture him for his long overdue trial.

"Now isn't the time for a family reunion," Aiden continued. "If they see us together you're—"

"I know." I cut him off.

I called Casey over and explained that we needed to leave. We all hid our faces under our hoods and I led us through the crowded streets. The Huntsmen that Aiden thought recognized me started following us. I saw Aiden instinctively fingering his hidden daggers, but I flashed him a warning glance. I wouldn't let him kill my fellow Huntsmen.

When we finally made it back to the edge of Bronzeshore, we went over to the patch of grass and trees where we had tied our horses. We quickly saddled them and had tied our belongings down when I heard a familiar voice.

"Harrow?" I turned to find Wren Bradshaw, his silver hair tied in the back, and Jhago Provo, his black hair in a long braid ending at his waist. I'd spent many years training with both of them and I tried to make my face show that I was happy to see them, though on the inside I felt the exact opposite.

"Bradshaw! Provo!" I greeted them and stepped forward, hoping to draw attention away from Aiden and Casey. The Huntsmen surveyed the scene.

"What are you doing in Bronzeshore? Last I heard you were heading to the Hunters' camp to help the Mistress of the Hunt with something. And who's this?" Wren asked, looking at Casey.

"Mel Basemeth," Casey answered quickly. We exchanged glances, but her answer had the desired effect, and Wren lost interest.

I spoke up. "You heard right. Just stopping through here before heading north for an assignment."

Wren started to say something when Jhago ripped a curved saber from his belt. "What assignment has you transporting this criminal north? That's Aiden Redding," Jhago told Wren. "He deserted years ago. Why aren't you bringing him to camp? I'm sure Cade would love to mark his name off the list."

Aiden stood a few feet from Jhago's saber, and he eyed it as though it was a twig. Casey was waiting for me to inform her next move, and I was still deciding how I could get us out of the situation without a fight.

"I'm bringing him to Cade when I return."

Wren asked, "Why not bring him now? We can help escort."

"That won't be necessary—"

Jhago suddenly lunged at Aiden, suspecting he was getting ready to pull a knife from under his cloak. Aiden held his hands up. Wren's hand was glowing but Casey stepped forward, her hand poised to fire as well. I kept my sword sheathed, hoping I wouldn't have to use it.

"Jhago, Wren, stand down," I cried.

"What's going on, Brennon?" Jhago asked.

"He was forced to ask for my help for his assignment, and wouldn't you seek out the best, too, if the world depended on it?" Aiden joked. Jhago took a threatening step forward, but Aiden didn't flinch. If anything, he was welcoming this fight.

Wren and Jhago sneered at Aiden and exchanged tense glances. Wren spoke first. "Brennon, he's a deserter."

Jhago added, "If Cade found out you were traveling with him, and he wasn't in chains—"

"I love being talked about in third person," Aiden said with irritation.

"We'll tell Cade you were on your way to camp when we saw you in Bronzeshore."

"Yes, Brennon," Jhago added. "You must take him to camp."

"I can't." They both looked like I had sprouted a second head. "And I can't explain why."

"This doesn't sound like you, Brennon. What does he have on you?" Wren questioned.

"Whatever it is, we'll make him regret it," Jhago said.

Before I could answer, Aiden's impatience had won him over. He lunged forward and disarmed Jhago in seconds. Wren shot a spell at Aiden, but Casey expertly fended it off. Jhago's saber was turned on him, as Aiden held the blade inches from his neck.

"You're defending him?" Wren said incredulously to Casey.

Casey explained calmly, "You can't have him."

"This is treason! The Mistress of the Hunt will punish you for this." Casey brushed the empty threat aside. "Brennon, help us bring these traitors in."

Aiden looked like a dog waiting for the order to attack. Casey seemed reluctant to fight, but prepared nonetheless.

I pulled my sword from its sheath and stepped in Wren's path to Aiden. "I'll explain everything later."

Jhago attacked first. He ripped two more sabers from his belt and flew at Aiden with dangerous ferocity. The horses startled and raced to the edge of the battle. Casey blocked another spell from Wren, veering it off course. I spun to help Aiden, knowing Wren outmatched me with his sorcery. Aiden deflected Jhago's swing, while I lunged at him. I spun away from a blade, as Aiden ducked below another. He spun, hooking Jhago's foot in his and sent him tumbling to the ground. I kicked away one of his blades before Aiden dove on top of him to wrestle the other from his grip.

I was suddenly thrown backwards into a tree and pinned by an invisible force. Casey was painfully pulling herself to her feet. It looked like Wren had flung her aside, through several trees.

"You've forced my hand, Brennon," Wren said apologetically.

Spots started appearing in my vision as I felt my consciousness slipping away. My grasp on everything had almost vanished completely when I suddenly slumped forward onto my hands and knees, and my mind began slowly clearing.

Casey had tackled Wren from behind and struggled with him a few feet away. He tossed Casey from him with ease. He went to grab her neck, but she knocked his hands away, kicked him in the gut, and launched herself at him. They fell together in a heap. She had one hand pressing into his chest; the other, glowed red, hovering over his face.

"Don't—even—think—about—it," she threatened between gulps of air.

His eyes starting fluttering and soon he fell unconscious, but not before giving me a murderous grimace.

My own dizziness finally subsided, and I rose to my feet. Casey was brushing herself off when Aiden surfaced from his own fight. Jhago sat propped against a tree, his head lolling to one side.

Aiden grumbled. "Friendly lot you've got here." He wiped blood from the corner of his mouth.

"You didn't kill—"

"No, but I can. It'll be safer that way," Aiden answered. "They won't even feel—"

"No!" I shouted at him as I glanced over Casey for injuries. I jumped to my friends' defense. "They're only doing their job."

"They'll report back to Cade and this mission will no longer be a secret. We'll have to keep looking over our shoulders." I shot him a hard look, so Aiden conceded. He gruffly tossed the sabers next to Jhago. "Fine, but let's strive to make this the only Huntsmen reunion for the duration of our travels."

Though I didn't want to admit it out loud, I agreed with Aiden. I knew word of my mission in Eileen would eventually get out, but I wanted to conceal the fact that I was working with Aiden until after it was over. Now that Wren and Jhago knew, it seemed my treasonous activity wouldn't be kept quiet for much longer.

We calmed the horses, gathered our things, and set out again. It was a much less enjoyable trip than the one to Emberrun had been, because the air between the three of us was still tense. Aiden was still annoyed that we had gone through Bronzeshore, and Casey was still on edge about her argument with Aiden.

It wasn't until the seventh night of our travels together that it seemed we could all converse without bitterness creeping into our voices. We huddled around the fire. The temperature kept steadily dropping with each day we traveled north. Aiden roasted quails that I had hunted, while Casey filled our canteens with water.

"What *do* you know about this rumored document that has Queen Gisele's and Azlaya's agreement on it?" I asked Aiden as he turned the bird in the fire.

"For one, I know its not rumored. It's real. It exists. It has for years."

Casey turned to Aiden. "They didn't make their alliance recently?"

He shook his head, but didn't clarify how he knew this information. Casey and I exchanged glances.

"I've been thinking about the best ways to search for it. While there are many places outside the castle where it could be, the likelihood that it's in the castle is high as well. So, having access to the castle is crucial."

"How would we do that?" Casey asked.

"The Tournament of Eileen," Aiden answered, but his gaze was set on me.

I considered what he said. Then it hit me. "Of course," I sighed.

"What's the Tournament of Eileen?" Casey broke into our silent exchange.

"It's an event Eileen holds every year, predating even the kingdom walls. To ensure it had the best army, Eileen's early rulers held a tournament consisting of games and trials to test the courage, strength, and intelligence of its soldiers. Since then, it's grown more into a form of entertainment, and less a test for Eileen's soldiers," I explained to her.

"What does that have to do with the castle?" she asked.

"The competitors stay in the castle for the duration of the games," Aiden contributed. "If you enter the tournament," he said to Casey, "we'll have the access we need to search the castle, if we don't find the document hidden outside it."

Casey looked taken off guard. "*I* have to enter the tournament?"

"I'm not popular with the queen, so I can't. Brennon's a Huntsman, and they've been barred from the games, so he can't. That leaves you." Aiden ignored her flustering and kept talking. "You'll have to enter under an alias, but this way I'll have someone on the inside who can help me get access to the castle so I can search for this document. That *is* the plan, isn't it?"

We considered the plan in silence for a few moments. "It could work," I said thoughtfully.

If what Aiden said was true, and the document was hidden in the castle, he would be the best person to send in after it to find it. So, not only *could* our plan to enter Casey in the tournament work, it *had* to. Otherwise, we would have to break into the heavily guarded castle, search for the document, steal it, destroy it, and escape—all without alerting the guards or the queen herself—a task that seemed more and more impossible as I thought about it.

Chapter 20: Kate

THE PAST COUPLE nights had been tiresome. I chose to do most of my operations at night, and let the Muskoxen work during the day. The darkness was my best ally, but still, I longed for sleep. I tried to sleep during the day, but normally I just grew restless and ended up staying awake, practicing and reading about dark spells. Very early one morning, I was so delirious from sleep deprivation that somehow I cast a spell that depicted my dreams on the wall while I slept. I woke to find a mural of myself plunging a dagger through Casey's heart as we fell, suspended in time. The colors were quite beautiful, especially when the warm sun spilled in through the small window and illuminated it. Still, my sleepless nights were beginning to wear on my functionality. That was probably why I met Zayne Ryder to being with.

I stood over a trembling woman. She was middle-aged, fair-skinned, and had curly hair framing her face. Tears streaked down her face as she clutched herself and tried to shrink away from me.

"Shh, you'll wake your kids," I hushed her.

Even though I had placed a deep Sleeping spell on her young boys, who slept soundly across the dark room, their mother still quieted her sobs. Her husband rolled over in their bed so that his back faced us. The woman, who sat crouched at the side of her bed on the floor, whimpered as though willing him to wake. I had sensed her powers while doing my usual rounds through the city, but as I stood over her, in this hysterical state, I wondered why I had sought her out. She hadn't tried to fight back, like most of the other sorcerers I had encountered. Rather, she sat still, resigned to her fate.

After several drawn-out minutes of listening to her muffled cries, a Sagen warrior finally appeared, at which point her crying became more audible. She began to beg again, this time appealing to my maternal side. I brushed her off and faced the Sagen who loomed behind us.

"She is strong," the Sagen observed.

"Not strong-willed," I noted.

She still hadn't uttered a spell to protect herself. It was then that I realized that she knew fighting back would put her family at more risk than if she just accepted her capture. *How touching*, I thought.

"Go on then." The Sagen approached her, wrapped its skeletal fingers around her arm and pulled her to her feet. Before I had even finished mumbling the counter-spell to release her family from its deep sleep, the Sagen and the woman had disappeared. That made over a hundred sorcerers captured, just in the past couple of days. I scanned the scene one last time before thinking how merciful I was to have left the young boys with a father. I hadn't been so lucky in my youth.

I exited the creaky house through the front door. The weather had taken a turn for the worse that night. Nasty wind whipped down the street, making strands of my hair attack my face. I gathered my fur-lined cloak around my shoulders and flipped the hood over my head. I was tired. I could feel my body yearning for rest as I walked down the street. This state of mind was weaker than normal, and therefore, vulnerable.

I passed under a lamppost. I wrapped my hand around it, hoping that the burning sensation of the frozen post would lift my mind from its drowsiness. My breath came out in white puffs in the frosty air. I decided it was time to turn in, even though I had only uncovered a handful of sorcerers that night. I could imagine Azlaya's disappointment with such clarity that I could have sworn she was there speaking to me. That was when I sensed yet another sorcerer. Though, this feeling was familiar. I recognized the sensation that overcame me.

The fogginess that threatened to swallow me before was swept swiftly away by the realization that another source of power for Azlaya's army was nearby. I unwrapped my now-frozen hand from the lamppost and turned down an alley. It was narrow enough that if I stretched out my arms, I could run my fingers along the buildings on either side of me. I came to another street, walked past a row of residential buildings, and then slipped into the shadows of another alley. This one was much longer that the first. As I walked, I realized it was leading me farther and farther from the main street. Finally, I came to a sharp corner and a dead end.

The building before me was as common and plain as any other house I'd seen. It had four rickety steps leading to a single, wooden door. To either side of the door, there was a square window, and above it there was another window, the size of two doors. A soft, orange glow from a fireplace told me my target was inside.

I approached the door, unlocked it with a flick of a finger, and entered. I was correct about the fire, though it was smaller than I anticipated. It looked like it had been left untouched for quite some time, as the logs were all but ash. Only small embers gave off the orange hue I saw from outside. I gazed around the house. It was just a single room. To the right of me was the fireplace with a worn fabric chair in front of it. Next to the fireplace there was a shelf with only a handful of books. In fact, the lack of books made the shelf appear superfluous. To my left must have been the kitchen. There was a table with a single chair and a single plate. On the plate there was a piece of bread and a slice of moldy cheese. I noticed more plates were stacked haphazardly in a basin, with even more spoiled food. The whole scene looked like someone had gotten up and left in a hurry, and hadn't returned in months. But that didn't explain the fire.

In the corner of the room, I spotted a ladder that disappeared into a lofted area above. Though I knew my mind was groggy, I was sure that I'd sensed a sorcerer, and that it was close. I approached the ladder and hoisted myself up to the lofted area. I realized that the space was fairly large, once my eyes adjusted. A bed lay on the floor, and the sheets, as I might have expected, were in a disheveled mess. The bed was all that occupied the space, beams converging over it.

I spun and raised my hand threateningly, spell poised to fire. In the shadows, I could see the silhouette of a body. "Come out. Now," I ordered.

Very slowly, the person came forward. Had I been more alert, our first encounter would have happened very differently. I would have alerted a Sagen to collect him and take him to the Shadowlands to harness his powers, and I would never have seen him again. Instead of fighting, however, he stepped from the shadows, arms raised in surrender, reserved smile on his lips, and curiosity in his eyes.

"I know who you are," he said cautiously. I didn't let my defenses down. It was plain to discern him as a sorcerer, despite his seeming unwillingness to exhibit his powers.

"Is that because you've been following me?" I accused him, now knowing why his presence was so familiar to me. I'd been feeling him lurking in the shadows for days.

"Observing you," he said innocently. "And because, your reputation precedes you, Kaitlin Coles."

I was surprised to hear him utter my name. He stepped forward again, and the moon cast a silver light across his face. He had fair skin. His eyes were piercing and silver-blue. They appeared to be aware of everything in the room, though they remained locked on me. His jawline was defined, and he had some close-shaven stubble above his mouth and around his chin. His hair was short, black, and had a wavy pattern. Though he smiled with the lips of an angel, his eyes were unquestionably devilish.

I appraised him closely. "You know my name. How is it I don't know yours?"

"Well, there isn't a prophecy written about me, for one," he said lightly. A reserved smile spread on his lips. My stance relaxed, though my hand stayed raised. I beckoned him on with my eyes. "My name is Zayne Ryder. I know why you've come, and I want to talk."

"About what?"

"I want to join you. I know you're gathering sorcerers for Azlaya's army, and I want to help."

I narrowed my eyes. "Why?"

"Because I believe that you're going to win this war," he said confidently, and oddly enough, warmly. "I know many things, Kaitlin, but above all I know where to stack my cards."

"Why should I believe you?"

"Have I given you a reason not to trust me?"

"You stalked me," I said plainly.

He paused. "You interest me."

My hand glowed at little brighter at his comment. I stepped forward threateningly, but as soon as I did, my hand stopped glowing. I tried to summon the spell again, but my hand did nothing. My confusion made him smile crookedly. He pointed at my feet, and I looked down and saw that I stood in a circle with symbols around its perimeter, drawn with what appeared to be chalk. When I tried to step out of it, an invisible force resisted me. I was stuck. My eyes flashed back to Zayne's face.

"Now that I've given you a reason not to trust me, do I interest you?"

"What do you want?" I asked.

"I already told you, but now that I have your undivided attention—" He stepped forward and brushed his foot on the floor, wiping away part of the chalk circle. "It's your move, Kaitlin."

He had completely lowered his hands now, so that he stood before me defenseless. He titled his head to the side, waiting for my response. My hand was glowing again, but I slowly let it fall to my side, too. His stunt, strangely, had the intended effect, and I was curious about this young man. He had me defenseless. He could have held me for ransom, or threatened Azlaya. Instead, he demonstrated his tricks, only to let me go and retaliate if I wanted to.

"Kate," I told him.

"Kate," he repeated gently. His voice was low, but still had the charm of a child's. "From this moment on, I pledge my loyalty to you and your cause." He bowed respectfully, but when he straightened, my suspicious, though curious expression still hadn't changed.

"I'll take you to Azlaya." I pressed two fingers to my wrist to summon a Sagen to escort us back to the Shadowlands so that I could preserve energy. "She can decide if you'll be useful to us."

Zayne nodded in understanding. "You know, all the stories about you haven't given you enough credit for one thing."

"Oh, and what's that?" I asked more defensively than I expected.

"Your beauty."

He didn't compliment me shyly, or even gently. It was a bit forceful, if anything. It was as though he was making sure there was no room for me to argue or brush his comment aside. I was still fumbling for words when the Sagen appeared. I studied Zayne's face as he observed the Sagen. The only things that consumed his face were curiosity and pure eagerness. He wasn't all that dissimilar from me when I had first encountered the Sagen.

"To the Shadowlands. I'm taking him to see Azlaya," I instructed the Sagen. I could sense Zayne's satisfaction with my reaction to his compliment, albeit small.

The Sagen dipped its head. It placed a hand on my shoulder, and I held my hand out to Zayne. My expression was reserved, to make sure he didn't perceive this as an advance on him. He grasped my hand, and slowly, we began to disappear, while simultaneously appearing in the Shadowlands.

As soon as we were grounded in the Shadowlands, I pulled my hand from Zayne's. "This way." I gestured towards the jagged castle.

We had kicked up some of the black soot with our landing. I grumbled silently to myself about how I had not missed the ubiquitous ash at all while I had been away. Zayne fell into step behind me.

"These are the Shadowlands?" I made an affirmative sound. "Not a very lively place, is it?"

"You have no idea," I said bleakly.

"You stayed here?" Zayne quickened his pace so that we walked side by side. I wondered how he had known that. Of course he knew. He was a sorcerer, and I was being reckless enough to think freely without shielding my thoughts. I quickly reassembled my mental defenses and marched onward.

"For a time, yes."

The servants saw me approaching and opened the front door in time for us to walk in without slowing our pace. We took the stairs that led to the upper level of the castle and turned down the hall. I knocked on the first door, waited for my cue to enter, and pushed the door open.

The room was large enough to fit a desk, a chair, a lounging chair, and a short table comfortably. All the furniture was made of the same black stone that comprised the rest of the castle, though the edges were smoothed. Behind the desk was Azlaya.

She looked like she had been focusing on something for a long time, and was taking a break. Her expression screamed that she was clearly distressed over something. She ran a hand through her hair, which spilled in unruly curls around her face.

She lifted her gaze and realized for the first time that another person was with me. Immediately her expression changed from drowsiness to accusation. "Who is this?"

"Zayne Ryder. I came across him in Eileen." I stepped to the side to let him present himself. Azlaya's eyes were still glued to my face. She was trying not to make her anger too obvious, but it was still unmistakable.

"I have only heard rumors about you, My Lady, so forgive me if I seem in awe. For a very long time, I have wanted to stand before you and pledge my loyalty to your cause."

Azlaya looked skeptical. "Why is that?"

"Because, as I told Kate," he exchanged glances with me, emphasizing my name, "I believe you are going to win this war. I am not a fool. I want to fight for the side that will prevail, and so I will be a most useful ally. I will help you continue to build your army, or in any other way that I can."

"Ambitious man, aren't you?"

"I swear, My Lady. I will be of great use."

Azlaya's expression flickered for a second. She looked at him as though he was a missing piece to a puzzle, but the moment was brief. Her cool eyes and calm face returned.

"If you swear your fealty, we will have you."

Azlaya's words shocked me and brought my attention from a distant place back to the present. Zayne contained any excitement he had and bowed gracefully.

"Kate, show him to a room. It's late. You two can return to Eileen tomorrow." She waved dismissively towards me.

My eyebrows had furrowed together. Azlaya saw my hesitation and shot me a look of warning. With an uneven voice, I told Zayne to follow me. I wasn't sure what Azlaya was planning for him. We walked to the other end of the hall where my room was. Across from my old room was the door to the spare room. I opened it and gestured for Zayne to enter. He brushed past, I followed him in, and the door swung closed. He looked around as he took in his lodging for the night. It was a plain room, much like my own. However, it was much cleaner than the house I had found him in back in Eileen. A bed was tucked into a corner, a chest was at its foot, and on the other side there was a chair for lounging.

Zayne carefully observed the room as if he was trying to commit it to memory. "So, what stories have you hear about me?" I asked.

I leaned against the wall, one leg propped against it to appear as casual as I could. My head was reeling trying to figure out what about Zayne had made Azlaya agree to his proposal. There wasn't anything unusually special about him, or his powers, however strong they may have been. Had he just interested her as much as he had me?

"All kinds. I've heard that you knew sorcery coming out of the womb. I heard you were an angel in your youth, but something hardened you against that disposition. I've heard that your powers will someday rival that of your mother's, and all the greats before her. I've also heard that your specialty is making people go mad. I've heard that you're plain—but that one isn't true." I licked my lips nervously. "I also heard that your hair is the color of a white rose." He had slowly closed the distance between us. He took a strand of hair that had fallen out of my ponytail and gently brushed it back in place. "But that one isn't true either. Its color more closely resembles honey."

My heart beat unevenly against my chest. I had never known someone so forward. No, that wasn't true. I just hadn't experienced this kind of forwardness in such a long time. The last time a guy had behaved like this towards me, we had quickly fallen for each other; he broke something inside me, and it left him dead. This thought and the reminder of the inner turmoil I'd felt made me immediately draw away from Zayne.

"Have I said something wrong?" Zayne asked. He noticed I'd recoiled, and the concern was genuine.

"No, I—just thought of something."

I spun away from his close presence. He watched me carefully as I clumsily pulled the door open and made way to leave. "We'll leave at first light. Goodnight."

I ducked into my room, shut the door, and slumped against it. Who *was* this guy? Who had the audacity to confront me like he had, convince me to take him to meet Azlaya, and then persuade her to let him join our efforts? Why was my skin prickling? What was the feeling rising inside me?

I rubbed my eyes and knew that had I not been so tired, I would have summoned a Sagen to take him away, and never thought of him again. He had an air about him that made him appear overly confident in his abilities in everything he did. It was as if he had never been familiar with the concept of failure. In the very short time I'd known him, he'd already started backing me into a corner. He was encroaching on a space I had walled off and carefully lined with barbed wire.

Then why was I yearning to swim in his serpentine eyes again? Why did my skin tingle under his breath? I was suddenly afraid that he was getting precariously close to my barbed defenses. Even more so, I was terrified that he had the capability of grabbing hold and swiftly, easily dismantling what I had convinced myself was a fortified barrier. The most petrifying thought, however, was realizing that some part of him knew this, too.

Chapter 21: Casey

BRENNON, AIDEN, AND I were still ironing out the details of my alias's story. Aiden said I would need more than just a fake name. I'd need a background, a family, names, dates, places, and events, all memorized and accessible within seconds. In other words, I would have to construct an identity so believable that even Aiden and Brennon were fooled.

We each provided details of my fabricated identity, letting the others edit and tweak parts to make it even more believable. Aiden and Brennon quizzed me regularly, and I when I couldn't keep details straight anymore, I forced them to talk about something else.

On the twelfth night of our travels, we came to a hollowed niche under a fallen tree's roots. We halted the horses and set up camp. Soon we ate around a fire, and my testing resumed.

"Where did you say you were from?" Brennon asked, mimicking questions I might receive once we made it to Eileen and I entered the tournament.

"I live in the Northern Mountains of Eileen by Riversmith Castle with my father, mother, and older brother. My father and brother work in the mines, and my mother works in a glass blowing store, and—"

"Casey." Brennon cut me off. I looked at him, wondering why he interrupted me. "I only asked where you were from. You can't spill your whole life story from one simple question," he lectured lightly.

I took a long breath. "I'm from the Northern Mountains of Eileen—"

"No," Aiden interjected.

"Now what?" I snapped, not hiding my annoyance anymore.

"If you were really from Eileen, you wouldn't need to say the Northern Mountains *of Eileen*. People would assume you're *of Eileen* without the clarification. Saying that would make them suspicious of your story," Aiden explained wearily.

Naturally, I opened my mouth to argue with him, but he had a point. I reluctantly turned back to Brennon. "I'm from the Northern Mountains, near Riversmith Castle."

"What do you for a living that would qualify you to participate in the tournament?"

"I hunt for my village, so I spend my days in the forest chasing game like bears and wolves." I eyed Aiden, waiting for him to poke holes in my response, but he remained silent. "I've always been drawn to the outdoors, and feeding my village has its own rewards." Brennon smiled approvingly at my reply.

"What would you do with the winnings if you won the tournament?" Apparently the victor won five thousand gold pieces.

"I'd use them to help my village."

Aiden made a disapproving sound. "Too innocent." I opened my mouth to protest, but he continued. "You hunt for your village, which means you face the possibility of getting mauled by a bear or killed by a pack of wolves each day, which means you're a realist, not a romantic. People will see right through those responses. Keep them real," he instructed.

I kept my gaze trained on Aiden as he bit into an apple. "I don't like to think too far ahead into the future. If and when I win, I'll think about what I'll do with the winnings then," Aiden goaded me on with his unwavering gaze. "For now, I'll take it one day at a time." I came to assume that when he stopped staring at me and didn't utter a word, he accepted my answer as good enough.

"Good," Brennon asserted. "How about we discuss the one thing we've neglected?" Brennon said. I cocked my head in questioning. "Your name," he said piteously.

I was tired and could feel a yawn toying at me. "James Bond." I chuckled at my own joke. The other two just blinked. "Never mind."

"Kai Frost," Aiden said. He had a thin grin on his face, though his eyes conveyed deeper, sadder emotions.

I'd known Aiden for only over a week, but that was plenty of time to become familiar with his tendencies, and more importantly, his sense of humor. "I won't go by the name of a prostitute you slept with." Brennon choked on his food. "I wonder how much you had to pay her to keep her in your presence," I stated boldly.

There was that face again, the one mixed with offense and amusement. "Don't be mean," Aiden scorned me playfully.

"I wish you would take this more seriously," I shot back sharply. "If you weren't Kyraine's brother, I'd have cursed you long before now."

He chuckled darkly. "Oh, so now my *sister's* protecting me?" His tone was unapologetically mocking me. "My fears of you casting some spell on me are negligible, compared to other things."

"You aren't afraid of me?"

The fact that he wasn't the least bit intimidated by my powers made me more irritated than it should have. He gave me a weary look, as though the conversation was about to bore him to tears.

"How about instead of concerning yourself with how much I fear you, you worry about our plan, or Azlaya, or your sister who wants to sever your head from your body?" he said coldly.

"Aiden," Brennon warned.

His vicious depiction of my death caught me off guard, and my words froze in my throat. Aiden must have realized that he had stunned me into silence. I was more shocked that he backpedaled to apologize, than by his comment.

"I'm sorry, that was harsh. We all have our demons." He rose to leave.

I snapped out of my bewilderment. "And what are yours, exactly?"

He smiled thinly, concealing something inside him. "Let's hope you never have to know." At the edge of our small campsite, he paused. "For the record, Kai wasn't a prostitute. She was the best spy I ever worked with." With that, he left.

Brennon searched my face, looking for any effects Aiden's comment about Kate may have had on me. I assured him I was fine, my gaze lingering on Aiden's path.

That night, I felt something humming in my head. I rolled over, thinking a bug had buzzed by my ear. I opened my eyes. Whispers and agonized screams drifted through my mind, like the memory of a dream. My head told me to figure out what it was, but my body protested. When I couldn't fall back to sleep, I threw the blankets from me and stepped out from my tent. The air was cool, and a soft wind rippled through the leaves. I heard something billowing in the breeze, and noticed that Brennon and Aiden's tent flap was partly open. I went over and peeked in and saw that only Brennon was curled up inside.

I closed the tent to shield Brennon from the wind and then turned to face the vast forest that stretched out before me. Once again, I was left to worry about Aiden's whereabouts. Suddenly, the thought that Aiden was a criminal wanted by the Huntsmen struck me like a blow. We were no longer within the secure confines of the city walls. Images of Aiden being dragged off by the male warriors gripped me as I forged ahead into the woods.

I rushed over to Aiden's saddlebag and rummaged around for something that belonged to him. One of his knives would have to do. My fingers wrapped around the blade hilt as I muttered a Tracking spell. I waited a few agonizing moments while I felt my powers radiate from me and search the forest. I felt it in my gut before I saw him in my head. My eyes shot open, and I took off on the path I had just envisioned. I walked until I couldn't see our little campsite, and then farther until I finally felt Aiden's presence. My feet slowed, and my head swung back and forth as my eyes scanned the trees.

To my right, I heard a branch groan. I spun around, expecting to come face to face with a mountain lion. Instead, I craned my head back and saw Aiden's silhouette against the night sky. I breathed a silent sigh of relief, but however silent I thought I was being, he still managed to hear me.

"Are you going to make a habit of tracking me down every night?" he asked wearily from his perch, a branch maybe fifteen feet off the ground. One leg dangled, swaying in the wind. His gaze was directed elsewhere, as if he were searching for something in the distance.

"If you keep disappearing like this, then yes." I paused and softened my voice. "This plan won't work without you, and your vanishing doesn't help my nerves."

My words filled the space between us, but he didn't utter a response. I took the chance to quietly observe the young man who stared placidly outward. It was the first time I could really study him without feeling the weight of his own gaze.

He sighed. "You're so concerned with others all the time."

"What's your point?" He didn't respond. He just cast a disapproving glance my way. "A lot of people are counting on me to protect them."

"Sometimes it's easier to stay out of things," he contested.

"I never really had the option to stay out of things." He considered me thoughtfully from his perch. It was a rare look, untouched by sarcasm.

"That's what you always think. Then you look back and see all the choices that were yours alone, all along."

I had the feeling he no longer talked about my prophesized fate. He took a swig from his flask. I wondered what demons he chased away with whatever he drank. Instead of prodding at a subject I knew he wouldn't talk about, I mentioned something else.

"I'm sorry for what I said earlier, about your friend. Where is she? Kai?"

"She's dead."

I tentatively asked, "W-what happened?"

Another swig. "She trusted me and I let her down. I understand the weight of having others depend on you."

I wondered how someone who was usually so emotionless and callous could suddenly shed that shell and confess the things he did. I attributed it to whatever he drank. In the morning, none of this would matter, though I wished it would. That way, I could be one step closer to solving the mystery that was Aiden Redding.

"I'll save you the trouble of saying you're sorry," he interrupted my thoughts. "Go back to bed. I'll find my way back."

As I expected, the next morning we acted as though our midnight conversation hadn't occurred. He still doled out quips, and Brennon still tried to keep the peace between us when he felt our discussions headed towards cruel remarks neither of us could take back. As we traveled, Brennon and Aiden would ask me the same questions about my fake identity in different ways, to confuse me, or they would have me tell the same story in more detail each time I retold it. Aiden was always ready with a quick interjection to correct me. I pitied Kyraine for having such a smart-ass brother, and felt grateful for my sister. Then I remembered she wanted me dead. I supposed having no siblings was the best scenario.

The closer we drew to Eileen's walls, the more layers of clothing we had to buy at smaller trading posts along the way. Interestingly enough, our closeness to Eileen had a positive correlation with Aiden's drinking, and a negative correlation with our bickering.

On the morning when the city walls finally came into view, we woke to a waterlogged forest. Pounding rain had drummed against our tents throughout the night. We groggily packed up camp and saddled the horses in preparation to set out. My body had become so sore from riding that the numbness had finally been replaced by pain. I was fantasizing about getting a nice massage when my horse tripped over something and went crashing to the ground, pulling me with it. Aiden and Brennon turned their horses back. My horse whinnied frantically, but it couldn't seem to roll back onto its feet. Brennon jumped down from his stallion.

"Are you all right?" Brennon asked. He knelt beside me and helped work my leg from underneath the animal's crushing weight. Aiden inspected the horse for injuries. When my leg was finally freed, and Brennon made sure I was fine, I turned to Aiden.

"How bad is it?"

Aiden knelt by the horse's leg and balanced it gently in his hands. "Broken leg," he diagnosed emotionlessly. He set the leg down and drew a knife from his belt.

My arm bolted out to stop whatever he planned to do. "What are you doing?" I shrieked.

"I'll put him out of his misery." He tried to move closer to the horse, but I blocked him.

"No. I can help him. Let me try to heal him."

Aiden eyed me curiously, as if questioning my motive. Finally, he stood and gave me room to move around the horse's leg. I took the injured limb into my hands and let my powers feel around for the broken bone and ruptured ligaments. They weren't hard to find, but I couldn't mend it like I could a human leg.

Brennon must have seen the creases in my face and asked, "What's wrong?"

"Myra had me commit human anatomy to memory, so I could heal anyone, but—I don't know horse anatomy that well," I explained, disappointed.

"Can you heal him or not?" Brennon asked carefully, not wanting to upset me.

I studied the swelling leg with determination.

"I think I can work through it," I added softly.

Aiden shifted his weight impatiently. "Well, thankfully I *do* know horse anatomy." He knelt beside me and before I could stop him, he plunged his knife into the horse's chest. I choked on nothing except his sheer audacity. The horse's whinnies faded, and I watched painfully as its eyes dulled into a blank stare. "Don't worry. It went right through his heart. He didn't feel a thing."

I angrily turned on Aiden as he went to wipe the knife in some grass. "I could have helped him!" I yelled after him. "I just needed some time!"

He gazed upon me, bent over the dead horse. "We need to keep moving."

I rooted myself to that spot and glared at Aiden. Brennon tried to comfort me, but I was too angry to absorb his condolences.

"You're too soft," Aiden observed. My eyes flashed to him. "For who you are and what you need to do, you can't be."

Brennon helped me to my feet. "Come on." Aiden gestured to his horse. "We have half a day's ride left, and Brennon's horse is getting lethargic. You can ride with me." I still glared at him from where I stood. "Don't make me beg," he said in a condescending manner as he held his hand out.

I swallowed more protests and approached Aiden's horse. He gracefully swung himself into the saddle and effortlessly pulled me up behind him. I found my arms were awkwardly hanging at my side, not really wanting to hug Aiden for the rest of the ride. He sensed my discomfort.

"Just hold on to me so you don't fall off, please."

I did as he asked and clasped my hands over his stomach, and tried to direct my thoughts elsewhere. My mind, however, wouldn't stop dwelling on his comment about who I was.

"I have a heart," I said by his ear, so Brennon wouldn't overhear me. "What you said about me being soft—it's having a heart."

He twisted so that he spoke over his shoulder. "You don't want to have one. It's dangerous."

Several hours later, we had reached the inner city of Eileen. I must have fallen asleep against Aiden's back, because when I awoke, stone buildings and streets surrounded us. We stopped at a quiet inn, and immediately, I could see the differences between Calem and Eileen. In Queen Gisele's kingdom, everyone lurked around, glancing over their shoulders, as if to catch someone following them. Furtive eyes flicked over every passerby, and even our horses felt uncomfortable in the strangely suspicious atmosphere.

Aiden's shift of weight jolted me fully awake. He hopped down from the horse and held a hand out to me. I took it and, not nearly as gracefully, slid from the animal's back. Brennon tied our horses to the watering post as Aiden and I went inside to book a room. After that, we met in the dining area near a roaring fireplace that fended off the cold from outside. An elderly woman asked for our orders, and Aiden told her to bring us their best dish.

I glanced around the dim room. A wooden staircase was tucked in the corner of the room. Next to that, a small bar rested against one wall, with the head of a large elk hanging above it. Its dead, blank eyes bored into mine, making me as uneasy as the horses were. Round tables crowded the room, each with people huddled close as they talked and ate. No one seemed to speak above a muffled whisper. Everything about Eileen screamed distrust.

The old woman returned and roughly placed three bowls of an unappetizing stew on the table. My nose involuntarily wrinkled. After she briskly walked away, I asked, "What is that?"

Aiden answered me. "It's either moose liver stew or beaver liver stew." He chuckled at the disgusted face I made. I longed for plain chicken, but Brennon and Aiden didn't seem to mind.

"I think I'll pass this time around." I pushed my bowl away from me, offering it to whoever wanted it.

I crossed the room, and it was when I was ordering bread at the bar counter that I overheard Azlaya's name.

A lanky man with greasy hair sat at the counter, a few chairs down from me. I leaned back on my stool to see whom he spoke to and realized it was the bitter woman who had served our stew. I cocked my head in their direction to hear the hushed conversation between them.

"Azlaya has been sending them into the city for weeks now," the man said.

"I see so many at night. Hardly anyone comes out anymore. It's terrible for business," the woman grumbled.

"Well, you know as well as I that only certain people need to be concerned," the man replied mysteriously. He glanced around the room in search of prying eyes. When he turned back to the woman he whispered, "What do you have for me?"

Someone returned with my bread and a cube of butter, but I was too engrossed in the conversation to say thank you.

"A young girl in the west district. Red, curly hair. She works in the bakery over there," the woman replied under her breath.

The man nodded curtly and rose from the stool. "I'll come by to give you your cut when it's over."

The woman left him to tend to other customers. My eyes trailed the man as he went unnoticed through the humming room. He exited out a side door; I jumped up and darted past disgruntled people after him. I didn't even turn to get Brennon or Aiden's attention as I slipped through the door.

The little light that spilled into the alley was instantly cut off when I closed the door. As my eyes adjusted to the darkness, I sensed something lingering at my neck. Then the cool, flat object pressed farther into my throat. Experience told me it was a dagger, and none other than the greasy-haired man held it. His teeth were bared, and they sat uncomfortably in his mouth, crooked and misshapen. He had a narrow nose that hooked at the end.

"Why are you following me?" His voice was high pitched and sounded like that of a weasel.

My voice was caught in my throat, not out of fear of the man, but from fear that my necklace had become dislodged and rested in plain sight on my collarbone instead. When he said nothing about the prophecy, my training kicked in. I swung my arm up and knocked his hand away, spun from his grasp, and shoved him against the wall. I quickly pried the dagger from his weak grip. He grunted and looked sharply at my face. I lowered the arm that I had pressed against his neck and backed up. He grumbled when he realized that a woman had disarmed him. I should have cursed him just for that.

"I want information," I answered. His eyebrows pinched together. "What were you just talking about with the innkeeper?"

He laughed, but it was more of a cough, and my nose wrinkled from the putrid smell of his breath. "Why would I tell you, *girl?*"

I stepped closer, and his expression faltered. "Because I'm holding the knife."

"Do you know how to use it?"

My eyes flared, and I lifted the dagger threateningly. I heard the clicking sound of boots on stone. Brennon and Aiden suddenly stood at the alley's entrance, wondering if they needed to intervene. They must have noticed that I had disappeared and had wound their way back to the alley in search of me. I was instantly glad I could use them as another method of intimidation to get the man to talk. From the corner of my eye, I saw Brennon's hand resting on the hilt of his sword, and Aiden's fingers reaching for his hidden weapons.

"What the hell is this? You people are crazy. I don't know anything." The panic in his voice was evident. "I'll scream for help."

He had finally irritated me enough. My hand started glowing, and I raised it so he could see. He eyes widened. "I could make you spill your darkest secrets right here, right now. Now I strongly suggest you tell me what I want to know." I wiggled the fingers of my raised hand. "Or we can do it my way."

The man's fear was oddly replaced by sudden greed. His lips, which were once pulled back at the corners, lifted into a wicked grin. "You're a sorceress," he whispered, as though the realization was his best discovery ever. My hand glowed stronger, making his face waver, but his yellowing teeth still poked out underneath a twisted smile. "Careful, love. They're starting to disappear."

I exchanged glances with the other two, and the greasy man suddenly shoved me back into the opposite wall. I was so stunned by his sudden speed that I didn't make any moves to stop him. He darted away from us and quickly vanished in the maze of alleys. Brennon started to take off after him, but I called him back.

"Leave him. It's not worth it," I said, straightening myself.

"What was he talking about?" Brennon asked as he slid his sword back into its scabbard.

"I thought he knew something about Azlaya's plans." I shrugged to shake off my baseless suspicions and peered over at Aiden, who stared at something thoughtfully.

"It's true then," he said, lost in thought.

"What is?" Brennon pressed.

Aiden broke from his trance and looked, in turns, at our faces as he explained. "I've heard rumors that sorcerers were disappearing, but that's all I took them as—rumors."

"We can't just believe something a random guy says," I pointed out.

"He wasn't lying though," Aiden replied. My eyebrows pinched together as I looked at him. "I know how to detect lying, and he wasn't." I made an expression that probed him to go on, but he changed the subject. "What are you holding?"

I held out the man's dagger, forgetting that I had grabbed it off him. Aiden took it and inspected the hilt. "He was carrying this?" Aiden asked me. I nodded, wondering what he was thinking about. "He's a member of the Muskoxen. They're a mercenary group that operates in Eileen, like the Boas in Calem." The last part he directed at Brennon, who nodded in understanding.

Aiden showed Brennon the knife, and he confirmed that it indeed did belong to a Muskoxen member. They explained that large mercenary groups operated in each of the four kingdoms, and each had its own symbol distinguishing it from the others. I couldn't make the connections that Aiden was making, but his mind raced. He suddenly broke his focus and pocketed the dagger. I had wanted Aiden to share what he had been thinking, but I had learned that when Aiden was done talking about something, there was no way to get him to continue; his mind had gone elsewhere.

I followed the two of them back into the inn, and we were met with the same curious stares as before. We climbed the winding stairs to our room. It was a small, rectangular space with two beds pressed against one wall and a chest against the other. There was a small window above the chest with a view to the vacant street. Aiden offered to bring our things up from downstairs and slipped from the room.

I pulled my boots off and collapsed on the bed. Brennon sat next to me and started undoing his shoes, too. "I wish he would tell us what he was thinking. Then we could all be on the same page."

Our eyes met. His lips parted, but then he pushed them back together, as if his body was refusing to let him disclose some secret to me. He stood and started taking off his travel clothes.

"Brennon." I protested his silence.

"That's just how he is. He keeps things to himself," he said as he pulled his shirt over his head. Smooth ridges rose and fell across his abdomen. His chiseled chest bore the scars of past battles, as well as the effects of arduous training over the years. "There are some wash rooms down the hall. I'll be back soon." And with that, he left.

I huffed. It seemed like Brennon and Aiden knew every intricacy about each other, and I was still piecing together the parts of a puzzle. I closed the thin curtain over the window and untied my cloak. I faced away from the door and started to remove my socks and heavy coat. As I was unlacing my tunic, I heard a thump and whirled around.

"Don't smite me, please," Aiden said sarcastically, but his words had an undertone of seriousness. My eyes darted from him, to the door, to our saddlebags. I hadn't even heard him open the door, let alone enter the room and close it. I knew he probably made the unceremonious sound to alert me before I completely undressed in his presence.

"Thanks," I said, flicking my eyes to our saddlebags. Aiden and I passed each other as he went to the window, and I dug through my saddlebag.

I stole a glance at Aiden before changing, but realized he wasn't even paying attention. Instead, he was focused on something outside the window. I exchanged my travel clothes for a warm nightgown and gathered my clothes to start folding them. The silence, though it didn't seem to bother Aiden, was choking me.

"How can you tell if someone is lying?" I asked.

"The pitch of their voice changes, their eyes may rise to the left or right depending on their handedness, or their heart starts to race," he replied quickly. "Will you come here?"

I stopped folding my shirt and rounded the bed to stand next to him. "What is it?" I asked, as he lifted the window.

"Hold this up," he answered. I sighed, tired of having my questions brushed aside. I placed my hands under the window and held it open. Aiden bundled his cloak and tossed it out the window, and before I could stop him, he was out the window, too.

He clung to the sill and glanced at the ground below, judging its distance. "What the hell are you doing?" I whispered harshly. *My god, he's suicidal,* I thought frantically.

"I'm going to investigate these kidnapping rumors," he replied casually, as though he were telling me that he was going out for a cup of coffee. "Oh, here." He pulled a wine bottle from under his cloak and set it on the sill. "To prop it open," he explained. "I'll return later tonight." Then he released his grip and dropped to the ground.

I shot my head out the window, but I had already lost him in the darkness. "Aiden? Aiden—"

I called out to him softly, but I knew he was gone. I heard the door open and close behind me as I positioned the half full wine bottle under the window to keep it propped open for when Aiden returned.

"What are you doing?" Brennon asked slowly, staring at me quizzically. I must have had a wild expression on my face. My disbelief seemed to have no bounds when it came to the things that Aiden did. "Where's Aiden?"

"Playing Sherlock," I snapped.

Brennon made a confused sound, clearly not understanding the reference I'd made. I waved it aside and resumed folding my clothes. Brennon had returned with extra blankets that he placed on the bed. I thanked him and crawled into bed, pulling the covers over me. Brennon lay down on the other bed and pulled out what appeared to be a newspaper. The writing was incredibly small and spirally, wrapping around the page.

"Brennon?" He had an arm behind his head, and one leg crossed over the other as he lounged on the bed and read. He acknowledged that he heard me with a soft sound. "Should we be worried about Aiden?"

He smiled sideways at me. "He can take care of himself, Casey. I'd only be worried about the person that gets in his way."

I could see that sleep taunted Brennon, but he continued to read his paper. I rolled over and slid deeper under the blankets. My eyes stayed trained on the cracked window as I dozed off, wondering about the mysterious spy that ran about in the night.

Chapter 22: Aiden

"WELL, I'LL BE damned. I must be seeing a ghost. The notorious Silverslinger, returned from the dead," a voice in the darkness said.

The backside of the building was barren except for a small balcony that could hold four people at most. A door led from the balcony into the building, and I could see the pattern of lit candles flickering inside. A body perched on the railing, effortlessly balancing itself on the thin wooden beam. It took me a minute to recognize who had spoken, but I'd never forget that voice. James Shepherd.

"How've you been, Shep?" I asked casually, as though a simple hello could bridge the years in which we hadn't seen each other.

He leaned forward, as if to inspect me closer from his lookout. He swung his legs over the railing and dropped to ground. As expected, his landing was muffled, and he stayed balanced. I remembered that my first lesson when I'd joined the Night's Guild was leaping from various heights and landing silently, but firmly.

"It's been twenty years, man. Where've you been?" Shep asked as we grasped each other's outstretched forearms. He chuckled under his breath then pulled me close, and we clapped each other's backs.

We stepped back from each other, and I met his searching gaze. His blonde hair fell to his shoulders and was cut jaggedly. He had dark eyes and a smile that never truly disappeared, only wavered with his emotions. He wore a leather, quilted shirt, dark pants, riding boots, and a cape clasped with a pin that identified him as a member of the Night's Guild. I'd thrown mine into a river a long time ago. "Amelia keeps me busy," I replied.

I saw a look of suspicion flicker across Shep's face. "Then what brings you here?"

I knew better than to disclose too much information, especially to a fellow spy. I'd learned early on that the less people knew, the safer it kept you. "Another assignment." Shep accepted my curt answer and beckoned me to follow.

"I think the Commander's going to want to see you," Shep said over his shoulder. "Yes, he's still alive," he answered my unasked question. My chest tightened. I knew the chances of encountering my old employer were pretty high, but I still hoped it wouldn't happen. We hadn't parted on the best of terms.

Shep effortlessly climbed up to the balcony, placed his feet precisely, and swung himself back over the railing. I followed his lead and leapt onto the narrow balcony behind him. I heard a soft hum of whispers coming from the other side of the door. Shep stepped aside to allow me to enter the room where I had begun my training with the Guild years before.

To our right was a large desk, piled high with paper. Behind it, huge shelves loomed over it, filled with record-keeping books organized alphabetically. Two wooden chairs sat in front of the desk. On the other side of the room, the wall opened into a larger space. Stands holding different knives, swords, and other weapons surrounded the room. A red target was painted on one wall, and I could see the divots in the wall where thrown weapons had struck it.

My eyes finished scanning over the room, and I took notice of its other occupants. A beautiful girl sat in one of the wooden chairs facing the desk, quietly conversing with the Commander. She wore multiple gold necklaces and bangles on her ankles and wrists. Her eyelids were dark with makeup and her lips were seductively red. She turned to look at me, and, as if I was her cue to exit, she got up to leave. The girl wore a tight top emphasizing her chest and leaving her torso bare. Her skirt reached the ground, but there were two long slits, so that her thighs showed as she sauntered. She was one of the Commander's girls who lived below.

"Good work. Have a drink on me tonight." The Commander stood and gestured to the door.

In addition to running the Night's Guild, the Commander operated a brothel. While his trained spies prowled the streets and collected secrets from the townspeople and families of the royal court, his girls gathered information from the men, and sometimes women, that visited them at night. The Commander's girl had always impressed me, and they were often able to extract the most compromising secrets, even faster than I could sometimes. I remembered writing to Kyraine that I had left the

Huntsmen to join a brothel and imagining the horror on her face when she read it.

The girl batted her eyes at me as she passed. I smiled; friendly enough to be a greeting, but guarded enough so as not to imply anything further. She winked and left the study. The Commander finally directed all his attention towards me, and a look of amused disdain crossed his face.

"I never thought I'd see you here again. The door *was* open," he said, flashing his eyes at the door through which the girl had exited.

"I always preferred the balcony."

I took him in. I could see the years that had passed etched into his face. His once-black hair and beard were streaked with gray, and his movements seemed labored. I thought about what it would have been like if I still worked for the Night's Guild under the Commander and had watched as he aged, while I remained virtually unchanged.

"I shouldn't even let you in here. Twenty years and not a single word," he chided me, with the same tone he'd always used with me.

"I work for Queen Amelia. She paid her dues, so I don't belong to you anymore."

We held each other's gaze for what may have seemed like an uncomfortable amount of time, for anyone that didn't understand our history. After Shep and I deserted the Huntsmen, we fled to Eileen. We decided to seek employment that utilized the skillset acquired from our Huntsmen training. The Night's Guild found us first. We were dragged before the Commander after successfully ambushing a group of his assassins. He was so impressed with us that he offered to train us on the spot. But once again, I was chained to an organization that commanded my body and blade. Except this time, I couldn't run. My mother had recently passed away, and I needed the money to care for Greyson, who was only five at the time. Also, I had no doubt that if I did try to run, the Guild would kill me long before I got away.

In my years under the Commander, I was sent after people, like a bloodhound. I was forced to butcher entire families that angered the Commander. I was an extension of the Commander's own blade: his reaper. He prized me as his best investment, and when he felt me slipping away, he reigned me in by appointing me his second-in-command. I presided over his operations as an overseer does slaves, though I had shackles on my ankles, too. When Amelia permanently hired me, stealing me away from the Commander, I felt those shackles finally fall away. I decided then that I would only accept missions that had a justified cause. No longer would I be someone's executioner, against my own will. The Commander hadn't been happy to lose me then, and he wasn't any happier to see me now.

"Why are you here?" The bitterness dripped from his voice like venom.

"I wouldn't have come if I knew a better place to get information."

"Information about what?"

"The kidnappings throughout the kingdom. I've heard the rumors for weeks, and now I have reason to believe they aren't rumors. Who's responsible and why is it happening?"

Shep silently observed as his oldest friend and current employer conversed, tensions running high. The Commander regarded me in silence. I imagined the hard look in his eyes was mirrored in my own.

"Surely I've earned more than your silence."

Another minute lapsed before he submitted to my request, though unhappily. "It appears that the Sagen are responsible. My sources tell me that sorcerers of any age, class, or gender are their targets."

"Where are they taking them?"

Shep looked to the Commander to ask permission to answer. "I've asked around, but they just disappear without a trace. I've talked to members of the Guild doing operations in other kingdoms, and they say it's been happening everywhere else for months. It's only just begun in Eileen."

"That's all the information we know," the Commander finished curtly.

I nodded and stood to leave.

"Aiden." I turned back to the Commander. "I'm sure I don't have to say this, but you know that when it comes to conflicts such as these, we don't choose sides. Profit chooses our side. It's how we survive. Right, Shep?"

"Yes, Sir," he answered quickly, standing at attention.

I stole a glance at Shep's unmoving face. He had always been tense around the Commander. "All due respect, Sir, but I don't let money command my hand anymore," I said firmly, "and I don't work for you."

"I would still like to know what you'll be doing during your time here in my city," the Commander added.

The tone of his voice was unwavering and unyielding. During the years I had worked under him, I came to welcome it, because it presented a challenge that my insurgent personality craved.

I smiled wryly. "Commander, I'm trying to save the world," I said whimsically.

I shot him a mischievous grin and then stepped back onto the balcony. I elegantly swung my body over the side and dropped to the ground. I heard a muffled thud next to me and saw that Shep, naturally, was at my side.

"Didn't think he'd be so tense," he confessed apologetically. "You can share my quarters for the night, like old times," Shep offered.

"No," I said softly. "I should get back." I started walking down the back alley I had come through. Faithfully, Shep followed. "Shep, I think I'm going to need your help with something," I began. Shep quickened his pace so that we walked in step. "But the Commander can't know about it, or that you're helping me."

"He won't." I could tell he yearned for me to share what I knew with him. "What are you *really* doing here?" he asked under his breath.

"Do you remember what you told me about Gisele the last time we saw each other?" Shep matched my gaze and nodded.

"Yeah, that she had signed an agreement with Azlaya, sealing their alliance. You're trying to find it?"

"I need to destroy it. I'm not sure how or where to start, but—"

"I'm in," Shep cut me off. "Count me in. The Commander will never know." We walked a few more blocks. "The Hunters and Huntsmen want to bring Eileen into the war?"

I always underestimated his intuition. I nodded.

"Hell, if Kyraine is desperate enough to ask you for help, this war *must* be real."

We exchanged glances and then we were both smiling. Shep was one of the few people that knew of the complicated relationship my sister and I shared. We roomed together, completed our first missions for the Commander together, and helped each other when the weight of our work became too much for one person to bear. The biggest difference between Shep and me was that I could discern between killing for the right and wrong reasons. To Shep, it was all just following orders.

Still, he stood by my side, and I knew I could trust him with my life. He had, after all, helped me cover up all the horrible mistakes that had led to my friends' and brother's deaths during my last time in Eileen. I would never forget that night.

I had asked Shep to do the unthinkable, but loyal as ever, he complied. I had asked him to retrieve a boy's body that had been sent to the mortuary from the castle. He had carried it for miles before meeting me on the outskirts of Eileen. He didn't know it was Greyson, or why I was consumed with grief when I finally cradled my brother's cold body in my arms to take him away and give him a proper burial. That was the last night I saw Shep before fleeing Eileen.

"You know things changed when you left. Bron became second-in-command—until he caught a mace to the throat on a mission." We turned a few corners, always keeping to the back alleyways. "You never told me why you left." I heard the disappointment in his voice. Images of dungeons, daggers, bloodied hands, and piercing screams cut across my memory.

I kept my eyes forward but positioned by face so that it didn't look like I was trying to hide something from him. We were both experts at detecting lies, but he had the unfair advantage of being one of my oldest friends. Twenty years apart hadn't changed that. We passed a group of what looked like the Commander's girls. They were cooing to someone across the street as we passed.

"I needed a change of scenery from Eileen."

We walked a few more paces in silence. He knew better than to keep fishing for an answer he wouldn't catch. "Well, man, I'm glad you're back. These streets haven't been the same without the Silverslinger walking them. The vermin may finally get back in line," he said through a large smile.

We were at the intersection, one path leading deeper into the maze, and the other spilling onto the main street. Shep glanced at the main street, his attention caught by a pretty girl. "Send a hawk when you need me."

We grasped each other's right arms as a customary way to greet and say goodbye—and to make sure a dagger wasn't concealed in the sleeve. We split from each other.

I retraced my steps and wound my way back to the inn. I saw the window to our room. Casey had left the wine bottle propped underneath it. I got my footing and starting scaling the side of the building. Years of climbing all kinds of structures had made my fingers strong and my feet confident. I quickly reached the windowsill, slid inside, and dislodged the wine bottle.

Casey slept soundly on the bed and Brennon had fallen asleep with his paper lying across his chest. One arm was propped behind his head while the other was draped across his stomach. I took a thick blanket from the foot of Casey's bed and sat on the chest below the window.

The street lamps provided little light on what lay below. In the distance, I could see Gisele's castle nestled into the mountains. It loomed ominously, like the woman inside who continued to haunt my dreams.

I wrapped the blanket around my shoulders and rested my head against the window frame. I forced my eyes closed and stayed that way for what felt like years. At some point, I finally nodded off.

Rough hands dragged me from my bed and hauled me into a dungeon that smelled like mildew, excretion, and death. I could never remember if I was chained first, or if the screams started assaulting my ears first.

"Aiden, help us! Help us!" The familiar voices of my friends, my comrades, burned in my ears. Every second, another one's voice fell from the chorus of pleas.

"Can you feel their pain? Does it hurt? Does this?"

I heard a crack as a whip bit into my skin. More blood poured into my mouth from where my teeth dug into my lip.

"Ask for it to stop. Beg for it to end. It can all be over if you confess your secrets."

She took a serrated knife, the length of her arm, and slid it across my back, slowly, as if slicing butter. My strangled cry made a smile crack on her lips. She carved into my back again.

"Ask me for mercy."

My head was jerked back so that I looked into her eyes as they burned brightly at the sight of my pain. I met her gaze with a cold glare, a habitual expression. The whip licked my back, cutting deeper into an already open wound. I smelled vinegar. Then, it was being poured over my back. I screamed, trying desperately to escape my chains, but it was futile. Heavy breathing, sour smells, and disorientation overwhelmed my senses. She let my head drop limply.

"We'll try again tomorrow."

My eyes flashed open, and I felt like my airway was being obstructed by something. I had to think about taking deep breaths until my respiratory cycle steadied itself. Beads of sweat formed on my forehead. I pulled the curtains closed, but I knew that not being able to see my nightmare didn't make it any less real.

Casey rolled over and sat up. She yawned and rubbed her eyes. "Are you all right? It felt like you were in trouble—"

"I'm fine. Go back to sleep," I ordered her softly. Her reluctance was visible, but her body won out over her stubbornness, and she burrowed back under the blankets.

I groped for the wine bottle I had set near the chest, pulled the cork out with my teeth, and took a long swig. I drained it much too fast. Once I'd emptied that, I withdrew another flask from my pocket. My throat no longer burned, because it had fallen numb. The only thing that seemed able to dull the nightmares was drinking—and lots of it. I pulled a dagger into my lap and covered it with the blanket. This time, I refused to surrender to sleep.

Chapter 23: Casey

I WOKE BEFORE the sunrise to practice sorcery, but then I remembered what the man had said the night before. *They're starting to disappear.* I immediately thought better of exposing myself to Eileen as a sorceress, and instead studied the spells by reading about them. Soon, Brennon roused and we dressed for our daily exercises. We found a deserted alleyway behind the inn that was large enough for a sparring match. Every morning he had me do the training routine he did with the Huntsmen. We jogged, did pushups, self-defense sequences, and finally, we sparred. By the end of our match, my back was coated in a layer of cold sweat, and we were both breathing hard.

"Too slow—you're not balanced—watch my core—faster—faster!"

Brennon's impatience grew as he delivered heavy blows simultaneously. We twisted, turned, lunged, jumped back, and parried. Locked in the repetitious dance, we didn't realize how much time had passed. Finally, Brennon swung his sword up, deflecting my attack with a graceful sweep, and stepped back.

"That's good for today. I want you prepared for the entrance round, not sore." He sheathed his sword and I did the same. "Didn't sleep well last night?" He observed me.

"I'm fine." I brushed his concern aside.

I joined him where he leaned against the wall. He dug around in his small pouch and handed me an apple. "Why didn't you sleep well?"

I knew why, but I was hesitant to tell Brennon. Rather than lying, I told him part of the truth. "Bad dreams." He nodded, accepting my answer.

In truth, I was exhausted. It wasn't my dreams that had left my last few nights sleepless. I felt someone's nightmares spilling over into my own head. It was impossible to sleep soundly when the sensation of being tortured every night consumed me. I soon came to realize that the nightmares belonged to Aiden, but I still didn't understand the reason, or the source of such awful imaginings. I hadn't been able to confront him about it, nor did I really want to. Besides, Brennon was usually present, and I didn't want to expose such personal details in front of him.

As if on cue, Aiden entered the alleyway. He held two steaming bread pockets and handed one to Brennon and one to me. "Done for the day?" Brennon nodded as he eagerly bit into the bread. We ate in silence for several minutes.

"I'm going to take a walk around the block to stretch out my legs," I told them before leaving.

The alley became narrower as I approached the main street. The road was grey cobblestone, but it was easy to see the worn trails of carriages and hoof prints. I glanced down the street and saw a crowd gathering. Instinctively, my feet tugged me to follow the crowd. A semicircle of whispering spectators had formed around a building with a sign designating it as a bakery. I tried to see what had drawn everyone's attention.

A bearded, bald man spoke frantically to someone in a black robe. In the doorway of the bakery, a woman with wild eyes stood protectively in front of a young girl with fiery hair. I assumed it was the older woman's daughter. The mother and daughter cried silently. I looked closer, and my breath caught in my throat when I realized that that father wasn't speaking to a man at all. It was a Sagen warrior.

"She means no harm. She can control her powers," the father pleaded. He received cold silence. The father glanced at the crowd in sheer desperation, as if looking for someone to come to his aid. "She won't use them anymore."

"Step aside."

The father held his ground, and the mother's weeping became more audible. The Sagen swung a long scepter at the man. It made a deafening crack when it made contact with his head. I had stayed frozen long enough. The bread pocket fell from my grasp, and as I was about to start pushing my way through the crowd, a hand jerked me backwards. Thinking it was another Sagen, my hand started to glow. It was gripped tightly and forced behind my back and out of sight.

"Don't," Aiden warned. My muscles relaxed, but only slightly. Aiden had pinned me against a wall, and I saw that Brennon stood close by, trying to shield us from inquisitive eyes. The mother's sobs filled the air as her daughter was ripped away from her.

"Aiden, let go of me!" I tried to shove him away, but he twisted my arm painfully. He was a head taller than me and much stronger than he appeared.

"*Stop*," he hissed. "You can't save her. They'll take you away, too."

"I won't stand here and do nothing. Now move!" I growled angrily. My voice was drowned out by the cries of the mother and the screams of the daughter. They made my gut wrench.

"Casey, we can't jeopardize your safety, or the mission," Brennon added softly, though it visibly pained him to do nothing, too. I still struggled against Aiden. "They'll bring you straight to your sister."

I still fought against Aiden's iron grip, though Brennon had a point. I'd be served to Kate on a silver platter if I interfered and exposed myself now. I started seeing spots in my vision and blinked rapidly to clear them.

"Casey, are you okay?" Brennon asked uneasily. "What's wrong with her?"

I hadn't noticed until Aiden removed his hand from my shoulder that he had been digging his thumb into a pressure point on my neck. My ears began ringing, and my head spun. I felt my knees buckle. The last thing I remembered was gripping Aiden's shirt, wanting to cast a spell in retaliation, but in my weakened state, dragging him to the ground with me was good enough. As he caught me, he was intensely watching something in the distance. I wouldn't know whom he recognized until later. My vision went black to the sounds of strangled cries from a heartbroken family.

I regained consciousness that evening. Either Aiden's ability to make someone pass out was that effective, or I was regaining hours of lost sleep. I had been placed on the bed and gently tucked in. Brennon's work, I assumed. The idea of Aiden having a tender bone in his body seemed impossible. I shot upright and immediately regretted it, as pounding exploded in my head.

"Take it easy."

I recognized the voice, and my anger got the better of me. I felt my powers wrap around Aiden's neck menacingly. He looked shocked, but not afraid. "I should kill you," I fumed, my jaw locked.

"At least make it a fair fight," he gasped, glancing at a sword in the corner.

While the idea enticed me, I realized that I had killed Sagen and small game with the Hunters, but I'd never killed a person. My powers released their grip on his neck and retreated back to me. He sucked in a huge breath and coughed.

I scowled as he recovered. "I could have saved her."

"I don't doubt it." He took a sip of something from his flask. "But weren't you listening? They're collecting sorcerers. You'd be dragged away, our plan would be ruined, and you would have failed all the people counting on you to protect them." He threw my words back at me, mercilessly.

"You and Brennon could have done something," I snapped.

"I choose my fights wisely. You can't save everyone. The sooner you learn that, the better."

I lay back down and turned from him so that he spoke to my back. My head still felt lightheaded from Aiden's stunt. I placed two fingers over the spot where he had dug his thumb into my neck, feeling for bruises.

His voice had lost its sharp edge. "I didn't mean for you to pass out. It takes most people a longer period of application before that happens."

I shook off his paltry apology. "Where does the queen's *thief* learn that anyway? I didn't realize making someone black out was a skill in your repertoire," I replied venomously.

"Is that what you think I am?" He chuckled, as if he was humored. I turned to see his face.

"A glorified one, at least."

"I suppose, under certain circumstances, that's pretty accurate."

He flashed his sideways grin at me. Getting a straight answer out of him was like pulling teeth. So instead of interrogating him all night and being left with an even worse headache, I closed my eyes.

That night I felt them again. The remnants of a horrifying nightmare tugged at the edges of my sleep, but they weren't mine. Just as quickly as they descended on me, they vanished. My eyes flashed open, but my body remained still. I looked over and saw that Brennon snored softly next to me. Aiden was where I left him, sitting on the chest under the window. I was about to close my eyes again, when he suddenly moved.

He rested his head in his hands. From where I lay across the room, it was plain to see that he trembled. I watched as he tipped his head back to whatever drink he fancied that night. His breathing was ragged, and I guiltily thought it was from my trying to strangle him earlier, but the thought quickly passed when his attention was captured by something outside the window.

He jumped to his feet, went to Brennon's bed and returned to his perch with the previous day's newspaper. I watched as he read the paper, wondering how he could read in the dark room. Concern grew in my gut with each passing second. As I was about to lean over to shake Brennon awake, he rolled over and sat up.

"Aiden?" He called sleepily into the night. Aiden hushed him softly. He was gazing out the window again. "What is it?"

"We're being watched," he whispered. Though he said it more with excitement than apprehension.

I realized that he had not been reading the paper, but was using it to shield his face while studying the street below. He slowly folded it up and pulled the curtains closed. Then, he unexpectedly shot up and started wildly pulling things from the chest.

"Wake Casey," he told Brennon.

"I'm awake," I replied.

"Good. Start packing. We need to leave."

"Who's watching us?" Brennon asked through a yawn.

"I didn't get a good look at his face, but I'm almost positive it's that guy Casey cornered in the ally the other night."

I thought back to that night when I confronted the weasel man. "What would he want with us?" I asked. It amazed me how quickly Aiden had recovered from whatever had gripped his thoughts moments before.

Brennon and I joined Aiden in packing our things. We pulled on our travel clothes, laced our boots, fastened our cloaks, and were off. After I paid the innkeeper for our stay, I could see the beginnings of a sunrise unfolding. I followed Brennon and Aiden out a back entrance that dumped us far from the main street. Neither Brennon nor I questioned Aiden as he confidently led the way to wherever we were going.

About an hour later, we arrived at our destination. It was another inn, but larger and cleaner than the last one. Aiden led us inside, and immediately I was overwhelmed with propaganda advertising the tournament. Flyers, posters, banners, and flags were strewn about the main room. A group of travelers hovered around some of the displays and buzzed excitedly about the tournament, which was set to start with the entrance round the following day. I was studying one of the posters that had a building the shape of a football stadium on it when Brennon called for me to follow.

Our room was on the top floor of the five-story inn. It had more space and was definitely better kept than the last one. The bed looked to be queen-sized, with deep green blankets. The pillows matched the blankets and had golden threading around the edges. A large rug lay at the foot of the bed, and a fireplace sat opposite it. I looked forward to sitting in front of that fire on chilly nights. Over the bed hung an animal pelt that looked like a cougar. Beside the fireplace stood another door that led to a second room. While not as large as the main room, the second was just as nice, only lacking the fireplace.

Aiden was at the window studying everything below. "This is an information hub for the tournament. People come here to talk about the details of the games, place bets, spread rumors—the usual. We'll stay well informed while you're in the games," Aiden said to me.

He messed with a lock on the window, and after a few seconds, pushed it open. He stuck his head outside, noted something above him, and then leaned back in. "Roof access," he replied to our silent question.

I went over to see what he meant and looked up. "So what?"

"It's an escape route. Running across rooftops is much easier than shoving your way through a crowded street," he explained. I commended him with my expression. It seemed that whatever he battled with in his head, they didn't dull his skilled instincts, as he always kept one step ahead of a potential attacker.

"Do you think we lost that guy on the way over here?" I asked Aiden. Brennon had started to fill the dresser in the corner with his clothes.

"No, he'll be back. I told the innkeeper to tell him where we went."

"You did what?"

"Why?" Brennon asked.

"We didn't come here to get away from him. We came here to wait for him. I have a few questions I'd like him to answer."

Chapter 24: Aiden

LATER THAT AFTERNOON, Brennon went into town to send a letter to the Hunters and buy Casey more northern-looking clothes. On his way out, he asked me to work with Casey on her one-on-one combat skills. He knew as well as I that combat was one of the most common events in the tournament, and Casey would need to battle competitors twice her size—without sorcery to aid her.

I relayed Brennon's request; I could tell by the face she made that she was annoyed Brennon had left her with me. I still wasn't sure if she was going to be bitter about being stopped from rescuing the young sorceress the day before. Casey slipped into thick pants with leather padding on the thighs and a dark blue shirt with similar pads on the forearms and chest. While she dressed, I gathered my own things. I strapped hidden daggers to both forearms, another to my right thigh, and tucked one more in my belt. Casey had just finished tying her boots when I returned.

"All right, let's go."

I led Casey away from the inn and towards the edge of town. We were closer to the mountains now, so the mining community was much more prevalent. People walked around in their gear, and the roads were darker from minerals being trekked down the mountain on people's shoes. This part of town had the best weapons vendors. I had a few personal favorites I had used when I lived in Eileen, but most of the smithies seemed quiet, which I guessed was what happened when the queen imposed a trade embargo on weaponry.

As we walked down the street, I could tell that Casey was doing her best to figure out where we were going. She wasn't just uncomfortable with me leading her to some unknown destination. She was uncomfortable with me leading, period.

Village kids dove in and out between us, chasing a dog. A group of schoolgirls huddled outside a bookstore discussing the latest lesson from class, and a young man cast a greedy look in their direction. I managed to deter him with one, swift expression.

"Where do you think the queen hid her agreement with Azlaya?" Casey asked, breaking the silence that had spread between us.

"It could be in the Royal Hall of Records; or there's her family's vault; or there's her summer castle down south. Wherever it is though, its hiding spot is as hidden and as seamless as this one."

I pushed a stone in a wall we had approached, making it sink deeper into its crevice. I hooked my fingers inside the wall and pulled it open. Casey was doing her best not to seem curious or impressed, so instead she tossed me a snide comment.

"Do you always time your monologues like this? How did you know this was here?"

"Well, you didn't hire me because I'm *unfamiliar* with this city."

I gestured for her to enter. She brushed past, into the opening. I followed and pulled the heavy stone door shut behind me. The room we stepped into was dome-shaped and lit well from the row of windows circling it, though, in my opinion, darkness was the best light to work in. My brother would have disagreed with me politely, while Kyraine would have launched into a heated counterargument. Casey strode across the room and gently ran her fingers over the weapons that lay on a table. Her hand stopped on a golden knife, its hilt icy silver.

"What is this place?"

"It's one of the Night's Guild shelters. They are scattered throughout the city so that its members can stock up on weapons wherever they are."

"What's the Night's Guild?"

"Just another mercenary group," I said with an unintentional sharpness. Casey decided to let the subject drop.

I removed a thick sword from the wall and handed it to her. She grasped it, testing it for balance, and made an unsatisfied face. I grabbed my own sword, identical to Casey's, and stepped into the center ring of the room, signaling that it was time for practice to start.

"This is heavier than I'm used to," she noted as she firmly grasped it with two hands rather than one.

"Eileenian swords usually are. These are the kinds of swords that will be available to you in the tournament. Swing with your shoulders and your torso, not your arms," I explained.

Suddenly, an old memory flashed through my head. Greyson stood in front of me, small and frameless. The sword he held weighed his stance, and his swings were slow and cumbersome.

"I can't do it, Aiden. I'm not good like you or Kyraine," he had told me. His eyes were downcast and swam in tears of frustration. He had been so ashamed of his performance. I knelt in front of him and took the sword from his hand.

"Greyson, I'm glad that you aren't." He'd lifted his blue eyes to look at me. His curly hair hung around his shoulders, the sun glinting off the blonde strands. "I'm glad that someone in this family will finally be able to solve their problems without using a weapon. You can fight all your battles with everything in here." I touched his forehead lightly, and his lips turned upward.

"Did you know Hugo Blakemore was declared the most distinguished scholar of our time last week by all the universities in the kingdoms? Could I buy a copy of his book on the way home?" he had asked me excitedly.

That night we lay under a canopy of stars while he read to me about things that should never be of interest to a nine year old. He was so intelligent; almost too much for his own good. I had been truly grateful that at least one of the Redding children would be spared from the hardships and violence that supplanted the lives of Kyraine and me. If only I had known then what would happen three years later, I would have tossed the book aside and kept training him until he was better than me. Then, he might still be alive.

I blinked the memories away as I sprung forward. Casey lifted her sword to deflect my own. Though she complained about its weight, she handled it well. Her movements were slightly slower, but she was stronger than she gave herself credit for. We sparred for an hour, before I signaled that we could stop. I waved her over to the weapons table. I picked up the gold-silver knife she had admired earlier and held it out to her.

"This is where you'd want to strike to disable an attacker," I instructed, pointing at the various areas on my body, "and this is where you'd strike to kill an attacker."

"Kill?" She sounded alarmed.

"A popular event is combat, and usually the people you are fighting are criminals. If you win, you move ahead in the games, but if they win, they win their freedom." Casey looked appalled. "It makes no sense to me either, but it's a battle to the death."

At first she seemed hesitant, but with each weapon, she got more comfortable with identifying the various ways to disable and then kill an attacker. A part of me wondered if I should be concerned about showing her how best to murder me. Another part laughed at being ambushed by her attack. I walked her through daggers, swords, sickles, axes, hammers, maces, and javelins. The tournament could be unpredictable when it came to the available weapons, so it was better to know the main ones than to only be comfortable with one. When I felt that she had learned the moves and attacks, we decided to head back to the inn.

Casey followed me back in silence. Something seemed to be on her mind. Unasked questions clung to her lips, and when she finally decided to say something, we had made it back to our door. She opened her mouth, but I held up my hand sharply. Something was wrong. I pressed a finger to my lips and examined the door. I'd picked enough locks to recognize a picked one when I saw it.

I grabbed a dagger from my belt, whispered for Casey to stay behind me, and then pushed the door open. Brennon was crumpled in a heap on the rug. I sensed the intruder, pushed Casey out of his range, and spun around the door. I knocked the attacker's hand away and slammed him into the wall. I held my dagger to his throat, pressing hard enough so that a thin line of blood trickled down onto his shirt collar.

"Casey," I called to her, but she had already dropped next to Brennon. After a few tense seconds, she confirmed that he was alive.

"What did you do to him?" I asked the man Casey had cornered in the alley a few nights before. I pressed the dagger a little harder.

"It was just a sedative dart. He'll wake up in a few hours," he confessed hurriedly.

"What was her name?" I shoved him against the wall again. "What was her name?"

"Aiden, what're you talking about?" Casey asked, startled.

I kept my attention on the man. "The baker's daughter. The girl you turned in to the Sagen?" I watched as his face contorted with apprehension. "That's right, I saw you yesterday in the crowd. What was her name?"

"I don't know," he choked out. Casey finally understood. "It was just a job. I was just doing it for the money, that's all." His eyes pleaded with Casey.

I retrieved the dagger Casey had taken from him and held it up to his face. It had the insignia of the Muskoxen carved into the hilt. "This is yours, isn't it?" His expression was answer enough.

"Why are you turning sorcerers over to the Sagen?" Casey asked, joining me at my side.

He glanced between us nervously. "We were hired. Please, I'll tell you anything, just let me go!" My eyes flashed, quieting his pleas instantly.

"By who?" I urged. I half expected him to say the Commander of the Night's Guild.

"A young woman. I never saw her; she only spoke directly with my superiors. Her name was Kaitlin," the man admitted quickly. I exchanged glances with Casey.

"My sister," she filled in. She turned away to think. After several tense seconds, her face collapsed. "The Sagen. She's gathering sorcerers for the Sagen, for their Dark Magic. She's building an arm of dark sorcerers."

"I don't know about any of that, but we were promised safety after the war. That's the only reason I'm doing this, I swear," the man implored urgently.

I was familiar with this type of vermin. Just like Thatch and his band of Boa thugs, they got caught doing crooked jobs, begged for mercy, then woke up the next morning and repeated the cycle.

"Well, if she's your sister, then maybe you could help her out. We could all work together, and then we'd all be safe when the Sagen take over again. I'll go back to my superiors and tell them—"

Casey had somehow acted before me. Her hand wrapped around my wrist, withholding me from slitting his throat.

"You'll be safer if he's dead. He knows about your powers and now he knows your face," I told her firmly. She held her ground. "He's responsible for that girl getting taken. She's probably dead, and it's because of him."

The merciful expression melted away. The look underneath was foreign to me, but one that I had been trying to goad from her since our meeting. I needed to know that she was as dangerous and lethal as her destiny required. More importantly, I needed to know that she could endure the tournament without getting killed; that she was able to end someone's life. I didn't need another death on my conscience.

She dropped her hand. "Don't do it in here."

In the end, I walked the man to a deserted alley and forced him to drink the entire bottle of the sedative fluid. I didn't need the royal guards questioning a midnight murder, so making it seem like the man had drunk himself to death was the most logical solution. After he had fallen into a comatose state, I tossed his dagger into the river that cut through the city and returned to the inn.

I helped Casey lift Brennon onto the bed. Part of the Night's Guild training was being able to identify poisons, so I was familiar with the concoction the man had used on Brennon and assured Casey that he would wake soon. Despite my comfort, something still seemed to disturb her.

"What is it?" I asked, tired of feeling her unasked questions playing on her lips.

Casey hesitated. "Why can't you sleep at night?"

"Not this again."

"Aiden, I know about the nightmares." When she saw my expression, she backpedaled. "I—I can feel them at night."

I dismissed her concern and added coolly, "Everyone has bad dreams."

"Not like these. I just—I want to help, if I can."

I was taken by surprise at her insistence. It was as though all the tension over the last couple weeks hadn't occurred. She didn't look at me in anticipation of our next fight. She didn't have a bitter retort stored on the tip of her tongue. She only looked at me. I drew away from her sudden warmth as though it was the plague.

"I'm fine."

"You are *not* fine!" she roared as she rounded the bed. "You say you have demons, fine. Let me help you fight them."

"You can't save everyone!"

"I could try to save you, if you would just—"

I huffed in irritation and tore from the room, ignoring Casey as she called after me. I walked blindly through the streets, letting my feet guide me wherever they pleased. My hand clenched and unclenched a dagger on my belt.

In truth, her words struck me like a blow to the gut. She had articulated the question I'd wrestled with for years as I planned my scheme to turn the Eileenian throne over to Lysander. I could save myself. I could make a thousand different choices in the days to come that would save me. But that was just it. I didn't want to. I didn't want to be yanked back from the edge of the abyss anymore. Death had tempted me for so long that it no longer beckoned—it only waited.

How much did she know about my dreams? How much did they reveal? I scolded myself for letting the nightmares get so out of control. They hadn't been this bad since the weeks following my last assignment in Eileen.

Nothing could compare to those days when a knife through the heart seemed more inviting each day. I'd run from death for so long that it was only poetic justice that I suddenly needed it to end my suffering. I was close to doing it, too, but the memories of Greyson and my fallen comrades deterred me. I decided long ago that their deaths would not have been in vain. They enabled me to keep fighting. They enabled me to delay death a little while longer, in pursuit of what I knew would be a better world.

Chapter 25: Kate

ZAYNE AND I had returned to Eileen, and together, we quickly made up for lost time. In the city, we targeted some of the sorcery academies Azlaya had told me about. Rounding up the young and fairly untrained students was easy. Their teachers were a little more challenging, but Zayne and I found that we enjoyed such things. We scoured the outskirts of the kingdom, pillaging for sorcerers in distant villages. We hiked into the mountains to uncover sorcerers. We even happened upon a couple lone Hunters and Huntsmen—those were particularly enjoyable catches.

I had to admit that rounding up sorcerers was much easier with an extra set of hands. Zayne was gifted, and he had finesse unlike anything I'd seen before. His powers had a certain precision to them that made him dangerous beyond even my imaginings. Where I excelled in power, he excelled in accuracy. When we cornered people, we fought as two halves of a larger whole, and learned quickly that we worked well together. Azlaya and I were like water and oil. We could mix and blend together, but our individualities were evident when we fought. But Zayne and

I were like fire and gasoline. We were volatile, powerful, and rightfully feared.

The more I admired his skills, the less I thought about my emotional defenses. I let myself smile when his eyes fell on me after a battle. I followed his movements, even when he knew I watched him. My tingling skin, pounding heart, or warm cheeks all screamed warnings at me, but I ignored them. And I received the same looks from him. It was as if we were constantly studying one another, wondering if someone so bold and intriguing really could exist. I'd fought the urges for days, and my discipline was wearing thin.

I was pulled back from these thoughts when Zayne's foot brushed against my own. We were on horseback, staring at an incline that led to an expansive villa in the rural outskirts of Eileen. I pushed my fur hood down so I could see more clearly.

"Nice place," I thought out loud.

We nudged our horses forward into a canter up the hill. The sun had set a few hours before, and stars speckled the sky. It was the first time since I'd arrived in Eileen that the sky was not overcast with grey clouds.

The horses were breathing hard by the time we made it to the top of the hill. The villa had an open courtyard occupied by carts and livestock. The building was made of dark stones that sat roughly against one another. The villa was shaped like a horseshoe surrounding the courtyard, and at its center stood a towering door.

We slowed to a stop. Zayne jumped from his horse and walked over to mine. He held out a hand in a very gentlemanly fashion. I gave him a wry smile and took his hand to humor his good manners. His hand lingered on mine for half a second too long before he turned away. I followed him up to the door and waited for him to utter a simple Unlocking spell. Instead, he placed both hands on the door. I waited a few more seconds before asking what he was doing.

"There's a powerful Warding spell on the entire villa. If we can penetrate the barrier, we'll be able to enter without any issues." He turned back to the door and stared at it intently, as though he studied the door and not the contained spell within. "Here, come help me."

I joined Zayne at the door and placed my hands as he had. Immediately, I felt a repellant force surge through me. It took all my concentration not to rip my hands away.

"It's strong," I observed. As much as the spell made me want to pull away, my will to break through it motivated me even more. I looked to Zayne, and he saw the flicker of an accepted challenge in my eyes and smiled crookedly. "On my count."

I counted off and then simultaneously we starting infusing our own energy into the door to break the spell. My hands were tense as my powers tried to chip away at the fortified defenses. I bit my lip, forcing all my energy to merge with Zayne's, creating a laser effect to pierce the magical barrier. We stayed that way for at least ten minutes, careful to keep an eye out for servants and stable hands as we worked. We were sweating and our breaths were coming out in ragged puffs, as though we were running. When the half-hour mark approached, I finally heard the beautiful sound of the door making the smallest clicking sound. We drew our hands back and exchanged glances. We were both impressed and pleased with ourselves. My chest was heaving. Zayne pulled the door open without any trouble.

"After you," he said through choppy breaths.

We slipped inside and immediately felt the spell around the door begin to pulsate with energy again. I gazed around the dark hall and saw a balcony above me, a wide staircase leading to the second story, and other arched doorways. Zayne directed the way through an archway under the staircase. We found ourselves in a study that had a desk, a chair, and a map of Eileen on the wall. There were bookshelves to one side, and to other there was a case holding several bottles of various libations. We stepped farther into the room, our senses on keen alert for any sounds or movement.

I heard him, and Zayne saw him. An old man sat in the corner in a wooden chair. His hands were clasped across his full stomach, and he had a thick mustache that commanded the most attention on his face. He wore red robes, and his skin was wrinkled and hung loosely. Given the powerful spell that protected his house, I was a little a disappointed with his reveal.

"Zayne Ryder. I always knew you would return to me," the man said. He spoke slowly. His voice was frail and rough at the same time. The expanse of his years was reflected in his voice. "Ten years is a long time to be away. You never completed your training."

I shot a curious look at Zayne, but he maintained his composure. "I think that's irrelevant at this point. Don't you, Leonantus?"

"Who are you?" I interjected, cutting their reunion short.

"He's not told you?" the man said. "I am Cadmus Leonantus. Zayne's old mentor. That is, until he ended his training and abandoned me."

I folded my arms over my chest and angled my body towards Zayne as though to prod him into an explanation. "You brought me to your old mentor's house?"

"He was one of the most powerful sorcerers in Eileen for a time. And clearly you still have some strength left in you." Zayne flicked his eyes back towards the door through which we had entered.

"Well, don't expect me to be merciful," I told Zayne sharply. He made a face as if to say, *never.*

"You're here to drag me to the Shadowlands, to use my powers for Azlaya's Sagen army. That's right; word about your endeavors has travelled far." Leonantus paused for a moment and regarded me with careful consideration. "My god, your aura is unmistakably old," he said pointedly to me.

My eyebrow perked. "What does that mean?"

"Your powers have the energy of a newborn babe, but your soul is older than any I've encountered…curious. You yearn for something that will cause much more destruction to get. And a part of you remains unfulfilled because you still do not know who you truly are." Cadmus Leonantus, though old and frail, boldly and unapologetically commanded his words. Zayne observed us as a scientist would a subject under a microscope, as he listened to his mentor toss insults in my direction.

"I could have gone to a palm reader to be told that," I said derisively.

Leonantus began to pour himself a glass of wine. "The same darkness I saw in Zayne, I now see in you. I have seen wickedness in many forms. They all come and go, but you, my dear, you are different. You would cast aside your humanity so quickly without even understanding the true immensity of your actions."

My eyes rolled habitually. His rambling was losing my attention very quickly. Leonantus focused back on Zayne.

"I always expected you to do great things, Zayne," Leonantus continued.

"You told me once that greatness is only a matter of perspective." Zayne stepped closer to Leonantus so that eventually he loomed over the desk. "From where I stand, we will be remembered through the passage of time, while your ashes with join the others upon which we will tread."

I couldn't peel my eyes from him. I wasn't sure how I had expected this encounter to go, but I know it wasn't like it had. Rather than a showcase of who possessed the most powerful sorcery, we seemed to be locked in a battle of whose words could hurt the other more.

"I pity you, Zayne Ryder. And you, too, Kaitlin Coles. I hope one day you will see the error of your ways." Leonantus raised his glass to his lips, but Zayne unexpectedly snatched it and the wine bottle out of his reach.

I looked on curiously. Zayne swirled the liquid in the glass and sniffed it. His nose wrinkled as he drew it away and looked at Leonantus with disappointment. "Arsenic? That's very unimaginative of you." Zayne carelessly threw the bottle and glass aside so they shattered in the corner. "The Sagen need you alive to harvest your powers."

I summoned a Sagen with my tattoo and within minutes, the once-distinguished Cadmus Leonantus was led away by a warrior, to his death. Zayne and I were left in the empty house.

The wind whined outside, and the house responded with hollow groans.

"What did he mean about my aura?" I asked, turning on Zayne.

He shrugged in response. "He was always rambling on about things that made no sense." I appeared unconvinced. "He probably just meant that your powers are stronger than your years would suggest. Shall we head back to the city?" Zayne asked.

"Yes. Let's go."

The house was beginning to unnerve me. Zayne led the way back to the courtyard, where we mounted our horses. Soon we were racing back towards Eileen, and, several hours later, the rural landscapes became more urban again, with villages and buildings spreading around us. If I had to guess, I'd say we made it back to the inner folds of the city in the early hours of the morning. Since Zayne was directing us, I soon realized that I wasn't familiar with the route we were taking. I didn't know Eileen well enough to be planted anywhere and instantly know were I was. Zayne, on the other hand, knew exactly where we were.

"My place is nearby. We can rest there for the night." I eyed him, but he didn't appear to have any tangent thoughts beyond resting for the remainder of the night.

I nodded and followed him back to his single-room apartment, wedged tightly in between two other buildings. We stepped inside, and once again I encountered a disastrous mess. The room was just as I remembered it. The bread and cheese that still sat on the table were growing some fuzz, and the basin behind the table was still stacked high with dirty dishes. I ran my finger along a piece of furniture and found a film of dust left on my fingertips. The fire from the last time, however small it was, had given the room some warmth that it now lacked.

I couldn't hide the disgust on my face. "Do you *actually* live here?"

Zayne gazed upon the sight without finding fault. If anything, he looked rather pleased with himself, as if the sight was an improvement over the usual scene.

"You know, your lodgings had dust everywhere too."

He took my dust-covered finger in his hand. Again, when his rough hands grabbed mine, the shadow of his touch lingered a little too long, even after he let go. I closed my hand, trying to trap the sensation inside. This had been the longest I'd gone without the company of a boyfriend, or at the very least, a distraction, and the cravings were getting harder to silence.

"It's cleaner upstairs. I'll be up with some drinks in a minute."

He went over to a cabinet and started rummaging around, while I climbed the ladder to the lofted area. I pulled off my boots and cloak and tossed them in a corner. The wide, unmade bed was the only object in the area. If it came to it, I wasn't opposed to sharing a bed for the night. It was spacious enough that neither of us would know the other was there. Besides, back home I'd slept many nights on the same bed as Nick, Brenna, and Connor. Oftentimes, several of us wound up piled on top of each other in a single bed. It was strange to think about my friends, because a part of me knew I'd never see them again. Still, I knew that sleeping next to Zayne didn't concern me. It was the tingling in my hand, the expectancy of my eyes when I heard him climbing the ladder, and the extra thump of my heart that concerned me.

He balanced two steaming mugs. My toes curled with the anticipation of the mug's contents seeping through me. I greedily wrapped my hands around it. The strong smell of cinnamon soothed me, but there were more ingredients compounding the lusciousness of the drink. Zayne settled onto the bed next to me. I was far enough away so that our knees didn't bump into each other, but if I leaned toward him, I'd be inches from his face.

The drink was thicker than I expected. It coated my tongue and mouth like syrup. I made a sound of delight. He grinned at my reaction.

We sipped in silence while I thought more about what Cadmus Leonantus had said about me. Most of his insults swept though me like the wind, but his comment about my aura stayed with me. What about my aura was unmistakable? And why did he think I had an old soul? Even though Zayne brushed is aside casually, my mind was plagued with the mystery of Leonantus's words. Thinking about it caused my mind to wander to the strange spell book Azlaya had shown me, with the ancient symbols I could read, but she couldn't. I wondered if Zayne knew anything about it.

"Do you know anything about Aelonian?"

"Sure, it's the ancient language of the first sorcerers, right?"

I made an affirmative sound. "Have you ever seen it?"

He shook his head. "No, it's a dead language. The only people who can understand it have dedicated their whole lives to deciphering it, and sometimes even they can't fully understand it. Why do you ask? Interested in taking up a course?"

"I just came across it some reading." Zayne started peering at me curiously, in a way that would soon turn more questions on me. I decided to stay in control of our conversation. "How long were you Leonantus's apprentice?"

"I went to him when I was ten years old, and left five years later. A traditional apprenticeship lasts seven years, unless you're," he gestured towards me, "unusually gifted."

I smiled demurely at his comment. "Why did you leave?"

"He was holding me back. Like you, he knew I was stronger than my years would suggest, but he still limited me. I went farther north, deep into the mountains to train with a group of sorcerers who worship Dark Magic and its powers." Something in my face made him continue. "I want you to meet them. In fact, when this army is stronger, I'm going to take you there to see for yourself. When I was with them, it was the freest I'd ever felt. They didn't stunt my growth like Leonantus had, and it was the first time my powers had been allowed to breathe."

I briefly thought of my grandmother and her years of suppressing my abilities. And then there was Azlaya, who imprisoned me in a cage guarded by Sagen for months. "I know the feeling."

"She'll regret locking you away," Zayne said in a low voice. He placed a warm hand on my knee. "She's going to realize the mistake of ever trying to keep you from reaching your full potential, and I vow, right now, to help you do just that."

The tingling was overwhelming, and I had grown tired of shying away from it. I placed my mug on the ground and rested my hand on top of his. His other hand had found the nape of my neck, and he was pulling me to him. I let out a long, pent-up breath of modesty before his lips pressed into mine. His lips, like mine, were still lightly coated in the buttery drink. As the sugar dissolved, we became hungrier for more.

Our soft kisses became greedy and desperate. My fingers knotted in his wavy hair. My other hand dug into his back. I felt his lips on my mouth, my chest, my neck, my chin, my jaw, and my ear. They were brushing over my skin as quickly as explorers rush over new lands. Soon, his shirt was unbuttoned, and my own was being tugged over my head. I fell back into the sheets. His stubble prickled my skin. My head spun from feeling his bare, muscular chest pressing against mine. His weight was on me, but in that moment, we felt weightless. Our limbs tangled.

He caressed me as waves kiss the shore. My heart galloped gleefully. I wedged a hand between our chests and pushed him back so I could see his face. His expression was soft, but his eyes burned with desire. They were daring me. I wrapped my legs around him and gracefully flipped our entwined bodies over. I sat up tall and cast a brazen look down on him. My hair fell around my shoulders and in my face; I wondered when my hair tie had come out. I placed my hands on his chest and let his heart count out the seconds.

He lay still, not fighting the exchange of power. He was captivated, though, it wasn't a look with which I was familiar. Normally, and foolishly, guys had looked at me as though I was their true love. Zayne looked at me like I was a challenge, an opportunity. It was as though he was telling me with his eyes that he was going to do everything in his power to become my equal. Amusement and eagerness contorted on his face.

"Do I still interest you?" I asked sweetly, though my eyes were mischievous.

He exhaled blissfully. "Always." His hands rested playfully on my hips. "You are the most exquisite being I've ever met."

"I bet that line works on all the girls," I teased him.

He looked smitten—greedy, but smitten. "Yes, but I've never meant it."

I thought back to when our powers had melded into one to penetrate Leonantus's defenses. Together, we were able to do something that would have been nearly impossible to do on my own. Where Azlaya and I had intertwined, Zayne and I had merged. The converging of our minds, our powers, and now our beings, was beginning to make me realize the formidable force we could be together.

Now it was my turn to dare him. "Prove it."

Zayne sat up quickly, his hand snaking around my back. His other was in my hair again, holding my head firm while his eyes washed over my face. My lips parted while he peppered my jaw-line with kisses. I was chuckling airily when his ravenous lips found mine, and he pulled me down into the sheets with him.

Chapter 26: Casey

BY THE TIME Aiden returned to the inn that night, Brennon had awakened. He complained about a headache and empty stomach, but other than that, he was fine. I ran out to the streets in search of dinner and came back with a pot of soup and loaves of bread. While we ate, Brennon talked to me, I talked to Brennon, Brennon talked to Aiden, Aiden talked to Brennon, but Aiden and I didn't talk to each other. Brennon knew better than to bring whatever had happened between us to the surface, so we behaved like our indifference towards each other was normal. After dinner, Aiden escaped to his room, leaving Brennon and me on our own.

We crawled into bed as the last of the firewood was diminishing to embers. I lay awake and stared that the ceiling. Brennon could sense my lingering anxiety about the next day's entrance round to the tournament.

"How are you feeling?" I was formulating an answer when he added, "And don't lie."

"Is it bad that I'm nervous?"

"Nerves are important. They keep you alert—and alive. You just can't let them impede your judgment." Brennon had turned his head so that he looked at me. "Casey, you have trained hard. You're going into this well prepared. Besides, anyone that can face an army of Sagen can surely survive the Tournament of Eileen," he scoffed and reassuringly knocked his elbow into mine.

I smiled warmly at his efforts to comfort me. Eventually, he rolled back over and pulled the blankets up to his ears. Though the tournament was on my mind, I thought about Kate and what she was doing to build a Sagen army, and Kyraine and how she would keep herself and Brennon from facing execution, and Aiden and his seeming unwillingness to save himself from the darkness that threatened him.

I woke a few hours later. Aiden's dreams were spilling into my own again. The physical and mental suffering that overcame my body wouldn't allow me to sit by in silence anymore. I didn't understand how he thought it was healthy to have such horrible imaginings dance through his subconscious each night.

I pushed the covers aside, careful not to disturb Brennon, and quietly picked my way across the floor. I reached the door to Aiden's room and silently pushed it open. A window to the left side of the bed spilled the moon's light onto Aiden's face. I'd never seen him actually asleep, but I wished it had happened more, because for once, he looked peaceful. The hard look of sarcasm he usually wore was gone. It was the first time I saw his face completely free of plots or deeply-kept secrets embedded in his expression.

Suddenly, his face winced, and his whole body jerked. It happened again a few seconds later, and he mumbled something incomprehensible. Though it was muffled, I could detect evident fear in his voice.

I crept to the side of the bed and was reaching down to shake his shoulder. Then out of nowhere, I saw the glint of something. Before I knew it, Aiden was swinging a dagger up at my face. My trained reflexes saved me, and I shot an arm out to grab his before he swiftly took off my head.

Aiden's wild eyes met mine, and he immediately drew back. "Shit, Casey!" he exclaimed.

I let out a shaky breath and stood, paralyzed, staring at nothing, while my heart pounded against my chest. "You sleep with a dagger," I said absentmindedly. Though knowing him, it shouldn't have come as a surprise. Yet, it still shook me to my core, especially since it had been flying towards my face moments before.

Aiden, dagger still clenched in one hand, jumped up and peered into the other room to see if we had awakened Brennon. He came back over to where I stood, unmoving.

"Are you all right?"

"You sleep with a dagger."

"Here, sit down." He gently pushed me onto his bed. By the way he looked at me, you wouldn't have known that we were busy hating each other hours before.

He began to pace the room, combing fingers through his hair every few seconds. When my heart finally slowed, I whispered, "Why do you sleep with a dagger?"

"Casey, it's late."

Once again, he was trying to bat me aside, but I could see the attrition of his stubbornness as he faced me. His shoulders sagged. His dark brown hair was disheveled. He gestured in the direction of my bed, as though to suggest we should just part ways for the night.

"No," I said defiantly. "You almost impaled me with your knife. I've earned an explanation. I know something is wrong, because your nightmares have been spilling into my dreams for days now." I had finally caught his undivided attention. "I've felt everything you have every night."

"You've been reading my mind while I slept?"

"No—it's like your head overflows and mine soaks it all up."

He stared silently, grappling for words. It was one of the few times he was caught without an immediate retort. The pause between us was thick. I felt him retreating.

"Stop trying to push me away, and just tell me what is going on."

He tried to protest. "Casey."

I lowered my voice, as though I spoke to an injured animal. "What are you so afraid of?"

The weight of his gaze on me suddenly became crushing. Maybe it was seeing all the agony swimming in his eyes, or the quiver of his lips from not knowing where to begin, but it clinched my heart in a way none of his spite ever had. He rubbed his face; saw that I was unyielding, and settled onto a wooden chest beside the bed so that we faced each other.

"It's a very long story, Casey."

I crossed my legs, folded my arms, and waited.

Aiden took a deep breath and mentally prepared himself for everything he was about to reveal—everything he had wanted to leave in the past, forever.

"I suppose it all began when I deserted the Huntsmen. Shortly after taking their oath, I realized that life, as a Huntsman, wasn't a life at all. I didn't want to live under their laws. I wanted freedom, not orders. I fled to Eileen with a friend. Greyson was five at the time, and my mother had just passed away. I needed money to support him, and the Night's Guild offered me payment that I couldn't refuse, so I joined them.

"I carried out and oversaw missions that left scores of people dead. Once again, my life didn't belong to me, and I wanted to escape. That was when Amelia came along. Word of my work had traveled to her ears, and she sought me out for a mission supported by the other sitting kings and queens. I saw it as my opportunity to escape the Guild, so I made a deal with Amelia: she would buy my freedom from the Guild if I successfully executed her mission."

He paused to take a breath.

"She hired me to eliminate the royal family of Eileen: Gisele's father, Gisele, and all the male heirs of their lineage. Universal law states that if all the legitimate heirs to a family's throne are deceased, the sitting kings and queens of the other kingdoms must select whom they want the next ruler to be. I was hired to eradicate Gisele's family in order to allow this to happen."

"I thought you were just the queen's spy?"

"Officially, yes."

"And unofficially?" I pressed, fearing I already knew the answer.

"An assassin." My muscles tensed uncontrollably. Though he had never given me a *real* reason to believe he would kill me, knowing that he was trained to kill still put me on edge.

"The Night's Guild isn't just a mercenary group, is it?" I questioned the explanation he'd given me before.

"No. It's a league of trained assassins."

"What happened—after she hired you?"

"It was the same summer Kyraine was appointed Mistress of the Hunt, so the care of our younger brother, Greyson, fell to me."

Kyraine and Aiden's brother had only been mentioned a few times, and in passing. He was like the topic everyone knew about but no one wanted to discuss, so they skirted around him as people would a disease. I only knew, from Brennon, that Greyson had died in a Sagen raid and that his death put a permanent strain on Kyraine and Aiden's relationship.

"I brought him with me to Eileen. Kyraine warned against involving Greyson in my work. He was my one vulnerability, but I was desperate to complete this mission for Amelia and be free of the Night's Guild. He was enrolled in an academy, so I could focus on my assignment.

"With Amelia's approval, I enlisted the help of my friends in the Guild. We started tracking down heirs to the Eileenian throne, disposing of them subtly as not to raise alarm. It just looked like a string of bad luck. Then I started closing in on Gisele and her father, the king.

"He secluded himself in his castle and was always surrounded by his personal battalion. So, I tried to infiltrate the castle from a more personal angle. I created the alias of Dorian Romauld, suitor to the princess of Eileen."

"And it worked?" I asked.

Aiden nodded. "I had easy access to the castle, to Gisele, and the king. I planned to poison him in his sleep. Old age would be blamed. I couldn't, however, bring myself to kill Gisele. Her father was a tyrant, but she had barely reached adulthood and bore no faults of her own, other than sharing the wrong blood. I decided to spare her life—let her live out the rest of her days in exile."

My next question escaped my lips before I had time to think about its implications. "You had feelings for her?"

He shook his head. "No," he said stonily. "I just couldn't justify her death. The rest of her corrupt relatives were a different matter."

I wasn't sure why, but this confession felt better to hear than the others. I struggled to imagine Aiden so taken by young Queen Gisele that he wanted to save her from his own blade. Instead, it was his conscience that stood in the way.

"My group and I were returning to the city after disposing of some of the last distant heirs when we were dragged before the king and Gisele. My identity was compromised, my friends were seized, and we were held in the dungeon for weeks— beaten, interrogated, and tortured. At some point, the king died, and Gisele assumed the throne. She ordered the guards to start killing my friends to get us to talk, but loyal to their leader, none of them betrayed me."

"Kai?" I asked quietly.

Aiden met my gaze and nodded solemnly. "They knew how desperate I was to be free of the Guild— They were the best assassins I've ever worked with. I began to devise a plan to escape, kill Gisele, and flee Eileen with Greyson when I was taken from the dungeon. All I could think about was how Gisele's death would win me my freedom, until I saw that they had Greyson."

Something inside me shattered at the sight of the unadulterated pain on Aiden's face that was twisting into a mask of grief.

He was so consumed by his story that he no longer kept his face from betraying his inner emotions. Whatever hardened feeling I'd had towards Aiden all but vanished in rawness of the moment. I was beginning to realize that I didn't want to know how the story was going to end.

"They tortured him in front of me until I finally confessed that Amelia, in league with the other kingdoms, had hired me to assassinate all the royal heirs. When I begged Gisele to release Greyson, she agreed and ordered my execution the following day. I prayed all night that Greyson sought out Kyraine and had gotten far away from the castle. When I was being led to the gallows, I realized another execution was in proceedings."

I jumped to what I hoped was the absolute wrong conclusion. "No," I breathed, but Aiden's expression confirmed my worst fear. I tried not to imagine a young boy standing on a platform awaiting his execution as he searched for his brother, but my mind constructed the image anyway.

"I escaped from my convoy and tried to reach him in time, but I was too late." He took another shaky breath, his hands trembling. "I fled the castle in search of the last remaining heirs to Eileen's throne. I don't remember much from that night— just that there was blood—lots of blood. I slaughtered them like animals, wanting to completely rid the world of Gisele's lineage. Among the bloodshed I came upon the last surviving heir, but I couldn't kill him. He was no older than three, and Greyson would never have forgiven me for murdering a child. I asked a friend to recover Greyson's body from Eileen so that I could give him a burial he deserved. When we met up, I learned that Gisele had formed a blood agreement with Azlaya in retribution for the other kingdoms plotting against her life. I brought the

last heir back to Calem with me and, until now, I hadn't returned to Eileen once." He paused again and steadied his
breathing. "In all these years, I've never been able to figure what
went wrong."

I was speechless. Aiden had all but exposed his soul to
me, and I couldn't believe that these were the terrible things
that haunted him. Of course he had terrible dreams. How
couldn't he, after witnessing the murder of his friends and
brother, and feeling responsible for enabling the alliance between Gisele and Azlaya to exist? But there was one component of his story that contradicted the little information I
knew about Greyson.

"I thought Greyson died in a Sagen raid?" I asked gently.

His head fell into his hands, as though to hide his shame.
"That's because it's what I told Kyraine. I couldn't tell her the
truth. The fact that he was dead nearly destroyed her. If she
knew how he died she'd— I couldn't bear to make her endure
that truth, too."

I waited for him to say more, but he stayed silent. I rose
from the bed, and our gazes met. His eyes were the most
vulnerable I'd ever seen them. I reached down and steadied the
hand holding the dagger. Carefully, I pulled it from his grasp
and tossed onto the dresser out of reach. He rose to his feet,
standing a head taller than me.

"If I'm captured while trying to steal this document—"
Aiden began. I plainly saw the images of his worst nightmares
flashing through his head. He was being tied down and whipped
mercilessly. His fingers were being cut off. He was being
drowned in scalding water. All these mounted into a horrifying
scene that ended in him begging for death. His body was

broken and scarred in so many different ways, physical and mental, that I had to pull away from him to break the connection I'd had with his thoughts. "I'm not letting Gisele walk away with her life," he finished.

I breathed shallowly, floating through time, untethered to anything, but I felt myself nodding. I tried to blink away his horrors from my own mind. "This was never about the money."

"Nothing can change the past now, but what can change is who sits on Eileen's throne." He still visibly shook. "I—I just—"

I'd never seen him stumble over words before, and, without thinking, I placed a hand on his arm. I grasped his wrist and felt his pulse. His fingers lightly touched the under side of my own wrist. I closed my eyes and, as when I absorbed part of the dark spell that had hit Connor, I tried to take away some of the pain that overwhelmed Aiden's dreams. As the onslaught of emotions swept over me, I had to brace myself. After several silent seconds, I let go of his wrist and stepped back.

"I know," was all I said to express my empathy.

I needed air. I needed a space that wasn't filled with the horrors of the past. I turned to go, when Aiden's words stopped me.

"No one knows about this, Casey," he whispered.

I faced him again and nodded, understanding what he was asking of me. "Brennon should understand the risk of being in Eileen with you if the queen has a price on your head."

With that, I left. It was strange, though. As I pulled the door shut behind me, it felt like Aiden didn't want me to leave. I crossed the room and slid back into bed. Brennon still slept soundly beside me. I pulled the blankets back over me and resumed my vigil of staring at the ceiling.

So many conflicting emotions warred inside me. I couldn't forgive Aiden for the crimes he committed, but then I also couldn't fault him for wanting revenge. I hated him for lying to Kyraine, but then I understood why he did. I wasn't sure if I could ever look at him the same way, knowing he had the blood of so many people on his hands. Though, I felt his desperation as though it were a palpable thing. I didn't know how to merge the Aiden I'd known up until this point with the murderous Aiden that plotted to avenge his brother and friends by dethroning the queen.

I had become familiar with the horrors of Aiden's nightmares, since they regularly became my own, but I could have never guessed their immensity or gravity. The man I once thought didn't possess a sympathetic bone is his body remained tortured over his past mistakes for years. The callous mask he had donned had now been removed in my mind. The person underneath was new and foreign to me. Finally revealing the secrets of Eileen had made Aiden unrecognizable—and perhaps even to himself.

Chapter 27: Aiden

I WAS STARTLED out of sleep, not from a nightmare, but from the absence of one. I bolted upright and stared into the darkness for an indefinite amount of time. I knew something was wrong, because I could always tell how much time had passed, and yet my mind let the seconds and minutes pass by carelessly. I glanced at my wrist where Casey had held it momentarily. Whatever she had done had quieted the nightmares unlike any other remedy I'd tried. Though they still crept around the edges of my subconscious, it was the best night's sleep I'd had in years. Eventually, my thoughts drifted to my conversation with Casey. Other than Blakemore and Lysander, no one else knew about the details of the mission that plagued my existence.

Why did I finally confess to her? Was it her earnest eyes that begged me to share my burden of secrets? Was it being trapped in her warm, embracing presence? Or did I just want to feel the validation of her soft eyes on me, even after seeing the darkest parts of my being? I doubted that would happen, though.

I dressed silently and left the inn in search of food to distract my mind. While I was out, I sent a hawk to Shep, asking him to check the Givaldi family vault in the Royal Bank of Eileen. By the time I returned to the inn with fresh bread and sausage links, Casey and Brennon had woken and dressed. After we ate, we left to register Casey in the tournament as Kai Frost, the village girl from the north.

"It's a short duel," Brennon answered Casey's question that had completely missed my ears. "I think you fight one of the young soldiers of the Eileen army. Right Aiden?"

I shook myself from whatever trance I had fallen into. "Yes. It's just a third year soldier who is still in training. Disarm him or her and you'll advance. Whoever it is, though, they won't even compare to Brennon," I reassured her without stealing one glance at her face.

We arrived at the square where the tournament officials had constructed a wooden pen in which the duels would take place. As we approached, an Eileen soldier battled a dark woman who fought with the ferocity of a mountain lion. Her attacks were powerful and brutal, and I noticed she didn't have to concern herself with defense, because her opponent wasn't able to turn the tables of the match. She disarmed him quickly, and applause rose from the crowd surrounding the circular pen. I silently commended her and her expertise fighting skills that clearly had their roots in Canabar.

Brennon, Casey, and I approached the registrar who sat behind a desk raised on a podium. He wore small, wire-rimmed glasses and his hair was thin and graying, but the efficiency with which he recorded and filed Casey's "identification papers" told me he had been doing this for many years. He asked her many of the questions Brennon and I had been rehearsing with her for weeks, and she answered them without so much as a nervous pause. Once she was registered, he directed her to wait until her number was called. We stood to the side and watched as people entered the ring. Some succeeded in disarming the soldier, but most were humiliated and sent home with bruises and fresh cuts.

Finally, Casey's number was called out, and she entered the pen. A group of squires helped fasten armor on her chest, shoulders, arms and legs. She was handed a sword, similar to the heavy one we had used in our own duel, and she stepped into the center. A soldier, who stood several heads taller than Casey, scowled intimidatingly and squared to face her. A bell sounded.

He darted forward. Casey expertly parried, elbowing his side with her free arm. He stumbled away from her. He rushed her again, but this time she met his advance with her sword. The clang reverberated through the square. He jabbed, she dodged; he swung, and she deflected. The duel became an intricate balance between offense and defense. The crowd began to thicken as the battle dragged on. Brennon and I exchanged unconcerned glances after realizing what Casey was doing. The fight wasn't taking a long time because they were evenly matched. In fact, Casey was much better, though the young man's size made up for his speed. She was letting him exhaust himself, waiting for him to make a mistake. When he finally made one, he struck out at her while she was in the perfect position to break his grasp by striking his wrist with her elbow. The sword clattered to the ground, and she stopped his attempt to pick it up by placing her blade at his jugular. The bell sounded again.

"Winner, Kai Frost!"

Casey dropped the sword and did something that won her an even more loving response from the crowd. She held her hand out. The soldier peered at her, flustered from his loss and confused by his opponent. When he reached out to grasp her hand, the cheers bolstered. Brennon had a look on his face that didn't show any surprise at all.

She exited the ring and approached us, followed by squires who unfastened her armor.

"Well done," Brennon congratulated. I nodded my agreement.

"They're going to escort you to the castle now to start getting ready for tonight's feast," I told her, flicking my eyes to a waiting group of attendants. "We'll see you there."

She nodded and gave Brennon a warm smile. When she turned to me, I saw the remnants of last night's conversation swimming in her eyes. She beseeched me to warn Brennon about my notoriety with one swift expression, before being herded away by a group of attendants.

As I watched her walk away, a strange sensation came over me. I felt like I had when I'd left Greyson at that academy. A voice in the back of my head doubted my decision to let her go; I couldn't protect her anymore. But she wasn't Greyson. I had to keep reminding myself that she wasn't my defenseless little brother. She was capable. She was strong. She was dangerous. Still, an unfamiliar feeling fluttered inside me.

Brennon and I split up before meeting back at the inn later. He went to send a letter to Kyraine to update her on our mission, and I walked the streets in search of Shep. Rather, I waited for Shep to find me.

While I waited, a familiar face cornered me in a vacant alley. It was the young woman who was speaking to the Commander before I had arrived. She wore a long overcoat that showed off her curves and dark makeup.

"I remember you from the other night," she exclaimed. "We weren't properly introduced. You're one of the Commander's?"

I was overly aware of how close her face was getting to mine. "No, I don't work for the Guild." That was evidently the last thing I should have said, because her eyes flared with thoughts of unspeakable pleasure.

A couple weeks ago, my skin would have tingled at the thought. I would have smiled crookedly. I would have given her a compliment that would have made me irresistible. But as I felt her body press against mine, I felt nothing.

To try to stave her advances, I warned her, "The Commander might have your head if he saw us now." She regarded me, saw that I wasn't joking, and pulled back.

She pouted and fastened the ties she had undone on her coat. "Shame, you look like you'd have been a lot of fun." She sauntered away without a glance back.

I returned to the main street and perched on a stack of crates while I ate an apple. By the time I finished feeding the core to a stray dog, Shep had found me. He wore a fur cloak that swallowed his figure. His various weapons, whether on his belt or strapped to his limbs, were concealed from the common eye, but I knew he had them was because I carried the same ones on myself. We grasped each other's arms in greeting.

"No luck, then?" I asked. Shep took his hood down and shook his head. Apparently he hadn't found anything promising in Gisele's family vault in the Royal Bank of Eileen.

"All she had were heirlooms, paintings of dead relatives, and a few rare pieces of jewelry. Nothing special," he said nonchalantly.

All of these things had been offered as payment, or bribes, during my time with the Guild, and again under Amelia's employment. It was strange that I had developed a callous to such riches, when in my youth, they were all I dreamed about.

"Was it easy to get in and out?" We started to slowly melt back into the crowds on the street.

"The guard was easy to bribe, if that's what you mean. I guess you didn't find anything, either?" We weaved our way around a group of young women talking about what they were going to wear to the festivities that night.

"No. Apparently the House of Public Records does not keep records for the sitting ruler. All documents concerning him or her are recovered when their reign begins and kept in the castle," I said scoffed bitterly. I had visited the building after I had stormed out on Casey, leaving her to watch over a sedated Brennon. I'd had a brief, but heated, argument with the official on duty. I came away with nothing but an even sourer mood.

"Where should we look next?" Shep asked.

"I'm going to check the Hall of Records in the castle tonight."

Shep nodded. He caught a glimpse of my face, which was caught somewhere between guilt and eagerness. "Just say it."

"How close do you think you can get to Gisele?" I asked after a minute.

Shep's brow furrowed. "Why? What did you have in mind?"

I stared straight ahead as I made my request. "I wonder if she keeps a document of that nature on her at all times."

I finally turned to exchange glances with him, and I could tell he understood what I was asking. I couldn't approach Gisele the same way he could. She'd have my head on a spike in no time. All Shep would need was a few minutes with her, and he'd know if she carried anything on her that might be what we were searching for. His pickpocketing abilities were remarkable.

"I'll do it. I'll even time myself. A gold piece says I can do it in under a minute," he said playfully. I grinned at him.

"You're on." We walked a few more blocks before our paths forked in different directions. "I'll see you tonight."

"Mask and all," Shep said before he disappeared into the traffic of people.

The Commencement Ball was the first official event of the tournament. It was a masquerade. It was a tradition that supposedly represented how the competitors entered the games as masked individuals, but would reveal their true characters during the events. My theory, however, was that the masks were originally introduced so that people could engage in promiscuous activity without compromising their identity.

I returned to the inn and found Brennon reading a pamphlet about the tournament. I closed the door and hung my cloak on a hook. "Is there anything useful in there?" I asked him.

"Not really. It's mostly speculation about what the events will be, and returning competitors' chances at winning. They don't look too terrible. There's a low chance she'll be killed by one of them." I was all too familiar with the printed hype around the tournament. "A vendor was selling masks down the street," Brennon said to me and pointed to the table. Both masks were black, simple, and would command little attention. "Do you think we need anything else for tonight?" Brennon asked.

I shook my head. "I'm having a friend meet us at the ball. He's going to help us look for the document."

"Guild member?"

"Yes. While you and I search the Hall of Records, he is going to distract Gisele and see if she keeps the document on her."

Brennon deferred to my judgment, however reluctantly. Anyone who was wise would have reservations about involving members of the Guild.

"There's one more thing, Brennon," I began. My voice had lowered enough that Brennon immediately stopped scanning over the pamphlet, set it aside, and matched my gaze. "You should know why I haven't returned to Eileen since my last assignment here." I paused, allowing the gravity of my words sink in. "Gisele has a price on my head."

"What for?" Brennon asked.

I took a deep breath and launched into an abbreviated version of the story I'd told Casey. Brennon had his chin balanced on his fingers while I spoke. He never interrupted me, but his face wavered. When I finished, I waited in silence for Brennon to pass his judgment.

"Why didn't you tell Kyraine?"

"I've destroyed a lot of things in my life, Brennon. I thought I could at least spare her."

Brennon was visibly conflicted by the information. I knew of the relationship he and my sister shared, and I was interested to see how deep his loyalties were to Kyraine. Would he go running to her at his first opportunity, or would he suppress this knowledge for my sake?

"I won't say anything," he finally said. I had to admit I was a little shocked. Brennon abruptly changed the subject, steering our discussion in a new direction. "In the very real event that one of us gets caught—" His voice trailed off.

The immediacy of my words surprised me. "The other gets Casey out. I understand her importance in the larger battle, and she needs to stay safe—and alive."

And this was true. I had grown up knowing the prophecy, just as every other man, woman and child in Alagia. I understood the gravity of having her fall under my protection, and the way she had looked at me last night made me realize that maybe my concern with her safety was more than just obligation. I began to entertain another very real possibility.

"And in the event that *I* get captured, there is something I need you to do. It's of the utmost importance; I cannot stress that enough. Can I trust you?"

"What is it?"

"The boy I brought back to Calem with me—"

"The heir?" Brennon clarified.

I nodded. "He's still alive." Brennon grasped the enormity of my words. "He's been living in exile, with a tutor to prepare him for his future. My point is that when Gisele dies—and she will, that I am sure of—there is a legitimate heir to the throne."

"Do any of the other rulers know of this? Because I'm sure they're all under the impression that upon Queen Gisele's death, they will choose a new ruler for Eileen."

"No. No one knows he's alive." He was looking at me as though I had just hatched a plan to sprout wings and fly. "Brennon, I'm pragmatic. I know the chances of getting caught on this mission are high. If she captures me, I will ensure her death, but I need you to make sure that this heir is recognized, and that he assumes the throne to which he has rightful claim."

I hadn't realized how much my words had tightened until I stopped to take a breath. Brennon was faithful. He had proven this time and time again with my sister. I knew, even before making my request, that he felt some kind of loyalty to me, however small. Brennon appeared to have taken every word to heart. He nodded and swore he would complete the final steps of my twenty-year scheme.

I turned from him to go find suitable clothes for the approaching evening when he asked, "Can I ask why you spared the boy?"

"Because my brother would have spared him."

A few hours later, Brennon and I made our way to the castle. The trek had been fast until we got close, at which point the entire city population seemed to converge. Everyone was dressed in his or her finest pants, shirts, gowns, capes, gloves, jewelry, and shoes. While most of the people would remain outside the castle and participate in the festivities on the streets, the lords and ladies of the court; the advisors; and the competitors and their family and friends would spend the night inside the ballroom. Brennon and I snaked around to the main entrance where they were admitting people into the castle. We made it inside after following a spiraling cobblestone road to the castle's front doors.

The ballroom was like I remembered. A wide staircase descended into a large open space that could comfortably fit hundreds of people. Across the room, a shorter set of stairs led to a dais upon which sat a throne. Red curtains hung to either side, framing the throne. Banners with Eileen's sigil animal, the snow leopard, hung on the walls. Massive, flickering chandeliers illuminated the room, hanging ominously over the guests. Blue streamers and other banners looped from chandelier to chandelier, casting a blue haze on the room. At each of the four corners, there were alcoves containing refreshments and food. Unlike Calem's ballroom, this one was very contained. There was no escape out to a balcony or the gardens. Everyone was trapped, like animals in a cage.

Brennon and I descended the stairs into the ballroom and quickly slipped off to the edge of the party. The floor was already full of people who stood around and talked. We had probably been among the last people to enter, and the ball was officially about to begin. I grabbed two drinks from a passing waiter and handed one to Brennon. Several ladies passed us and gave us looks meant for someone else. An announcer took to the dais area, and silence fell over the room.

When I saw her, uncontrollable resentment gripped me. Gisele still carried herself with the elegance of a viper. She slithered like a snake, and her eyes—her vacant and cold eyes—moved slowly across her audience. Because I had known her when most considered her beautiful, I could see the places where the years had hardened that beauty. Her lips had lost their natural, rich color and were now just a dull, thin memory.

Her cheeks were sunken. In fact, her skin looked as though it had been pulled tightly over her face. It no longer possessed the full and round features she'd had in her youth. She had crow's feet wrinkles extending outwards from the corners of her mouth and eyes. Her entire complexion looked splotchy and pale. It was like someone has sucked the life out of her, leaving behind an atrophied woman with the flaws of the world in her eyes.

"Good evening, and welcome," Gisele began. "This night is meant to celebrate the beginning of a much-treasured tradition. Tomorrow, the Tournament of Eileen shall begin. Tomorrow we shall bear witness to the kinds of competitors that will compete this year. Tomorrow we will embark on a journey with our competitors as we watch one of them claim glory. But tonight, we shall feast." Her voice was lower than I remembered, and her words rougher. Her pitch didn't change as she spoke, but remained flat and monotonous. "Let us meet this year's competitors."

Now that Brennon knew of Gisele's capacity for cruelty, I felt him tense next to me as the competitors marched from behind the curtains on the wings, and onto the stage. We kept our eyes peeled for Casey. Finally, I spotted her. She wore a black, corseted gown with a full skirt. I could tell by the way she walked that she didn't like her shoes. Her mask was gold and drew most of the attention, even more than her lips, which were blood red. The other people on stage also wore black garments and golden masks. The announcer came back on stage. As he called out the competitors' names, they stepped forward, turned to Gisele, and bowed. After the display, Gisele released them into the crowd, and soft music began to spread through the room.

I handed Brennon my drink and slipped into the crowd. I wove my way through couples, keeping my eyes on Casey. Despite the discomfort with her shoes, she still walked with grace. She tried her best to hold a straight posture, but I think she was just trying to look over people to find Brennon and me. I finally reached her, placing my hand in the middle of her back and directing her back the way I had come. When we reached Brennon, he looked relieved to see her.

"Everything is going as planned," Casey reported, and I saw her quickly cross and uncross her fingers. Then she shot me a glance, but Brennon interrupted our exchange.

"He told me, Casey," Brennon reassured her. His attention was stolen by something behind me. I turned, hand on dagger, and came face-to-face with Shep—well, masked Shep. It was black and simple, much like the ones Brennon and I wore.

"Brennon, Casey, this is my friend, Shep." I introduced them, filling Casey in on why Shep was there.

Brennon grasped Shep's outstretched hand. Then Shep turned to Casey and placed a delicate kiss on her hand. "All right, where do we start?" Shep asked eagerly.

I gestured to each of the four alcoves in the corners of the ballroom. "There is a system of pulleys that sends food up and down from the kitchen, and a staircase that leads down to it. We'll—"

I was interrupted by the sudden blare of music. A procession of woodwind and string instruments sparked the room into action as people started pairing off and spinning onto the dance floor. I realized this was as good a time as any for Shep to try to figure out if Gisele kept the document on her, with all the commotion. We must have been thinking the same thing, because when we met each other's gazes, he nodded and melted into the crowd. Brennon was being towed away by a woman with an elaborate mask and a mischievous gleam in her eyes.

The music dragged on for a few more counts, and as I stood next to Casey, my obligation in that moment dawned on me. Casey turned to me and quietly said, "I can go get—I think I saw some food—we don't have to—"

I watched her stumble over her words and pictured color spreading over her hidden cheeks. She knew how to avoid conflict, I'd give her that, but there was a good-mannered part of me. I held out my hand to her. Though she tried to hide it, her eyes betrayed her surprise. After a brief moment of hesitation, she placed her hand in mine, and I led us onto the floor.

She squared to face me and placed her other hand on my shoulder. I gently rested my free hand on her hip. When neither of us objected to our sudden closeness, created not because we were trying to disarm each other, I took the first step. We moved about awkwardly for a couple counts, our feet shuffling haphazardly.

"I don't know the dance," Casey finally admitted, even though I didn't need her confession. Her unsure feet were evidence enough.

I gave her rigid hand in mine a reassuring squeeze. "It's just like sparring, but with a four count. When I move forward," I said, stepping towards her, "you step back."

She stepped backwards. Then, I stepped backwards, and she moved forward. We repeated the maneuver several more times, and then I started to turn us in a large circle, as the other couples were doing. I ignored the curious glances we got, because, of course, anyone who lives in Eileen knows the traditional ballroom dances. But I didn't care to be bothered with them.

"Now, take your eyes off your feet." She lifted her gaze but kept her eyes on something just over my shoulder.

We felt the music change, and we adjusted ourselves to the new rhythm. The dance steps had changed, too. I turned Casey and moved my feet to complement hers. After only twenty-two seconds, she had picked up the new pattern and danced as gracefully as she fought. When she finally lifted her gaze from her shoes again, she had a warm smile on her lips, but it quickly transformed into a reserved expression. I wanted to say something—do something that would let her know that her reaction wouldn't be received coldly, as it may have before, but she spoke first.

"My room is on the backside of the castle. It overlooks a courtyard that's right up against a mountain side." We stepped apart for two steps and came back together. "It has a balcony," she finished when she was in my arms again.

I nodded with approval. "As soon as you can, you should get to the library and try to learn more about how to break a blood agreement." Casey nodded.

When the song ended, we broke apart and joined the thunderous applause for the musicians, who were seated in a corner. They dipped their heads in gratitude and then dove into the next song. It was slower-paced than the last.

We resumed our position and danced in silence for a few more counts. She wasn't as tense as before, and I noticed she chewed the inside of her lip when she wasn't talking. Her hair was silkier than Kyraine's thick hair, though they had similar coloring. Her small nose sloped gently, and her eyes expressed a kindness without having to move a muscle on her face.

She broke my trance. "Has anything changed?"

I blinked several times and repeated her question to myself, because I hadn't really comprehended it the first time. My eyes washed over the room. "Not really. Just the people in it." My eyes settled back on her, which unsteadied her a bit.

We spun, and I felt her hip pushing into my hand. Her hand rested a little more firmly on my shoulder. I didn't even notice the song had changed again. Casey studied her feet again, but when she raised her head, I found myself staring into two silver-blue orbs. The blue haze cast across the room swam in her eyes. Her mouth was parted slightly. Everything in the room slid from view. The music melted into white noise and those around us became irrelevant ghosts. In moments, she had completely stolen my attention.

Something in my eyes must have changed, because she asked, "Am I doing something wrong?"

"No," I breathed, struggling to make my words cooperate with me. She kept her eyes locked on mine for what felt like an eternity. She finally released me from her gaze as she stole glances at people around us. She blinked and said something about how some people were staring at us.

Of course they're staring at you. It's not often that someone rivals the beauty of everyone else in the room.

We danced for several more counts. That was when I caught Gisele out of the corner of my eye. Clearly the only thing that had a stronger effect on me than Casey's soft eyes was Gisele's hard eyes. She was peering at us through the crowd as she spoke sideways with one of her guards. Casey squeezed my hand to get my attention.

"What is it?" she asked, looking around to see if she could spot what had caught my gaze. Gisele and two of her guards started making their way towards us, cutting through the crowd. I located Brennon in the mass of people and mapped out my escape route in my head.

"We shouldn't make a habit of this. It's much too civil for us," I said softly in her ear. I spun Casey so that her back brushed against my chest. She angled her face so that I could see her profile. "If she asks, you had no idea who I was. Just a random stranger," I instructed.

"Who?" Casey turned around to ask what I had meant, but I had already darted away, leaving her to greet Gisele.

I ducked around several dancers and servants before I looked back and saw Casey respectfully bowing. Her shoulders were tense and she bit her lip again. It was the perfect response for anyone meeting the queen for the first time. I weaved past some young women who looked at me like I was a dessert, and found Brennon. He was politely trying to fend off the advances of the woman he had been dancing with. He saw me approaching, and his body sighed with relief.

I leaned over the woman's shoulder and whispered, "Your husband is looking for you." She stiffened and immediately skirted away from us.

"She's married?" Brennon asked, alarmed.

"I guess so." I silently disapproved of my own sloppy deductions, but I was still shaken after having been within murdering distance of Gisele. "Let's go."

Brennon followed me around the edges of the crowd. As we moved around people dancing, eating, and drinking, I caught sight of Shep in the crowd, moving towards Gisele, who was still talking to Casey. She appeared uninterested in whatever it was Casey was saying. With Shep present, I felt comfortable leaving Casey alone with her. Brennon and I finally made it to one of the corners of the room. We found the staircase that twisted down to the kitchens and soon found ourselves in the chaos.

Cooks and servants rushed about exchanging empty plates with full ones. The ovens were radiating heat, and the rows upon rows of pots sizzled and popped. Brennon and I were invisible in the madness, so we easily found another door that opened into a staircase. Before we climbed the stairs, we discarded our masks and found ourselves in an empty corridor. The floor was carpeted with a long red rug and paintings depicting animal hunts were hung on the stone walls. I was immediately colder after escaping from the close proximity of hundreds of guests. The warmth from Casey's hand in mine had finally faded, too. The space, however, gave me room to think. The emptiness of the castle didn't unsettle me, because I was used to walking the corridors at night when no one but the guards were about.

Brennon and I silently ran down the hallway, and as we made our way, my mind kept filling the hallway with old memories. I saw myself pacing the corridors, trying to figure out how to get close to the late king. I saw Gisele and me slumped against a wall, still cold from our stroll around the castle grounds. I saw myself bribing one of the late king's advisors as I sought the whereabouts of one of the heirs to the throne. When we had turned two corners and passed through an archway and into the Hall of Records, all my thoughts refocused.

The room went so deep that from where I stood I couldn't even see where it ended. Shelves upon shelves of papers and books lined the room. I heard Brennon make a very unenthusiastic sound. I echoed his remark silently.

Brennon cursed poetically under his breath. "Where do we even start?"

"We'll go row by row. You take one side; I'll take the other. Look for anything that mentions Gisele's suitors, her father's abdication, deals with Azlaya, Dorian Romauld or—" I paused. Greyson's name clung to my lips, but Brennon understood after seeing the expression on my face. We parted ways and started digging through files.

On any other night, I would have read all the scandalous secrets about the royal family, to use as leverage in the future, but on that night, I quickly scanned through official reports. As we searched, I kept track of how much time had passed since we had left the ballroom. When seventy-two minutes had passed, we still hadn't found anything promising. It wasn't until the one-hundred-and-eighth minute that we finally come across something relevant.

"Aiden," Brennon called to me. I pushed some books aside so that I could see him through the shelf. "This document says, 'King Leopold Givaldi received Dorian Romauld, son of Lord Gerard Romauld and suitor for his daughter, Princess Gisele Givaldi, on the eve of the Summer Festival and then something about a feast."

"Pull all those files," I instructed as I shoved what I held back on the shelf.

Dorian Romauld was the alias I had used during my time in Eileen while posing as a suitor. I joined Brennon on his side of the shelf and started rifling through papers. I was amazed by how much of my time at the castle had been documented. Even mundane things like, '*Dorian Romauld and Princess Gisele went for a walk*' were recorded alongside '*King Leopold Givaldi ordered the assassination of Lord Richard Marfont of House Rutherbard for public insubordination against the throne.*'

"Do you see anything about her meeting with Azlaya?" I asked Brennon as I quickly skimmed through another paper.

"I just found her coronation address, so we're getting close," Brennon tried to say reassuringly.

He must have been able to sense my growing impatience. It had been one-hundred-and-forty-seven minutes. Finally, I came across a file I had dreaded finding. It was the detailed report of Greyson's execution. When I was a kid, I was sitting in a tree and watched a jaguar drag a deer up to its perch. It was horrifying, and yet I couldn't take my eyes away from the sight. The same thing happened with the report detailing my brother's death.

A boy, between the ages of ten and thirteen, was sentenced to death by Queen Gisele Givaldi for treason, conspiring against the crown, and aiding and abetting a criminal. He was held overnight in the castle dungeons; he was executed the following morning by having his throat slit. Approximately three minutes after the throat being cut, the boy was pronounced dead. His body—

I finally pulled my eyes away. The world seemed to shrink in the twenty seconds it had taken me to get halfway through the report. The once spacious-feeling room seemed suffocating. Brennon grabbed my attention when he said he had found something.

He handed me the paper, which read '*Queen Gisele Givaldi met privately with a sorceress whose identity is unknown.*'

We both frantically looked up at the shelf and started pulling out books and folders, emptying them of their contents in hopes that the agreement between Azlaya and Gisele was somewhere within. After several minutes of searching, I knew it wasn't there. It was my turn to curse, and I did so without reservations. When I was calm again, I turned back to Brennon, who appeared to be holding back his own swearing.

He pushed his hair back from his face. "I need a drink. I need five drinks."

"I'll treat," I replied, and pulled from my pocket some coins that I had swiped from a man who had been slurring insults at a servant in the ballroom. I offered a hand to Brennon, who was slumped against another shelf, and pulled him to his feet.

I knew that we had spent way too much time away from the ball, and that guests were surely being ushered out onto the streets by now. If we tried to leave through the ballroom, we'd be questioned about where we'd been and everything would only get worse from there. I made a mental map of the castle in my head and envisioned where Casey's room was. It was on the backside of the castle, had a balcony, and was above a courtyard that was nestled next to a mountain face. My mind raced over all the rooms on the exterior until I finally pinpointed which room she had described. I directed Brennon to follow me.

We went back down the hallway with the paintings, turned a corner, and found ourselves in a hall full of taxidermy.

Animals' heads were mounted on the walls, and several had their entire bodies stuffed. They loomed, threatening, as though they could spring alive at any moment and attack. We went through an arch at the end of the hall, made a right turn, and entered another staircase. The whole journey, I could sense Brennon's unease as we kept turning corners and passing things he didn't recognize and couldn't commit to memory fast enough.

"We're almost there," I whispered back to him.

I pushed a door open and breathed a sigh of relief as we finally entered the guest quarters. I quickly scanned the doors, cross-referenced with my mental map, and made my way towards what should have been Casey's room—if my memory served me well. We stopped at the third door on the left, and Brennon rapped on it twice. I heard celebratory toasts and cheers from the streets somewhere off in the distance as we waited several tense seconds.

I heard someone moving cautiously towards the other side of the door. Then, it was wrenched aside abruptly. "What're you two still doing here?" Casey asked alarmed.

Brennon held a finger up to his lips as we pushed past her and bolted the door.

Casey tucked her hair behind her ears and rubbed her eyes. By the look of the partially wet candle wax on her nightstand, she hadn't been in bed for long. "It wasn't in the Hall of Records?" she asked as she fought off a yawn.

Brennon shook his head in response. I was already analyzing our exit route from the window. The roof slanted at a fairly sharp angle, and we were too high off the ground to launch ourselves from it. We would have to slow our momentum, move around to the spire to our right, and climb down the outside. The stones on the wall's exterior were uneven enough that we would have handholds as we descended the tower.

I turned away from the window and saw that Brennon was already nursing a drink that had been put out for Casey. His body didn't look fatigued, but his eyes did. Casey had nestled into a couch and curled her feet under her. Her hair was no longer elaborately braided and wrapped around her head, as it had been earlier. Now, it fell in soft waves around her shoulders. She had exchanged her dramatic, black gown for a white nightgown and a red robe. I was happy to see that all the makeup that had been caked onto her face earlier had been washed away. She shifted, making her robe fall off her shoulder exposing the gentle curve of her neck. I saw her muscles tense and relax as she listened intently to whatever it was Brennon was saying. He finished telling her about our failed attempt at finding the document.

"What did Gisele have to say to you?" I cut in abruptly.

Casey turned towards me, her hair covering the bit of exposed skin. "She introduced herself and then asked who you were. I told her what you said—that you were just a stranger who'd asked me to dance. She got bored right away." I nodded.

Though her tone was causal, her gaze was more intense, as though already trying to calm any nightmares that were starting to creep to the surface. It was a much harder look than the unguarded, softened one I'd received earlier at the ball. I briefly wondered under what circumstances that expression might return to her face. Brennon set down the bottle he'd been drinking from with a satisfied thud.

I went back to the window and called Brennon over. Casey rose and joined us. "Need me to prop this one open too?"

I grinned sideways at her joke and pushed the windows open. I climbed out onto the balcony and swung over the side.

"Get some rest, Casey. The first event is tomorrow," Brennon said to her before climbing out behind me.

I let go of the balcony and slid down the roof, digging my heels in to slow my descent. Brennon followed my lead, and before we slinked off into the night, the last thing I saw was Casey leaning out of the balcony, making sure we hadn't flown off the roof. Her hand twitched with a goodbye wave. And, like earlier, I held her gaze for a second too long before Brennon and I disappeared into the night.

Back at the inn, I was on edge in a way that I hadn't been in a long time, and I wasn't sure it was because of Gisele anymore. My mind hummed with worries for Casey's safety. But she wasn't fragile and untrained like Greyson had been. Still, as I stared at the stone façade from my window, I couldn't help but wish that I were only a room away from her.

My feet pounded the ground beneath me. My arms pumped madly. My heart raced. My lungs begged for air. I couldn't tell if I was running towards something, or away. Both sensations gripped me, and I wasn't able to discern which was worse.

Suddenly, I hit a thick wall. I turned and found I was trapped. A rancid smell invaded my nose and I gagged. I clawed at the wall, hoping that there was a divot, a hole, or anything I could use to start climbing it. Yes, there was! I grabbed hold. Then, I heard his voice behind me.

"Aiden?" Greyson whimpered. "Aiden, I want to go home."

I dropped from the wall and faced him. His blonde hair was caked in mud, and what I assumed was blood. His eyes were red from what I knew was hours of crying. But he wasn't alone. My friends from the Night's Guild, Kai among them, surrounded me.

Then, one by one, they started dying. Shamus buckled under an onslaught of arrows. Tobias collapsed in a pool of blood pouring from his mouth. Zachary's head fell to the ground with a thud. Luca screamed as his skin melted from his bones. And Kai just stared at me while a stake was driven through her heart.

Blood started gushing from a wound on Greyson's neck. I rushed to him and tried to stop the bleeding, the blank gazes of my friends still on me. Nothing worked. I couldn't save him. I couldn't save any of them. I never could. I staggered backwards. How many times would I have to realize this truth?

Suddenly I was restrained. The deaths of my brother and friends repeated themselves, but this time, I was shooting the arrow, I was holding the poison, I was swinging the axe, I was stoking the fire, I was gripping the stake, I was wielding the dagger. It was all me.

I struggled against my bonds, trying desperately to free myself and stop my other self from killing. I felt Gisele's presence before I heard her.

"Their blood is on your hands."

"STOP!" I called out to myself. "DON'T!"

Each of them begged me for mercy with their eyes as they were cut down. Gisele's delighted cackle filled my ears. I couldn't block out their screams. I couldn't run. I had to sit and endure their deaths in a continuous loop. My throat grew hoarse from trying to call myself off.

My desperate begging faded into fitful whispering. "Please stop. Please stop. Please stop."

Gisele surrounded me. Her face shifted back and forth between her older and younger self. Her unkind eyes and hard mouth remained unchanged. I felt the unmistakable coolness of a dagger at my throat.

"Do it." I surrendered, wanting the torment to be over.

"No. This I want you to live with forever."

I closed my eyes. When I opened them again, a new nightmare had materialized before me. I could never save the people I cared about in my dreams, and this crushing truth settled in when I saw Casey.

I jumped awake and reached for the spot on my arm where Casey had infused the Sleeping spell. My hand trembled as I tried to remember the sensation of her touch while burying my ghosts in the deep crevices of my memory. I opened my hand where I had held hers and wondered if the tingling I'd felt was a figment of my imagination, or if she really did have that kind of effect on me. It seemed her appearance in my dreams confirmed it though.

I nestled into a vigil of watching the castle. Soon, I had a drink in hand and sat in silence as I tried to tuck Casey into a corner of my mind. I found out, several hours later, that I wasn't able to fold her away as easily as I could other people. She floated through my thoughts, unlabeled and untethered. What I knew for sure, though, was that when she looked at me while we danced, something in her eyes reflected things I couldn't say.

It was probably a good thing that we were held captive by our history of animosity. I would have to rely on that as a barrier between us, because I couldn't risk thinking about Casey as I had during the ball. I couldn't give her the power to draw me away from the abyss that lay at my feet.

Chapter 28: Kate

IT WAS STRANGE to me how quickly I had become desensitized to people's screams. Especially, the shrill, strangled ones that blended with sobbing. This was the concerto that started when a captured sorcerer laid eyes on the Sagen who were waiting to escort them to the Shadowlands. My first couple of captures, I had winced and drawn away from them, but I hardly heard their suffering anymore. Zayne was even colder. He didn't even blink.

In the beginning, I used combat spells to disarm other sorcerers. Though, Zayne soon convinced me to use Dark Magic as a way to preserve energy. Instead of engaging in a full-blown battle, we started pushing into our opponents' minds, twisting their realities until they couldn't even fight us. By that point, they were so weak that their captures became much easier. He'd also taught me how to make a circle like the one he'd first caught me in. I'd used it a few times while tracking down sorcerers, but soon came to realize that I enjoyed the labor of the hunt. Incapacitating my targets was so uneventful.

I stood over a middle-aged man, while he pleaded with me to release the hold on his mind. I felt his powers trying to resist and tightened my grip on his thoughts. I presumed that the piercing siren sounds I created in his ears, the sensation of a collapsing chest, and the visions of him murdering his wife and children, would be enough to cripple him into compliance, but he was stubborn. Zayne could sense my mounting frustration.

"You're getting close," he encouraged me from behind.

We were in a square courtyard, which was behind the man's house. Zayne had felt his presence, and we had found him in his garden. He hadn't felt the need to attack us, until I was already assaulting his mind with my powers. It had become my specialty, especially after feeling all the satisfaction I'd gotten from doing very similar things to Casey not so long ago.

"Please—stop—please," the man said in labored breaths. I pushed deeper, thinking how most sorcerers we had encountered would have broken a long time ago. He sank to his knees and clutched his head. His cheeks were bright red from when he had tried to scratch his eyes out. My hand had grown tense, lost all feeling, tingled, and then gone numb again in the time I'd spent trying to break this sorcerer's defenses. I finally gave my hand a violent twist, and immediately I felt the wall crumble.

The man fell onto his hands so that he was on all fours. Zayne stepped around me and hauled the man to his feet. He swayed and looked at Zayne without any recognition of what had happened moments before.

"Are his powers intact?" I asked. During one of these encounters, I had gone too far in penetrating a sorcerer's mind and had decimated his powers, rendering him useless for the Sagen.

Zayne let the man slump back against a wall. "Yes, they're fine." He turned back to me and smirked, his face full of pride. "Well done. This must be the strongest one you've done yet."

A Sagen collected the man, and Zayne and I returned to our hunt.

I smiled faintly, but on the inside I was beaming. I was getting better and better at breaking people's will. It was an extremely useful tactic that Zayne had shown me. He had me practice on weaker sorcerers we encountered. I'd watched him do it a few times before he decided to teach me. It was kind of like snapping a twig. You're left with two parts of one whole, but since they're separated, the connection between them is gone. It's the same concept with one's mind: break the connection between the willpower and the conscience, and all power of resistance is lost.

Zayne told me about one of his old mentors who had been able to split someone's mind with a snap of his fingers. When I asked about his mentors, he would only tell me that they lived in the mountains, isolated from the rest of society. He didn't tell me much else, except that eventually he would take me to meet them. Soon though, I was confident that I'd be able to surpass even his mentors' abilities. My powers were hungry for more practice, and every time I exercised them, they still yearned. Their appetite was insatiable.

Only a handful of minutes passed before we both sensed the presence of another sorcerer. Zayne and I jogged down the quiet street and veered off onto a smaller side street. We came upon a wide alley that stopped in a dead end. We spotted an old woman and exchanged glances. Her hair was grey and tied in a headscarf, and her hunched body was huddled under a thick coat. A quick glimpse of her thoughts told me she was a widow, so there was no husband to cast a Sleeping spell over while we dragged her away.

I nudged Zayne forward with my eyes. Though I wanted to, I couldn't have all the fun all the time. I watched him from a distance as he disarmed the sorcerer. He was always so sharp and precise. I had summoned a Sagen before the duel even started, and it had arrived just as it finished. It couldn't have taken more than two minutes for Zayne to overpower the sorceress. After the Sagen left, he rejoined me at the other end of the alley where I leaned against the wall. If anyone had passed, they would have thought I was waiting for someone, not that I was guarding the alley so no one saw the duel beyond.

"Thanks for that one," Zayne said lightly as he stretched his arms, as though they were sore.

"I *do* know how to share, you know."

His mouth twisted devilishly. He pinned me against the wall and planted a kiss solidly on my lips. My heart was electrified into a gallop in my chest. I don't know how long we stayed like that. The rare passerby hardly gave us a second glance, because, after all, we just looked like a love-struck couple. I thought fleetingly that Jackson and I had only kissed this aggressively when we had gotten into a fight and used it as a why to make up. It was rough and raw with emotion.

Zayne and I had nothing to make up for, yet the way he tugged my hair, and the way I dug my fingers into his back, only made us want each other more. We really were a strange pair. We both loved the spark we'd feel when our powers jumped to life, and we both loved being in control. We shouldn't have been able to mix as well as we did, but somehow our clashing amplified our abilities, rather than destroying them. I fed off him, just as he fed off me. We were stronger together than we were apart. That much I knew was true; everything else was peripheral.

I finally pulled away from him when I felt snow brushing my cheeks. My hands were on the sides of his face, and I forced him to look towards the sky, too. When I felt his body arch with even more desire, I slipped under his arm and took several steps away from him. I swung my hips to taunt him.

"Come on. Azlaya wanted us to check in with her after we finished up here," I said to him.

His mouth twisted into a wicked smile. "*I* wasn't finished yet."

I summoned another Sagen to transport us back to the Shadowlands so we didn't expend any more energy. The Sagen touched our shoulders, and the reverberating sensation overtook us. I felt my body leaving Eileen and starting to solidify in the Shadowlands. A few seconds passed before we were thoroughly in the Shadowlands.

I opened my eyes and found myself in my old room in the castle. I brushed past the bed, and Zayne and I went to the depths of the castle. I called out for Azlaya and heard her voice through a door I hadn't noticed beforehand. She quickly emerged and wiped what I could only assume was blood off one of her fingers. She carried an ancient-looking book under her arm. I caught a glimpse of the author: *Mikhail.* I raised an eyebrow, recognizing the name as the one from the book filled with the ancient Aelonian language that contained the steps to binding myself to the Sagen. She swept aside my unasked questions and motioned for us to sit. Azlaya placed the book before her and sat at the head of the table. I took my place to her right, and Zayne beside me.

"From what the Sagen have been telling me, you two have collected some very powerful sorcerers. Your alliance with the Muskoxen has also proved very beneficial. I commend you." Azlaya then angled her body so that what she said next was clearly directed at me alone. "You need to discover where your mother's remains are." I nodded and received a curious glance from Zayne.

I decided not to question the strange request. "Who would know where they are? The Hunters?"

"Start there. Once you find them, everything else will begin to fall in place." I crossed my arms over my chest and peered at Azlaya questioningly. It was so unlike her to give me this much freedom. I knew she was preoccupied with something, but I still didn't know exactly what. "I know you've been wondering what it is I've been doing," Azlaya added, breaking into my train of thought.

"How couldn't I? We've been rounding up sources of power for this army, and meanwhile you've been here— *reading?*" I gestured towards the book.

She flashed her sharp eyes at me. I felt Zayne's interest pique as a sudden wave of tension filled the atmosphere. "I've been busy searching for something as well." Her voice was gentle, but hardened by the edge of her biting tone.

"What?" I asked.

"An ally who could overpower you, me, and even your mother, at her prime."

"Do you require help?" Zayne interjected diplomatically.

Azlaya hardly changed her position to acknowledge him. This had become *our* conversation. "No. I can handle this alone."

"That's all you're going to tell me?" I asked a little exasperated. "Does it have anything to do with Mikhail?" I flicked my eyes towards the book.

I received another look of warning, though by her expression, it seemed I had guessed correctly. Still, she wouldn't reveal her plans to me.

"In time," she said icily. "For now, finding your mother's resting place will be your responsibility."

Zayne and I retreated back into my room. I stood at my window and tried, unsuccessfully, to ignore the bars obstructing my view as I thought. I drummed my fingers restlessly on the sill. Zayne had apparently sat patiently on my bed for too long and broke into my trance.

"Why does she want you to find your mother's remains?" I turned to face him. The pale light from outside cast a sickly grey color over his skin. The indecision in my head displayed on my face, and Zayne noticed it. "You can tell me, Kate."

I quickly thought through all the reasons not to tell him, but I couldn't think of any legitimate ones. I'd come to trust him. "Azlaya is helping me reunite with my mom."

"But isn't she—" His voice was edgy, but he softened his face to compensate.

"Dead? Yes, but I'm going to bring her back," I told him plainly.

His eyes narrowed. "Can't be done."

I crossed my arms over my chest. "It can. And I'm going to do it." My resolve was undeniable.

Zayne's face relaxed into what I took as submission to what I'd said. "You're serious?"

"Completely."

He laughed tersely and pushed at locks of hair that had fallen in his eyes. He shook his head back and forth, but a frozen grin hung on his face. "You're going to reverse death."

"Interesting, no?" I asked seductively.

"A master of death—" he breathed absentmindedly. His eyes settled on me, which brought his mind back to the matter at hand. "You have my attention. What needs to be done?" His eagerness seethed into his words.

"Apparently, the first thing we need to do is find her remains." That was a sentence I'd never imagined saying before.

"So we need to find out who buried her. Who was she with when she died?"

"The Hunters," I answered, thinking about the story Azlaya had told me about how they had murdered my mother, because they feared she was growing too powerful. "They killed her."

"Find a Hunter who remembers that day—"

"And we find out what happened to her." I finished his sentence, regardless of whether that was what he was going to say. "Who would remember?"

"Kyraine Redding—isn't that her name? The leader."

"The Mistress of the Hunt?" I scoffed. "She'll be too difficult to capture. We need someone who was there, but whose absence wouldn't be as conspicuous."

Zayne rubbed at his growing stubble. I resumed my impatient tapping. "What if we went to the Hunters' camp and peered into everyone's minds. We get a comprehensive view of everyone's internal knowledge, and we can narrow down whom to target, efficiently and effectively."

A smirk spread on my lips as I thought through his idea. As I worked through all the details, I realized how realistic the plan was. "Yeah, that could work."

Zayne rose from the edge of my bed and closed the distance between us so that our hipbones grazed each other's. "With both of us, it *will* work."

"You think we're unstoppable?" I asked mockingly.

"Well, don't you?" Zayne greedily stole a kiss from my lips before I could reply. I pushed him away, but realized I wanted more, too, and yanked him back towards me. "We could become the most powerful pair of sorcerers in all of Alagia—in the history of Alagia."

I leaned away from him to see how serious he was. His lips didn't tug at the corners with a lighthearted grin, and I found no traces of facetiousness on his face. His even stare beckoned me to agree with what he'd said. He was waiting for me to jump on board and verbally commit myself to a cause that I had probably already committed to emotionally.

His soft breath brushed across my nose, and I realized then that his hunger for power was undeniable. He wanted respect from those around him. He wanted to be recognized after being brushed aside for so long. He wanted appreciation for his abilities. And above all, he wanted to live free of any shackles that had been placed on him in the past. I saw every part of myself reflected in his eyes. We wanted all the same things from life. No—we demanded the same things from life. I had been forced to hide my true abilities, and thus a part of myself, for so long.

With Zayne, I could completely release my powers and reach my full potential. The only other time I had felt my powers surge inside me with such strength was when I had first stepped into Alagia.

My words fell from my mouth like honey, slow and sweet. "You are the most exquisite being I've ever met."

"I bet that line works on all the guys."

I smiled devilishly. "Just the foolish ones."

Zayne guided my lips to his. Who signs a pact with a handshake anyway?

Chapter 29: Casey

SERVANTS WOKE ME early the next morning. They brought a platter of thinly sliced meats, cheeses, and fruits. Another group arrived shortly after with the clothes I would wear during the tournament. I learned in Calem that protesting while someone was trying to dress you was pointless, so I kept my mouth shut and allowed the servants to proceed.

My nightgown was being tugged over my head and brown pants were pulled over my hips. More clothing was added and tied and fastened until finally they stepped away, and I looked at my reflection in the mirror. The whole outfit was a brown, earthy color. The pants hugged my legs and were tucked into fur-lined boots. The shirt was long-sleeved and made of a warm, wool fabric, and over it I wore another sweater and a thick jacket, with coattails and a fur hood. I became acutely aware of how hot I was under all the fur and layers, as a thin coat of sweat formed on my back.

I followed an escort from my room and down the corridors of the castle. Other people, whom I recognized as other competitors who had taken the stage with me the night before, started to spill into the hallways as well. After several twists, turns, and two flights of stairs, we were outside. Immediately, I was thankful for the brisk air. By the looks of the sky, some form of precipitation looked imminent. In the circle drive in front of the castle, horse-drawn carriages were waiting. They were incredibly ornate, decorated with gold, blue and red patterns. The horses were black and had been covered in gold glitter so that they shimmered, even with the overcast sky. They wore brightly colored feather-headdresses. It was clear that whoever chose the styling did not want us to be missed as we passed.

I was directed into the third of eight carriages. I nestled into one of the seats and was soon joined by two other people: a young man and a young woman. The inside of the carriage was complete with red velvet cushions. The door was closed and before long, we were making our way towards the arena. When we were beyond the boundaries of Queen Gisele's castle, people were already gathered on the streets waiting for us. I had been to, and been in, enough parades in my lifetime to be familiar with the sensation of being carted through crowds of people, though my stomach was doing flips as we neared the arena. Unlike the others in my carriage, I wasn't taken by the fame that had suddenly engulfed us, but rather by the hoards of people that had come out to see us on our way to the tournament. Even in the brutally cold weather, families, couples, children, and older individuals alike filled the streets, cheering as we rode past. No wonder Queen Gisele had insisted that the tournament occur as usual, despite the impending conflict with Azlaya's growing army. People were totally enthralled by it.

I turned away from the window and noticed the young woman, who was sitting diagonally from me, seemed quite unenthusiastic about the whole thing. Her dark skin absorbed the silver light from outside and made it appear warmer. Her lips were pulled taught and her eyes seemed determined to narrowly gaze at everything they slid over. The young man sitting next to her suddenly nudged her excitedly and pointed to something outside his window. She looked lazily out the window, and responded with an indifferent look. Her eyes and face softened enough for me to believe that they knew each other. Even the way he touched her so willingly, despite the abrasive vibe she gave off, told me that this was a side of her with which he was familiar.

"I can't believe how many people came out!" the young man exclaimed. "Oh, Sev, look! Those kids have a sign with our names on them. They must have traveled from Canabar."

He turned back to her, and she feigned a smile. He was bubbly, to say the least. His skin was a caramel color and his black hair was cropped close to his head. He had bright eyes and a face that looked friendly, even when there was no expression on it.

"I can't even picture how many people will be in the arena when it's full. I've never even seen it before. Have you?" He asked me.

I took my eyes off a crowd of excited students chanting some sort of cheer, and turned to the young man. "No. I've never been this far south before. I'm from up north, from the mountain region." He smiled, while the girl glanced me over disapprovingly. "I'm Kai Frost."

"Ikede Ono, and this is my friend, Sev Amani. We're from Canabar." A violent shiver suddenly shook his body. "And very ill adjusted to the weather. A snowstorm and sandstorm—very different," he said, while smiling widely.

My eyes moved from Ikede to his friend, which was like moving away from the warmth of a fire. "Sev? Is that short for something?"

Her cool brown eyes swept over me as though determining my worth. "Seven," she said so firmly that I pursed my lips and turned back to Ikede.

"What made you want to enter the tournament?" I asked.

Ikede's eyes brightened as he leaned towards me. "Well the adventure, of course." My face fell a bit. "Too many people die without ever truly living. They spend their lives at court, behind castle walls, cooking for others, washing linens. Mundane things that eat away at one's existence. But I don't want to be like that. I want to live freely. I want to brush up against Death and stare it down until it blinks first. I want everything this life has to offer and nothing less. We only get one after all," he exclaimed.

I could only imagine the startled look on my face at Ikede's declaration. "And both of you feel this way?" I said unevenly, stealing a look at Sev's face.

"Oh no." Ikede leaned back. "Sev finds my outlook on the world naïve and foolish. Those were the words you used, weren't they?" Ikede said to Sev.

"The very same."

Ikede shrugged playfully. "We can't all be dreamers. And what about you, Kai? Why have you come?"

"My family could use the prize money," I answered simply. Ikede nodded understandingly, as though he had keen insight into the hardships my fake family endured.

"Money," he scoffed, "the poison of the world—"

"Ikede, do shut up. You're missing everything outside," Sev cut him off harshly. He immediately retreated back to his window to take in the sights, though his mood hadn't been affected in the slightest.

I couldn't figure out the relationship between the two of them. They were clearly very familiar and comfortable with one another, judging by the way they spoke. They could be siblings, but Ikede's skin was a warm, caramel color while Sev's was a deep brown. His eyes were wider than hers, and his nose broader. They were at least friends, though the dynamics of the friendship were still unclear as we approached the arena.

I soon followed Ikede's lead and found myself staring out the window at the arena. It was oval in shape and massive in size. There appeared to be five stories, indicated by different stonework at each new level. At the top there were hundreds of flags that flapped in the wind with snow leopards, the Eileenian sigil, stitched onto them. Thousands of people crowded the streets now, waiting for us to arrive. I could only guess that thousands more were inside the arena. I briefly thought that I would never be able to find Aiden and Brennon in this chaos. The carriages slid to a halt, and the door was opened. The once dulled applause and cheering spilled into the carriage at a thunderous volume.

Sev gathered her furs around her as she stepped into the brisk weather, with Ikede on her heels. I stepped out behind them and tried not to let my inner anxiety show on my face. I couldn't, however, keep my lips from parting as I stared up at two gargantuan statues—a male and female warrior, engaged in a sword fight—that created an entrance archway. They were so huge that I barely came up to their ankles. They looked fierce, each with a snarl frozen on their lips, and I could imagine the ear-splitting clang that had occurred moments before when their swords came into contact with one another. It was a masterfully-rendered battle, captured in time, and it undoubtedly set the mood for what was to come. Guards in black armor quickly shuffled us through the crowd as other guards had cleared a pathway for us under the entryway statues. People hollered out to us and some even tossed flower petals as we passed beneath them.

We entered and found ourselves within the arena walls. I followed closely behind Ikede as we rounded the building, but as I looked deeper, I could just see the innermost parts of the structure where the tournament events were to be held. I couldn't understand why there were so many trees, though. We were finally led to a cramped area where the other competitors stood waiting behind a large, iron-grate door. Cheering and applause shook the stone walls. It all reminded me of stories of ancient Rome and the games of the Coliseum, except that hoped I wasn't fighting to my death—at least, I hope, not on the first day.

Lost in thought, I hadn't realized that the crowd had finally quieted. Someone was speaking to them. An announcer, I guessed. Suddenly, a roar emerged from inside. The noise died down again, only to be followed by another bout of loud cheering, but this time, the iron-grate door was lifted, and we were allowed to march out into the arena. As we stepped out from the cover of the stone walls, the snow fell harder, and began sticking to my fur-lined clothing and my hair. I batted a couple of snowflakes from my eyelashes as I gazed up at the scores of people crammed into the arena.

"Wow. One-hundred thousand people," someone behind me breathed in awe.

The atmosphere was electrifying, and robust with energy. It was a feeling I was familiar with, having played at several soccer state championships, but this was something else entirely. This must have been how athletes felt as they walked into the Olympics or professional football players into their stadiums. I lowered my gaze and was stunned to find what looked like a forest in the middle of the arena. I had been expecting sand, stone, or even mud, but the wooded area took me by surprise. Perhaps they had recreated a forest for the event, but what required trees and shrubbery?

Our single-file line came to a halt and we turned to face a purple canopy that sheltered the queen and some of her subjects. Her eyes were icy and dull, just as they were the night before when she had asked me with whom I was dancing. Her fiery hair was in a tight bun at the nape of her neck and she wore a white fur hat. Her dress was dark blue and around her shoulders she had a white fur cloak that reached the ground. Her hands were clasped in a matching fur muff, but she drew one out and held it up to quell the boisterous crowd.

An announcer stepped forward and began to list the names of the competitors. I watched anxiously as names were called. Some people blew kisses at the crowd, others made aggressive punching motions, and one man even flexed his muscles, which were hidden under layers of fur. Each person, however, bowed to the queen first. When Sev's name was called, she curtly bowed and stepped back in line. Ikede bounced forward, bowed, and touched his forehead with two fingers and then gestured to the crowd. That earned him an extra loud applause from the present Canabarians.

My "name" was finally called. I stepped forward, and my eyes met with the queen's. In that moment, everything Aiden had told me about her gripped my thoughts, and my expression revealed my distaste for her before I, too, lowered my head. When I straightened, I could just see the remnants of a curious, but guarded, smirk on her otherwise expressionless face. I stepped back in line, but our gazes stayed frozen on one another. As several more names were read, we studied each other for another minute, until the announcer turned the crowd's attention back to the queen.

She rose from her silver chair and motioned for silence. "Welcome to the Tournament of Eileen," she cried. "Today our competitors will duel in an event that will not only test their skills, but their eye for strategy as well. In this event, two teams will compete to reclaim flags that have been scattered throughout their enemy's territory. Capturing these flags is the goal, but you may be captured as well. You will each be given a key that unlocks the shackles of captured teammates. The first team to reclaim all of their flags and team members wins. The losing team will have ended their journey in the games."

A soldier in armor was going down the line and tying a red or blue ribbon around our arms to distinguish the two teams, and hooking a key onto our belts. Once we were all labeled, we were allowed to choose our weapons, which had been carted out in wagons. I realized that they were all wooden, so this must have been an event in which we were only disarming one another, not killing. I breathed a sigh of relief as I grabbed a blue, wooden sword. Others picked wooden maces, staffs and hammers.

"You have sixty seconds to get to your territory, marked by the trees. When the horn sounds, the game begins," Queen Gisele announced before she nestled back into her chair.

I turned on my heel and ran to join the other blue team members, who were disappearing quickly into the trees. After everything, strange and new, that I'd seen that day, running through trees, jumping over rocks, and brushing aside shrubs was comforting. For a few seconds, I felt like I was back in the woods, running through the Hunters' camps. Then, the horn sounded.

I ran for a couple more paces and then slowed myself to a halt. My heart thumped in my chest; I waited for my breathing to even, and I listened. I heard rustling in the distance. My eyes scanned the trees and realized that every few trees were painted with blue paint, designating that I was in my home territory. I peered through the canopy of trees and could see the crowd, who had fallen into a muttering trance as they waited for something exciting to happen. I walked through the artificial forest, trying to commit a path to memory to keep myself oriented. My feet led me towards the edge of the trees, and it was there that I found the "captured" post. An iron chain was wrapped around a thick tree, with shackles hanging from it. I assumed that the field was set up symmetrically, which meant that when my teammates were captured, they would be at the farthest end of the forest on the opposite side.

A sudden cheer erupted from the crowd. I spun to see if someone was coming, but I still hadn't seen anyone. I was tempted to use my powers to scan the trees, but Aiden had warned me a number of times to not use my sorcery, especially with all the disappearances of sorcerers. Not to mention, the tournament officials would surely report me if they suspected I had used sorcery, which was considered illegal in the games. Instead, I thought back to everything I had learned with the Hunters. I crouched low to the ground, trained my gaze ahead, and listened silently.

There was activity to my left, and more to my right. Whatever was happening on my right, though, held my attention. It sounded like a chase, in which one person didn't know how to run through a forest. The crashing through and slashing at branches would have made the Hunters shake with fury. It was probably the way I sounded when I had first started to learn how to maneuver through the forest. The sound came closer with each second until finally I could see who it was.

"Ikede?"

He wore a blue ribbon and the person chasing him wore red. I rose from my position and darted forward so that I could intercept the tall man that chased Ikede.

I ran parallel to them for a while, trying to exceed their pace so that I could intersect their path farther ahead. My feet pounded into the frozen ground, and the fur started to make my body sweat heavily. I finally passed them, stopped, and waited. Ikede darted clumsily through the underbrush, saw me, tripped and tumbled to the ground. I raised my sword just as the other man burst through and almost plowed me over. I swung at him, swift and hard, knocking his mace clean out of his unsuspecting hand. I lunged forward, driving my foot into the ground and the man flew through the air. Applause sounded above me. As the man moved to stand, I gently rested my sword by his neck.

"Consider yourself captured," I said.

Ikede had straightened himself up and was brushing dirt off his pants. "Masterful move, Kai," he exclaimed shakily after his fall.

I motioned for him to collect his sword and help me escort our captive back to the post. We walked in silence to the post where I shackled the man, who looked several years my senior, to the tree.

A young woman, who looked close to my age, darted out of the trees and skidded to a stop before us. I checked for her blue ribbon before greeting her with a slight nod. "I just came from the red territory. I can watch the captured post while I catch my breath," she wheezed.

I nodded and called for Ikede to follow me away from the captured post and towards the red territory. We kept to the outskirts of the forest, trying to avoid any red team members. We reached trees bearing red paint, and I slowed our pace until we walked quietly. The crowd cheered at something in the distance, and Ikede jumped a bit. I thought nothing of his nervousness, figuring it was just the stakes of the game. He suddenly grabbed my arm and pointed to something in the trees. My gaze fell on a blue flag flapping in the breeze. It was tied to a branch several feet up the tree.

"Good eye," I said to Ikede as I raced towards the tree. "Keep watch," I said, as I fastened my sword in my belt and started to climb the tree.

Thankfully the branches were thick and there were many, making climbing easier. When I was halfway to the flag, I heard a yelp from below. I looked down and saw that two red team members were attacking Ikede. I scrambled up the tree and ripped the flag down, stuffing it into my pocket. Then, I scurried down and took off after Ikede.

I guessed that we were still on the outskirts of the arena and far from the "captured" post of the red team, so I called out to them to get their attention. A woman with light skin and pale hair, who looked to be in her forties, and man with darker skin, who looked a little older than me, turned. The man clenched Ikede's cloak at his throat, aggressively tossed him aside, and growled at him not to move. When Ikede made no move to jump up and help me in defense, I swore under my breath in disbelief.

The woman rushed me with a sword. The wood on wood contact was a foreign sound to my ears, since I had never used anything but metal swords. The wooden ones were much lighter though, and therefore quicker. They sliced through the air at speeds I didn't even think I was capable of maintaining, but I knew that my sword skills matched, and probably surpassed, those of the woman's. The man joined the fight, and soon I was fending off a sword and staff, each threatening to make a deafening blow to my head. I swung, ducked left, jabbed right and lunged back. Each move was calculated to maximize the chances of disarming one of them while not getting hit by the other. It wasn't often that I practiced fighting two attackers, and I could just picture Brennon sitting in the stands somewhere taking note of each mistake I made.

The staff finally broke my defenses and swept my feet out from under me. My back hit the ground hard, and my breath was knocked from me. I raised my sword to protect my face, but it was kicked from my hands. A sharp pain exploded through my abdomen after the man struck me in the stomach with his staff. A nasty fit of coughs burst from me.

"Get him; I'll take care of her," the man ordered. He towered over me with a much-too-smug look on his face, and something that made my skin crawl gleamed in his eyes. He lowered his staff so that it rested inches from my face. "Don't try anything, sweetheart."

Just then, the woman shrieked in surprise. I turned my head to see what had happened when Sev appeared, sword held high. She attacked so abruptly that both the man and woman were caught off guard. I jumped at the opportunity. I wrapped my hands around the staff and violently shoved it in he man's direction. It connected with his throat, and he collapsed to his knees, clutching his windpipe and wheezing. I scrambled to my feet and collected his staff and my sword. Sev had overpowered the woman and now clutched the back of her collar.

"Ikede," she snapped. "Pick up your sword. Let's go."

She pushed the woman forward, and I grabbed the younger man in the same fashion and followed her. He shot me a dirty look and snarled hoarsely, "Were you trying to kill me?"

"No," I replied, "because if I was, you'd be dead."

Ikede stumbled after us. His face was aroused with all kinds of excitement and curiosity at everything he had just seen. When I saw that he was dragging his sword on the ground behind him, I knew he wasn't trained to use it at all. We followed

Sev back to the "captured" post and chained up our newest captives. The young woman, who had taken over my post, still lingered nearby. I noticed for the first time that a rope with hooks on it was strung between two trees. On two of the hooks, blue flags fluttered. I pulled a third from where I had tucked it into my belt and went to hook it on the rope with the others.

"Two more to go," Sev breathed. She faced me. "I passed a group of six earlier who were taking turns going into the red territory to search for flags. Five others were patrolling our territory to capture red team members."

"And the four of us here," I said, gesturing to the other young woman in the distance, "makes fifteen. It adds up." A chattering noise made me spin to find Ikede huddled under his furs, rubbing his arms to stay warm. His sword lay idly on the ground. I observed him silently for a few moments. "Ikede, pick up sword," I ordered him softly.

His eyes flicked from me, to Sev, and then back to me. He hesitantly reached down and raised it in front of him. His stance, his grip, even his breathing was wrong. I lifted my own sword, studied him for a minute, and then lunged forward. He immediately flinched and stumbled backwards. I lowered my sword and exclaimed in exasperation, "What the hell is a person who doesn't know how to fight doing here?"

He looked hurt momentarily. "I told you; I'm here for the adventure." His words were limp, without the conviction he'd had before. I turned to Sev. "You're his friend. Why did you let him come here?"

Her face hardened, and her fierce eyes narrowed. "He couldn't be talked out of it. Trust me, I tried many times and in many ways."

"Don't blame Sev. I entered upon my own volition. She only came along to keep an eye out for me."

"You do realize that people die in these games? And others will kill to win them."

"I wanted this. I *needed* this. My life needed some excitement."

My brow had furrowed in confusion. "Then go travel the world—see a horse race—meet a king."

"I've done all that," Ikede cried indignantly. "I wanted to explore something more. Something more thrilling."

My face was a still mask of disbelief. I couldn't believe I was having this argument here and now. I blinked several times to make sure I was seeing this mad man clearly.

"I don't expect you to understand. Sev has known me my whole life, and even she doesn't understand it. Do you, Sev?" She didn't respond to his inquiry. "Sev?"

I broke from my fixation and looked to Sev. She had her eyes trained on something in the distance. She kept changing the angle of her head slightly as though she was listening for something. I went to her side and peered in the same direction.

"What is it?" I asked her.

"Whatever it is, it's not human."

In the distance, a sound floated through the air. It sounded like a growl, but it wasn't low and guttural like Adalia's or the Hunters' wolves. This growl was higher and sent chills down my spine. It grew louder. Sev and I raised our weapons, as she ordered Ikede to get behind us. Then, the rustling became more audible. Suddenly, a white cat, speckled with black spots, jumped out from a bush. It was long and lean, though it only seemed to come up to my waist. Its yellow teeth were bared, and I noticed fresh blood stained some of its fur by the corner of its mouth.

"That's a snow leopard!" Ikede exclaimed. "My goodness, I've never seen a real one before. I've read about them in—"

"SHUT UP!" Sev and I hissed. The cat began to pace in a wide arch, and we moved to counter its advance.

The cat crouched low, its tail flicking back and forth. Then, it sprung forward. The spectators responded accordingly. It headed towards Sev, but veered to the right when it spotted Ikede cowering behind us. I dove to the side and shoved Ikede out of the way, just it time to try to strike the cat as it leapt towards me. I hit one of its legs as I fell to the ground and watched in fear as a mass of fur came crashing down on top of me. Sharp claws sliced at me, and I was immediately grateful for the multiple layers. I kicked at its body and tried desperately to push its bared fangs away from my face. A searing pain ripped across my cheek as one of its claws cut through my skin. I rolled to the side and felt more claws dangerously close to breaking the skin on my back. I heard a hissing screech, and then the cat's weight fell away from me.

I lifted my head to see Sev wrestling with the leopard. I stared in awe, as I had never before seen anyone handle a wild animal as she was. She fearlessly tangled with it as though they were playing, and not trying to kill each other. She had her arms wrapped around its neck, and her legs straddled its midsection. She struggled to keep it pinned down, but eventually it collapsed under her weight and growled ferociously against her. She finally got a firm grip around its neck and as I realized that she was about to snap it, Ikede shouted.

"SEV, DON'T!" She hesitated. Her wild eyes met Ikede's. "That's the sigil animal of Eileen. You can't kill it. The Law says—"

"I know what the Law says," she growled, cutting him off.

"We would execute anyone who killed our sigil back home. This is no different," Ikede pleaded with her.

I tried to follow their conversation. From what I gathered, it sounded like the sigil animals of the kingdoms occupied a kind of sacred status. I silently cursed the queen for releasing a wild snow leopard into the arena to kill us, even though we couldn't return the favor. I disliked her even more after that.

Sev gritted her teeth and muttered something angrily under her breath. She reluctantly released her grip on the leopard and rolled away from it. The leopard lost no time in getting away from us as we watched it race off into the trees. Breathing hard, Sev quickly glanced over at Ikede to make sure he wasn't hurt. Then, she approached me and held an outstretched hand to me. I grasped it as she hauled me to my feet.

"Your cheek," Ikede pointed out. I touched my face and saw blood when I took my hand away.

"It'll heal," I assured him.

We heard another crashing noise in the distance, and I gathered my sword from the ground and crouched into a fighting position. Sev did the same. A man with olive-tone skin and long black hair appeared. I saw the blue ribbon on his arm and relaxed my stance. He asked for directions to the flag post where the other captured flags hung. A few minutes later he returned with an errand.

"We have one more flag to capture before we win," he told us.

"Do you know where it is?" I asked urgently.

He nodded. "One of our team members has it," he started to say as I felt my face light up. We were about to win this event and move forward, which meant I had more time in the castle to search for Queen Gisele and Azlaya's agreement. "But he was just captured."

"Well, let's go get him."

"He's being heavily guarded," he tried to warn us.

Sev asked combatively, "Afraid of a fight?"

The man stood a little taller at her comment and hardened his stance. "No. I just wanted to make sure you knew what you were getting yourselves into." His tone was defensive.

"These two got out of a fight with a snow leopard with just a little scratch to show. You didn't seem to be so lucky." Ikede flashed the man a twisted grin.

I looked at the man more closely and saw he had ripped away at his cloak to bandage a wound on his arm that was bleeding badly. I realized he had claw marks on his clothes, as well, and guessed that the blood I saw on the snow leopard must have been his. I smiled inwardly at Ikede's keen observation.

The man cut his eyes at Ikede and then turned, motioning for us to follow. We crept through the forest, listening for the crowd's cheering to alert us to the activity around us. On the edge of the red team's territory, we ran into three other of our teammates. Two middle aged men and a middle aged woman eagerly joined our rescue party. I started to feel better about our chances of rescuing our teammate and getting back to our territory to win the game.

The man with the long black hair debriefed our group about our plan of attack. He and the other three members would draw some of the red team members away from the "captured" post while Sev, Ikede and I would release our captured man. With everyone understanding his or her role, we moved into enemy territory.

As we weaved between the trees, I couldn't helping thinking it was odd that we still hadn't seen red team members. I ran a few paces behind Sev, and her agility reminded me of the Hunters', but she was even more graceful, if that was possible. Though I had spent the most time with her and Ikede, I knew nothing about them other than the fact that Ikede was inept with a sword and Sev was great. Their story was enticing but would have to wait, because the "captured" post came into view. Then I saw all the red team members for whom I'd been searching.

Our two groups split from each other. The long-haired man led his unit away to try to distract some of the red members. Sev, Ikede and I hung back for a few moments, while four red members darted away. We saw our chance and bolted forward. I didn't love our odds in a five-on-three battle, which was really a five-on-two battle, since Ikede was really only an accessory.

I rushed a lean man, ducked as he swung his staff at my head and landed a solid kick to his side. He stumbled forward as I snatched his staff and whipped it around so that he went careening into a tree. A woman lunged at me from behind, and I swiped the staff in her direction, just missing her. She jabbed at me again. I swung the staff up, catching her shoulder. She snarled at me; then someone jumped me from behind. I felt an arm at my throat and another groping for my sword.

I whipped my head back, hitting something, and then jabbed an elbow into the person's side. Their grip on me fell away, as I spun from their embrace. I sliced the staff through the air and connected with the side of their head. I watched as a larger man fell, unconscious, to the ground. The lean man from before had regained his composure and, with the other woman at his side, rejoined the fight.

My breath came short puffs of air. I tugged at the shredded cloak around my shoulders and threw it to the ground, relieved that I had lost added weight that would only slow me down as I took on two opponents. Ikede was watching me from behind a tree and saw his chance to unlock the shackles of our team member.

I tossed the staff aside and lifted my sword. The both charged me at once. I blocked one sword, and narrowly missed getting clubbed by another. My body twisted and turned away from one's advance while fending off another. My feet knew exactly where to go; unlike dancing with Aiden the other night, they were sure of their placement. The man's sword jabbed towards me just as the woman's knocked me over the head. White spots burst into my vision. I thought I saw Ikede's figure, with another person, race off into the trees, so I hollered at Sev.

More pain shot through me when someone kicked me in the stomach for the second time that day. My knees hit the jagged ground as another kick was landed to my side. Before I knew what had happened, someone was on top of me, meaty hands wrapped around my neck. My eyes bulged in surprise as the man tried to squeeze the breath out of me. I wondered whether they would chain up dead captives, too. I scratched at his face, but to no avail. Strangled gurgling sounds kept invading my ears, and it took me a while to realize they were coming from me. The spots in my vision began to return when the man suddenly stopped choking me and slumped to the side.

Someone above me, who was jerking me to my feet, had shoved him off of me. Sev's alert eyes snapped my mind back to reality as she screamed at me to run. She took off and I tried, clumsily at first, to stay in pace with her. I tripped on rocks and tree roots as the double vision went in and out.

"We just have to get back to our territory!" Sev called back to me, urging me forward.

Her words illuminated something in my memory. I blinked away the deliriousness that threatened to overwhelm me and pumped my arms harder. Pounding footsteps pursued us, but I didn't dare look to see how many. The crowd cheered, but I wasn't sure whom they goaded on.

I saw a tree with a blue painted trunk in the distance, and my heart fluttered with relief. My lungs whined for air, and my throat was dry from the harsh breaths I gulped as I ran. When Sev and I reached the tree, we spun to find our pursuers had slowed their pace and stared at us with murderous expressions. Just when I thought another fight was imminent, a resounding horn echoed through the trees and bounced off the walls of the arena.

"We won," I hoarsely said to Sev, though the expression on her face indicated that she understood what the horn meant.

After several minutes, all the competitors emerged from the forest and stood before the queen's canopy again. The crowd was cheering loudly again. The announcer congratulated the winning team on its victory, and then turned to the losing team. He thanked them for their participation in the tournament, and then sent them on their way. Once they left the arena, the attention returned to me and fourteen other blue team members. The crowd went crazy as little pieces of blue paper fluttered down around us. Queen Gisele rose from her throne, silencing the crowd.

"Enjoy the rest of the day's celebrations," she said, emotionless, and turned to leave.

I joined my other teammates and bowed as she left with her guard escort. As I straightened, the blood that rushed to my head caused a fit of nausea to sweep over me. The double vision returned with vigor. My knees buckled before I could stop them. I was grateful for the chaos of the confetti and boisterous crowd, which diverted attention away from me as I hunched over, trying not to get sick, and to remain conscious.

Ikede knelt beside me and tried calling to me, but his words sounded miles away. Soon, a medical team surrounded me and lifted me onto a stretcher. My eyelids fluttered as I willed myself not to black out, but inevitably a black wave of nothing washed over me, and the last thing I remember was confetti tickling my face.

Chapter 30: Zayne

I'D LEARNED EARLY on that people like Kate and me were rare. As a child, I had been sent to sorcery academies all over Eileen, and each time I was sent home for insubordination. I never understood why I was being punished for the pursuit of knowledge. No. I was being punished for exploring things my masters never thought about. They lacked vision. They lacked vigor. Above all, they lacked my strength, my endurance, and my power. The things I dreamed of doing, they never considered. They were weak. Even Cadmus Leonantus, once renowned as one of the most powerful sorcerers in the land, regarded my abilities as special. He saw potential in me, something he rarely saw in anyone. Yet, he, too, let me down. It wasn't until I escaped up north and found the tribe of sorcerers who worshipped Dark Magic that my potential was realized.

I didn't know anyone who wouldn't desire more power, if they could do what Kate and I could. Like me, she had been told to tame her powers. And, like me, she wasn't going to be caged again. Not after she had been allowed to breathe. Who would return to a cave after stepping outside and seeing the world for the first time? Who would allow their powers to be muzzled like a dog? Who wouldn't demand absolute autonomy after realizing that you were the most powerful being alive?

We craved the same thing: the ruin of our enemies and the bent knee of everyone else.

When I looked at her, I saw all these desires wrapped in her knowing gaze. Kate and I had disguised ourselves as travelers, wearing earth tones to blend in with the other villagers that lived outside the Hunters' camp. I had also performed a complicated spell that temporarily gave her the face of another person to ensure she wasn't recognized. No one in these parts knew me, so I was safe. We bought lunch in the village and huddled under a tree to eat on the outskirts of the tents. If anyone passed us, they would think we had stopped to rest on our journey to somewhere else. Instead, we fiddled with our food as we invaded the minds of countless Hunters, searching their memories to see which of them had been present the day that Kate's mother had died.

It was tedious work that required sorting through thousands of memories. Kate was masterful at reading minds. She was able to, within minutes, reach into the innermost crevices of a person's thoughts and find out who their true love was, whether or not they had murdered someone, or if they were cheating on their spouse. I, on the other hand, was able to discover the same things, but in double the time. Her exploitation of a person's mind, once she was inside, was unlike anyone else's I'd seen before.

With her, our search for a Hunter who was present the day her mother died was that much easier. After several hours of coming up with useless information, I decided to sit back and let her more-practiced skills take over. Her eyes had glazed over and become so unfocused, I would have thought she was blind. Her body was as still as a statue, so the only way I could tell she was still alive was the steady rise and fall of her chest.

By the time I had finished eating a piece of fruit, she found our target. "Got it," she said as she blinked and her eyes refocused. Her powers crept back towards her. "Jenmira Sun."

We waited for evening before heading into the camp to find the Hunter. Kate spent the better part of the day trying to keep track of the woman as she went about her duties within the camp. She had hunting duty in the morning, attended a training session, ate lunch, resumed training, went into the village to send a letter, returned to training, and finally took her post for night patrol.

When night finally fell, we closed in. We confirmed that she wasn't a sorceress, which, unfortunately, would make the whole night slightly less exciting. I scanned the forest for other Hunters and determined that they were spaced about one hundred yards apart from each other. As long as we moved quickly and quietly, no one would know we were ever there. Kate approached the Hunter from the rear while I approached her from the front. When she caught sight of me lurking in the distance, she made her way towards the suspicious activity, but not before getting knocked unconscious from behind by Kate's spell.

Kate lowered her hand, and the glow from the spell dissipated into the air. "Bind her arms and blindfold her," she told me. She had a deadly look in her eyes that made me swallow a playful protest and do as she said. Our mission concerned her mother, so tonight she wasn't fooling around.

I followed Kate along the outskirts of the village, on the edge of the Hunters' camp. The village was quiet, with the occasional stray dogs and cats scampering down the street. I carried the Hunter in my arms, and even though there was no one awake to question Kate and me, she had still removed the Hunter's outer garments and tugged a brown shift over her head, just in case.

Kate turned down a deserted alleyway and entered a building that looked like it had been abandoned for years. A faded sign hung above the door, saying that it was once a seamstress shop. The windows were broken and had a film of dust on them. All the furniture inside seemed to be worn out, or destroyed by years of neglect. We climbed the stairs to the upper level, and I followed Kate into a bedroom that no longer had a bed. There was a lone, wooden chair in the corner that Kate dragged to the center. She gestured for me to place the woman in it. Then she had me dissolve her disguise, and her normal face returned. Kate waved her hand over the woman's face; her eyes started to flutter, and Kate patted her cheek a couple times to bring her back to her senses.

"Come on, wake up."

The woman, Jenmira Sun, finally blinked away her confusion and cast an accusatory look in our direction. Her skin was pale, and she had straight, black hair braided down her back. Her eyes were a soft almond shape, but her black irises were piercing.

"Who are you?" she snarled.

Before I realized what was happening, Kate's hand connected with Jenmira's face, making a satisfying crack. Jenmira's head whipped to the side, and she gasped in surprise.

"Notice how you're the one in the chair," Kate threatened. "I'm asking the questions."

If Jenmira was afraid, she didn't show it. She only locked her jaw and narrowed her gaze on Kate. I had completely faded into the background, and I was eager to see how this encounter was going to develop.

"Do you know who Layna Coles is?"

Jenmira held Kate's gaze. Another crack met my ears. When Jenmira brought her head around, blood pooled at the side of her mouth.

"Yes. Yes, I knew her." She was studying Kate as though she was trying to remember something.

"Were you there the day she was murdered?"

"Yes," Jenmira said through gritted teeth. Kate exchanged a pleased glance with me.

"And what happened to her after she was killed?"

The tunic Kate wore hung loosely on her frame, and I could picture the curve of her neck into her shoulders, and her hips into her legs. I had taken up a post at a window facing the alleyway, pretending to watch for people below. I stayed this way, watching the two of them from a distance and allowing Kate to have her space, because she was sucking all the energy towards her anyway. Something about the interrogation had invigorated her, so I kept back and let her do as she pleased.

"I know who you are." I brought my attention away from Kate's figure and towards Jenmira. "You're her daughter, aren't you?"

Kate suddenly unhinged her dagger and held it inches from Jenmira's throat. This surprised me, because she normally liked to mutilate people mentally. Rarely, if ever, did she launch a physical attack. It seemed she wanted to feel the Hunter's blood spilling over her hands. She wanted to feel her heart pounding against her chest. She wanted to feel her body shake as she screamed. Kate wanted to feel all these things, and not from across the room, in her mind. She suddenly wanted to feel the pain she would inflict.

"Kaitlin Coles," said Jenmira. The dagger pressed into the thin layer of skin. "Evidently, you are nothing like her."

A crooked grin slid onto Kate's face. She glanced sideways at me, and I didn't have to read her mind to know what she was thinking. I swept my hand over the room, creating a soundless barrier that would block any screams from escaping the four walls.

Kate swiftly cut open the front of the woman's dress so that her collarbone and some skin above her chest showed. Then, she carefully started to carve into the skin. Her gaze matched that of a painter trying to perfect a portrait. Jenmira's screams sliced through the air, bouncing off the walls and echoing through each other. When Kate was satisfied, she withdrew the knife and stepped back. Jenmira's breath was ragged, but her eyes were still ice cold as she glared at Kate.

"What happened to her after she was killed?" Kate asked, as she coolly wiped the bloodied knife on Jenmira's clothes. Jenmira clenched her jaw and focused her gaze on something behind Kate's head. Though she tried to appear fearless, her body trembled uncontrollably, whether from fear or from pain, I couldn't tell.

"I'm not telling you anything."

Suddenly, she swung her leg up to kick out at Kate, but Kate had anticipated it, and she gripped Jenmira's foot in her hands and gave it a violent twist. The snapping sounds of bones and tendons were swallowed up by another fit of screams. Kate dropped Jenmira's foot, and it fell limply to the floor. Kate didn't seem to mind the awkward angle at which the foot lay bent. My stomach did a few flips, knowing that Kate had done that. I was used to her mentally and emotionally disfiguring people, but not physically.

Kate bent over, so that she was eye level with Jenmira, and the look I saw in her eye was familiar; though, it seemed to be amplified by the darkness of the room and the twisted smile on her lips. I knew the day we met that she was dangerous. This was the first time, however, I was seeing the gravity of being in her way when she was at her worst—or best; however you saw it.

"I don't want to ask again," she whispered gently.

Jenmira was fighting back sobs and trying to get her breathing under control. Her body was going into shock, and it trembled even more. "You're going to have to kill me."

"Oh trust me, I'm going to get pretty close, but you're going to tell me what I want to know before I let you die. That," Kate said, nudging the broken foot, "is a promise."

Over the next several hours, Kate drew more of the woman's blood with her dagger, asking for my blade when hers became too dull to slice the skin easily. When she got tired of that, she fell into her old habits of mental attacks. She broke into Jenmira's head and started bringing her worst nightmares to life before her eyes. Jenmira's fear multiplied over and over again, compounding the terror she already felt. As her mind betrayed its worst imaginings to Kate, she twisted them into realities so horrible that I finally had to step in.

"Kate?" She looked at me for the first time in hours. "Maybe get what we came for before you destroy her mind?" I offered coyly, as not to insult how she was handling things.

Her face wavered, but she deferred to my judgment, and the nightmare that consumed Jenmira collapsed.

A weak voice came from Jenmira's direction. "Enough— please—please make it stop—"

She was hunched in the chair, and her hair had fallen loose from thrashing around and now hung in her eyes. She was sweating profusely, and her eyes were red-rimmed. If anyone had walked in, they would have thought she was a mental patient escaped from a madhouse.

"This can all be over if you just answer my question." Kate emphasized every word. "What happened to my mother after she was killed?" Jenmira's head hung limply on her chest. Kate wrapped her talon-like fingers around her chin and forced her to look her in the eyes.

"I—I don't know," Jenmira sobbed. Kate huffed in exasperation and dropped her chin. She lifted her hand to resume the onslaught of nightmares, when Jenmira added, "After her body was found, your father brought her somewhere to be buried."

"My father buried her?"

"Y-yes." Kate exchanged a convinced look with me.

I was about to unhinge my other dagger and give it to Kate to let her finish the job, but she brushed off my gesture. Kate studied Jenmira for several minutes, as though contemplating how she wanted to kill her. I watched with equal amounts of awe and trepidation as Kate gently placed her fingers on Jenmira's head and started to pull what looked like black smoke from it. My face distorted as a creature practically crawled from the woman's skull. Kate dropped her hand and joined me at the window.

Its body was made of bones and then of flesh that had been butchered and massacred. It looked like it was shrouded in a black robe, but it was also oozing a thick dark fog that flowed like black liquid. It stood solidly like a human, and then floated like a ghost. Its face was a black mass, and it had wide, yellow eyes and a gaping mouth that seemed to have flesh stretching across the space. At first, it made no sound, and then its wails made me cringe. It was grotesquely and magnificently horrifying. Kate had to tug on my sleeve to rip my eyes away from the awful beast that had materialized. She finally managed to pull me from the room when its shifting gaze landed squarely on us.

We raced down the stairs and back onto the streets. When we had put enough distance between us to keep the hairs on our necks from standing on end, I turned to her.

"What the hell was that?"

She flashed me one of her wicked smiles that seemed to model my own. "Did you like it?" My expression must have been wild. "It was a physical manifestation of her nightmares."

I thought about all the spells and Dark Magic I'd learned over the years. I was basically a library of the most dangerous magic out there, and yet I had never seen anything like what I'd just witnessed. I'd done my fair share of twisting thoughts into nightmares and torturing a person mentally, but Kate had just introduced something that surpassed all of that. She had just created her own spell.

"How—just, how?"

When she tried to explain how she managed to do what I'd just seen, we both realized that she couldn't. She couldn't understand how she'd created the monster. She told me that something inside her compelled her to just reached into Jenmira's mind and literally pulled out all her worst imaginings, which manifested into the horror we had left there to finish her off.

I don't know if it was the jagged shadows across her face or the way her mouth tugged at the corner in a half smile as talked, but I couldn't stop looking at her.

She was unbelievably powerful, and incredibly beautiful, and she was mine. All mine. I knew from the second she gave me that shameless smile while we were tangled in my sheets that she belonged to me. I thought about the electrifying feeling of her skin on mine and the sound of her voice in my ear. I thought about the way she arched her back as I kissed her neck. I thought about everything pertaining to her, except the words coming out of her mouth.

"Would you wipe that dazed look off your face. You look dumbstruck. It's very unappealing."

I couldn't even begin to understand her power, and in that moment, she couldn't be happier with that fact.

"The day I don't look at you like that is the day you lose me."

"Is that a threat?" Her eyes flashed dangerously, but it was a look that drew me in.

"I wouldn't dare."

She laughed heartily and swept herself close to me. Her lips were inches from mine, and I felt her hands at my waist and around my neck. I knotted one hand in her golden hair and pulled her away from me so that I could see her whole face. Her brown eyes swam with excitement, and her tongue slid along the back of her teeth. She looked at me the same way I was looking at her. Possessively. Greedily. Everything I saw, I wanted forever. Whether she read my thoughts or was thinking the same thing was hard to say, but when our bodies folded into one another, we were in consensus.

"Let's go find your father."

Chapter 31: Kyraine

I ROCKED FROM side to side and finally pulled the horse to a stop. I sat in silence watching the trees. Normally the hum of the forest was calming. The twitter of birds, the scuffle of squirrels and small foxes, the babble of the creek all coalesced together into a comforting song. But recently, the music had grown disturbing, because it was never interrupted by a horn signaling a Sagen sighting or the clash of sword on scythe.

It had been weeks since we'd spotted a Sagen lurking near the border of our territory, and strangely, the lack of their presence caused me more concern. I sent scouts out to Azlaya's castle to see what had happened, and they came back with reports that confused us all. The Sagen had slowly been evacuating the castle and heading back towards the Shadowlands. I didn't know retreat to be in Azlaya's nature, and that was why I had a hard time believing that any of this was good news.

I withdrew a letter I had tucked into my belt and unfolded it. It was another update from Brennon. Casey had successfully entered into the tournament and would be in her first event soon. His words were terse and short of emotion, much like our last encounter.

It was getting harder and harder to remember a time when Brennon and I could interact without the weight of our duties pressing down on us. I wondered if I couldn't recall those days as easily because I had to forget them, or because I wanted to, in order to ease the pain. It was hard seeing him every day while he was here and ignoring the history we once shared. It was harder still to catch his gaze on me and think nothing of it. However, it was impossible not to see how ardently he believed that we still had a chance.

Did I still believe that we did?

He had loved me enough to let me go, with the hope I'd return to him one day. Since then, I'd only repaid him with doubt, misery, and possibly even regret. He'd earned better. He deserved better. But something selfish inside me wouldn't let him go completely. I'd known sympathetic love, like the love I had for my mother after our father abandoned her. I'd known selfless love, like the love I had for my Hunters. I'd known complicated love, like the love I had for Aiden, even through all his mistakes. But the love I had with Brennon surpassed all of those things and more, and it turned into something that couldn't be defined, described, or understood, even by me. I couldn't love him, because I only caused him pain. You don't hurt someone that you love, but then again, isn't that all love is? Is it not hurting those that mean the most to us, knowing they'll never leave?

I chided myself for thinking about these things when much more pressing matters should have had my undivided attention. I could be summoned before a council of Hunters and Huntsmen and tried for treason just for thinking these thoughts. But I couldn't rid myself of the fact that I was too weak to let Brennon go, and too strong to turn my back on my Hunters.

I heard hoof beats behind me, and a Hunter joined me where I sat. She handed me a letter, and said that it had just arrived. I took it from her, and she went on her way, to continue searching the forest for what we both knew wasn't there.

The wax seal had a hawk emblem on it, meaning it was from the Huntsmen's camp. I inched my thumb under the seal and unfolded the letter.

Kyraine, Mistress of the Hunt—

We have been working tirelessly to replenish our weapons stock, but still require Eileen's production efficiency if we are ever to be ready to face Azlaya's army.

I've recently received word that Cassia Coles and Brennon Harrow successfully arrived in the kingdom of Eileen. I notified Cassia's father of this, and he plans to travel to Eileen to reunite with his daughter. I will share this news with Brennon as well.

I know you explained your plan to bring Eileen into the war to me several weeks ago. However, I do not remember you mentioning your brother's involvement. Two of my men notified me that they saw him in Bronzeshore, travelling with Cassia and Brennon. I am sure that I do not need to tell you of the punishments Aiden has earned for his crimes as a deserter of the Huntsmen. Brennon will also be at the mercy of our laws for working with a criminal, and will be held accountable upon the completion of their mission.

I do not look forward to their trials, but as your friend I wanted to warn you that their actions, while heroic, will have consequences.

—Cade, Master of the Hunt

Cade's impassive tone rang in my ears. I knew what I was asking of Brennon when I asked that he work with Aiden. I knew I was asking him to commit treason against the Huntsmen, and now his commander knew. Brennon would likely be stripped of his rank and title as a Head Swordsman, while Aiden would likely face the noose—or worse. However, if they successfully completed the assignment with which I tasked them, I would stand before Hunters and Huntsmen alike and demand that their crimes are pardoned.

Cade would not be convinced through a letter, though. I would have to have this fight in person. I tucked the note away, wondering if I had sentenced the only two people, who had my infinite love, to their deaths—regardless, it seemed, of the out-come of their assignment.

I raced back towards camp. Armor still needed mending, swords forging, and bows restrung. Not to mention that I needed to start drawing up plans to begin moving the Hunters in position to fight Azlaya's army. As much as I wanted to help Brennon and Aiden prove their innocence, I couldn't do that without winning the war as well. The safety of their lives was conditional upon the outcome of the war. But then again, I guess all of ours were.

Chapter 32: Casey

WHEN I FINALLY woke, I wasn't sure how much time has passed since I had fallen unconscious at the end of the capture the flag game. My hand gently touched my face, and I felt a small bandage on my cheek. A nurse in the room realized that I was awake and came to my bedside. She helped me sit up and propped several pillows behind my back to keep me upright. I was about to ask her how long I'd been out, when movement across the room caught my eye.

I tried to hide my surprise as Queen Gisele entered the room. The nurse finished looking over my bandages and scampered out. My eyes followed the queen as she crossed the stone floor and settled into a chair beside me. All the air seemed to be sucked towards her, and I found myself breathing shallowly in her presence.

She found some satisfaction in the mildly crazed expression on my face. "Your Grace." I clumsily bowed my head, but that caused a mild headache to come over me.

"Please," she said icily. "The crowd seemed to like you today." She seemed oblivious to my physical state—or she didn't care. "I wanted to make sure that one of our promising competitors was faring well."

"I—I am, Your Grace. Thank you."

She suddenly leaned forward and placed a bony, cold finger on my skin. I froze. Her fingers brushed over the spots were I knew bruises ringed my neck. When she pulled her hand away, I couldn't hide the surprise on my face. Again, she seemed pleased with my reaction. It seemed as though Queen Gisele prided herself on being unpredictable.

"My physicians tell me the bruises will heal soon enough. It is a shame about your face though, that such beauty should be defiled." Her blank eyes settled on my cheek.

I briefly thought about all the scars that the Hunters and Huntsmen proudly sported. "It's just a scar," I replied plainly, thinking the subject would drop.

"Those are the worst kind of injuries. They may heal, but they never go away." Her hand hovered near my face.

I wasn't sure if I should sympathize with whatever it was she was thinking about, or pretend I didn't understand. She made the decision for me when she withdrew her hand and continued to speak.

"Where are you from?"

"A small village in the mountains, by Riversmith Castle," I answered, spewing my alias's well-rehearsed story.

"You must hunt for your village. I could tell by the way you navigated the forest." I didn't sense a question so I just nodded. I was feeling tenser with each passing minute under her stony gaze. "Remind me of your name."

"Kai Frost."

Familiarity tugged at her expression, unsettling me. As quickly as it came, the expression left her face. "A strong northern name." I exhaled silently in relief. "The first young man you danced with at the Commencement Ball—do you know where he is from?"

Her question caught me off guard, and I stumbled over my words. "No, Your Grace. Like I said before, I don't know him." Her insistence about Aiden made me nervous, and I wanted to know why she was still asking after him. "Have you seen him before?"

"Of that I am unsure, but I do know that he is not from Eileen."

My heart skipped a beat. Had we been found out already? "How could you tell?" I asked nervously.

"Couldn't you? You danced with him." The expression on my face gave her reason to continue chiding me. "You were probably too taken by him; too distracted by his words. Don't you know that young men always know the right things to say to pretty women?"

I pursed my lips and nodded, as though to validate her statement that I was just a naïve girl who couldn't navigate the world and take care of myself.

Queen Gisele continued. "He knew the dances well, but he carried himself and moved with the fluidity of a southerner. I would assume Calem. I studied dancing as a girl," Queen Gisele explained. "If he ever approaches you again, notify me immediately. If he is who I think he is…" Her voice trailed off. "Let's just say that I have some unfinished business with him."

I nodded stiffly. The queen rose from her chair. She still wore the same blue gown and fur coat from earlier, so I guessed it was just later in the same day of my being injured.

Before Queen Gisele left, she added, "I do hope you will have sufficient rest by tomorrow."

Then I remembered Aiden's instructions about finding a way to destroy Queen Gisele and Azlaya's agreement. He'd told me that Eileen's library would likely have books on how to break such spells.

"Your Grace, I was wondering if I could use your library— for leisure reading?" I called after her.

"You would spend the night reading before celebrating your team's victory?"

Her judgment made me quickly add, "It calms my nerves."

She turned another dismissive look towards me. "It is at your disposal." With that, she left.

A few more hours passed before the nurses decided I was well enough to return to my room. I walked through the cold corridors, wishing I wore more than a thin nightgown and robe. I climbed the stairs and turned down a hall lined with doors that belonged to other competitors' rooms. A door up ahead swung open, and Ikede's head peeked out. When he saw me, his brown eyes lit up with a smile big enough for both of us.

"Oh, thank the heavens you are all right. I was beside myself with worry when you collapsed. Come in, come in."

I followed him into his room. A group of couches faced each other in one corner and Sev was stretched out on one. I settled onto one and Ikede took his place on a third.

"I did not get the opportunity to thank you for your courageous efforts today. You saved my life, and for that, I am forever grateful." Ikede grasped my hands and genuine gratitude displayed on his face. He spoke diplomatically, something I hadn't really noticed before.

I leveled his gaze with mine, though, and he pulled away. "Ikede, these games are going to *kill* you," I said evenly. "You can't fight, you can't protect yourself—hell, you can barely run without tripping every two steps. This isn't child's play. How did you even qualify?" I thought about the Eileenian soldier I'd had to disarm to enter the games.

He puffed his chest when he spoke. "I disarmed the soldier, just as everyone else did. It was a fair match."

"You conveniently left out the part where he slipped on ice and practically disarmed himself," Sev added stonily from her perch.

Ikede's triumphant smile dropped from his face, but he waved Sev's comment aside. "Kai, I appreciate your concern, but it is wasted on me. I wanted to do this, and you cannot dissuade me."

"I can't even try to convince you with your life?" Sev had a look on her face as though to say, *don't bother. I've already tried telling him all of this.*

"Kai, I have nine older brothers, all in line for my father's land, his title, and his legacy. They are all skilled warriors and soldiers in whom he takes great pride. I, on the other hand, preferred books and diplomacy to combat, so he brushed me aside. There is very little for me at home, but here, I have the chance to make something of myself."

"Then why not get involved in politics and diplomacy?" I pressed him.

He flashed me a genuine smile. "After this, that shall be my next endeavor."

I respected his resolve and nodded my understanding. I finally asked, "How do you two know each other?"

Ikede went on to explain their history. As it turned out, he was a son of a lord in Canabar. He had grown up in a life of luxury, while Sev had been raised on Ikede's father's lands as a poor farmer's daughter. The two should have never met, let alone become close friends, and yet, they were.

"She and I met when we were no older than five years of age. In Canabar, combat is like a religion, and children learn it at a young age. I preferred reading to wrestling, which got me into trouble with some of the other children. That is, until Sev set them in their places for me. We have been friends ever since."

Sev's chiseled arms and legs boasted strength and agility, and it was easy for me to imagine her beating up other kids, in Ikede's defense. It seemed that relationship had persisted into their adulthood.

Ikede had revealed quite a bit about himself, though I still felt that I knew very little about Sev.

"Why were you named Seven?" I asked.

Her cat-like eyes flared in the candlelight. When they flicked to me, I immediately felt like I had become her prey. Strangely, though, her gaze softened.

"That's not actually my name. My real name is Shyna. Seven was a nickname I'd earned as a child. I lost control of my powers and left seven of our livestock dead. It was my father's way of reminding me of what I had done, and what I was capable of doing." A thick pause settled before she spoke again. "I've told two of my secrets; now I want two of yours. And the fact that you're a sorceress doesn't count. I already know that one."

I hesitated, realizing that she had just confessed that she was a sorceress. More importantly, she knew that I was one. Did I really trust them enough to share my secrets? Would they turn me in to the queen, knowing that I possessed powers that the Sagen sought? But then, I could turn Sev in just as easily, so why would she gamble with this information? I decided against lying, realizing that these two might be the only real friends I had inside these walls.

"All right, here are two of mine. I'm not really here to win the tournament. I'm here on a mission from the Mistress of the Hunt—and my name isn't really Kai Frost. It's Cassia Coles."

Smugness settled onto Sev's face, as though I had confirmed what she already knew. "I knew you weren't from Eileen."

Ikede, on the other hand, jumped forward. "Good heavens! It's you. The girl from prophecy, in my presence. Just wait until my brothers hear—"

"Ikede, keep your voice down," I hushed him. "You can't tell anyone. Promise you won't tell anyone until the tournament has ended."

"Yes, I promise," he reassured me quickly. His eyes still marveled at me. "What kind of mission has the Mistress of the Hunt sent you on? And what is she like? I've always highly regarded her and her—"

"Ikede, be quiet," Sev silenced him.

I indulged Ikede and briefly described what Kyraine was like. As I did this, I couldn't keep my mind from wandering to Aiden. Though he and his sister had initially been talked about as though they were polar opposites, I now saw that they had more in common than either would probably like to admit, and that either probably realized.

Sev and Ikede listened intently as I told them why I needed access to the castle. I explained the dire situation the Hunters and Huntsmen were in, and how the outcome of the war would be determined by Eileen's involvement. They held their tongues while I spoke, and by the end of my story, I could tell by their expressions that they wanted to help. My worries from before vanished as they eagerly listened to my plans to dethrone a queen, one whom neither of them supported.

"How do you even break a blood agreement?" Ikede wondered.

"I don't know," I admitted. "That's why I was going to search the library and see if there were any answers there."

Before I could even ask, Ikede said that he and Sev would cover for me if the servants asked after me. I gave them my thanks and stood to leave. I knew then that I had just gained two more allies, but what I didn't know was how important Ikede and Sev's support would come to be. When I finally left the room, I was relieved that I had been able to share my mission with someone inside the castle.

My muffled steps where the only sound I could hear as I crept down the hallways. I had to find the library and figure out how to destroy Queen Gisele and Azlaya's agreement. Once I discovered how, Aiden could finally destroy it—after he found and stole it, that is.

On the night of the Commencement Ball, I'd seen some of Queen Gisele's advisors coming from one side of the castle with books in their arms, so I began my search there. I turned

corners and ascended one flight of stairs before I found a wide
archway leading into the library. Though it was thin, I was glad
to be wearing a robe, because the room was drafty, and tall windows let the cold creep in.

High ceilings arched above me and tall bookshelves that
looked like they had been undisturbed for years stretched back
into the space. A table with a thick catalog, the written record of
every book in that aisle, sat at the end of each shelf.

I walked the rows of shelves, trying to decide where to
begin such a daunting task. I scoured the catalogs for anything
pertaining to magical agreements, but nothing came close: *A
History of the Kingdom of Eileen, Early Conflicts of the Four Kingdoms
and the Northern Tribes, Healing Remedies of the South*. Every time I
heard a noise, I bolted upright, prepared to find Queen Gisele
or a guard watching me from behind. I walked deeper into the
room, towards the back, where the dust started to make me
sneeze occasionally.

Finally, I came across something promising. At the back of
the library there was a gated section separated from the rest of
the books. It was padlocked.

I whispered, "*Aperire.*" Open.

The padlock fell from the door and I entered the restricted
section. Just as with the other shelves, a catalog sat at the end
of the three selves behind the iron gate. I realized that this
section of the library was where all the books regarding dark
sorcery had been stored. My eyes scanned through them until I
finally glimpsed a title that could have the information for
which I searched. *Accords and Dark Sorcery, by Mikhail,* the
catalog read.

After several tense minutes, I located the book and pulled it from the shelf. I paused to listen for any disturbances in the library's silence, turning back to the book when there were none. The pages were worn and smelled of mildew, and the book itself looked archaic. It took me a minute to realize that the words were not words at all, but ancient-looking symbols. I guessed that Myra had me read a book on them at some point, which is why I understood them with ease. I thought nothing of it and tore through the pages, scouring for anything useful. I found a chapter reading *Blood Accords*; my heart thumped against my chest. This had to be it.

I skimmed through the passage. What the book described sounded like what Queen Gisele and Azlaya had done. In order to make a binding agreement, such as the one they shared, each of them had to seal it with her own blood. By doing this, if one of them went back on her word while the agreement still existed, she would die. I read farther. In order to nullify the agreement, one person had to wet the record of their agreement with her blood and burn it. I read and re-read that passage, trying to wrap my head around the rather simplistic solution.

I flipped the page to check for a "disclaimers" section. I grumbled to myself when I found one. The agreement could never be broken if either person died before the agreement was dissolved. So, Aiden's wish to kill Queen Gisele would have to wait until after we were sure the agreement was destroyed.

I turned to the next page, expecting to find more conditions. Instead, I saw the next chapter title that read, *Accords with Sagen.* Curiosity made me continue reading the beginning of the chapter. It started by detailing the various deals that could be made with the Sagen; the most powerful of all was binding one's soul to them. I was halfway through the effects it had on the person's mind and body before I closed the book and returned it to its spot. The details were too gruesome to imagine, and besides, I'd gotten what I came for. I didn't need to distract myself with the disturbing pacts the Sagen could form with humans.

Once outside the restricted section of the library, I locked the gate again and retraced my steps back to the front. The light that spilled into the library from windows in the ceiling had lost its warm, orange glow from before. Now it had a pearly luminescence, so it must have been the dead of night, with the moon peeking out from behind the clouds. I guessed that the sun would rise in a couple hours. I mildly worried about the amount of sleep I had lost.

I returned to Ikede's room and gave him and Sev my thanks for turning away two servants who had arrived during my absence, before bidding them goodnight. Once I was back in my own room, I slipped under my fur covers. Though my body ached with ghost pains and yearned for sleep, my mind was humming. I knew how to destroy Queen Gisele and Azlaya's agreement. I was desperate to share the news with Aiden and Brennon, but the night was too far gone for me to slip into the city and return to the castle before morning, so our meeting would have to wait.

Chapter 33: Aiden

IT HAD TAKEN all my persuasive skills, and the unfair advantage of wielding a knife, to convince Brennon not to break into the castle to see if Casey was alive. I knew from the minute she staggered from the trees in the arena that something had happened. Whatever it was, though, it didn't appear to be life-threatening. Assuring Brennon of that was very difficult, however. I told him that if she had died in the night, bells would toll and the news would have spread by now. Neither of those things had happened, so we had to stay put.

The hours dragged on, and I was adamant about sitting at the table all night to ensure that Brennon didn't try to escape. The next morning, though, I was anxious. Maybe Casey had died in the night, and the tournament officials wanted to wait until that day's event to announce it. I wasn't going to tell Brennon that, but it was a very real possibility. It'd happened before.

I ignored all the small voices that kept killing Casey in my head and filed into the arena with Brennon and thousands of other spectators. On the way, I'd overheard rumors that one of

the men on Casey's team had been eliminated and taken prisoner for killing one of the snow leopards that had been set
loose in the first event. His punishment had yet to be determined, but I couldn't imagine it would be pleasant. The killing
of the kingdom's sigil animal could warrant an execution, if
Gisele was in a particularly sour mood.

The day began with the usual pomp and circumstance. A
royal ensemble played while Gisele took her place under her
canopy. Then the competitors were marched in. My eyes
scoured the field for Casey. Relief swelled inside me when I
caught sight of her walking in line with the others. Brennon
sighed audibly. Nothing about her seemed amiss, so I concluded
that whatever had overcome her the day before had been
resolved.

My attention turned to the arena's interior, and I became
fairly interested in the event when I realized it was a maze. It
almost filled the entire oval space. The thorny hedges looked
about ten feet tall, but, from above, we could watch the
competitors try to navigate their way through.

After the usual introductions and acknowledgement of
Gisele, the horn sounded and the competitors were turned
loose. They dove into the hedges, each tearing off in their own
directions.

Casey had formed a small group with the young man and
woman she had fought with during the capture the flag event.
The three of them wove through the hedges together. Every
now and then, a scream would alert the crowd to various
misfortunes in the maze. One person fell into a pit of thorns.
Another became cornered in a dead end with a venomous
snake. Two others had triggered a trap that left one with a spear

impaled through his foot. Casey and her group evaded most of the deadly traps.

It wasn't until an hour in that the young man walked into a vat of quick sand. I watched as Casey and the other young woman struggled to pull the young man out. A little while after, they ran into another group of competitors. I followed Casey's every move as she expertly fought the other group off, while defending the young man who hung back. The other young woman, Casey's fighting partner, crouched low in her attacks and struck with deadly blows. Right away, I recognized her as the person I'd seen fighting in the entrance round before Casey. It was plain to tell that she was from the sandy dunes of Canabar, where her style of fighting had originated. The Canabarian woman and Casey successfully fought off their attackers and advanced through the maze. I couldn't see what Casey was doing, but she held something in her hand and at every turn in the maze, she glanced down at it, as though consulting a map.

Three hours later, Casey, the young female fighter, and the inept young man miraculously found the end of the maze and were the first ones out. When nine more people had stumbled out after them some time later, the top twelve competitors had been chosen. The crowd went wild, Brennon along with them.

Later that afternoon, whispers of Kai Frost, Sev Amani and Ikede Ono ran rampant through the streets. Within a couple hours, they were the talk of the kingdom, and the new favorites to win the games. Brennon and I didn't pass a street corner where people weren't excitedly discussing those three names. Even in the lobby of our inn, other guests were arguing about supporting the new favorites to win long before their popularity had spiked.

When I told Casey this that night, she tried to hide a prideful smile. It was mid-evening by the time Casey was finally able to get away from the castle and meet up with us. We had stayed holed up in our room at the inn, waiting for her arrival. Brennon was especially grateful to see her after watching her collapse the day before.

"Did anyone recognize you?" Brennon asked, as he took the coat from her shoulders.

"No. I kept my hair down and my hood up. But, my god, it's madness out there," she exclaimed. Her cheeks and nose were red, making her face look even more doll-like. She lowered herself next to the fireplace and held her hands over it.

"How are you feeling after yesterday?" Brennon asked.

"I'm fine." She tugged at her collar, exposing purple bruises around her neck. "They're still sore, but they'll go away soon enough."

They looked bad, but they hadn't caused her windpipe any damage, and her voice sounded normal, so I knew her skin would recover soon. Brennon wasn't so readily convinced. I interrupted his examination of Casey and asked what she had been holding during the maze event. She told us how she had kept track of where she had gone in the maze by marking it on a leaf with her fingernail. I could tell by the way she walked through the maze earlier that day that she had been calculating something. As it turned out, it was her position she had been keeping track of. I didn't try to hide my approval at her ingenious strategy. I'd underestimated her cleverness.

As much as we all wanted to dwell on the excitement that came with the tournament, we had more pressing matters hanging over our heads. The games were just a distraction, after all.

"The queen paid me a visit in the infirmary," Casey said.

"What did she want?" Brennon asked apprehensively. Now that they both knew the cruelty of which Gisele was capable, it seemed the mere mention of her put them on edge.

"Nothing, really. She basically said the crowd seemed to like me and would hate to see me die so early on. She asked about you again, Aiden." This she said quietly, as not to startle me. "I told her again that I didn't know you, but she—she knew you were from Calem, based on the way you danced."

I rubbed my thumb over my bottom lip and cursed myself for not dancing with the heavy-footed rigidness that Eileen's ballroom dances required. Casey had done this perfectly, but that was because she had just learned the steps moments before. "If that's all she's noticed, then we're still safe," I reassured both of them. Though, Gisele's perception did unsettle me. I couldn't allow myself to be so careless, especially since it seemed that she was expecting to see me again.

Casey nodded. "I was able to make it to the library last night, and I think I know how to destroy their agreement."

Brennon sat up straighter on the chest at the end of the bed. I inclined my chin in her direction to show she had my full attention. I reprimanded myself when I caught my eyes lingering on her lips.

"I broke into a restricted section in the library and found a book about different accords people can make. You said it was a blood bond they made?" she asked me. I nodded. "The book said that to break the magic that binds their agreement, one of them has to wet the document with her blood and burn it."

"That's it?" Brennon said, incredulously.

It was a pretty simple fix to what had amounted to a colossal problem. While Brennon and Casey were discussing their disbelief, I realized that I now had a plan, and one that I liked the sound of more with each passing second. Spilling Gisele's blood would be easy, but I'd seen enough spells to know that there were always hidden clauses that could ruin everything.

"Well there's one more thing—" Casey began.

"They have to be alive in order to break it, don't they?" I asked, already knowing the answer.

"Yes. If either person dies while the agreement still exists, it can never be broken."

There it was.

I cursed under my breath. So I could only spill enough of Gisele's blood to break the agreement, but not enough to kill her when I did. My thoughts raced. How was I going to accomplish this? It took me a couple minutes to realize that I already knew. Actually, I had known all along.

Brennon, Shep, and I had been searching all the places that Gisele *could* have hidden the document, just to rule them out completely, even though, deep down, I'd already known it wouldn't be in any of those locations. Before I went into the Hall of Records with Brennon, I had known the document wouldn't be there. Before I had Shep break into Gisele's family safe, I had known the document wouldn't be there. Hell, before I had even arrived in Eileen, I had known exactly where it was. Yet, I had to convince the part of me that still trembled at the thought of Eileen to do what I knew had to be done. I'd been running away from the inevitable for long enough, and now, it seemed, it had finally caught up to me.

There was only one way that I was going to get Gisele's blood on that document, and that meant getting caught. I had danced around the edges of the trap for long enough. I had to walk right into it in order to get through to the other side. This didn't come as a surprise to me. What did, though, was realizing that I didn't hesitate from the fear of facing Gisele's dungeons again. I was suddenly reluctant because, for the first time since my plan's inception, a part of me didn't want to die anymore. This new part of myself consumed my waking days.

Marching into hell was just another part of my daily job, something I'd done many times before. This time, however, was different. My confidence in my resolve to execute my scheme was wavering. I still wanted Gisele dead. I still wanted Lysander to become king. But I wasn't sure if I still wanted to meet my end in order to make these things happen. This was the first time I didn't know if I'd be coming out unscathed—or even at all. My only solace was knowing that if I didn't, Lysander was ready to assume Eileen's throne, and I would get to see Greyson again.

Casey interrupted my thoughts. "How are we going to get the queen's blood? We can't exactly attack her without getting killed."

Brennon and Casey's gazes had landed on me. "I'll worry about that. For now, you've done everything you can."

A knock at the door turned all our heads. We started to move into defensive positions, hands on our concealed weapons. When I heard three subsequent knocks, I recognized the signal and called to Shep to come in. We all relaxed. He entered, noise from the hall spilling in with him before he pulled the door shut.

"Casey, Brennon, Aiden," he greeted us, handed Brennon a note, and joined Casey by the fire. "You are all anyone can talk about," he said to Casey. And then to me, "Fifty-two seconds, and she doesn't keep the document on her."

"What about a key? Or jewelry that would unlock something?" I pressed him. Shep just shook his head. I swallowed my frustration at hitting many dead ends in our search and tossed him his well-earned gold piece. "Fifty-two seconds?"

"I know, I was cutting it close. I'm slipping," he joked. Casey watched our exchange as though it was strange, but not unexpected.

I looked at the letter Shep had given to Brennon and caught a glimpse of the insignia on the letter. "From the Huntsmen?"

"A messenger was coming to deliver it. I told him I knew you," Shep said, shaking snow from his tangled hair.

Brennon nodded and opened the letter. He removed a quill from his things and swept the feathers over the parchment, revealing the previously invisible words. "It's from Cade. He says Casey's father is coming to Eileen. He's also agreed to send a unit of nearby Huntsmen in case we need some combat assistance. They're already en route and should be here within the next day or two. They're being led by—Callum Greaves," Brennon exclaimed. "He used to be in my unit." Brennon continued, "But—" His face furrowed as he read on. "Upon the completion of our mission, Cade says that we are to stand trial for the crimes we've committed."

Brennon's face was grim. Casey's expression fell, too, as she remembered that most of the trials concerning treason resulted in death sentences. No one seemed to know how to clear the apprehension that had descended upon the room.

"Yeah, yeah," I said casually, trying to lighten the mood, "and I should have been imprisoned for removing Amelia's crown from the castle, to impress a girl. What else does he say?"

"That's it. He's promised us soldiers. That's the good news." Brennon still hadn't fully recovered from the news of his imminent trial.

"Casey, you should return to the castle before the streets actually start to get wild." I told her.

Every night, without fail, street fights broke out all over the city; or someone's gamble on the games didn't pay off, so they set whatever was closest on fire. The irrational rage spawned from the games was what made them unique in my mind, but not everyone would agree.

I herded Casey out the door, but not before reassuring her that I would quell Brennon's anxieties about Cade's letter. Shep offered to make sure she got back safely. We'd both heard scattered stories about academies for sorcery being attacked and its students and teachers being kidnapped. Apparently, another one had been targeted the other day, and Shep wanted to ensure Casey's safe return to the castle. We exchanged glances, as I silently thanked him.

She spun on me before leaving and placed a firm hand on my arm. The weight of her hand was a crushing sensation, as though it weighed a hundred pounds. Or maybe it was just the touch of someone that wasn't trying to disarm or kill me that made me pause.

"Tell me what I can do to help." Our eyes met. I wasn't sure if she was talking about stealing the document or comforting Brennon.

Suddenly, all the things spiraling in my head fell away, and all I saw were her round eyes looking at me. How had she retained that soft gaze, knowing how cruel the world was and what her future held in store? Greyson had managed the same thing, and perhaps that is why I was intrigued with her from the moment we met. I stepped away, and the effect her gaze had on me subsided. I concealed my inner thoughts, but they still haunted my subconscious.

I realized the answer to helping me and helping Brennon was the same one. "Just stay alive."

Even though I knew what I had to do, and where I had to go to steal Gisele's document, I wanted one more night before everything I knew collapsed into uncertainty. That decision was what led me to Casey's room later that night. I had easily slipped into the courtyard and scaled the castle walls up to her balcony. She was curled up on one side of her bed. I dipped my finger in a candle by her bed, and the wax was still warm, so she couldn't have gone to sleep that long ago.

I gave her shoulder a shake and cupped a hand over her mouth, in preparation for her to berate me for being there. She shoved my hand away from her mouth and pulled herself upright.

"What are you doing here? Is everything okay? Where is Brennon? Is he okay?" She asked frantically. Any sign that she was tired disappeared in an instant.

"Everything is fine," I said breezily.

Her eyes narrowed suspiciously. "Then what are you doing here? Did anyone see you?" she demanded.

I hushed her. "Keep your voice down. And no, of course no one saw me."

"You shouldn't be here. Someone—the servants might walk in and see you. You'll be caught!"

"If you keep speaking that loudly, I will." She bit back a retort. I stepped away from the bed, allowing her to stand. "I can hardly let you stay in all night. Come out with me. You never really got to celebrate your first tournament victory. And now you have two under your belt."

The confusion on her face was monumental. She clearly had no idea what had possessed me to climb into her room at this hour, to make this request. I wanted to keep it that way. When my inviting grin didn't fade, she collapsed back onto the bed.

"You're crazy, and I'm tired."

I could see the restlessness in her gaze. "No, you're not." I pulled the covers away from her. "You're tired of being cooped up in this castle. You're tired of pretending to be another person. You're tired of always being on your guard. But you are not *tired*." She made a face that expressed that she didn't disagree with that I'd said. "Come with me."

"Aiden— What if we're caught? What if *you're* caught?" Casey already knew my darkest secret. The shadows of it clung to me, and she knew she had targeted a pressure point. But I wouldn't be dissuaded that night.

My face was impassive. I could only imagine what she'd say if I told her my plan to get Gisele's blood *was* to get caught. It would probably be along the lines of *that's a horrible idea*, or *that'll never work*, or *that's completely suicidal*. Honestly, I couldn't say that my imagined protests from her were baseless. In fact, they were all within the realm of realistic and probable possibilities, though I'd never admit it out loud. I blinked away any remnants of my nightmares. I was determined, which meant she had as much choice as the sun has to rise.

She huffed in defeat. "Get my cloak," she ordered me.

As I did that, she pulled on leggings, boots, and a warmer tunic. I approached her from behind and before she could object, my cool hands were fastening it around her shoulders. I stepped away and waited for her at the window. She carefully crossed the room, making sure to tread as lightly as possible.

I was counting softly under my breath when she asked what I was doing, but I pointed a finger in response. A castle guard was stationed on the roof towards the other end of the castle. Though he was far away, he would still be able to see two people slipping out in the middle of the night. The guard eventually walked far enough along the roof that he fell out of sight. I pushed the widow open and pulled myself out onto the balcony. When I turned back to Casey, she looked past me nervously.

"Casey," I interrupted her worrying. She didn't look afraid. She was actually giving me a face I'd received from Kyraine plenty of times. It was the one that screamed *this isn't a good idea.* She looked at me thoughtfully. "Don't you trust me yet?" I whispered as I stretched out my hand.

She stole a glance over her shoulder at the room, sighing when she turned back to me. "Probably more than I should."

I smiled crookedly as she grasped my hand and climbed out the window into the frigid night. I climbed upwards onto a flat part of the roof and pulled her up behind me. As we walked along the roof, we had to stop to crouch behind various towers and turrets to stay out of the guards' sights. As we came to a slanted part, we held on to the roof and shuffled carefully across. I'd climbed so many things over the years that my body didn't even need to be told what to do. We came to the roof's edge.

"Hold on," I whispered. I pulled Casey close. She locked her arms around my chest, as she had the day we had to share a horse. I let go of the roof tile I had been holding, and we slid down the spire as if it were a slide.

As we came dangerously close to flying off, I dug my heels in to slow our descent. Her breath was ragged from the adrenaline rush. She unhooked her arms from around me. I nimbly grabbed the edge of the roof and dropped down so that I dangled. Then I swung my body forward and disappeared. Casey had frantically, but cautiously, leaned over to search for me, when I popped out of the window I'd swung into.

I beckoned her to do the same. I chuckled as she cursed to herself before dropping down. She swung towards the window, but her balance was off. I grabbed her arms and pulled her through as she teetered backwards.

"I won't let you fall," I assured her. I held her for a moment too long before letting her stand on her own.

She followed me down the stair landing. At the bottom, I resumed the counting, that I'd been doing in my head, under my breath. After several seconds, I slowly pushed open the thick wooden door. I peered outside, saw no one, as calculated, and then slipped through with Casey on my flank.

We raced through the courtyard towards the castle's outer wall and darted through an archway that led outside. As we made our way from the back of the castle towards the front, the noise from the festivities grew louder. We approached the busier streets, and I swiftly pulled Casey's hood up to cover her face and grasped her hand to keep her close.

All around us people yelled out to each other; some were singing, others drank clumsily. Children dashed about without mothers on their heels and dogs followed people around, looking for scraps of food. I suspected that everyone who was carelessly spending money had won it within the last couple days. After bumping into and pushing past rambunctious people for what felt like miles, we finally escaped the heavy crowds and made it back to the edges. The crowds had thinned out enough that I let Casey's hand drop to her side. Soon, our steps were faint noises compared to the boisterous celebration coming from the area around the castle.

We rounded a corner and came upon a short, one-story building. Music floated from it, as did sporadic laughter. I had spent many a night here with my fellow assassins, planning how to kill Gisele and her father, in between drinks. I started to walk towards it, but felt Casey hesitate behind me. I turned and she tossed me an incredulous, yet playful look.

"Do you want to get the other side of your face banged up, to even it out?" she asked, as she tapped her jaw.

For the first time in a long time, I laughed without restraint. "It would only be fitting." I wound an arm around her to show the other men in the area that she was under my protection, and we entered the establishment.

Wooden tables and chairs were scattered about the room and a fire pit flickered in the middle. Pitchers and glasses were being passed around like water. I led us over to a counter crowded with other animated people. I ordered two drinks, which were delivered quickly. I pushed the warm, cinnamon milk drink towards Casey and watched her face eagerly as I took a sip of my ale. Her eyes lit up as the liquid spilled into her mouth.

"Milk of the Gods. It's an Eileen specialty. Probably its only redeeming quality."

As she took another swig, I furtively studied her features. Everything about her seemed soft: her cheeks, her neck, and her lips. She didn't appear to possess a hard feature, until she got angry, that is. I'd fallen under her sharp gaze a number of times already. And though she appeared gentle on the outside, I'd seen her in action enough times to know that her opponents had reason to fear her.

I felt my eyes lingering, so I busied myself with studying the room instead. I had always been careful about hiding my identity when working jobs, and never risked recognition in public. Yet as I sat next to Casey, watching her joyously drink and feeling her warmth, I hardly cared about the glances and prying eyes around me. The weight of my identity had no bearings on me for the first time in years.

Casey dipped her chin in the direction of another room of the bar. I followed her gaze and saw men and women gathering to play another game. Clearly the celebratory atmosphere was starting to affect her, because she leaned over and said, "Do you want to join?"

Shockingly, the answer was no. Even I was surprised with myself, but there was curiosity in her eyes, so I rose from my stool and led her into the room. I made sure to keep her just close enough that none of the others would get any ideas.

They were playing a card game I'd learned as a child, when we played with cards made from leaves that my friends and I had crafted. Money never went far enough to buy toys; so all our entertainments were handmade. I settled into a chair and Casey sat beside me. I quickly explained the rules and strategies of the game while the deck was being dealt. I drew up my cards, organized them, and the bidding began. Cards were tossed into the center, judged against one another, and then collected rhythmically. We had played several hands when Casey leaned into me and pointed at a card I should play. Just as the night when we had danced together, I was impressed with how quickly she picked up the game. I gave her a sideways smile and played the card. She sat close enough now that our legs touched and my arm brushed hers as I moved to place cards down. Neither of us pulled away.

The night went on like this, and Casey and I melded into a single mind during the rounds, thinking and strategizing the exact same way. She finally brushed her lips against my ear to tell me she was going to get some water. I let her go, even though I didn't love the idea of leaving her alone in a room full of people who weren't thinking straight. She ducked into the outer room, but I kept one eye on her the whole time.

More rounds of cards were thrown down. A few minutes had passed when shouting in the other room drew my attention away from the game. When I heard Casey's voice, I jumped up and darted away from the game, ignoring the angry curses directed at me. Before even assessing the situation, and before he even knew what was going on, I had landed a swift punch to the man who had latched onto Casey's arm.

Chapter 34: Casey

I HAD PASSED drunken people falling over each other, as I headed to the bar to get some water, when I jolted to a stop. A lean man blocked my way. At first, I guessed he may have recognized me from the tournament, but the thought quickly faded. His inability to focus his eyes, the uncertainty of his feet, and the reek of his breath told me to stay away.

"Can I buy you a drink, *Miss*?" The way he said 'Miss' made my hair stand up on edge.

"No, thank you," I replied, making a second attempt to get past him.

This time he was right in front of me, leaving no room for escape. I felt as though his scruffy chin was about to stab me as I jerked back. "I *said*, can I buy you a drink?" he repeated more forcefully.

"And *I* said no." Anywhere else, I would have cast a spell on the man, but this was Eileen, and exposing myself as a sorceress would only end badly for me.

I tried once again to get away from him, but he reached out and snatched my wrist. He held on tightly. His grip was strong and rough.

"Get off of me!" I shouted trying to twist away from him. He pushed me against a wall and tried to whisper something in my ear. I tried shoving him away from me, but the weight of his body restricted me.

"Let go of her!"

In a flash of movement, Aiden had found me and was swinging at the guy who held me. I jumped back to avoid getting caught up in the tangle of bodies. Aiden's fist connected with the man's cheek, and he doubled back in shock. Aiden dove into him and landed a punch to the guy's face. His fists swung furiously but without the precision I knew Aiden possessed. His attacks were laced with passion that lacked the more practiced skills with which he typically fought.

One of the man's friends rushed to his aid and attacked Aiden, making him fall away. They fell into the counter, and the people sitting there scrambled to get out of the way. The skinny man rose and tried to get back in the fight, but before he could, I swept his legs from underneath him and struck him on the side of the head. He hit the ground with a hard thud.

I looked up and saw Aiden roll to the side as the other man connected with the bartender's face. That was when all hell broke loose. Everyone in the bar jumped up to join the fight. Curses and threats started filling the room, and a table overturned to my right as another fight broke out. I ducked out of the way of another melee and found Aiden. I wasn't sure who was pulling whom out of the bar when we tumbled outside, but someone was pursuing us.

I twisted and saw the larger man on our tail. With a quick twitch of my hand, I created a thin sheet of ice in front of him. No one would question the ice in this weather. I didn't even turn to watch him crash to the ground as Aiden and I tore down the street.

We ran side by side, and I didn't even know if one of us was leading the way or if either of us knew where we were running. We finally came to a bridge that arched over a river below. We ducked underneath and finally stopped to catch our breath in its shadow. The cold air burned my lungs as I heaved deeply.

Once I could, I started laughing uncontrollably. Aiden watched me hesitantly, as though trying to decide how to decipher my reaction.

"We shouldn't make a habit of this. It's much too civil for us." Throwing the words he'd whispered to me at the Commencement Ball earned me another real smile. "I've never been in a bar fight," I laughed breathlessly. "Not a real one, anyway."

"Yeah, the first time you kind of cheated. Magic isn't typically allowed."

He touched his jaw carefully. Then he started moving it around, testing for soreness and dislocation. Blood trickled by the corner of his mouth. His face was turning a red-purple color where the man had hit him. Aiden collapsed on the bank and I lowered myself next to him, taking in his new injuries. He turned to look at me, but I couldn't read his expression.

Hesitation gripped me, but I ignored it and grasped his hand in mine to heal the bruises that were already forming after his throwing so many punches. I tried desperately not to think about his gaze on me as I worked. Then I raised my hand to his face and lightly rested my fingers on his cheek and jaw. I kept my eyes trained on his injuries as the Healing spell infused into him. He winced. When I drew my fingers back, the bleeding had stopped, the swelling was going down, and the discoloration was fading.

My gaze lingered, though nothing else on his face needed mending. I was trying to make sense of the almost dreamy look on his face.

"Is it that bad?"

I smiled, returning the same crooked look he always gave me. "Some things just can't be helped."

Aiden smiled. It was a smile that wasn't tainted by deviousness, judgment, or even sarcasm. It was just a smile. It was so genuine that I had to drop my eyes to keep from blushing.

Indistinct music and laughter floated towards us. Everything suddenly felt dreamlike. The streetlights flickered and the river below us babbled, but it all felt distant. Whatever space we were in felt, suddenly, unreachable by everything else.

Our breathing had finally evened when I asked, "Why did you do it?"

"Do what?"

"Become an assassin," I replied. There was a long pause as he searched for an answer.

He turned his face towards me. "The easy answer would be because I'm good at it—killing, that is." I realized how used to his nonchalance I'd grown when I didn't even blink. "But the real answer is that I was scared. I'd deserted the Huntsmen and I needed protection. The Night's Guild offered me that and money. But soon I realized that it wasn't worth it. I was too much of a coward to face the consequences of the Huntsmen and too much of a coward to run from the Guild. In a sense, I'd dug two graves—it just became a matter of which one I would fall into."

"Do you regret joining the Guild?"

"Sometimes, but I'm not delusional enough to think that it isn't a part of me now. Do you regret finding Alagia?"

"Sometimes." We shared a brief shadow of a smile. "I think about what my life would be like if I'd never found it. I guess it doesn't really matter how much I wish I hadn't found it. My sister wants me dead. I can't change that."

"The queen of Eileen wants me dead. And I'm sure the other kings and queens will, too, soon enough."

"How did we come to this?" I replied lightly.

We stared at each other—into each other. My whole world disappeared. All I cared about were his eyes on me and mine on him. Our bodies leaned together in a way that felt so natural, that I wondered how long we had fought these urges.

His warm breath drifted over my lips. We were both still hesitant, knowing that once we fell together, there was no going back. He gave in first and pressed his lips to mine. They were soft and warm and gentle and everything I never thought he could be. I closed my eyes, letting our dream descend and wrap us together.

Aiden abruptly pulled back, releasing his grip on my neck. His expression revealed his surprise at his actions. Oddly though, he seemed to struggle between happiness and pain as he looked down at me. He leaned away. Reality was quickly coming back into focus, but I didn't want it to. I didn't want to leave the dreamy space we'd fallen into. With one swift stroke, Aiden shattered it altogether.

"I shouldn't have done that."

My cheeks flushed. I turned away from him, hoping he didn't notice. I was embarrassed that I had so eagerly kissed him back.

"I—should get back," I said rigidly. Our once-cozy spot under the bridge felt cold again. Aiden stood and held a hand out. I grasped it, but my skin no longer tingled at his touch. I caught a glimpse of his face, and his eyes were guarded again. He'd retreated back into his defensive shell.

I wasn't sure what I had done to warrant this kind of reaction from him. I felt guilty for even letting it get that far. And yet, as I followed him back to the castle, I longed for that boyish gaze to linger on me, and for that genuine smile to soften his face.

Chapter 35: Aiden

I LED CASEY back to the castle and helped sneak her back into her room again. We had made the whole journey in silence, and her body tensed if I accidentally brushed against her. Once back in her room, I waited quietly as she pulled off her outer layers. I noticed her eyelashes brushed her cheeks when she blinked and her lip twisted at one side when she was thinking about something.

Aiden, stop *it! Stay focused. You are here to do a job, not busy yourself with a pretty distraction.*

"Aiden, you're doing it again," Casey said flatly.

"Doing what?"

"The thing you do, when you stare with that look on your face. The face someone makes when they're planning a murder."

I blinked, realizing that I hadn't been studying her discreetly, as I would anyone else. I tried to ignore the sensation that wanted to hold her face in my hands, or the sensation to feel her hair in my fingers or her lips on my neck. It was painful to push them aside, but more painful still to know that they existed.

I would have marched into Gisele's chambers hours ago, spilled her blood and destroyed her agreement with Azlaya, but something had stopped me every time I made a move to leave. It wasn't until I now that I realized what suddenly blocked my way.

Greyson had been my excuse to die. Casey was my excuse to live.

But is that really what I wanted? After twenty years of plotting to kill Gisele, knowing that I'd likely die in the process, was I suddenly willing to accept the possibility that I could survive our encounter? No. I couldn't let thoughts like this distract me from my goal. I couldn't go after Gisele hoping I'd survive. I had to go after her, ready to give my life in order to end hers. But how was I supposed to make Casey understand?

I stood at the window. "Come here." My words were gentle. Though reluctant, she joined me and looked out. "You already know how to get out of this room and down to the courtyard. It's a longer route, but safer. Once you're in the courtyard, exit through the archway and head west. Don't let anyone recognize you as a competitor in the games. Don't stop until you've reached the western gate. At the gate, you can buy a horse. Ride southwest for three days until you find one of the Huntsmen's outposts. Don't stop riding until you've found them. They'll get you back to Kyraine."

"What are you talking about—where is this coming from?"

"Just promise me. If anything happens, promise me you'll get out." The intensity in my voice seemed to startle her.

"Anything like what?"

"Casey!" Her lips pinched together which meant she was about to argue. "Please."

"What do you think is going to happen?"

I imagined her getting caught as my accomplice. I imagined her being dragged before Gisele and disfigured while the queen laughed heartily. I imagined Casey cowering in the dungeon with muck at her feet and darkness as her only companion. I imagined her hating me for handing her over to my demons so they could feast upon her.

I had to turn away from her. That's when I felt her hands on my back. They rested gently on my shoulder blades where the scars crisscrossed, as though she was afraid I'd lash out any minute.

"I won't pretend to understand everything going on inside your head, but that doesn't mean I'm afraid and can't help you."

Damn it all to hell.

I turned back to her and wrapped my arms around her. I was surprised and relieved that she clung to me just as desperately. She knew who I was. She knew what I wanted. Above all, she seemed to know that this was very likely a farewell. Perhaps this was her way of telling me that she could let go.

"Casey," I tried coaxing her face from where she had buried it into my chest.

"One night—I just want one night when we don't think about any of it."

I lightly kissed the crown of her head. "I can do that," I whispered into her hair.

Effortlessly, I scooped her into my arms and carried her over to the bed. I sank onto it, her body still curled next to mine. The nightmares that danced at the edges of my sanity slowly disappeared. It was the same feeling I'd had when she infused a Sleeping spell into me. My mind didn't hum. My thoughts didn't race. For once, I was at peace. When I was with her, I was no longer haunted.

My eyes closed as I listened to Casey's heart count out the seconds.

Several hours later, I jumped awake. The sun hadn't risen yet, but it would soon. Casey had rolled away from me in the night, leaving most of the blankets wrapped around me. I carefully untangled myself from them and pulled them over her before leaving the way I'd come.

Brennon didn't ask where I'd been when I made it back to the room, even though I saw the questions in his eyes. Instead, he directed me towards some leftover food and rolled back over in bed.

The following morning, as had become a routine, Brennon and I joined the hoards of people streaming into the arena. As soon as we settled into our seats, I knew the event was dueling. The maze hedges had been removed, and a flat, dirt space remained. A large white circle had been painted onto the dirt, designating the area in which the duel would take place.

The rules were simple. Each competitor would face a criminal that had been sentenced to death. Either the competitor would kill the criminal, or the criminal would kill the competitor. If the criminal won, he or she would be released. High stakes created interesting fights, and Eileenians loved their duels to the death. Immediately, I was concerned. Even though Casey was a good fighter, and as confident as I was in her skills, this event was not designed for her. Mercy would have no meaning in the arena today, and she wouldn't be able to shake her opponent's hand, as she had in the entrance round, when it was over.

The one-on-one combat was typically spread over several days. As there were twelve competitors remaining, I guessed that would mean four fights per day, over three days. I'd assumed correctly, and the names of the first four competitors were called out. My heart sank a little when Kai Frost was called among the others.

Two competitors in, my anxiety still hadn't subsided. Already, both duels had resulted in the release of the criminals. In the third battle, the competitor won, but not before losing a severe amount of blood. Game officials quickly spread new dirt over the bloodied areas, and my fingers drummed nervously on the hilt of my knife.

When Casey entered, the arena burst with heightened excitement. Her notoriety had more than doubled overnight, and the crowd's reaction was proof of that. I didn't have to see her face to know she flashed a demure smile at the cheering.

Her opponent entered the ring: a bald man with tattoos covering his scalp, and arms the size of tree trunks. They were each handed a sword and a shield. A horn sounded. The man jumped forward with unexpected speed. Casey adjusted her stance and countered his attack. She moved her feet gracefully. The man lunged, and she knocked him away with her shield. She deflected several more blows and landed a couple of her own, but the man was skilled, so he blocked her shots. They battled this way for several minutes. I found myself coaching her movements under my breath. Brennon followed the deadly dance with a fixed stare that could level a building.

I watched as Casey was knocked to the ground. My heart stopped. The man stood above her and swung his sword in a wide arc. She just missed being sliced in half, as she rolled to the side, and jumped to her feet. I could picture the wound before I actually saw it, as the man cut the air with his sword again, this time connecting with Casey's arm. Her shriek stabbed me. That was when my heart started racing. In that moment, I realized that I'd never been so afraid of losing something in my entire life. The man attacked again, mercilessly pounding at her shield. I could tell she was getting tired of bracing her body against the staggering blows.

I sucked in a breath with everyone else when a trap door suddenly opened to the left of Casey, and she lost her balance on its edge. She clawed at the dirt to keep from falling all the way into whatever lay at the bottom. The man approached her, and looked as though he was getting ready to kick her into the hole. Casey swung her sword and sliced his leg open. His roar echoed off the walls as he stumbled back, clutching his bleeding leg.

She had lost grip of the sword, though, and it lay several feet away. She scrambled to pull herself from the pit and rolled back onto solid ground. She raised her shield as the man rushed her. She fended him off, but I knew she couldn't continue this way for long. She was given a short reprieve from his advances when he, too, almost fell into another trap door.

As she blocked another strike, the man swung out at her and connected his fist with the side of her head. She wheeled around, but he was on top of her again and knocking her to the ground. They scrambled for a minute, but the man had the upper hand. Brennon stood next to me, his fear controlling his thoughts. Mine petrified me. He made a move to start climbing through the crowd and down into the arena. I grabbed his arm.

"Brennon, we can't interfere!" I called over the commotion, even though I wanted to do just what he was thinking.

Just stay alive, my mind screamed at her.

Casey and the man wrestled on the ground. My eyes latched onto Casey's face. She glared at the man, and suddenly her face contorted into a murderous expression. She used all her strength to throw the man from her. She followed by striking him with her shield across his already bleeding face.

I couldn't hide my surprise when she grabbed his sword and ran it through him until it protruded out his back. He stumbled to his knees, and she fell away from him and collapsed onto all fours. My world froze. An eerie silence settled. The man fell face-first into the ground.

"Get up, Casey," Brennon breathed next to me. "Get up."

Several more tense seconds passed, before she lifted her head and made an attempt to rise to her feet. She stumbled at first. I didn't start breathing again until Casey painfully, and shakily, stood. Then the trance was broken. Men hollered, women squealed, and children chanted. She straightened and cast her fallen opponent a look I'd never seen her give anyone before. It harbored a kind of hate I didn't think she was capable of possessing.

Casey turned in a wide circle to look at everyone who cheered for her, but I could tell the victorious expression was a guise. Underneath, I knew she wished she didn't have to kill that man. Underneath, I knew she ached with different pains. Underneath, I knew that a small part of her was gnawing at her conscience about the fresh blood on her hands.

Still, she had won. She was alive. She was safe, at least for another night, and I was going to keep it that way.

A group of physicians bombarded Casey at the arena's edge and started dressing her wounds. Brennon and I stayed until we were sure that she was well taken care of. When we got back to the inn, I went to my room, lit a candle, and started scribbling letters. I had four I needed to write; five that I wanted to write. The first four were to Lysander, Kyraine, Cade, and Callum Greaves.

To Lysander, I wrote telling him that his reign as king would begin within a matter of days. I instructed him to travel to Queen Amelia in Calem and seek her help to prove his legitimacy to his throne. I assured him that he was well prepared for his future role and that his people would come to love him.

To Kyraine, I wrote telling her about what had happened on my last mission in Eileen twenty years ago. I confessed the details of Greyson's death and how I'd done everything in my power to right my many wrongs against her and our brother. I wanted her to know the truth, but I didn't want her forgiveness.

In the letter to Cade, I asked him to show mercy to Brennon in his trial.

To Callum, I wrote telling him to keep his ears to the ground in search of Kai Frost, and to escort her and her friends to the Huntsmen's camp. She would fill him in on the rest.

The fifth letter, I wanted to write to Casey. The only thing that I could write that was completely true, though, was that I had come to Eileen prepared to die in order to get Lysander his throne. But after knowing her, death wasn't as inviting as it had been for years. In the end, I burned her letter. I would be able to feel her wrath from the grave if those had actually been my parting words to her.

I sent the other four letters and met up with Shep. He was spoiling himself with the riches he'd won form Casey's victory. I had to pull him out of a brothel and wait a couple hours for him to sober up before telling him that I needed him to help Casey and Brennon escape Eileen that night. If I executed my plan the way I needed to, there would be no reason for Casey and Brennon to stay. After explaining it several times, and when I was convinced that he understood, I returned to the inn, in the late afternoon, to find Brennon.

"Brennon, I want you and Casey to leave Eileen tonight. I know where the agreement is and I'm going to destroy it. You two won't have any reason to stay. I've already laid out the plan to Shep. He'll help you get into her room and get away tonight."

"You're kidding! Can't we help with—"

"No," I breathed, "this I have to do alone."

"What will you do after?" he asked.

Our gazes met and his fell slightly, knowing the answer. There was likely no *after* for me.

"If something happens to one of us—" I began.

"The other gets her out," Brennon finished. "I know." We shared a solemn nod of agreement.

I drank a lot that evening. Brennon was decent enough to keep buying me more drinks, even though the dutiful side of him protested silently. But if it had been him going to face the beast of his nightmares, I would have kept buying drinks for him, too.

When I'd had enough, I chased the evening's drinks with a concoction I'd discovered for use while on assignments. It completely flushed the alcohol from my system and allowed me to think unimpaired, and walk without stumbling. When I was sober again and had collected my things to leave, I met Brennon at the door.

We shook hands. "You're the only man who has ever deserved my sister. I hope you know that."

He gave me a reserved smile before I walked from the room and out onto the streets.

Later that night, I pulled myself through Casey's window. She slept with her back to me, and her hair fanned out behind her. I knelt beside her, inhaling her intoxicating scent. My eyes glanced over her injuries, the worst of which being the cut to her arm.

I closed my eyes and thought about the first smile she gave me. My thumb stroked her hand and thought about the night it had folded into mine as we danced. I brushed loose hair from her face and thought about seeing it cascading around her in unruly waves. I kissed the side of her peaceful face and resolved that this was the image I would keep with me.

My lips brushed her ear. "Please don't find anyone better looking than me. My ego can still be hurt from the grave."

She stirred in her sleep, but didn't wake. An unsettling realization settled in. Sarcasm had no power here. After several minutes, I dropped the pretenses. In that moment, only the truth could exist. Only the truth could span the chasm I was about to create.

As I gazed at her in this arrested moment of time, I realized that she had uncovered parts of myself I didn't think existed. When I had confessed the sins of my past, she'd listened. When I had been in pain, she'd held me. When I wanted to end the suffering I'd endured for years, she'd given me a reason to go on. All this had said so much more than what three little words ever could.

I had so much more I wanted to say to her. I suddenly wanted years to show her and tell her all of this. Instead, I had a few silent minutes.

"I'm sorry."

I scaled the ramparts of the castle and pulled myself onto the roof. I was armed with a hidden blade on my right arm, a dagger in my belt and two more strapped to the sides of my boots. I wore all black and had a hood and mask covering my nose and mouth. As I raced across the roof, I was picking off guards like flies. I hit one in the shoulder with a dagger, finishing him off as I passed. Another fell under my weight and then my blade. One dropped to my left, another to my right. I jumped another and swiftly sank my hidden blade into the back of another's neck before I rolled and kept going.

I finally came to the window that led to queen's chambers. I lowered myself along the wall, digging my feet into the nooks and crannies of the stones, and silently opened the window and climbed inside.

The bathroom had an oval tub in the center that could comfortably fit five people. Around the edges of the room stood cabinets with different perfumes, bathing oils, and candles. Rugs with snow leopards stitched into them hung along the wall for decoration. I approached one of the rugs and held it aside. Just as I remembered, the door to the hidden passageway greeted me. The wooden door was disguised so plainly that it

was almost impossible to believe that it was there. But there it
stood.

I went to pick the lock, when I realized that the door had
been left unlocked. The door wasn't meant to keep me out, but
rather allow me inside. I took a deep breath before silently
opening it, and peered inside. After waiting several seconds, I
confirmed that no one was in the hidden passage.

The descent down the hall sent memories of a younger
Gisele and myself reeling through me. The passage ended in a
circular room that had a single desk with a quill and parchment
on it, and shelves lining the room. On the shelves were hundreds of small vials, about the size of my thumb, and each of
these vials contained one of Gisele's secrets.

The first time she had brought me down to the secret
room, I had been utterly confused. Why would anyone keep a
written record of all his or her secrets? That is how they get
stolen and exploited. It was perfect ammunition for anyone
that wanted to cause harm. But it was her way, however, of
keeping her darkest deeds off her conscience. As an
adolescent, the vials contained secrets of the lords of the court
she'd flirted with, or of the gifts she'd received from an
admirer. As she grew older, though, they began detailing the
confessions of rebel villages she'd ordered to be burned
down, or disloyal families she'd had killed in the night. After
the deed was done or the order complete, she'd write it down
and add it to her collection of secrets. Once she recorded it, it
no longer weighed on her. Though her rationalization still
puzzled me, she liked to lock away these parts of herself in
this room, and I knew her agreement with Azlaya wouldn't be
an exception.

I looked on the shelves, scanning through the dates etched into the wood, until I found the one that matched with the date I had in mind. I took the vial from the shelf and worked the cork out. The parchment inside slid from the vial into my hand. I unrolled it, and the paper grew in size until it was several feet long. Surely an enchantment of some sort. I skimmed through the words: *alliance, provide no aid, in exchange for protection.* This was it. I quickly rolled the parchment, shrinking it back to its original size, and shoved it back into its vial.

I retrieved a vial from my pocket. The concoction I had consumed to cleanse my drunkenness came in a vial identical to those Gisele used to store her secrets—a coincidence that worked in my favor. I scribbled a few words on the parchment on the desk and placed it in the fake vial, which I replaced on the shelf, so that nothing would appear amiss. Just as I did so, the door down the hallway opened behind me, and I heard the unmistakable clicking of shoes on the stone floor as they approached. She'd set the trap. I'd sprung it. Now, it was time for the encounter.

My back was to her when her familiar voice cut the air. "You couldn't stay away forever."

I turned to find Gisele watching me carefully. She wore a dark gown and her bright hair was in intricate braids, so she hadn't retired for the night. I saw the twenty years that had passed in her features even more now that we were only feet apart. Her face swam with a mixture of emotions, but triumph dominated them all. She had waited a long time to see me in her clutches again, and it was clear that her retribution had become her obsession. My muscles tensed, out of habit, but my mind and thoughts remained calm and collected. She glanced around the room, and when she didn't say anything about the vials, I let out a silent breath of relief.

"I knew you'd return. I knew the Hunters and Huntsmen would get desperate enough to send someone after it. I told Azlaya that you were the only person who would know where to look for our agreement, and I was right."

Everything about her that had seemed lifeless was now awakened with a new sense of intensity and purpose. Her eyes burned in the same way that Casey's had burned when she looked at the criminal in the arena. Pure hatred unfiltered by anything.

"I admit, I didn't think it would take you twenty years." She paused, gazing at me appreciatively, as though she welcomed my silence. "So my castle is still familiar to you, since it seems you still have it mapped out in your head. That's how you found your way here so quickly, isn't it?"

"Believe it or not, but this is the room I am most fond of. I'd never forget it."

I wasn't lying. In this room, I had allowed myself to forget my plight, my mission, and just spend a night with a pretty girl. At least for several hours, we had been stripped of our identities and allowed ourselves to enjoy each other's presence and company. It was after that night that I decided to change my plans to assassinate Gisele along with her father. I went to my friends who dwelled in the city and told them of the new plan. In hindsight, that decision was my first mistake. By the dark expression on her face, I could tell that she was remembering that night, too.

"Had you already decided that night how you were going to kill me?"

My voice was even. "I was never going to kill you." I articulated each word with icy clarity, but remembered I needed to keep my tone under control, less I set her off. "I was going to spare your life and let you live out your days in exile, once your father was deposed."

"Don't lie," she spat.

"What reason would I have to be dishonest now?"

Her eyes narrowed.

I stifled an impatient sigh. My thoughts were starting to spin. I needed a drop of her blood on the document. If I didn't do it now, I wouldn't be able to get it at all. Everything would have been for nothing. Then, the thought hit me like a blow. I was putting my persuasion skills to the ultimate test.

My eyes hardened to show my resolve in convincing her of my plans years ago. I touched my arm, right above the bend of my elbow. "Do you remember what I did to your arm, there?"

In response Gisele pulled her sleeve up, exposing her skin. I pushed aside the distracting voices in my head that repeated the attacks that would kill her fastest. I needed her blood first to break the blood agreement. Carefully I closed the distance between us. She seemed oddly calm as I approached, though my heart raced. On her arm was a scar consisting of three horizontal lines with a fourth vertical one cutting through the others. It was a small symbol, no bigger than a couple inches. I remembered making the cuts myself.

"The Night's Guild marks people who are to have their lives spared with this symbol."

I reached out so that my thumb stroked the raised scars. I held my breath as I slowly unlocked my hidden dagger and ever so carefully sliced the skin of her forearm so that she wouldn't feel the razor sharp blade. I had uncorked the vial and gently collected a trickle of her blood. All of this I did while holding her hard gaze, trying to distract her with my eyes while my hand worked.

"From the day I marked you, you were safe," I said. "It wasn't until you refused to show mercy to my comrades, who were only following my orders, and murdered my innocent brother, that everything changed." My voiced hardened from gentle to menacing. "After that, this symbol has meant nothing to me."

She smiled crookedly, as though she had been waiting for this outright declaration of war from the start. I had what I needed, and my hands were fidgeting for my daggers so they could kill her with one swift move. But I had to make the sure the agreement was destroyed before doing so.

I shoved her aside, throwing her into the wall, and raced back down the hallway. My eyes searched for candle fixtures where I could burn the document. When I spilled into the bathroom, ready to make my escape, I went barreling into castle guards. I clenched the vial tightly in my hand as they attacked. I fended off some blows, but I was outnumbered, twenty to one.

My knees hit the ground and then my head. Blood trickled into my eyes from my head and I heard chains being closed around my wrists. Then I was hauled to my feet. I struggled against my bonds, but it was no use. I couldn't even protect myself as they punched at my face, my gut, and my side. I don't remember when I started coughing up blood or how I ended up on the floor again.

Gisele was suddenly in front of me, but I could barely see her as one of my eyes was swelling shut. She whispered something into my loudly ringing ear, but I didn't understand any of it. I was dragged away in chains, my hand gripping the document that was so close to being destroyed.

Chapter 36: Brennon

I'D NEVER KNOWN Aiden to be a chivalrous person, so when he came to me with his plan to destroy the agreement and get Casey and me out, I didn't ask questions. I couldn't think of anything worse than having to tell Kyraine that her only living brother was likely dead, other than trying to dissuade Aiden from executing his plot. I chose to face Kyraine's grief rather than try to stop Aiden.

Something about his demeanor had changed. Even though he was charging forward relentlessly, he seemed to be looking back; as if he was suddenly unsure of what he was about to do.

Several hours after Aiden left, Shep arrived. I had packed a knapsack with a change of clothes and food that would last us a couple of days, and I followed him on horseback to the castle. We left the horses a few blocks away, then ran the rest of the way to the back side, through a courtyard, up a staircase, and climbed out a window and pulled ourselves onto the roof. As we darted along it, I kept a ready hand on my sword, in preparation for any encounter with the guards that were surely patrolling in the night.

My foot suddenly slipped in something wet. I looked down and saw a clear trail of blood. The body was a few feet away.

"Aiden must have beaten us to it," Shep called from ahead.

He waved me forward. We came to the awning over Casey's room and dropped down. Shep pulled the window open and we climbed through.

I ran over to Casey and jolted her awake. She sat up. Her eyes were wild. As she was about to launch into a diatribe, I cut her off.

"We have to leave. Now!"

I unceremoniously yanked her out of bed, forgetting that she had taken a heavy beating earlier that day, and handed her the travel clothes that Shep had pulled from a drawer. She didn't ask questions as she quickly changed. As she was tying her boots, she finally asked, "What's going on? Has something happened?"

"We're leaving Eileen tonight," I told her.

"Why?" She stopped short and looked around the room. "Where's Aiden?"

I made an uneasy face, because I wasn't sure what to tell her. *He's sacrificing himself for us* seemed too melodramatic, but it was basically the truth.

"Brennon, where is he?" She articulated every word, and her voice was steely, but the raw fear underneath was evident. I wouldn't be able to weasel my way out of this one.

I studied her face and saw an expression I'd seen hundreds of times over the years. It screamed of desperation and terror reserved for only the most important people in one's life. That was when it struck me. *Casey and Aiden.* That must have been why I sensed Aiden's reservations all day. He didn't doubt his plan; he doubted if he really wanted it to end the way he had envisioned for years.

Casey was suddenly inches from my face. "Brennon!" She seemed close to tears. "Where is he?"

"Casey, we have to go. I'm sorry."

I understood the feelings swirling inside her. I'd felt them before every battle I charged into with the Huntsmen, knowing that some of them would die, and I could do nothing to prevent it. But I couldn't express my empathy in a way that would let her know that I understood. Not now, at least, when fear controlled every fiber of her being.

She recoiled from me, as though I'd struck her. My heart clinched at the pure anguish on her face.

"Where is he?"

Shep finally took pity on Casey. "The queen has him," he replied. "He broke into her chambers to steal the agreement, but he got caught."

I briefly wondered how Shep had come by this information.

Casey stepped around me. "Where would they take him?"

"To the dungeon."

"Where is it?"

"No! Casey, we're leaving," I interjected.

"I'm not leaving him." It sounded more like a realization than a declaration, as though her resolve surprised even her.

"He's the one who told us to leave. He knew from the start this might happen. He wants us to be safe. He wants *you* to be safe."

Her eyes blazed, and when they settled on me, the smallest hint of fear crept into the back of my mind. She'd never turn a spell on me, even in this crazed state of mind. Right?

"I'm not leaving him." Every word was spoken with icy clarity.

I exchanged glances with Shep, who directed my attention to Casey's hand, which had a faint glow to it.

"I'd never ask you to leave Kyraine behind." Her mouth set in a hard line, but her eyes softened, knowing that she was attacking me from an emotional angle now. My face fell at the truth of her words.

"I know you wouldn't."

I rubbed a hand over my face. I couldn't stop seeing Aiden's desperate eyes in my mind, and now I was being faced with Casey's. Aiden's instructions were clear, but I hadn't anticipated Casey's unwillingness to abandon him. After wrestling with myself, I turned to Shep.

"Is it even possible to reach him and escape?"

Shep nodded. "It won't be easy, but it's possible."

"That's all we need," Casey added.

"You're sure about this?" She didn't need to answer. She didn't need to utter a word. It was written all over her face. I sighed heavily. "What's a mission from the Hunters without a run-in with death. Shep, lead the way."

Chapter 37: Casey

AS WE FOLLOWED Shep through the castle halls, I couldn't stop thinking about Aiden. Worry and anger were the only things that consumed me.

What had the queen already done to him? What the hell was he thinking? Was he even still alive? If he wasn't, I was going to dig him up and kill him again for pulling this stunt. Why did he think he could do this on his own? Doesn't that selfish prick know there is safety in numbers? Why did he think I wouldn't care if he died?

We encountered some castle guards. We didn't slow our pace as they demanded our business and told us to stop. Shep collided with one, and I shot a spell at another. Brennon launched his sword into one several feet ahead. As we passed his twitching body, Brennon grabbed his sword. My heightened state of fear made me blind to everything but finding Aiden. We ducked down a deserted corridor that ended in a dark staircase.

When we drew closer, the smell of human excrement and rot hit us like a wall. I gagged and Brennon coughed. We all gulped some fresh air before rushing forward.

I was grateful to be wearing tall boots once I made it to the bottom, because the ground was wet with mud and sewage. I produced a ball of light in my hand. Several rats and bugs scuttled away from the light. I ignored them and moved farther into the dungeon. We peered into each cell, calling out to Aiden softly. But soon, we came to realize that they were all empty. I spun to face the other two.

"He isn't here." I spotted movement in the darkness. "Brennon, behind you!"

I was too late. A thick club had knocked him over the head and into the wall. He had manacles closed around his wrist before he could straighten. We were suddenly overwhelmed with opponents.

I hit a guard with a spell, but another came rushing towards me. He collided with my Frozen Limb charm while another doubled over with an Incapacity spell. Brennon was being dragged away as I threw more spells. I had lost sight of Shep in the battle, and I soon found myself surrounded and outnumbered. I attacked two more guards before an invisible force struck me from behind. I was restrained, blindfolded and forced into iron manacles.

First, I silent tried using an Unlocking spell to release my hands, but nothing happened. Then I started shouting the incantation, but still nothing happened. My feet dragged through the muck as they hauled me back up the stairs and through the castle. I tried to conjure another spell to attack. I tried to make my body unbearably hot so they'd let go of me. Desperately, I even tried to shape shift into an animal, something I'd never done before. Nothing worked. I was powerless.

My body was suddenly thrown to the ground and then roughly straightened so that I knelt. The blindfold was roughly torn away. Brennon knelt to my left. I raised my gaze and saw that we were in the throne room. The queen stood a few feet away and the entire room was filled with armored guards at every entrance, window, and door. Queen Gisele looked way too happy, and my stomach dropped. Maybe I was too late. Maybe Aiden was already dead, and she had gotten what she'd been after for twenty years.

"What have we here? A sorceress and a swordsman sneaking around in my castle."

I stayed silent.

"Why were you in the dungeons? For whom were you searching?" She made a sound of inquiry. "Perhaps you were looking for him?"

My breath stopped in my throat when two guards dragged Aiden from behind a door. The corner of his mouth was bloody, one eye was purple and half-open, the skin above his eyebrow had split open, and a streak of his hair had dried blood in it. He was conscious, but just barely. His eyes weren't focused, so his attention wavered.

He painfully raised his head, and when he did, his expression seemed to say, *you shouldn't have come. I can't protect you here.*

This was a sick game, but I couldn't let her see my weakness. I clenched my jaw and dropped any expression from my face. If I could just unlock my manacles and release Brennon, we could fight our way out. It'd be tough—maybe impossible, but at least we could try. But when I tried to use my powers, nothing happened. I glanced down at the cuffs and saw a word etched into the metal: *Inermes*. Defenseless. My throat went dry when I realized I was powerless and that we were all at the mercy of the deranged queen.

She approached me and I saw the glint of a knife in her hand. "You lied to me earlier when you said you didn't know this young man. Then, you never reported to me when you saw him again, which, it appears, happened quite frequently." She waved her knife in Aiden's direction. Then she brought it down by my throat. Brennon made a move towards the queen, but a guard restrained him roughly. "You lied to your queen. That is, you would have lied to your queen if you had one, but you do not. I know *he* is from Calem, just as much as I know that *you* are not from Eileen, just as much as I know that *he* is a Huntsman. Brennon Harrow, is it? Have I guessed correctly, Cassia Coles?"

My face dropped. My composure evaporated, leaving my mouth suspended on a word I couldn't form. My insides melted. I couldn't stop my face from betraying my identity. The blade was pulled away, and she rounded me so that I had to crane my neck to look up at her.

A victorious smile spread on the queen's lips. "Hmm, you were telling the truth about them."

She no longer addressed me. A young man stepped forward and, as if to add to my shock, it was Shep. He didn't have a single scratch or bruise on him. He stood without restraints, and he held his head high as he matched the queen's gaze. Then, I heard Aiden's words echoing in my ears: *I've never been able to figure what went wrong.*

Who had told Queen Gisele that Aiden wasn't really Dorian Romauld? Who had known all the assassins he had enlisted for his mission? Who had known Aiden was hiding his brother in

Eileen? Who had turned them all in? Who had known every step of our plan? Who had we immediately given our trust to, from the beginning?

Aiden had drawn the same conclusion. If I thought I'd seen pain on Aiden's face before, what I witnessed then was a kind of distorted agony that fractured something inside me.

"Shep—"

The young man with the unruly blonde hair emerged from the circle of guards, looking as out of place as ever. He tried to keep his face impassive, but he couldn't keep the guilt from showing in his eyes. He licked his lips nervously.

"The whole time?"

"She hired me to investigate the deaths of her relatives, Aiden. The Guild—the Commander—I couldn't say no—I didn't know she was going to—Kai and the others—Greyson—I had no idea, I'm—"

"Oh, silence yourself," the queen snapped viciously.

That was one of the very few times I saw Aiden utterly lost for words.

Queen Gisele rounded me like I was her prey. "Now, what to do with you. I promised you to Azlaya. She never said I had to deliver you in one piece, though. Your sister needs you barely alive; after all, she only needs to deliver the final blow." She stooped down and looked directly into my eyes. I drew back. "Your eyes are pretty. I have a beautiful arctic wolf that would glow with those eyes."

"Gisele, *don't* touch her." Aiden roared. His voice was hoarse, but powerful.

He was looking directly at the queen with an expression that could kill. All the agony from before had vanished. Queen

Gisele's expression changed in a moment from amusement to anger. The possessiveness of Aiden's words spiraled her into rage.

"Oh, don't tell me," she laughed derisively. "You can't possibly be taken by *her*?" Queen Gisele snatched my face and her nails dug into my chin as she wrenched my face to look where she directed me. "So you pursue little girls from prophecies? Are you above queens now?"

"This is between you and me. It always has been. Leave them out of it."

She recognized what was happening then. She had seen this exact same look from Aiden when he had tried to get his fellow assassins and Greyson released. She had seen him at his most vulnerable and his most desperate, and now she was seeing it again. I watched her face distort into a cynical smile. Her eyes gleamed with a wicked joy.

Her cackle filled the chamber. "Did you lie to her, too? Did you manipulate her? Or did you carve symbols into her skin with the same knife you used to murder her family? Did you promise to marry her and then bed her while you planned to kill her father and destroy her life forever?" Queen Gisele screeched. She went on and on like a mad person, tossing accusations at Aiden like bait, and waiting for him to bite.

She suddenly jerked my collar, bringing me inches from her face.

"He did it to me. He will do it to you." She had lost her mind. "He's a lying, traitorous bastard who has deserved everything I've done to him. Even this—"

"GISELE—"

"NO—"

"WAIT, Your Grace!"

Three people shouted at once. Gisele pressed the knife where my jaw and neck joined. She kept her venomous eyes on my face.

"Your Grace, Kai Fr—Cassia Coles—this young woman is still a competitor in the tournament and she has become very popular among the people. Killing her might cause unrest, the very opposite of what these games are meant to accomplish."

I couldn't see who spoke, but the words had an effect on Queen Gisele. I watched her face as an idea formed in her head.

"Yes, Your Grace," another voice said. "If word about her murder got out, the people might riot against you."

"Very well," the queen snapped, and drew away from me. "Then I, Gisele Givaldi of House Morecolt, Queen of Eileen, sentence you, Cassia Coles, and you, Brennon Harrow, to death tomorrow morning."

"Your Grace, Azlaya instructed that she—"

"She is *my* prisoner. I decide her fate. You," she pointed to a guard, "alert the tournament officials that there has been a change. I want the final event moved to tomorrow. Only *Kai Frost* will compete." She said my fake name with mockery.

Queen Gisele silenced more protests from her advisors with one look. Then she approached Aiden. He was too weak to defend himself if she lashed out.

"Do you enjoy watching the people you care about die?" Aiden looked at me helplessly. "I'll allow you this one chance to say goodbye, since your friends and brother never got the pleasure."

A guard violently shoved Aiden forward. He stumbled. His hands were tied behind his back, and he couldn't catch himself as fell to the ground. I rushed to him, stepping around the queen, and dropped to my knees. His injuries were so much worse up close. His back was to me, and I leaned over him. His lips were moving, so I bent lower to hear what he was saying.

"Take my hand," he whispered.

I did as he said, wanting to provide what little comfort I could, when I felt something being pushed into my hand. I wrapped one hand around it and clasped my other one over it, to keep it hidden from view. Though his face was covered in blood and bruises, his eyes shone through, telling me what his mouth couldn't. I told him with my own eyes that I understood.

At that moment, I didn't care that the queen stood mocking us. I didn't care that Brennon observed us from a few feet away. I didn't care that Shep watched from afar. I didn't care that tears welled in my eyes. I didn't even care that I was supposed to die the following day and that we had failed our mission. Everything else seemed peripheral, because I was drowning in his expression that pleaded with any higher being to spare me.

I leaned in and kissed him so softly that our lips barely touched.

"I'm going to get you out of here," he whispered to me.

I caught one last glimpse of his resolute expression before he was yanked away from me. He disappeared through one door and Brennon and I were pulled through another. We were dumped into a prison cell below the castle.

I waited for the guards to leave before unwrapping my hands from what Aiden had given me. It was a tube with a cork in the top. Parchment was rolled and stuffed inside. I examined it closer and noticed the top of the paper looked stained with red liquid. I gasped, realizing it was blood—Queen Gisele's blood. He had done it. He had stolen the document right from under her nose, and given it to me to burn.

Panic set in, as I angrily shook my manacles. I couldn't burn the paper, and I couldn't do anything to help Aiden. I had probably just seen him for the last time. He had risked everything, sacrificed his life, and I couldn't even do the simple thing he expected I could with my powers.

I swore a hundred times under my breath. The angry frustration turned into hysteric frustration. Tears starting streaming down my face as I hunched over and cursed everything. In the next cell over, Brennon tried to get me to calm down, but I was too overwhelmed with my powerlessness in the situation. After what felt like hours, I finally slumped against the prison wall. I heard Brennon move to his wall too, trying to comfort me by being a little closer.

"Brennon…" I was completely at a loss for what to say to him.

I'm sorry I dragged you into this. I'm sorry I didn't leave with you. I'm sorry I can't break us out. I'm sorry you may never see the Huntsmen again. I'm sorry you'll never know if you and Kyraine could have had a future. I'm sorry for everything.

"Yes?" He had heard my tantrum and seemed hesitant.

"I'm sorry." I owed him much more than an apology, but it was all I could manage at the moment. "I'm so sorry."

"This will hardly be first time I'm facing my death," he said, trying to cheer me up. "Besides, you would have done the same for me, had I asked."

Oddly, this only made me feel worse. I could have gone anywhere, and Brennon would have followed. Now, he was following me to our ends.

Chapter 38: Aiden

I WAS TOSSED to the floor like a ragdoll. I was so delirious that I hit the mucky ground clumsily. The cell door was locked behind me. A putrid smell hung in the air, and by morning, I knew it would cling to me, too. I had spent weeks in cell like that one. Though, I had a feeling my stay would be much shorter this time around.

For hours, my eyes stayed trained on a sliver of light under the dungeon door. It finally opened, and guards came in to drag me to my feet. A blindfold was tied behind my head. My hands were cuffed with irons in front of me. My feet tried to keep up with the guards, but one of my knees had definitely been dislocated when I was bludgeoned, so I walked with a painful limp. Knees grinding in protest and wrists screaming with pain, I was shoved into a cart of some sort.

After being tossed around haphazardly, a sound I'd heard all morning starting growing in my ears. I realized it was the crowd in the arena, excitedly anticipating that day's event. Rough hands pulled me from the cart when it jolted to a halt.

Again, I was hauled forward with my feet dragging under me. The noise was deafening now. The blindfold was finally ripped away.

The arena was filled to capacity. Horns blared, banners waved, people roared. I had no doubt that word of Kai Frost's solo event had run its course through the city, which is why the stadium was overflowing with spectators. I realized that I stood under Gisele's canopy, surrounded by guards on every side. Gisele sat on her throne, casting a brazen look over the crowd. She beckoned, and I was pushed forward, chains rattling around my wrists and ankles.

I searched for Casey, but the pit of the arena was empty. The only things visible were jagged rocks scattered about. Nothing else in the arena suggested an execution. Even the cheering was too rambunctious for it to be calling for someone's death.

To our right, a bolt was unlocked and guards began filing into the arena. I counted ten. In the middle of their formation, I finally saw her. She had only been given a thin black shirt and pants to shield her from the cold. Her hands were chained in front of her and the guard leading her escort tugged her along like a dog.

I tried to catch her eye as she looked around the arena with a shaken expression. Had she destroyed the agreement? As long as I didn't know, Gisele's life was safe. Despite willing her with every fiber of my being to give me a sign, a signal, or anything, she never found me in the crowd. Brennon stood at the arena's edge with his own escort of guards. Whatever Gisele had planned, it was clear that she wanted Casey's life first.

"I thought you should have the best view of this," Gisele cooed to me.

Someone struck me from behind when I didn't respond. They hit me again but were waved aside by Gisele. Casey was chained to one of the rocks, giving her only a few feet to move in each direction. The guards exited the arena, and she was left alone.

I calculated in my head how long it would take me to reach Casey. One minute twenty-three seconds. In that time, she could be filled with arrows, attacked by the guards circling the arena, or killed in whatever manner Gisele had planned. Spectators, guards, and even Gisele could also block my way as I tried to get away. My conclusion: Casey would be dead before I could reach her.

An announcer stepped onto a dais at the arena's edge. The noise fell to a soft hum as the announcer began to speak.

"People of Eileen and afar, ladies and gentlemen of the court, Your Grace—" He looked towards everyone he addressed. The announcer looked uneasy, as though he didn't agree with what he had to say. "In the name of Gisele Givaldi of House Morecolt, Queen of Eileen, this woman is hereby charged with entering the tournament under the false identity of Kai Frost, aiding and abetting a wanted criminal, and conspiring against the crown. Do you deny these charges?"

Casey raised her chin and stared at the announcer evenly, unsettling the fat man even more.

Use your powers. Save yourself! I screamed at her in my mind. Why wasn't she freeing herself from the chains and fighting her way out with her arsenal of spells?

I struggled against my bonds. "Gisele, don't do this. You have me. Punish me. Kill *me*." I was struck from behind again.

My knees buckled and struck the hard stone. "I'm begging you to show mercy."

She grinned at me with that horrible, crooked smile. "This *is* merciful. I was going to have you carry out her execution, but I wanted to see your face when you watch her die."

"Cassia Coles." The crowd started murmuring again. "You are hereby sentenced to death." The whispers turned to angry shouts. People of the court called for Casey's head, the city and country folk called for mercy for their beloved competitor, and others screamed as they recognized the name of one of Layna Coles' daughters. This is was not how the prophecy was supposed to play out.

A low rumble drowned out the uproar and shook the ground beneath me. A massive, grated door was being hauled open by a chain. Guttural growls, unlike anything I'd heard before, poured from the cavernous opening. My mouth parted in terror, and my heart dropped when a gigantic, scaly beast crawled out.

Its eyes burned with hunger, and it bared its razor sharp teeth. Its talons could effortlessly puncture the strongest armor and sharp spikes trailed down his spine. It whipped its tail, striking the wall behind it and causing chunks of the stone to fall away. Gisele laughed joyously when the thing bellowed out an ear-splitting screech. Death by dragon.

I couldn't wait for a sign from Casey anymore. I was seeing red, my body hot with rage. I wanted Gisele dead. I wanted to feel her blood pouring over my hands. I wildly searched my surroundings for weapons or anything I could use to smash her head in. My eyes fell on a side table beside her throne. A pair of daggers rested next to a vial. I froze as Gisele caught me looking at it.

She plucked it off the table. "You almost took this from me." She waved it tauntingly. "That must be the worst part of all this—knowing that you came so close."

"Open it," I growled.

The intensity in my eyes wiped the smug expression from her face. She teetered between confidence and utter fear for a minute before she finally twisted the cork. She dug out the paper, unrolled it, and her whole body collapsed with disbelief.

I pictured my handwriting where I'd scrawled, *'You lose'*.

She lashed out and struck me across the face, sending me tumbling towards the ground. Blood rushed into my mouth as I was jerked back to me feet. I couldn't stand on my own anymore. Gisele was in my face, sputtering and in hysterics.

"Where is it? What have you done with it?" she screeched.

My eyes slid to the center of the arena. Gisele followed my gaze, realization setting in.

"Stop it! She has my document! Stop the beast!" she cried out. "STOP THE BEAST!"

A wave of heat hit us as the dragon shot a stream of fire towards Casey. She dove behind the rock to which she was chained. Brennon was trying futilely to escape his guards and rush to Casey's aid. The crowd erupted with screams. People sitting towards the bottom of the stadium rushed to escape the sudden heat as they clambered through the stands. It was complete chaos. Casey narrowly missed the fire again, and once more before the chain was tightly wound around the rock.

The guards tossed me aside. My head cracked against something hard. In my dizziness, my gaze fell on Casey. Guards had rushed into the stadium, but they couldn't get the dragon's attention. Its hide was impenetrable by arrows and swords made by men. The beast rounded on Casey. She was cornered with nowhere to run and nothing to shield her from the fire.

Please, no. Not like this.

It arched its neck, and I knew it was preparing to douse the arena and Casey in flames.

Chapter 39: Casey

THE WORLD WAS burning. Everything around me smelled burnt, and my hair and clothing were singed.

I tried to move around the rock, but I had no more free chain. I was stuck. The dragon reared its head, and I pictured the flames before seeing them build in its throat.

This isn't going to work.

It has *to work.*

I ignored the rational side of my brain and unfolded the agreement that I'd kept rolled in my hand. As I did, it grew three times in size so that it was two feet long and another foot wide. I was shocked at the transformation, but I didn't have time dwell on it. As the flames shot towards me, I thrust the parchment out and ducked my head, hoping for a quick death.

A brilliant light blinded me and an invisible force thrust me backwards. I slammed into the rock, my skin splitting upon impact. The dragon roared angrily at the strange light that had burst between us, and swung its head through the air. I looked down in shock. My clothes were only singed, the document had disappeared, and I was alive.

I wasn't given long to wonder how I hadn't been burned alive, because the dragon was preparing to try again. In the dragon's confusion, I raced around the other side of the rock, loosening the chain as I went. I barely dodged the flames as they swept past me. I shook my manacles furiously, hoping that the fire had weakened them, but they remained firmly around my wrists. The dragon had recovered from its momentary stupor and turned on me again. This time, its spiked tail wrapped around one side of the rock, blocking my way. It had discovered my hiding spot.

I hoped it wasn't too gruesome a sight for Aiden and Brennon to watch. My eyes pinched shut as I resigned myself to my fate.

A shrill cry exploded from the dragon. I looked up and saw an arrow piercing one of its eyes. Its head thrashed around wildly as it bellowed out in pain.

Over the dragon's noise, I heard a familiar battle cry. Suddenly, scores of Huntsmen started pouring into the arena. Civilians jumped out of their way as the warriors engaged with the queen's guards stationed around the stadium. Even more chaos broke loose. Huntsmen were in the stands fighting, along the top walls, and some were even battling with the guards that held Brennon. A variety of different colored spells started flying through the air, too. I stared in awe at the scene. I couldn't piece together how any of it was possible.

I dove away from another random stream of fire. A group of Huntsmen, huddled under shields, raced over to me. Brennon and a red-haired man led them.

"Callum, the hammer!" Brennon shouted over the noise. He still had shackles on his wrists, but his chains were gone. "Are you hurt?" he shouted over the noise.

The Huntsman, Callum Greaves, started banging away at the chain keeping me tied to the rock.

"No!" We all ducked under the umbrella of shields as fire haphazardly came our direction. After several minutes, the chains finally fell away. Callum started in on the manacles, but they wouldn't budge after several blows. I waved him off. "I have to find Aiden!"

Brennon nodded, signaling to Callum and the group of Huntsmen. "We'll cover you."

I tore off towards the stands with the small platoon on my heels. Another group of warriors started attacking the dragon with arrows, swords, and spells—anything to damage its armor.

Panicked screams filled the air. I located the queen's canopy in the madness, though I couldn't tell who was under it with all the frantic movement around me. All I knew was that Queen Gisele had Aiden, which meant he didn't have long to live.

I grabbed an abandoned sword and raced up the stairs and into the stands. I kept the sword close as I shoved and pushed people out of my way, desperately trying to reach the queen.

"STEP ASIDE!"

"MOVE!"

"GET OUT OF THE WAY!"

The Huntsmen and I clawed like animals and screamed madly to get people to move. I spotted Queen Gisele under the canopy. She held Aiden by his collar and spoke viciously to him.

Finally, we reached the canopy. Guards rushed forward. I knocked one aside and drove my sword through the shoulder of another. Brennon and the Huntsmen engaged with the rest while I dashed forward.

Queen Gisele held a blade at Aiden's throat and one at his abdomen. Her eyes trembled, but her hands were firm. I took a step forward and blood starting trickling down his neck. I dropped my sword. I wouldn't be able to stop her before she killed Aiden. I wished badly that I could use my powers, but they were still useless with the manacles on my wrists. My hands raised in defeat to show her I was unarmed. Aiden's face was wrought with pain, but his eyes were sharp with lethal focus.

"You don't have to do this—"

Her eyes were crazed. Her lips twitched unnaturally. "I've waited twenty years for his blood—"

"It's over," I called to her, as calmly as I could manage.

"Almost—"

"NO!"

The blade sliced his abdomen open as easily as cutting through butter. He moved in a flash though, and before I finished screaming, Aiden had grabbed the blade near his throat, spun, and sliced the queen's head clean off.

It hit the ground with a sickening thud, and her body collapsed. Aiden looked down at her with crushing disdain. The blood, old and new, made him unrecognizable. The mud covering his clothes and his smell made me want to run away. The unwavering, murderous expression on his face threatened to completely erase his soft touches and gentle kisses from my mind. It was the first time I was seeing him in his true form. He was suddenly unknowable.

He clutched an arm to his stomach, but his whole front side was soaked in blood. He staggered and crumpled to the ground. My trance shattered, and I ran to him, trying to support him in my arms.

"Aiden!"

His eyes fluttered, his breathing was ragged and shaky, and his body convulsed. Every time he moved more blood poured from the open wound.

"Stay still. Stay still," I hushed him. I hadn't realized I was crying until he blinked when a tear fell into his eye. I grabbed a nearby animal pelt, acting as a rug, and held it to Aiden's wound, but soon it too became soaked with blood.

"Casey!" Brennon called from behind. Next minute, he was at my side.

"I can't help him with these on," I told Brennon frantically, referring to the cuffs.

Brennon looked around. Callum's hammer hadn't been enough, and he couldn't see anything in the immediate vicinity that would be sufficient. His expression reflected my powerlessness. "I don't have anything I can use to break them off."

"I need a sorcerer—someone who knows healing spells."

We surveyed the scene. People were dying everywhere. Women and children tried to escape the violence. Arena guards were cutting people down for helping the Huntsmen. Others were getting trampled. I realized the heartbreaking reality that, in the chaos, there was little hope I'd be able to find a sorcerer. There was even less hope that I'd get him or her to Aiden in the minutes he had left.

Aiden suddenly lurched forward and snatched Brennon's arm. "Lysander Tennenbay—promise me that you'll make sure he is crowned king."

Brennon tried quieting him, but Aiden became more fitful and held him harder, until Brennon complied with the request. He released Brennon's arm and fell back into my lap.

"Tell me what I can do," I pleaded with Aiden. The turmoil around me had melted into white noise.

"You're doing it." He swallowed, but blood was beginning to pool in his mouth now. "You're here." A new onslaught of tears rushed forward.

He was fading. The life was draining from his eyes and the color from his face. His once-steely gaze became more and more distant.

"Aiden—Aiden! Stay with me!" He blinked, his head rolling. "Aiden, please! I can't lose you!" I pleaded tearfully.

I suddenly became blind to everything. I forgot about the pandemonium around me. I forgot about Kate. I forgot about my home. I forgot about my grandmother. I forgot about everything that was important in my life, because what had suddenly become the biggest part of it was slipping away in my arms.

Brennon was trying to coax me into getting to safety with him, but I fought off his efforts. Denial gripped me. I couldn't be covered in Aiden's blood. I couldn't be crying over his dying body. I couldn't be losing him. This couldn't be the end—I wasn't ready for this to be the end.

"Casey—Casey—go. Don't throw your life away—Change the world." I felt his heart slowing with each labored pulse. I leaned back so that I looked into his eyes—those eyes that had the ability to threaten and admire, intimidate and encourage, loathe and adore. "Walking away from you was the hardest thing I've ever done." He took a few more pained breaths.

The screams flooded my ears. The clanging of swords grew louder. The dragon's agonized cries echoed off the walls. The shallow breaths coming from Aiden became fainter. I closed my eyes against the tears, but the nightmare around me didn't collapse. I was the only thing collapsing as death descended upon the arena.

Chapter 40: Kate

WE'D KEPT OUR prisoner locked in the room and strapped to the chair for days now. Zayne and I had been planning to travel to the Huntsmen's lands to search for my father, when Zayne rushed to me on the night we were planning to leave, saying he had passed him on the street. I was baffled as I followed him into the city that night. We retraced his steps and found my father exiting a little tavern a few hours later before continuing on his journey east, towards the queen's castle.

Zayne cornered him, easily knocking him unconscious with a spell. He had carried him back to his apartment, and we restrained my father in a chair in the lofted area, sealing the windows and walls with a Silencing spell.

His dark brown hair was long and was pulled away from his face in a messy ponytail. His facial hair, which had been well-groomed, was starting to get unruly. I'd been having Zayne give him his food and water, though they were kept to small portions to make him a little delirious from the hunger and thirst. That way, it wouldn't take too much effort to get the information I needed.

He hadn't seen me yet. As far as he knew, Zayne was the only one holding him captive. In all honesty, I was anxious for him to finally see me—to realize who I was. My impatience was mounting, so I decided that three days had been enough time to wear him down.

Finally, after more than seventeen years, I would meet my father. I stepped into the dim light. Zayne stepped aside as my gaze settled on Aaron Coles. He stared at the two of us with a mixture of disbelief and anger.

"Oh, so there are two of you." He sighed in annoyance. "Whatever it is you hope to get out of this, you're wasting your time. I don't—"

I had put down my hood, revealing my hair and face. It was clear by his expression that he recognized me, or at least something within my face.

"Kaitlin?"

"Hi, Dad."

"Why are you doing this?" His voice was soft, and it lacked the manipulative edge that Zayne and Azlaya frequently employed.

His words struck an unexpected nerve. The betrayal on his face was evident. In truth, I had no reason to kill my father, other than the necessity of binding myself to the Sagen. My only grievance was that if it came to it, I knew he would side with Casey. This angered me, but hadn't affected me enough to want his blood—or rather his heart. I'd never really craved his approval. He was just a swordsman after all. My mother, on the other hand, had the ability to help me rule Alagia. Together, we could bring peace to this land, and my father would play a part in helping us achieve that goal.

"Mom didn't deserve to die. With your help, she's going to rise again, and together we can bring peace and prosperity to Alagia."

"Kaitlin, your mother is dead."

I smiled unreservedly. "Yes, she is. But I'm going to bring her back. And to do that, I need to know where you buried her."

Aaron's mouth hung on a word. "You—you can't bring her back—"

"I love how everyone keeps telling *me* what I can and cannot do." My words hit him with the force of a blow. "I can and I will." I crouched before him. "Now where is she?"

"Kaitlin, what you're doing isn't right. Whatever Azlaya has told you, it can only hurt you more. Trust me, she is using you to accomplish her own self-interests. Please, Kaitlin, listen to me. She doesn't care about you!"

"Aw," I sighed, "and here I was worried that *you* didn't care about me. Where is she?" I emphasized every word clearly.

He searched for something in my eyes, begging me to believe what he said, but when he didn't get a response, he gave up. His gaze fell from me. "There are caverns alongside the cliffs that border the Eastern Waters, northeast of the Hunters' territory. It's where you and your sister were born. You'll find her tomb there."

I was taken aback by how easily he had given up the information. He had a look on his face that said *please don't hurt yourself.* I'd seen a similar expression from my grandmother whenever I asked to do something she thought I might regret. Out of love, she would let me go, and I realized that my father was doing the same thing.

My sharp eyes softened. I placed a comforting hand on his knee. "Thank you."

I rose and drew a jagged dagger from my belt. Aaron didn't panic, but his face fell. He didn't appear shocked by the turn of events, but rather hurt that his own daughter wielded the knife.

"I have to do this to bring her back," I explained gently, and a little apologetically.

"You have her ambition—" he began to say. Aaron's gaze washed over me, his face melting as though I was the most beautiful thing he had ever seen. "I have always loved you. I hope you know that."

"I do now." And I meant it. He was submitting to me without a fight and allowing me to use him for my own purposes. He probably knew there was no point in resisting. I placed a warm hand on his shoulder, infusing a Numbing spell into him. "Don't worry, you won't feel anything."

He looked at the dagger apprehensively.

Though he couldn't say it, he was thinking about holding me in his arms as an infant and wanting to watch me grow into a remarkable woman. The memories were consumed with love, happiness, guilt, and sorrow—everything he felt when he looked at me.

"I'll give Casey your love."

Epilogue

"YOUR GRACE, TWO riders from Goldtree Castle just arrived—a Professor Hugo Blakemore and a Lysander Tennenbay."

Queen Amelia wondered why the famous scholar who was awarded the highest of distinctions shortly before his disappearance, and presumed death, was at her palace. She also couldn't figure out why the name Tennenbay was vaguely familiar.

"They are requesting an audience with you—they're saying that Spymaster Redding sent them."

Upon the mention of her spymaster, Queen Amelia waved the steward to bring them in immediately. She hadn't heard from Aiden in weeks. His silence wasn't unusual, though, even when he left on missions, or when he wasn't on any assignments. His correspondents were few and far between. Still, she was hoping these riders had been sent ahead with word that Aiden had successfully assassinated Queen Gisele, as he should have done twenty years earlier. That way, she and the other sitting kings and queens could select the new ruler for Eileen. But when the shriveled man and the striking man, who looked to be fifty years his junior, entered her throne room, Queen Amelia didn't understand.

"Your Grace." They greeted her in unison and bowed, though the older man couldn't dip as low.

Queen Amelia peered at them narrowly. "I am told that Aiden Redding sent you? Does this concern his operations in Eileen?"

Blakemore spoke. "Your Grace, we've come on a related matter—something that is impacted by the events transpiring in Eileen."

"I, along with the rest of the world, thought you were dead, Professor Blakemore. How is it you stand before me now?"

He smiled as though he had all the knowledge in the world. "To answer your question simply, Your Grace, it is because I am indeed *not* dead. I have been living quietly beyond prying eyes, while working in private, during the years of my absence." Then he stepped aside and turned the attention to his companion.

The young man revealed his cloaked face. Queen Amelia regarded him as one would a tiger—with apprehension and curiosity. Though, his features were strikingly attractive, she didn't let her face show it, and kept her guard up. His stunning green eyes and Queen Amelia's brown eyes locked for several seconds.

"Queen Amelia, my name is Lysander Tennenbay of House Morecolt." The queen recognized the name as one of the noble houses in Eileen.

"Your Grace, I admit we came to you upon Aiden Redding's instructions, but we are here not to discuss his operations in Eileen, but the fate of Eileen itself."

Lysander removed a rolled parchment from his cloak and handed it to Queen Amelia. She unrolled it and read the letter. Her eyes were caught on one short line written in Aiden's handwriting at the foot of the letter: *Lysander Tennenbay is the one true heir to the Eileenian throne.*

"This is impossible. Aiden disposed of all the legitimate heirs to Eileen's throne years ago."

"Not all of them, Your Grace," Lysander told the queen evenly. "He spared my life when I was only a child."

He produced several more rolls of papers. Queen Amelia looked through his birth, title, and family history records, all bearing the insignia of House Morecolt. She didn't want to believe it, but she held the proof to his legitimacy. Despite her urge to burn the records and resume her plans to choose a new ruler for Eileen, she submitted to the truth the papers bore. True to the honorable character Aiden knew her for, Queen Amelia would recognize his rightful claim to the throne.

"It seems Aiden owes me an explanation." She turned to Blakemore. "What was your role in all of this?"

"I have been Lysander's tutor these past twenty years. It's not very often one gets the chance to mentor and teach the future king; one who will likely alter the course of this land's destiny," Blakemore replied wistfully.

Queen Amelia couldn't comprehend the plotting that had gone into such an elaborate scheme: to spare the life of a legitimate, but young and impressionable heir, then raise him under the influence of the most intelligent and noble man in the land, all to have him return to his home and claim his rightful throne when he was old enough to lead a kingdom in crisis. But then what else did she expect from the most intelligent and skilled spymaster Alagia? Though she wasn't pleased with the outcome of Aiden's plans, she was impressed. Lysander wasn't sure how he was expecting this meeting to go, but it had gone well.

As the two regarded each other, they couldn't help but wonder about the person who had brought them together. Since receiving his letter, notifying him to prepare to assume the Eileen throne, Lysander had a sinking feeling that he might never see Aiden again. It was to Aiden that Lysander owed his life, and now, his future.

"I will recognize your claim to the Eileenian throne," Queen Amelia said to Lysander. She stood and the two faced each other as regal statues. "You shall henceforth be called Lysander Tennenbay of House Morecolt, King of Eileen."

About the Author

Taylor is currently a student in college. She started writing the first book in *The Sorcerers' Prophecy* series in 6th grade and has been writing ever since. The second book in the series is called *Secrets of Eileen*, which follows the story of twin sisters Casey and Kate as they build armies in preparation for their imminent battle.

She enjoys sharing her passion with others and has created a program to encourage and inspire elementary/middle school students to read and write. She has been profiled by WLWT Channel 5 for her mentoring program, has won numerous awards for her writing, and was recognized by the Ohio State Legislature for her work. Her goal is to transform young children into avid readers and writers by pushing them to keep searching for that one book that will open their eyes to reading forever.

Taylor lives in Ohio with her mom, dad, two sisters and brother.

www.ingramcontent.com/pod-product-compliance
Lightning Source LLC
Chambersburg PA
CBHW021120260626
47169CB00005B/1378